CW00418932

THE
FIRE
· OF THE ·
FALLEN

THE LIGHT OF THE NORTH SAGA · VOLUME 2

· J. C. DUNCAN ·

Copyright © 2021 by James Simonds (pen name J. C. Duncan)

All rights reserved. No part of this book may be reproduced or used in any manner without written permission of the copyright owner except for the use of quotations in a book review. For more information, address: jcduncanbooks@gmail.com.

First edition November 2021

Cover design by Damonza.com
Photography by Studio Zahora
Illustration by James Nathaniel
Maps by Red geographics

ISBN 978-1-8383522-2-6 (paperback)
ISBN 978-1-8383522-3-3 (ebook)

www.jcduncan.co.uk

PREFACE

THE FIRST BOOK of this series told of an alternate history where the Norse nations had refused to convert to Christianity, and retained their traditional religion and culture, as well as their famous practices of raiding; 'going Viking'. We saw the seeds of a climactic conflict between North and West being sowed, and the banners of the Crusade raised against the pagan Norse by the newly united Christian nations.

We met Ordulf, the young German smith, whose easy life was so rudely and violently turned upside down, rendering him a slave in a foreign land. We met the Norse leaders, Jarl Ragnvald and his brethren, remnants of the traditional way of Norse life, warriors of the old ways, trying to preserve their lifestyle and culture in a changing world. And we met the ambitious and powerful Christian lords, Adolf and his fellow feudal rulers, trying to extend their control over Europe after the chaos and war of the successor states of Charlemagne have been resolved.

The first short campaign of the war for the North was fought and Jutland burned, its warriors defeated, its people subjugated. The three old kings of the Norse all fell, to madness, to sickness, and to battle. The Norse nations were shocked, scattered, and divided. Three thrones; one lost, two vacant, created a vacuum of power. The spectre of civil war and battles of Norsemen against

Norsemen raised its ugly head, even as the shadow of the Crusade loomed across the narrow sea.

The Norse nations faced a simple choice. Put old rivalries and petty concerns aside and stand as one, or fight and die apart. Traitors and assassins carried blades in the dark to save a nation, and good men died under their swords to secure a future sealed in blood.

In the present day, echoes of this struggle remain, for those who care to look for them. Stories of heroes and conflict, victory and disaster, of the struggle of a people for hope of a future. Echoes of a dark past brought into daylight with the discovery of a once mythical sword in a frigid northern lake, 'The Light of the North', a saga of a lost people, a legend that threatens the foundations of history itself.

Book Two of the saga of the Light of the North covers twelve months in this alternate timeline, October 1116 to October 1117 AD. In the narrative, we will start where we left off; in Uppsala, as Ordulf struggles with his new life as a Norse slave. And also with the politics and machinations of Norse nations trying to build an alliance of survival in the face of an existential threat. In the conquered province of Jutland, the victorious Christians cast their eyes over the sea, to new lands, and new conquests.

The stage is set for the great war for the soul and future of the North, a clash so great its echoes will continue to resonate through the ages, and shape events even in the modern day, forging them in the fire of the fallen.

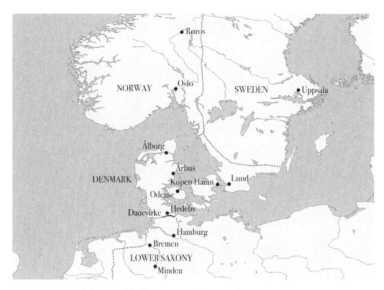

The world of Ljós a Norðan with major towns

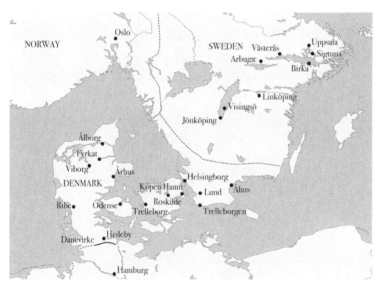

Named locations in Denmark and Sweden

Across the sea I find my fate
Beyond the waves and sand
I left aboard a ship of friends
To brave a foreign land

I went to raid the Albans
To take the riches of their kind
But I fell beneath a Saxon blade
And have no hoard to leave behind

To my fine sons I leave my strength
To my daughters; my scant lands
To my faithful wife a missing kiss
And the longing of my hands

My bones may lie in foreign soil
But weep not, my forlorn kin
For I fought with gods and dragons
and do not sleep the sleep of men

Death poem of a Norse warrior

PART 1

CHAPTER 1

THE SAGA OF LJÓS
A NORÐAN

Lundjen, Nordland
August 2015

THERE WAS A knock on the door of the office Halfar was borrowing at the University of Lundjen, and he looked up from his notes. He was preparing for a press conference later that day to present the sword and their findings, and he was nervous. The interest the find of Ljós a Norðan had inspired was well beyond what he had expected. The discovery of a once mythical sword had caused a national sensation and he was trying to be as ready as he could to face the media storm.

'Yes, come in,' he said, turning towards the door.

The door opened, revealing Professor Hallsson, who stood aside to usher two other people in, and Halfar beamed as he saw who had come to visit him. 'Ingrid!' he said, jumping to his feet in the haste of excitement. Professor Hallsson waved Ingrid and her father Aurick into the small office and the young girl looked around in curiosity at the cluttered, paper-strewn office and then smiled shyly at the diminutive curator.

'Wonderful to see you again, I wasn't sure you were coming. And Aurick, lovely, I'm so pleased you are here today.'

'Hello, Mr Asleson,' Ingrid said in reply. Aurick strode over and thrust his hand out, which Halfar took after a moment's hesitation and was subjected to a friendly but overzealous shaking.

'How have you been? Are you excited for today?' Halfar asked, getting a slightly odd look from Aurick, which dampened his enthusiasm as he looked between the three visitors.

'Uh, we have decided...' Aurick said, pausing and looking down at his daughter, who was still peering around the room at the eclectic collection of half-abandoned artefacts and old books littering the office, before nudging her back into paying attention. 'We have decided that we won't come to the press conference, and that we want to remain anonymous.'

Halfar nodded. 'Ah, I see.'

'I don't want us to be subjected to that level of publicity,' Aurick said. He glanced down at his daughter, leaving unspoken that what he meant was he didn't want Ingrid to be subjected to it.

Halfar waved the issue away and smiled again. 'Don't worry, I understand completely.'

Ingrid was looking as though she very much didn't understand, and Halfar could see that it must have been a contentious decision. There was an awkward silence that he quickly moved to quash.

'Well, we have everything set up in the conference room, and nobody's there yet, so how about we go and have a look at your sword, and everything else we found there?'

That perked Ingrid up immediately and she smiled broadly at Halfar and nodded, looking up at her father with an earnest appeal for approval on her face.

'Of course!' said Aurick. 'That would be great.'

Hallsson and Halfar took the two of them down the hall in the university archaeology wing until they reached one of the lecture halls, which had been set up for the presentation. The university was still in recess, and it would be several weeks before the new cohort of students arrived, so the halls were empty and the building quiet, beyond a few scattered clusters of researchers and PhD students in some of the labs and offices.

Along a row of lab tables at one side of the front of the hall were a series of clear plastic boxes of preserving solution with artefacts in. On the other side of the space, long rolls of felt were laid out, with dozens of artefacts laid carefully and neatly on top of them, each one with a label beside it.

In the centre of the space, in front of the table set up for Halfar and the others to sit at, dominating the room visually, the sword itself lay on a custom wooden cradle, lined with white felt.

Halfar had been stunned by the breadth of artefacts and details that had been revealed by the search of the lakebed. Dredging of the lake and a final count of the finds suggested this was probably the remains of the complete war gear of five warriors.

There was a wide array of weapons. Spearheads, axe heads, two partial swords other than Ljós a Norðan, and a couple of seax blades. Of armour there was one nearly complete hauberk of mail and fragments of at least another two. Partial remains of two helmets, one sufficiently complete to re-construct, four shield bosses and numerous buckles and fittings. Then there were the personal effects, the fabulous gold torque, and the other arm rings, buckles, and fittings.

Many of the items were damaged, beyond what they had sustained with age and degradation in the lakebed. As shown in the initial examination, the hauberk was pierced in several places, with battle-damaged rings evident. Some of the helmet pieces had dents and impact marks in them. The shield bosses were universally battered, and the broad axe blade had been cracked and hastily repaired near the haft. Everything about the collection supported the idea of this being the gear of a band of warriors who had fought many times, with little opportunity to repair or replace their equipment. That, added to the names of the four legendary companions on the golden torque – Leif, Gunnar, Vidar and Bjorn – more or less confirmed the identity of the sword and, more excitingly, provided real supporting evidence for the basis of the legend itself.

Halfar led his two guests along the tables, pointing out details and answering Ingrid's bottomless supply of questions. Then they stood in front of the sword on its cradle and Halfar flexed his toes in his shoes as he bounced slightly on the balls of his feet. The excitement of showing the sword to people had not diminished during the month that had passed.

Further fascinating details had emerged from the analysis of the star of the show, the sword. The sword, Ljós a Norðan, had been badly damaged before it was put into the lake. It was slightly bent and twisted around halfway up the blade and there were at least a dozen unrepaired notches and cracks in the steel of the edge. There was also evidence that it had been repeatedly re-ground to repair previous damage. The bronze pommel had several deep scores in it and the end was worn and deformed from repeated use. The elaborate cast and inlaid cross guard bore a number of dents and cuts, and some of the inlay had clearly been lost in battle damage. The sword was, to put it simply, worn out.

Ingrid looked it up and down with wonder and then looked up at Halfar with a nervous smile. 'Can I pick it up?' she said, reaching out a hand towards the ancient blade. Hallsson made a nervous move to protect the priceless artefact and Halfar gave him a questioning look. They had agreed no one outside their team and selected academics would be allowed to handle the fragile sword, but Halfar's expression suggested they make an exception.

Halfar had handled it himself with near religious reverence when it first emerged from the preserving process, turning the cleaned and dry sword over in his hands, drinking in the newly revealed details of the metal and the carving and inscriptions in the hilt and bronze work. Hallsson had to politely pry him away from the ancient sword, Halfar was not capable of leaving it alone unaided. He felt it was only fair that the girl who had discovered it be allowed to do the same.

'Ah, perhaps, if we are careful, it could be allowed,' he said, to Ingrid's delight. Hallsson went over to the box behind one of the tables and retrieved two pairs of blue latex examination gloves. Putting one pair on, he got Ingrid to don the oversized gloves, frowning at them but having no alternative, and carefully picked the sword up from its cradle. Resting the hilt in one hand and the midpoint of the blade in the other, he brought it over to Ingrid.

'I'm going to help you hold it, it's very fragile. Halfar, show her where to put her hands.' He nodded with his chin to the curator, who scampered over and directed Ingrid where to put her hands on the blade and the professor and the girl were left awkwardly sharing possession of the ancient sword.

'Look at me,' said Aurick, holding his phone up and lining it up while the delighted Ingrid and the nervous Hallsson shuffled to face the same direction so that Aurick could snap a photograph. 'Got it, great.'

'Okay, let's put it back now.' Hallsson firmed his grip on the sword, and gently lifted it out of Ingrid's hands with exaggerated care before carefully lowering it back into its protective cradle.

Halfar watched and pondered, as he often did when looking at the items, what had caused them to be left in the lake, and what might have become of their bearers, perhaps even the legendary Gjaldir.

The finds could tell them a lot, but sadly what they did not and could not do was tell them anything about the life, fate or even existence of Gjaldir himself. His name was nowhere on any of the equipment. Halfar had spent many an evening pondering the man's existence and the lack of any evidence was deeply disappointing. Had he been real, an amalgamation of real people, or simply made up? Clearly, the story had been exaggerated; the sword was good quality but it was neither magical nor made from 'super steel', as many of the trashier media outlets and Twitterati had branded it. Truthfully, it wasn't even the best quality sword they had found from that era in terms of steel or decoration, although it was clearly still a fabulous and battle-tested weapon.

After the initial wild excitement of the find had died down a bit, Halfar had struggled to come to terms with being no closer to solving the mystery of the warrior who had wielded the mythical weapon. He wanted, above all things, to know what had happened to the man. The saga did not relate the final fate of Gjaldir. The prophecy that ended the story remained open to interpretation and speculation. The saga simply ended with the promise that Gjaldir and the sword would return to fight for the Norse people when they were worthy of it. However, in some ways he was glad it remained a mystery. The legend would be somewhat ruined by knowing the ending, especially if it was mundane.

His thoughts were interrupted by Aurick turning and asking him a question. 'So, is it really real? I've read the saga, and some articles about it. But what do you think? Is the story true, is this the real sword?'

'Was it really magical?' butted in Ingrid, before Halfar could speak.

He laughed softly and put his hands up defensively. 'One at a time,' he said, looking at Ingrid. 'I don't think it was ever magical,' he added with a wink.

'Oh.' She looked deflated and turned again to look at the sword. 'I hoped it was true,' she said, disappointment etching her voice.

'Oh, well, it's definitely real,' Halfar said with a nod. 'We have done a lot of tests, it's a real, nearly thousand-year-old sword, and the name is real. This sword is older than the story about it, as far as we can tell.'

That confused Ingrid. 'But if it's not magical, the story isn't true.'

Halfar thought about this for a moment. 'Not in the way the story says. But that doesn't mean none of the saga is true.'

Aurick nodded. 'That's what I tried to tell her, that these stories can be exaggerated, but some of it can still be real.'

Ingrid gave her father a dark look. 'You don't know anything about it. Of course I understand not all the stories are true.' And Aurick rolled his eyes and looked at Halfar with a knowing shrug.

'Well, your father is right. I think some of the story is probably true. It fits into some events we know about from history. But the people who made sagas like this, they would often add magic and exaggeration to a story to make it more exciting. The same thing happens today.'

This explanation seemed to satisfy Ingrid, who shrugged noncommittally. 'It's even possible Gjaldir was a real person, although I think it's more likely he was an invention, a hero made for the story.'

'No, he was real,' said Ingrid, with a tone of utter certainty.

Halfar was taken aback momentarily. 'What makes you say that?' he asked out of curiosity.

The girl looked at him with a blank expression. 'Because I've had dreams about him,' she said, as if that explained everything.

Halfar didn't know what to say to that, so he exchanged an amused look with Aurick, who shrugged and smiled. 'She has been very excited about the saga, and she has had dreams about it, it's only natural. The imagination of children, eh?' he said with a deep smile of affection for his daughter.

Ingrid scowled and shook his hand off her head as he ruffled her hair. 'I told you, he knows nothing about it. I've seen him, I know he was real,' she insisted in a tone of hurt pride.

Halfar didn't want to cause any upset. 'I believe you,' he said, before he was interrupted by Hallsson.

'I'm sorry to end this, but we have to start letting the reporters in to set up their cameras and equipment. I'm afraid you will have to go now, if you want to remain anonymous.'

Ingrid looked up and slumped her shoulders, before nodding.

'I will try to arrange for you to come back later, though, would you like that?' added Hallsson, which got a renewed smile and an enthusiastic nod.

'Okay, Aurick, this way,' Hallsson said, directing the duo to the door at the side.

An hour later, Bertrand Lang, the deputy assistant minister of culture for art and antiquities, and the government's representative on the project, looked out over the sea of raised hands and indicated one with a pointed finger. The woman he pointed to spoke up. 'Professor Hallsson, some are calling this the most significant find in the history of Norse archaeology, would you agree?'

'Well, it's certainly very exciting, but the most important? I think every new great find always seems to be the most important, but this cache of weapons and armour, the most significant? I think only time will tell,' replied the professor, with a fixed smile.

'A follow up for Mr Asleson, please.' Bertrand nodded his head. 'What do you think of its cultural importance? This find shows that one of the sagas that tells of the end of the Norse rule in this country, long thought to be a myth, is real. Does this change the accepted understanding of the end of the Norse era?'

Halfar pursed his lips and glanced over at Bertrand's studied gaze before replying. As the representative of the ministry, who now owned the sword, he had become Halfar's ever present shadow during the round of interviews and press pieces that Halfar had quickly grown tired of. He had been clear from the start that he wished to avoid any difficult political questions, or any controversial historical topics.

This infuriated Halfar, to whom the guidelines sounded like asking him to lie. But the dour and fussy man had to be tolerated, for it was he who would ultimately decide how the finds would be displayed, or even if they would be displayed. But the question had turned to the disputed history of the end of Norse rule, and Halfar was unsure how to handle it.

Halfar looked back at the reporter before replying. 'It's too soon to come to any conclusions about the effect on the historical record, and this does not prove the saga true, it perhaps only confirms that it has some basis in fact.'

'But Mr Asleson,' said the same reporter, ignoring Bertrand's pointing at another raised hand. 'The official history of this country states that after the initial conquest, most of the country welcomed the conversion to Christianity, and supported the new rulers. Yet the saga tells of a great war, and then what could be described as a campaign of ethnic and cultural cleansing. Other finds have shown evidence of destroyed settlements and mass graves of people who died violent deaths. Does this sword perhaps confirm the saga's claim that the conquest of Nordlandia was based on genocide, not peaceful conversion?'

'Now, that would just be speculation,' Bertrand interjected with a flustered wave at the reporter to sit down.

'Well, it certainly is worth re-examination,' said Halfar. 'But no, it doesn't confirm anything yet. The whole process of history is to examine how new evidence might affect the understanding of the past soberly and factually, without jumping to conclusions.'

'Now, another question,' said Bertrand, giving Halfar a sideways glance of reproach.

'Well, that certainly got lively,' said Halfar with a smile as they left the press conference. 'Not what I expected at all.'

'No, I am concerned... Look, Halfar perhaps I didn't make it clear but really you were there to answer questions about the discovery, not talk about the historical record,' Hallsson said curtly.

Halfar looked at the man with surprise. They were walking alone, Bertrand had stormed off in a foul mood with his assistant without saying a word. 'What? I didn't speculate, I said the opposite, I said we shouldn't jump to conclusions.'

'That's not what it will read as. You said it might prove that the conquest of this country was a genocide, that will be the headline,' Hallsson sighed.

'What, no, that couldn't be the summary. And anyway, it might have been a genocide, there is plenty of evidence it was. But so what? It was nearly a thousand years ago.'

'Please, Halfar, don't play so naïve. It is a sensitive subject, the Nordic revival movement is generating a lot of friction, Germanic nationalism is on the rise and this government is very conservative.'

Halfar was genuinely taken aback, and quite annoyed. 'I don't care about any of that, if they misinterpret me that is not my concern. I am a historian, and I believe it is very possible that the officially accepted history is incorrect.'

'Yes, we are all aware of your views on that, and they are not without merit, but it caused enough trouble at the university in your courses. This, on the national stage, this is different.'

'Pfft. I didn't care if me speaking the truth about evidence-based challenges to the accepted historical record upset people then, and I certainly don't care now. Why does it even matter?'

'Because,' said Hallsson with an exasperated voice, 'the sword belongs to the country now, it will go in a national museum, the project has government oversight and you just put the government in a very difficult position. If they acknowledge that the sword is real and give it due attention, that might be seen by their voters as being support for the idea the saga is true, and that their history is thus a lie. Do you expect a government that is largely supported by conservative Germanic identifying voters to support a story that their history is a lie?'

'Politics! You are upset because of the politics of what I said!' Halfar was appalled and stopped to stare at Hallsson as they arrived at the professor's office. 'I'm not going to lie for political convenience.'

Professor Hallsson cast his eyes up and down the sparsely populated hall – the university was still empty for the summer holiday – and ushered Halfar into his office. 'I didn't want you to lie Halfar, just… be more careful with what you say.'

'That is the same thing,' said Halfar, wagging his finger at his old friend. 'I am not naïve, I understand that history is political, but I also won't let politics affect it, never have, never will.'

'I know, you have always been a stickler for telling the truth no matter what, and that is why you never sat in this office. I had just hoped it wouldn't extend to this,' Hallsson said sadly.

'I never wanted to be the department head!' Halfar protested. 'So why would I have changed my ways for that?'

Hallsson chuckled. 'Always the rebel, it's one of the things I most liked about you, and one of the things that I found most irritating about you.'

Halfar huffed and looked away. 'Someone has to speak up against the official record. It's quite clear to me that…'

'Enough!' said Hallsson with an exaggerated eye roll, raising a hand to calm his old colleague. 'Come, not again, not now. We know each other's views backwards.'

Halfar grumbled to a stop and there was an awkward silence. 'Well, I'm going to go and see where Ingrid and Aurick got to. They want to talk before they go. I suspect I'm going to be told a lot more about her dreams.'

CHAPTER 2
WOLVES AND WILD THINGS

Uppsala, October 1116AD

THE WATER SPLASHED around his ankles as he ran through the shallows of the river towards the ford, slamming to a halt in a shower of spray in fear as a line of Norsemen, weapons up and teeth bared, sprang up in front of him. He looked to his left, and saw the familiar dark figure on the warhorse, black eyes staring at him from the metal shielding his face, blood running from his sword. He begged for salvation from that hard steel glare, but the face turned from him, and the horse spurred away into the mist at the edge of his consciousness.

He turned back to face his enemies and saw they were almost upon him. He stepped back in panic, backing up, trying to raise his leaden hands to ward off the swords and spears that crowded around him. Then he tripped, thumped down into the sand and the breath was knocked from him, the pain twisting in his chest as a bearded figure stood over him, vicious great axe in hand. He tried to beg for mercy in a voice that would not speak, as the shadowy figure raised the axe high and then brought it arcing down.

Ordulf gasped and sat up, clutching his hand to his chest, feeling for the wound in confusion, and then recognising the dream for what it was, a familiar and repetitive reminder of the day he had been captured and enslaved at the ford in Jutland, just a few months ago. Sweat sheened his brow and dampened his chest despite the cold of the morning air. He looked around furtively, but either no one had seen his panic, or no one had cared. It would not have been the first time he woke in panic from the shadow with the long axe. In the crowded room of the slaves' longhouse, there were no secrets.

He dragged his furs to the side and stripped his sodden tunic, wearing the damp thing on a cold day would not do, and set about finding his spare one, and some food to start the day.

A short time later, Ordulf sat cross-legged by the fire in the nearly empty longhouse and focused carefully on the slim bone needle, trying to guide it correctly through the good strong strands of fabric on both sides of the tear, and swore as he misplaced another loop. The light inside was insufficient, but he knew if he went outside, someone would see him and tell him to do something, and as a slave, avoiding being told to do anything was one of his primary priorities. He was a bladesmith, and he had been set to work helping Dengir, the town's master swordsmith, and spent most of his days at the old master's forge. But Dengir was away visiting another town, selling his wares, and Ordulf had a few rare days with nothing to do.

'Ordulf, Geir, where are you, come out here.' Otto's voice came from outside the longhouse where the slaves lived in Jarl Ragnvald's Uppsala compound. Ordulf had spent most of his free time in the last month with Otto, trying to learn their language, trying to end his reliance on the man to translate everything. The Christian slave found it hard, perhaps the first thing he had ever truly had to work hard to do successfully, but he was making progress, and was often able to speak for himself now. He groaned even as he set the torn tunic he was repairing aside, another skill he was trying to learn, and stood to stretch his protesting back.

He looked around and saw Brunhild walking towards him, on her way to the cooking area with a basket of harvested fruit and grain. He smiled and made a move to greet her, but she flashed him a contemptuous glare that silenced him in mid-word, hand frozen in an awkward rise that he then tried to pass off as scratching his chin as she passed and left him standing alone. Brunhild had spurned him constantly since the night he had fought Geir to prove he was not a coward, the night that Brunhild had shared his furs in the spot near the fire that Geir had once claimed as the humiliated slave slept alone at the edge of the room.

He tried to hide his sadness and embarrassment at Brunhild's rejection from the few still in the house. He did not understand why Brunhild scorned him so, often refusing to even speak to him. He had done nothing but try to be friendly to her. He was deeply confused and hurt by the rejection he felt, but he tried not to show it as he walked to the door without looking back.

He stepped out into a glorious, sunny early winter morning. It was cold, but not unpleasantly so. The crisp air made working outside much more pleasant, although the nights could be bitter, and a week of rain made everything miserable.

Otto was in the yard, where two men were dumping tools, food, and water into a small cart. Geir followed Ordulf out of the longhouse. The two men had not spoken since the incident with the food and Geir's attempt to intimidate Ordulf had so spectacularly failed, but Geir begrudgingly gave him space and kept the peace, restraining his obvious hatred to scowls and muttered comments, which suited Ordulf just fine.

'What?' asked Ordulf in German, without thinking, before shaking his head and switching to Norse. Otto cocked an eyebrow in disapproval but replied in German. The man had been a Norse slave for many years, but like Ordulf, he had once been a man of Saxony. 'One of the farms has some work that needs doing on the buildings before winter closes in, the farmer's eldest son died in Jutland, so Jarl Ragnvald is helping them out by sending you.'

'Oh, why us?'

'Because that is who I was told to send. Go with these men, do what you are told, maybe your skills will be useful.'

'You are not coming?'

'No.'

'Then how will I know what to do?'

'You'll work it out. If you paid more attention to my lessons then maybe you would find it easier,' muttered Otto in Norse. Ordulf didn't understand the jibe, which rather enforced the point. 'You'll be gone for a few days – get some food, furs and blankets, and a couple of water skins, you are leaving now.'

The cart, thankfully, was pulled by a small mule while the two slaves walked behind it. One Norseman led the mule, the other followed behind the slaves. The men were two of Ragnvald's household warriors, but they carried no weapons other than their seaxes, which hung from their belts in leather sheaths, weapons that no warrior would go anywhere without.

As they left the city through a broad gate in the northern palisade and walked north with the soft rising sun on their left, Ordulf could not suppress a smile. The area around the city was quite beautiful. Immediately outside the walls were fields and winter pens for livestock, filling more every day with the herds coming back from their autumn pasture. The pine forest that existed in clumps here and there between the fields further from the walls was very different to the forests of his native land, stark, more uniform and taller. There was little of the dense brush and undergrowth. He enjoyed the clean, fresh air away from the stink of the city. It was a shock to him, he had forgotten how bad the city smelled, after living in it for so long.

It had been a while since the march of the Crusade from Hamburg to the tip of Denmark and Ordulf had not walked more than a few hundred feet in one go since. So his feet were sore within an hour, but he knew what to expect and he was able to bear it. It took most of the morning to reach the farm. When they arrived, the warriors were greeted warmly by the family and, despite their protestations of haste, were fed the remains of a good meal of leeks and onions with some fish and fresh bread. Ordulf and Geir looked on in jealousy, ate their own meagre food and unloaded the cart of their provisions and other items, all without acknowledging the other.

The family lived in a longhouse much smaller and narrower than the one Ordulf lived in. Its walls were built of packed earth and inside it was low, smoky and roughly furnished. Three thralls lived in a second, even rougher building, which they shared with the chickens and a few sheep. Ordulf realised the truth of what Otto had once told him; he lived better as a slave in Jarl Ragnvald's hall than these free people lived in their own homes.

The warriors left the slaves with the farmer and went on their way with the cart. Ordulf was able to understand that they were headed onto their own farms, but not why. The farmer was an older man, rotund and stooped with age, skin browned and wrinkled by decades of work in the fields. He had a daughter, who was perhaps a little older than Ordulf, with a pinched face and narrow frame, and two sons, who were maybe in their tenth and eleventh years. Ordulf did not see a wife; perhaps she was not there, perhaps she was dead.

The thralls were two women and a short man, who Ordulf at first took to be middle-aged from their posture and skin, but realised with some horror were younger, simply worn by a hard life of service outside.

The farmer had welcomed the men warmly, but he turned a

stone-cold expression on Geir and Ordulf, advancing on them as they stood idly in the beaten earth yard with a menace that scared Ordulf immediately. He stared the two men up and down, and Ordulf found himself unable to meet the man's gaze, looking down at his feet. 'There won't be any trouble from you two.' It was not phrased as a question. Ordulf understood well enough and nodded and Geir mumbled his assent.

'Back wall of the barn needs replacing, you work on it, you sleep in it, you get water from the stream down the hill and you clean it out.' More nods.

'Don't come in the house, don't go near my daughter, don't eat anything except what you brought with you.' The man scowled and walked away.

Geir looked at the barn and then grabbed an armful of their supplies and tools, carrying them inside. Ordulf sighed and followed with the rest. The barn was a simple structure of wooden posts dug into the ground, with wattle walls between the posts. The walls were built up to half their height on the outside with earth banks, so that the whole low structure was half buried in the ground. Long, rough-hewn beams sat atop the posts, supporting the simple trussed roof. It was barely high enough inside for Ordulf to stand, and sloped down towards the edges. The first thing that happened was that he smacked his forehead on a roofbeam, and Geir laughed heartily.

Ordulf muttered under his breath. He didn't want to do much breathing or talking in there, it stank. It reeked of animal waste, stale, thick, of damp and rot. It was terrible. The building was old, the roof trusses were sagging and the wall was peeling away from the roof between several of the wall pillars, two of which were leaning at precarious angles. Ordulf's stomach sank. He had no idea how they would fix this in three days, the entire structure needed re-building.

The farmer returned and gruffy herded them out to the back of the structure, where a pile of seasoned, debarked logs were ready for cutting and fitting as replacement posts for the rotten ones. The work wasn't unfamiliar to Ordulf, he had done similar things in the past. Under the terse directions of the farmer, they cut deep grooves into the top of the replacement posts and tapered the lower ends. Temporary props were forced into the underside of the old roofbeams, and the old posts levered and hacked out, before the new ones were put in.

One of the roof beams was clearly beyond saving, and after much cursing the farmer ordered the slaves to make a new one, before he left to go about his other business. Geir set about cutting one of the available logs down to size, but Ordulf was concerned. The log had a split in it, and his alarm grew when Geir over-cut the section that would slot into the groove on top of the roof beam. Instead of re-starting with a new beam, Geir tried to hack the tongue into shape with a wood-cutting axe, which only made the problem worse. Ordulf could see the beam was fatally weakened.

'Geir, no, we need a new one,' he insisted in his halting Norse.

'What do you know, I've done this before,' said Geir angrily, and waved his concerns away. Geir finished hacking at the ruined beam and grunted to himself, before lifting one end into place and looking expectantly at Ordulf and indicating the far end.

'No, it will break.'

'No, it fucking won't, do it,' the man said furiously.

Ordulf sighed and picked up his end of the beam, lifting it up and over the new post, carefully lowering it into place in the groove. Once it was set, he could see that it was too loose, and was twisting towards the weakened side with the crack, even under its own weight. He looked at Geir and shook his head vehemently, pointing at the crack. 'It will break.'

Geir huffed and stamped over to look. He shook his head

obstinately. 'It is fine.' Ordulf growled in frustration, he lacked the language to have an argument with the stubborn man. He looked up at the beam, trying to work out how he could somehow sup-port fix it so that it would support the roof. He was horrified to hear behind him the sound of Geir knocking out the wedges on the temporary supports.

'No!' He turned and saw the first support fall away, the roof creaked and settled on the far end of the weak beam, the whole structure sighing and crackling as it settled. Then Geir moved towards the last support, above the weak end. 'NO!' shouted Ordulf again, moving to block him and to grab the big hammer that Geir swung at the wedge. He collided with the smaller man and grabbed for the hammer, fouling the swing and causing the hammer to hit the support instead of the wedge, driving it sideways, and leaving it precariously hanging on one edge of the beam.

Geir shouted angrily at him and tried to pull the hammer away, but Ordulf was much stronger. The man cursed and gave one final heave. His hands slipped and he jerked backwards. Ordulf watched in panic as Geir fell back into the support with a thud, and the top sprung away from the roof it was supporting. The roof, instead of being lowered gently down by a gradually removed wedge, crashed down onto the roof beam, right at the weak point. There was a hor-rible, slow, rending noise of tearing wood, and then the structure settled for a moment, before the split in the beam gave way and the broken roof beam tore off the new corner post with a thunderous crunch and fell to the floor.

Geir dived away from the falling beam, and Ordulf backed up in horror as he thought the whole roof would come crashing down. But the fresh new corner post, strong and standing firmly in the ground, proved adequate, and caught the remaining structure in a squeal of tortured wood and a shower of sticks, dust, bird shit and detritus that cascaded to the ground throughout the barn, coating both men and causing Ordulf to gag and cough violently in the choking cloud.

As he tried to clear his throat and eyes, there was a roar from behind him. Ordulf wiped his eyes and looked around. The farmer had burst into the barn, peering through the murk. Ordulf was rooted to the spot, standing next to the fallen beam, Geir had dived away, and was by the far wall. Ordulf looked on in horror as Geir looked back and forth with a shocked look on his face, and then pointed one slim finger at Ordulf.

'What!' gasped Ordulf as Geir babbled something at the farmer, a flood of words that Ordulf could not follow, but he got the meaning well enough. Geir was blaming him. The farmer's thunderous look creased into a mask of fury as he stamped over and examined the damage. He shoved a finger in Ordulf's face and showered him with spittle as he roared at the hapless slave. Then he picked up a stave, part of the new wood for the walls, a bar of seasoned pine as thick as a boy's wrist and half his height, and swung it with all his might at Ordulf.

The stave hit him on the arm as he barely had time to flinch, and pain blossomed up and down from the stunning impact. Ordulf yelped in pain as the farmer drew back for another swing, and Ordulf instinctively caught the blow, and ripped the wood from the man's grasp, shoving him back with an open palm to the chest.

The moment he did it, despite not having deliberately planned or thought to do it, Ordulf realised the magnitude of what he had done. He looked dumbly at the wood in his hand, then with utter dread, looked up at the farmer, who was a stone mask of outrage and shock, nervously backing away from the huge slave who was facing him, holding the bar like a weapon. Everything slowed right down. Ordulf felt the panic rising, he saw Geir's shocked face, he saw the farmer, getting over his own shock, reach behind his back and draw his belt knife. He remembered Otto's warning, that to strike a freeman was death.

In that moment, he could not decide if he had already gone too far. He had shoved the man away, he had taken the bar, he suddenly realised he was holding it defensively, as if to ward off his attacker. He gasped and opened his hand, dropping it as if it was red hot. Should he run? Should he fight and flee? The tide of uncertainty and fear washed over him as the farmer looked him up and down, knife ready, trying to gauge his intent, teeth bared and snarling, down in as close to a fighting pose as his age and weathered body would allow.

Where would he run? Ordulf put his hands up placatingly, shaking his head and pleading with his eyes. The tension in the dusty space was unbearable. The farmer was still standing in furious indecision, just a single long step away, knife out and ready. Ordulf couldn't remember a word of Norse. Not one single word that he could speak in his own defence. He just mumbled and shook his head placatingly. The farmer finally advanced half a step, long knife held out in front, furiously shouting and pointing with the knife, yelling at him. *Kneel.* He picked out the word clearly in the deluge of Norse, a word he remembered.

Ordulf felt the fear grasp his chest, he judged the distance, he could grab the knife, he was sure, he could throw the old man to the ground and kill him. He could take food, weapons, whatever they had, and he could run.

But where would he go? A tear broke out unbidden from his eyes and his resolve cracked. He dropped weakly to his knees, hands still out in supplication to the advancing, screaming farmer. He looked over at Geir, and saw the man watching in rapt fascination, a hint of a smile on his face. Ordulf crouched down lower and pulled his arms into himself as the knife came forwards with the farmer behind it, not knowing if the farmer would kill him there and then, and dropped his head towards the ground, averting his gaze from the long, wicked looking blade, surrendering himself entirely to its intent.

For a moment nothing happened. He knelt on the floor, back arched and head almost on the floor, looking sideways at the fixated Geir, trying to control his racking breath and hold back the tears that threatened to burst from his face as he took what might be his final breaths, waiting for the knife. In the dust in front of him was the wooden bar. A rough hand reached down for it, and he saw it lifted up out of his vision, trailing dust as it rose out of sight. He broke his gaze from Geir and screwed his eyes shut, bracing for what was to come.

The bar slammed down into his back with appalling force. It rose and fell and rose again. The farmer was careful, studious even. He did not crack it over Ordulf's skull, knocking him out or killing him. He did not target the hands or feet. He laid into Ordulf's back and sides, his arse and thighs. He worked over every big muscle in Ordulf's writhing body with awful precision, as the slave fell into the dust and tried to cover himself. Ordulf realised, as the blows kept falling, that the man was not going to kill him, but the realisation was not much comfort as the pain burned through him from every blow.

It was like nothing Ordulf had ever experienced, far worse than the beating Hermann had given him over the anvil in his old forge in Saxony, much worse even than what the farmhand Leuter had done to him on the patch outside the tavern where the boys used to wrestle and fight to amuse themselves in the evenings. The nausea started to come in waves as the wood hammered down on him, and he was on the verge of throwing up or passing out when the farmer finally tired and sat down heavily, sweating and breathing deeply, still showering Ordulf with curses and threats.

Ordulf lay there whimpering, the humiliation barely registering over the terrible lances of agony that were spreading through every screaming muscle, every bruised rib. Eventually the farmer stood up, and, giving Ordulf one last kick, stormed out of the barn, leaving the two slaves in stunned stillness, Ordulf whimpering, Geir just staring at him in silence. Ordulf looked up through bleary eyes to find the man wearing a smirk of utter triumph. Ordulf twisted his face into a grimace, but must have looked as pathetic as he felt, and Geir just cackled and stared him down.

Ordulf lay there in pain and fury and humiliation, too hurt and too proud to move, as Geir chuckled in the corner. He swore to himself a thousand painful deaths for the cackling thrall, and tried to give himself scant comfort with thoughts of what he would do when he got the chance.

Ordulf dragged himself to a corner as night fell. He didn't eat, he pissed in the corner into some old hay, he didn't look at Geir again, trying to block him and the world out. He didn't sleep either. The pain was just too vast. The lancing gave way to burning then deep aching, before settling into exquisite tenderness, leaving him unable to find any position where he was not lying on a fresh angry bruise. He lay in his firs and writhed and winced and shivered.

It was the worst and longest night of his life. When morning finally dragged itself around again, Ordulf was standing in the corner, pacing slowly around, muttering to himself, stopping to lean on the wall with his palms and even his forehead. His hands and feet were the only things not hurting to the touch, he had spent half the night aimlessly pacing in circles on stiffening and protesting muscles, the cold that seeped into his bones at least providing some respite.

He got himself some food when that need finally penetrated the fog of his thoughts, and when the farmer arrived through the door he backed away into a corner and let out a humiliating and involuntary whimper, like a beaten dog. The farmer looked him up and down and grunted to himself in satisfaction, no hint of remorse or sorrow.

Ordulf was forced to help, as much as he could, as the two men re-built the damaged corner of the roof. The farmer proved far more skilled than Geir, and soon had a new beam cut and the three of them levered it into place, Ordulf trying not to cry out in pain from his screaming muscles.

For two more days they worked on the damaged roof, replacing some parts, shoring up others, before finally re-building the two failing sections of wall. Gradually Ordulf's pain faded, he found to his relief that nothing felt broken, beyond perhaps a cracked rib, he wasn't sure. The mass of bruises went deep brown and purple, but his muscles started freeing up.

On the last day, there was little left to do, and the two men were clearing the barn out of mess and old straw. Geir grabbed the buckets they were using, now emptied, and headed off to the stream to get more water. The farmer was out on his fields, the family still in and around the longhouse. Ordulf took the opportunity to sink stiffly to the ground carefully, with his back up against a wall post, and exhaled slowly. It would take Geir a while to fetch the water, he could rest and spend some time in peace.

He dozed off and was started awake by the sound of distant shouting. At first, he couldn't hear it when he tried to listen, and thought he might have imagined it, but then it came again, clear and high, the cry of a man in terror and agony. Ordulf scrambled to his feet, ignoring the rush of aches that prompted. He looked around, the cry had come from outside the barn to the left, the direction Geir had gone. He paused indecisively. Should he go and investigate? What could have happened? Could it be bandits or enemies, were there even bandits in these lands? If it was bandits, could he even do anything?

The swirl of questions clouded his judgement, the flinching terror of his savage beating for shoving the farmer reminding him of the penalty for hitting a Norseman. What could he do? His eyes landed on the small wood axe that they had been using. Single-handed, simple iron, but with a good edge. He could carry that, and still claim it was for cutting wood, not as a weapon. But would that be believed?

Fuck it. He grabbed the axe and started out of the barn. Another cry came from ahead, and a different noise, a guttural, animalistic howl. He jogged to the trees and up the gentle slope beyond, reaching the crest that led down into the narrow gully that the small stream ran through. He forced his way between some bushes, the trail lost in his haste, and burst out into the clearing by the edge of the water that they used to fill the buckets.

He stopped dead in his tracks. Geir was backed up against a tree trunk, one leg bleeding freely, holding a dead branch out in front of him, desperately swinging it from side to side to keep his attackers at bay.

Wolves, three of them. Ordulf looked at the beleaguered man, and then back at the wolves, fear slipping its cold hand into his once more. He had never encountered a wolf before. They were huge, almost as big as the biggest dog he had ever seen. Yellow fangs hung from snarling mouths, lips pulled back and black and pink gums exposed. They were darting in at Geir, trying to get past the branch as he shouted at them and fended them off. One of the wolves was now looking at Ordulf, snarling and snapping its jaws as it advanced on him, head down, padding slowly and deliberately.

Ordulf remembered the axe and swung it out in front of him, but it was pitifully short, and the wolf nipped at him, each just out of the range of teeth and iron. He shouted at it in pure panic and stamped forwards a step, swinging wildly at its head, but the wolf easily dodged the blow, mocking him with its toothy grin.

Ordulf looked behind him, over his shoulder, he could leave, he was sure the wolves would stay for the easy kill, not chase him. He looked at Geir, and the terrified man stared back, pleading with his eyes, he also knew he was about to be abandoned, and he knew he wouldn't last long when he was.

For a moment, Ordulf cherished the thought. Justice, in snarling teeth and rippling fur, justice so sweet for Geir's betrayal of the past days. He shuddered with anger when he remembered the slave watching in rapt satisfaction as Ordulf was brutally beaten for his mistake. He thought of the way the man cruelly laughed as he shivered with pain on the floor.

He almost did it. He almost backed away, to run back to the farmstead and leave Geir to be torn apart by those wolves. Then he remembered the day at the ambush at the ford when he was captured, of him being the one surrounded by snarling enemies, and of Sir Hans turning to leave him. He remembered the gutting pain of that betrayal, and the anger he had held ever since that someone he trusted had left him to die.

'Fuck it.' He stepped forwards again, screaming at the wolf and swinging his axe wildly to drive it back. The wolf scurried back and snapped at him, not letting him get close enough to hit it, but unable to get past the flailing axe. It tried to dive in but the axe caught it on the haunch and it squealed and backed away.

But the blade didn't bite through the thick fur, and it was soon pressing forwards again. Ordulf made it to the tree, where Geir was still swiping at the other two wolves and propping himself up on his injured leg. 'Let's fucking go, hold onto me, you bastard,' growled Ordulf.

Geir just nodded and put his left arm around Ordulf's shoulders, hanging from him and pressing on several of his still tender bruises so hard that Ordulf nearly fell to his knees under the sudden pain. He roared and swung at the wolves with his axe in his left hand, backing up, one step at a time, the three-legged slave pairing struggling to move up through the undergrowth as the wolves followed them, growling and snarling and starting to circle around them.

They got about halfway to the crest of the rise before one of the wolves managed to get around behind them and they were forced to stop, standing back-to-back to be able to fend them off in all directions. Ordulf cursed himself. He owed this man nothing, he had no reason to stay and defend him, but now here he was, stuck in a circle of murderous predators as they slavered and waited for an opening.

It didn't take long. A wolf lunged in and the two others followed it instantly. Geir slammed his branch into the head of one wolf and it scurried away with a squeal, but a second one hit him and bowled him over, Geir only just managing to get the branch between himself and the gaping jaws of the furious beast. Ordulf struck a glancing blow off the top of the third wolf's head with his axe and it pulled back, shaking its head in pain. He turned as the second wolf managed to get its jaws past the branch and onto Geir's arm.

There was a horrifying crunch and a scream of pure agony as the wolf sank its fangs into Geir's flesh. Ordulf stepped forwards and swung his axe down with all his strength, and the edge sank into the wolf's neck behind its ears with a dull crunch. The thick fur absorbed some of the blow but Ordulf felt something give. The wolf shuddered and let out a low moan, letting go of Geir's arm and stumbling back a half pace, unsteady and dazed, back legs not working properly.

It whined pitifully and half fell, shaking and scrabbling, all hostility gone. Ordulf could see the same fear in the wolf's eyes as he had seen in Geir's. The predator was gone, the pathetic, injured animal that remained looked up at him in pain and fear and confusion as it struggled to get its legs under itself. He could almost hear the wolf begging for mercy.

Ordulf stepped forwards and smashed the axe into the top of the beast's head with a thunderous crunch and it instantly flopped and went still with a wheezing breath. Turning around, he reached for Geir, who was cradling his arm and whimpering and, uncaring, he pulled the man to his feet by his good arm. Now half-carrying, half-dragging the other slave, Ordulf backed away from the scene. The other two wolves did not follow, alternately sniffing nervously at their fallen brethren and howling and barking at the retreating men, unsure what to do.

Ordulf held the axe out, threatening them with it until he was out of sight, then Ordulf tucked the axe into his belt and carried the now near senseless Geir the final distance to the farmstead.

When he arrived, he saw the farmer's daughter in the yard, standing in the doorway to her house and looking nervously in the direction he was coming from. She too must have heard the shouts and howls. She took one look at the injured slave and ducked inside her house. Ordulf stared in confusion, not knowing what to do, but within moments she reappeared with an armful of rags and a wicker basket. She hurried over to the slaves and Ordulf tried to mutter something about the wolves, but she shooed him aside and knelt down to examine Geir. After a few moments, she looked up at him. 'Water!' she said, urgently.

Ordulf blanched and looked back towards the stream, where the buckets lay abandoned, and the two wolves presumably still prowled. He wasn't going back into those woods. She shook her head firmly and pointed back to the longhouse. 'In there, water!' Ordulf nodded and took two steps, then hesitated, remembering the farmer's instructions never to enter the house. He paused. The girl looked at him in exasperation and waved him towards the house. He clamped his jaw and went through the door.

As his eyes adjusted to the light, he looked around and saw a broad half barrel of water by the end wall, and a simple wooden pail next to it. He filled the pail from the barrel and hurried back out. As he stooped to exit the doorway, he found himself standing behind the farmer, who heard him come out and turned in surprise and anger, red fury instantly colouring his face. Ordulf stepped back in panic and spread his hands out, sloshing some of the water from the pail.

The daughter chastised the old man, and after a short argument he grumbled and looked back at Ordulf, reluctantly indicating with his chin that the slave could go over and deliver the water. Ordulf put the pail down beside the woman, who started cleaning the nasty wounds. The farmer went inside and reappeared with some plants and leaves, and a bowl.

The two were clearly experienced with injuries. Ordulf supposed they had to be, living out on their own. And he stood back while they cleaned the wounds and applied various leaves and plants, the farmer grinding some of them into a paste.

The leg wound was just a series of deep scores that went through the skin but not too deep into the muscle. The arm injury was much worse. It was clearly broken, and the bite marks were deep and blood welled strongly from them. The farmer made a splint for it and wrapped it tightly once his daughter had cleaned and bandaged the gouges.

For Ordulf, that night was spent in quiet seclusion in the main barn with the farm's other slaves, who had returned from whatever job they had done. Ordulf sat in silence and wondered what was happening in the house. Geir had been taken in there for the night.

In the morning, after a fitful sleep, he woke up and went out to find out what was happening. The farmer appeared, and managed to convey that Geir was alive, and his wounds had stopped bleeding. Ordulf found himself strangely relieved, and surprised at that.

'Geir said you killed a wolf?' asked the farmer, regarding him with a new expression, for the first time not with contempt, more appraisal. Ordulf nodded. 'Show me.'

Ordulf looked uncertain, he had no wish to return to those woods, but the farmer pushed him in that direction and picked up a long-handled axe from the front step of the house. They walked the short distance to the scene of the desperate fight and Ordulf was surprised to find the half-eaten body of the wolf he had killed. Sunken eyes staring at him, almost in fixed indignation.

The farmer whistled and surveyed the scene. 'Big one. Should have told me before, the skin is ruined now.'

Ordulf apologised clumsily. He suddenly realised the two remaining wolves must have eaten their brethren and the thought somehow upset him.

'Bring it back, still useful.' The farmer turned to walk away, leaving Ordulf to drag his grizzly, stinking trophy back to the farmstead.

Later that day the two warriors who had brought them there returned, and were confused and startled to find two injured slaves and half a dead wolf in the farmstead yard. The farmer explained what had happened, leaving out the part with the collapsed barn and the beating. The warriors examined the dead wolf and the injured Geir with great interest, and one looked with open curiosity at the large bruises visible on Ordulf's arm. He pointed at it. 'Wolf did that?'

Ordulf looked from the warrior to the farmer, who smiled and shrugged. 'I fell, in the fight with the wolves.' The warrior looked unconvinced but grunted and walked away.

Geir was loaded into the cart, an uncomfortable fit, and the two warriors took him away, back towards the city. Geir met Ordulf's eye as the miserable man was taken away, and his face was full of shame and pain. *We will have words when I return*, Ordulf promised himself. He stayed at the farm. There was work yet to be done, and despite the farmer's now more genial attitude, he wasn't spared finishing clearing and cleaning the barn.

Five days later, the work was finally complete, much extended by the extra damage caused to the roof by Geir's poor workmanship, which still rankled Ordulf. The farmer had not become angry with Ordulf again over it, despite the fact he now had to help Ordulf fix the damage. The two men worked in near silence on the finishing of the repairs, and when one of the warriors returned to collect Ordulf, the work was complete and the farmer even appeared satisfied. As the farmer thanked Ragnvald's man and the warrior motioned Ordulf to leave, the farmer called out to him. 'Hey, here.' He walked over and pulled something from his belt pouch.

Ordulf's eyes widened. It was a wolf's tooth. It was huge, yellow and curved, tied onto a thin leather thong like a necklace. 'One less wolf,' the man said with a hint of a smile. 'It's good for me, thank you, wolf-killer.' He winked and walked away. It was hardly an apology, but Ordulf grinned nonetheless, and turning the tooth over in his hand, followed the warrior back to the city with a spring in his step the whole way.

When they finally got back to the compound, Ordulf composed himself and went inside. The longhouse had not changed. But there was an odd reception to his arrival, and he scowled and wondered what lies Geir had been spreading in his absence. Had the man told them of his humiliation? Lied about him causing the damage to the barn? The bruises were fading, but the memory of the pain and fear was still raw.

Otto came over from the corner, he looked tired. Brunhild was there too, eyeing him oddly. 'Where is Geir? I need to speak with him,' said Ordulf, loud enough that most could hear.

Brunhild looked at him in surprise and confusion, then shook her head. 'No, you don't.'

'I do, what has he told you? If he has lied about me again…'

'Stop, he hasn't. He told us about the wolf.'

'Then what is wrong? I still want to talk to him, he needs to apologise to me.' Ordulf could feel his anger rising now. 'Where is he?'

'He's dead, Ordulf,' said Otto.

Ordulf looked away from the angry Brunhild and blinked at him dumbly. 'He's what?'

'He died,' Otto said with a sad sigh. Ordulf looked around the room. All the slaves were watching him, the strange atmosphere in the room suddenly made sense. It was mourning.

'What, what happened? His wound was bandaged, they did well, I saw it. The bleeding had stopped. He looked fine as he left. How did he die?' Ordulf babbled, the anger gone from him and confusion reigning.

'Yes, they treated his wounds well, and so did we. His leg started healing but his arm…' Otto unconsciously picked at his stump of finger as he spoke. 'Ragnvald even called a laeknir, but his arm got the wound rot anyway. And then yesterday they cut it off. All night we watched him, tended to him, but he died this morning.' He looked up at Ordulf sadly. 'And he told us what he did to you, before the end. He told us about the barn and the wolves.' He gave a thin smile. 'Thank you for trying to help him, Ordulf. But please, say nothing more about him. He made mistakes, but he was our friend.' Otto put his hand on Ordulf's shoulder and walked away, leaving Ordulf churning and filled with regrets.

CHAPTER 3

FIGHT AND FLIGHT

November 1116

WINTER HAD COME and the snows came with it. Ordulf had nothing to do but work in the forge and huddle in the longhouse, where he spent his time learning the language from Otto, and anyone else who would speak with him. It had become his obsession, to be able to speak for himself entirely, to no longer rely on anyone, and he was finally getting there, only having to check with Otto for words he had not heard before.

He had been making mixed progress on his sword project at the forge, despite Dengir's obvious disagreement with his ideas. The old smith scorned his pointier designs, the style he had learned from master Gunther back in Hamburg during his days as a smith with the men of Saxony on Crusade, but he helped Ordulf nonetheless. Ordulf was trying to forge a blade that would cut like a Norse blade and thrust like a Christian blade, and none of his experiments in plain iron had worked well at both, not sufficiently. He was growing frustrated, and beginning to believe that Dengir was right to doubt it was possible.

Ordulf was walking home from a long day at the forge with a deep sense of gloom about the project and the harsh Norse winter. He had not been ready to face a winter in the northern city, already the intense cold at night was worse than anything he had been used to at home. Even inside the longhouse, the water in the buckets would sometimes have a thin layer of ice in the morning. The days were so short as to barely exist. He was in the forge before it grew light and went back to the compound after darkness fell.

The streets were a mixture of frozen earth, churned, icy mud and mush on the main thoroughfares, so he avoided those where possible, taking back routes where the ground was solid and wouldn't steal a shoe in the cloying half frozen morass, or seep freezing mud in between his toes.

It was taking a back route home that led Ordulf to come upon the men waiting in the shadows of the buildings across from Jarl Rangvald's compound. He turned a corner that looked down the side street leading directly to the yard outside his longhouse. At the end of it, in the late day gloom, he could see the jarl; he was in the yard, dressed in fine furs, laughing with his huscarl Leif, and apparently about to set off into the street to go somewhere. But that was not what drew Ordulf's attention. Standing around the next corner in front of him, no more than ten running paces away, was a group of armed men hidden from the view of the jarl. One of their number, axe held around the corner out of sight, was leaning against the building, feigning indifference, but watching the jarl intently.

Ordulf's mind slowed. He had not been seen yet but he could see one of the men turning at the sound of his feet on the frosty ground. ten paces away. The men were all looking tense, swords free of scabbards, axes in hand, violence written on their features.

Nine paces. A man in the group locked eyes on him. Would he be recognised? Could he simply walk past the men, or come close enough to passing them that he could break into a run and reach the yard?

Eight paces. He shifted his eyes to the jarl. Ragnvald was wearing his new dragon sword; two of the other men were likewise armed. That was it. Three armed men unprepared for violence against seven – no, eight men, who were ready, axes and swords in hand.

Seven paces. He was committed now, he did not have enough time to turn and run, he kept a calm face and simply carried on walking, a slave minding his own business.

Six paces. The turned man's face flashed with alarm and then anger. Ordulf cursed his foolishness for trying to walk past. *What the fuck do I do now?*

Five paces. The alerted man emitted a low noise of warning and started off towards Ordulf. He would get between him and the jarl, it was too late to make a break for it cleanly. *I'm going to have to fight him.* The realisation was sickening. Ordulf went for the hammer on the belt that was draped over his shoulder, letting the rest of the belt fall. By the luck of the gods, it was easily accessible, almost under his hand.

Four paces. The axeman was gesturing to his fellows to move on the jarl, who had not yet moved to leave the yard. The men looked around in confusion; their attack delayed for a critical moment.

Three paces. Ordulf had a firm grip on the hammer, arm cocked back behind his shoulder, belt hitting the ground behind him. The axeman started swinging his own weapon back as he powered into a run, clearly aiming to hit Ordulf at speed and kill him before he could make a sound. Ordulf opened his lungs to draw in a great breath

Two paces. The axeman realised his mistake too late. Ordulf wasn't going to try to block the blow from the axe, or hit him with the hammer – he was going to throw it. Ordulf whipped his arm past his shoulder with terrifying speed and as he exhaled with the force of the throw, used all his breath to shout, 'RAGNVALD!'

One pace. The axeman had a brief moment in time as the hammer flew, just long enough to realise that he had no chance to dodge the heavy steel tool, which came at his face with the speed a falcon swoops for a rabbit. The other men were breaking from cover, three paces behind and to the right of the shocked axeman. *Too slow, I can make it* – Ordulf was already at a run, ducking to avoid the still-swinging axe even as his hammer hit the leading man in the face with a sickening crunch and snapped his head back like the end of a rotten plank.

Ordulf skimmed under the wildly swinging axe and saw, in his peripheral vision, that he had half a pace on the other attackers and was moving faster. His feet pounded on the frozen ground, threatening to slip at any second. A few paces to go to reach the street and the jarl in the yard beyond. Ragnvald raised his eyes.

The jarl had heard Ordulf's shout of alarm; his wide, cold eyes had snapped around and were taking in the image. The falling man with the ruined face sprawling onto the ground. The armed men breaking from cover. His big Saxon slave sprinting towards him, face a mask of effort and fear.

The jarl had to decipher the situation in a heartbeat, decide what the threat was, and what to do about it. Jarl Ragnvald made his decision. He was an experienced lord of war; making life-and-death decisions in a moment was second nature to him.

'TO ARMS!' he roared, drawing his magnificent new sword, Drekitunga, Dragon's Tongue, and backing towards the entrance of the great hall. His two men rapidly reacted and joined him, swords drawn, covering his flanks.

Ordulf had nearly reached the cross street outside the yard when his foot slipped in the slight ditch along its edge, where mud from the main street remained churned and unfrozen. His leading leg went sideways; he put his arms out in horror as he started to topple, desperately flailing for balance, the armed men merely two paces behind him.

The jarl saw the smith fall and cursed, willing the boy to rise to his feet in time to get ahead of the men chasing him. He could see it wasn't going to happen. He had five more warriors in the great hall. It would be ten heartbeats, at least, before they arrived. His idea had been to defend the door until they came out, to avoid being trapped in the hall and burned out. Perhaps he would have to survive two exchanges of blows, neither side with shields. It was possible he could hold for long enough. The smith would be caught in five beats, just a couple of paces in front of him. The slave who had just saved him from assassins.

The jarl powered off his back leg and charged out towards the attackers, his two men just one step behind. Ordulf managed to turn his fall into a roll and came up on his feet, facing the wrong way, costing him speed and leaving him with no time to turn. A sword was coming for his guts, its wielder two paces away. Ordulf backed a step and brought up his arms to desperately ward off the coming blow, twisting to try and avoid its path.

The jarl's dragon tongue sword appeared over Ordulf's shoulder, held point forwards like a spear, and hit the running man in the throat, passing right through it and coming clean out the other side, such was the closing speed of the two men. Ordulf was hit by the dying man; his now-unguided sword scored Ordulf across the left arm, and his shoulder rammed Ordulf in the stomach. The slave went down under the soon-to-be corpse.

On the jarl's right was Leif. He leaped over the tangled bodies of the slave and the dying man and swung down from the top of his arc at one of the axemen, the cut severing the man's leading arm at the elbow, removing the threat from the jarl's right flank as he faced the five remaining attackers, who spread out after exiting the end of the alley and skidded to a halt in the face of the sudden counter. The jarl's second man arrived and traded blows with an axeman circling to Rangvald's left. Both men struck hard and both men reeled back holding hands to gushing chest wounds.

Four men now faced two. If they had attacked together, the assassins would surely have won. But men, especially frightened men, make mistakes, and hesitate in the heat of the moment. These men had just seen half their number downed in the space of twenty heartbeats, their plan and advantage of surprise shattered.

Three of them finally gathered their courage and attacked, but not all together. The fourth lost his nerve and tried to circle around behind the jarl. The door to the great hall burst open and the first of Ragnvald's men came out, sword in hand, face wild with anger and confusion. He saw the fight and charged. Two more followed behind him.

The jarl and Leif had to stand against the four attackers for just a few moments until help arrived, but it might be a few moments too long. Two men charged Leif and he skipped to his right, opening a gap between him and the jarl and allowing him to face only one blade at first. He took the swing of that blade at a glancing angle on his sword, pommel up towards the sky, flat of the blade pointing down, and the incoming swing glanced off it, momentum carrying the arm and the attacker past to Leif's left. Leif reversed the block into a sharp downwards swing and his blade bit into the shoulder of the attacker as he passed. With his backswing he knocked aside the axe of the second attacker and stepped into his advance, shoulder charging him and knocking him back a pace.

Ordulf had rolled the gasping and nearly dead man off him and levered himself to his feet. He saw the fourth attacker circling to the left. He saw the man with the injured shoulder reeling towards him, shouting in pain. He saw the discarded sword at his feet and he bent down to grab it. In front of him, the man with the injured shoulder ignored him. Leif was blocking a vicious blow from the axe-wielding man and his back was turned. The injured man drew back his sword to strike Leif's unprotected flank. Leif turned, eyes wide, backing up. He blocked another blow of the axe by taking the haft on his upraised sword arm with a painful-sounding thud. Then he desperately dodged the incoming blow from the injured man by ducking underneath it and trying to grapple. The man's sword went over his back, scoring his ribs.

Ordulf ran into the melee, calculating, time slowing in his eyes. Leif was tangled with the injured man, trying to pin the sword arm. Ordulf guessed Leif would win, men were about to arrive to help him anyway. He ran past the grappling men and stabbed his sword forwards at the axeman, who was surprised, but knocked the thrust to one side and took a step back before countering at Ordulf's face, a blow Ordulf barely managed to avoid, before wildly swiping his sword back across his front, missing the axeman but forcing him another step back. To his left, the jarl parried a thrust from the man he was engaged with, twisted his blade clear of the bind and then put his sword through the chest of his attacker in a burst of bright blood. Behind him, a strangled cry and a gurgle announced the end of the injured man fighting Leif as an arriving warrior pulled his sword across the man's throat. The jarl spun to face the man who had been circling around him, off to Ordulf's left. Too late, that man saw the warriors coming from the hall and was bowled over and killed on the ground.

The axeman facing Ordulf saw all this as he bobbed on his feet, axe up and ready to strike against Ordulf. He saw the last man attacking the jarl get taken down. His eyes flicked between Ordulf and the jarl. If he took the time to kill the slave, the jarl was safe; if he went for the distracted jarl, he was open on his flank and even the slave could kill him. If he ran, he would be hunted down like a dog. He chose a fourth option. He threw his axe.

His throw was good; his luck was not. The axe seemed to be sluggish in the air, the blade not swinging round as he intended. In the heat of the combat, the axeman felt suddenly cold, like a fell wind was on him. In that moment between fates, he felt an otherworldly presence and heard the screech of a raven so close he almost flinched. Then it was gone, and he saw that the throw would not kill, and that he had failed. The haft glanced off the side of Ragnvald's head and the edge merely nicked his ear. A different amount of rotation and the blade would have buried itself in the skull behind his temple.

Ordulf watched the axe fly with horror and then turned back to find the now unarmed man lunging and almost upon him. A hand grasped his sword, trying to push it out of the way; another went for his throat. Blinding pain erupted from his neck as the man's fingers punched into his windpipe. Ordulf almost let go of the sword. Almost. The man, like many before him and many who would come after, had underestimated Ordulf's strength.

Despite the surprise of the throat hit, it had not been a clean blow and was made with an overextended arm. Ordulf grabbed the man's hand away from his neck with his left and pushed back on the hand fighting for the sword, his fingers like iron on the hilt. He forced his attacker's arms apart as the man struggled, drawing their faces closer together. Then he viciously headbutted the man in the face. The axeman's nose shattered and his head snapped back. He let go of Ordulf's sword hand. Two warriors arrived and bore the attacker to the ground, dazed but alive, blood pouring from his face.

The fight was over. Seven attackers lay dead or dying. The jarl's badly injured man was sitting up with one of his comrades supporting him, clasping one hand and the other helping him grip his sword. He was coughing, dribbling blood and obviously breathing his last. The jarl was bleeding from a minor leg wound, leaning against the wall of the hall, breathing hard. Leif had a shallow cut the length of a forearm down his side, over his ribs, which was bleeding through his ruined tunic. Leif ignored it as he stood by his jarl, bloodied sword in hand, eyes scanning the roads. Ordulf's arm was cut deeply, down into the muscle. He was shocked by how little it hurt him. He felt lightheaded and his heart was hammering, the slow passage of time of the fight snapped back to the full speed of reality. Suddenly a furious warrior barged into him, simultaneously shoving him against the wall and stripping the dangling sword from his hand. The warrior growled and pointed the sword at Ordulf's chest. 'What were you doing with that sword, slave?'

'Hold, no, he is not to be harmed,' Ragnvald called over, waving the man away. Ordulf breathed a deep sigh of relief. The warrior gave him a scornful look and limped away, taking the sword with him. Ordulf realised it was Fenrir's brother and shuddered at how hot the man's hatred had felt as his sword tip was hovering against his chest. The jarl snapped out more orders.

'Bring the injured and the prisoner to the hall. Arm all the men, there may be further attack. Sten!' He pointed to the warrior who had disarmed Ordulf. 'Send word to the king's hall of this attack and warn the lords present there for the meeting; this may be part of a wider attack.'

The men all rushed to their orders. One of them pounded down the road towards the city square and the great hall there, parting a growing group of curious onlookers. The pain of his wound suddenly hit Ordulf and he clutched his arm to his chest with a stifled cry. The jarl beckoned to him.

'You too, in the hall. Now!'

Ordulf nodded and jogged to the door, holding his injured arm in his right hand, heart still pounding out of his chest.

CHAPTER 4

FOR WORD AND WYRD

NO MORE ATTACKS on the hall came and no more were reported in the city. Warriors were armed and patrolled the streets nonetheless. The planned meeting in the king's hall was cancelled as darkness turned into night. A dozen stood guard in the jarl's compound and at the doors to his hall. Inside, a læknir, a healer, was tending to the wounded. The jarl was sitting in his chair on the dais drinking a horn of ale and laughing with Leif. The mood in the hall was tense but jubilant. The læknir was kneeling at the jarl's side, dressing his leg wound, which did not look too serious.

Ragnvald scanned the room as Leif told him what Ordulf had done. His eye was caught by the one man in the room who looked out of place, but then, recently, he always looked out of place. Sten, the crippled brother of Fenrir, who had fallen to Leif's sword in a duel over unforgivable insults. Ragnvald could see him staring in their direction and on his face was a look of undisguised bitterness. *Perhaps he would rather Leif had died today?* Everyone else in the room was celebrating the victory, Sten alone looked disappointed.

Ragnvald frowned, and Sten saw his frown and turned away, shuffling his way back along the side of the hall.

The læknir at that moment finished the poultice she was laying on his leg, and she pressed it down, causing Ragnvald a stab of pain that took his attention away from Sten and back down to his wound. Leif was drinking and inspecting his own wound, which the healer now moved onto with a nod of deference to the jarl.

'He did well, don't you think?' said Leif. Ragnvald looked over at his huscarl confused, then remembered Leif had been talking of Ordulf.

'He did well to alert me, it would have gone badly otherwise,' he said.

'I meant, in his fight with the attacker.'

'Ah, yes, I didn't see it, but I'm sure he defended himself well.'

Leif shook his head ruefully, knowing the jarl had not been listening. 'He saved my life, and through that, he saved yours.' That got Ragnvald's attention.

'Truly?' he asked. Leif nodded solemnly.

'I see.' Ragnvald looked around again, seeing the slave standing at the back of the hall, clutching his injured arm and looking unsure of himself. 'Well, we must see he is dealt with accordingly, I will think about what he deserves.'

Leif smiled. 'That would be well, Lord Ragnvald.'

The healer was just finishing with Leif. She had smeared his wound with some sort of paste and then covered it with a mixture of grass and herbs before wrapping a length of linen around his chest to hold it.

Leif thanked the læknir and pointed at Ordulf. 'Perhaps I should send the læknir to him, he was wounded.'

'Yes, a one-armed smith would be no use to me anyway.' The jarl nodded at the læknir, who collected her things. 'There is another matter, Leif, while we are talking.' Leif met his eye. 'Since your fight with Fenrir, Sten has been a shadow of a man. I have seen his eyes on you, filled with nothing but hate.'

Leif laughed nervously. He still felt guilty about the fight with Fenrir, it had cost Ragnvald one of his best men, although the jarl was too honourable to hold it against him. Not publicly, at least. 'I have nothing to fear from the cripple brother.'

Ragnvald chided him with his glare. 'Sten fought in my shieldwall and took a wound in my service, he deserves respect.' Leif wiped the smile from his face and nodded submissively. He had never liked Sten, but since he had killed his brother Fenrir in an honour duel the man had become a potential threat, and made no attempt to hide his own feelings. 'However, there are many ways a cripple can kill a man, you must sleep, after all. A knife in the dark kills as sure as a sword in the daylight.'

Leif looked around nervously. 'Surely he would never do such a thing, he would be cursed.'

'He is cursed already, and he was never the most honourable of men. No, I will find some reason to move him away, when it will not seem a humiliation. Until then, be on your guard.' Ragnvald thrust his chin to the side, indicating the talking was over.

'Yes, Lord Ragnvald,' said Leif, standing and heading down to one of the tables to get a horn of ale.

Ordulf stood awkwardly by the side of the room, blood seeping from between his fingers and dripping onto the floor. He was practising his old skill from his time at his forge in Minden of trying to appear not to exist, a laughable thing to do as he stood there huge and sweaty, bleeding on the jarl's floor.

To Ordulf's surprise, three of the attackers were still alive, and the Norse were not only not finishing them off, they were treating them. The man who had lost his arm to Leif's sword was sitting against a wall post, stump heavily bandaged, face ashen.

The man Ordulf had thrown the hammer at was unconscious, lying stretched out on the floor at the side of the room, breath gurgling through his ruined face, his nose completely crushed, leaving a horrific pit in the centre between bulging eyes.

The læknir, a middle-aged woman in a floor-length dark and rough woollen dress, shuffled over to Ordulf and took his hand away from his arm to inspect it. She smelled strongly of herbs and other unfamiliar scents that were slightly acrid and unpleasant. She hummed to herself and released his arm. 'You'll be fine. Sit over here so I can stitch the wound and put on a poultice.'

She led him to an empty table towards the end of the hall and went to fetch her basket of supplies. She had a fine curved bronze needle with a spool of silk thread and a wooden pestle and mortar filled with a foul-smelling green-black substance. He laid his arm flat on the table at her direction and she washed and inspected the wound before she started closing and stitching. The washing and stitches were really unpleasant, but when she took a scoop of the foul-smelling stuff and then laid it onto his wound. Ordulf's arm exploded in pain. He started to open his mouth to cry out, and wanted to yank his arm back, but managed to suppress both reactions. Grinding his teeth together, he breathed hard and tried to ignore the band of fire across his arm.

Men were watching him; he couldn't show weakness. He remembered with amazement that the jarl had been laughing and drinking beer while he was having his wound dressed. The treatment hurt more than the wound, the jarl must be made of stone.

Leif appeared next to him and thrust a horn of ale into his good hand while the healer was poking and covering the gash in his arm. He gratefully took it and drank deeply. He forced his face into a neutral mask as Leif spoke to him.

'You saved my life today, Christian. I think we are even now.' He was smiling.

Ordulf grunted in what he hoped was a way that indicated agreement – but it was really the only noise he could manage short of crying out. He drank some more ale to mask a grimace he couldn't stop, and to let him screw his eyes shut.

'I'm glad you didn't actually have to fight that man. You hold a sword like a child holding a stick. He would have been through you in two more strokes. You never used a weapon while you were in Christian lands?'

Ordulf finished his draught of ale and shook his head, trying to force himself to speak without screaming. 'Never. Although, actually, I did help throw stones from a siege engine at the Danevirke, if that counts as using a weapon.' He choked out a pained laugh. The healer finished applying her evil mixture and began binding his arm in linen from wrist to elbow. The pain was changing from fire to icy numbness.

Leif chuckled and slapped his hand on the table. 'So you have never held a sword, but you helped fell the great wall? What strange people you Christians are. I think you should stick to your hammer. I didn't see the throw that felled that man,' Leif nodded over his shoulder at the still-gurgling man laid out on a bench, 'but the jarl said it was magnificent, like Thor's throws from the skald's songs. That's two warriors you have taken down with that hammer, eh?' His eyes blazed with mirth, referring to the day he was captured, when Ordulf had put Leif on his back on the riverbank, and broken the huscarl's shield with his hammer. 'Although one was clearly greater than the other – I still have my beautiful face!' He slapped Ordulf on his meaty shoulder and stood, turning to walk back along the hall.

The healer had also finished. Ordulf realised that the ale and laughing about the fight had made the treatment of his wound much easier to bear. He then realised with a smile of recognition that had been deliberate. The jarl hadn't been laughing and drinking with a warrior because he didn't feel his wound. Leif had been helping him to appear unperturbed by laughing and drinking with him. Leif had seen Ordulf struggling and helped him in the same way. He still had a lot to learn about the subtleties of their honour system, but it clearly ran deep.

The jarl called out into the hall above the chatter and everyone fell silent. 'Friends, gather round, bring some ale and sit by the fire. Let us drink and celebrate our victory. Food is on the way and tonight, we shall feast to the memory of our brave friend Harald and those of our enemy who deserve our respect!' There was a chorus of cheers and table-thumping throughout the hall. Ordulf watched, fascinated. They were going to celebrate their enemy? The men who had just tried to murder them?

'Ordulf, where are you, my mad Christian thrall?' the jarl shouted across the room. Ordulf tensed and stood, catching the jarl's eye. He hoped Ragnvald didn't blame him for Harald's death. The jarl beckoned with his hand over the throng. 'Come here, sit and drink with us. You stood with us in battle, so you shall drink with us tonight.' No one cheered this announcement but there were nods of approval and a few faces turned to look at him in appraisal.

Ordulf grabbed his ale and walked over to the group. Hands slapped his back and someone vigorously clasped and pumped his injured arm, making his eyes water in pain. A warrior directed him to a bench at the front of the hall, near the fire. Even Ordulf knew this was a place of distinct honour at such a gathering. Leif sat next to him, smiling and raising his horn to knock it together with Ordulf's. This was something he was used to from Germany as a form of celebration; apparently some things were the same wherever you were.

The jarl's people settled into their seats and benches, or gathered along the walls, sitting on chests, shelves and piles of furs.

There must have been fifty men and women in the hall, their bodies and the bubbling fire keeping the cold a distant memory. It seemed that every one of the jarl's men from across the city had come. He realised with a shock that the man he had subdued with the headbutt was sitting across the hall from him on the floor, leaning against one of the pillars, completely unrestrained and drinking a horn of ale. Dried blood covered his ruined nose and woollen tufts were stuffed into his nostrils. He looked quite ridiculous, but Ordulf could not understand why he was allowed, as an attempted murderer, to sit there drinking, mere feet from the very man he had tried to kill.

His thoughts were interrupted when the jarl called for silence so he could speak. The warlord raised his voice, and men beat the tables to hush the crowd. Ragnvald looked out over the gathering while he waited for all eyes to be on him, sweeping his piercing blue eyes over the men, while they gave their attention to the silver-haired lord.

'Friends. Today we were attacked by the family of Jarl Harnsted, the cousin of the previous King Philip. Jarl Harnsted died while out hunting not long ago, beset by unknown men. What some of you might still not know is that some of my hird and I may have been those unknown men.' A ripple of surprised muttering and even some angry exclamations went around the hall, followed by silence. The jarl continued. 'Good, I am pleased that so many of you are shocked, the secret has been well kept. Well, clearly not enough, because his family found out and sent these men to kill me in revenge.' He indicated the prisoners along the side of the hall. 'I am telling you this today because the time for secrets is over. Jarl Harnsted was asked to relinquish the throne to allow a unified king of the Norse to face the Christians as one people with one army. He was asked to give his throne to King Sigurd of Norway. He refused to do this. So a group of the other great lords of Sweden and I discussed and decided the matter. Most of us decided unity was in the best interest of the people of this land. Our enemy has to be the Christians, not other Norse. So, I tell you with no regret, we plotted against and killed a rightful contender to the throne of this country and his most fervent supporters, and called for King Sigurd to come and claim the throne. King Sigurd Magnusson will be here in the spring to do so.'

The jarl stopped and looked around the room to give them time to digest the news. Some men were shaking their heads in disbelief, others were nodding. A few even shouted out, calling their support.

'I have done what is required to defend my people. It is the highest duty of a lord, but I recognise that it was a dishonourable act, to plot against a man who had not wronged me. I offer any of you who cannot forgive this the chance to break your oaths to me without shame or dishonour and leave, for another lord or another land. You will face no repercussions or disrespect.'

There was a wave of chattering in the hall. Some men looked around them; others stood in stony silence.

Only one warrior left the hall with his gear, shaking his head in dismay and anger.

The jarl waited until the noise died down. The rest of them had made their decision. 'I declare the attempted revenge taken today to be honourable. The men who carried out this attack did so according to our laws and customs and shall face no punishment for their actions, in this life or the next. Those who fought well and died, I salute them, they served their oaths well until death, as is the duty of all of us. I hope they are already drinking in the halls of Valhalla. Those who survived are free to go. They are to be treated with respect.'

There was a swell of agreement in the assembled ranks. Men pounded tables and grunted in that peculiar Norse way Ordulf had heard several times, a loud, guttural noise.

'Further, we celebrate the life and deeds of Harald, my loyal huscarl, who followed me without pause or question to fight double our number in the street, and died with his sword in his hand, the man who gave him his death wound already slain at his feet.'

There was a crescendo of roars and cheers in the hall. Tables were pounded and men rose to their feet.

The jarl raised his silver-trimmed horn of ale into the air. 'Let us drink and feast to his name so that the Allfather himself hears us, and welcomes Harald to feast with him in his golden hall. For Harald!' he roared at the crowd and pumped his fist.

The room exploded into cheers. Ale was splashed from horns as men raised their hands in the air and emptied the drinks down their throats. Ordulf found himself also on his feet, carried by the tide of emotion. He drank to the dead foreigner's name and loudly celebrated Harald's death deed of saving the jarl who had enslaved Ordulf. Cheering with the men who had stolen his life and condemned him to an existence of service without giving it a second thought.

The feasting and drinking were indeed long, loud and raucous. Women sang and danced, men wrestled in front of the dais and drank vast amounts of ale. A skald performed a rousing and hugely exaggerated song about the fight. Ordulf wasn't sure what it took to get the attention of their Allfather but he expected this probably would. He found himself forgetting his wound and his woes as he drank and laughed and swapped stories of the fight with others in the room. Men stood up at intervals to tell stories of Harald's life, his deeds in battle, his honour to his friends, and in one case, to a chorus of whoops and cheers, his many supposed achievements with women.

When the stories were all told, and the food was all eaten, the men sat around exhausted, some sleeping in a drunken stupor and others still chatting and laughing around their tables. The jarl gestured from the dais to Ordulf, who was describing Christian funerals to a bemused and extremely drunk Leif, to come and join him.

Ordulf staggered over the rush-covered floor to the dais, and sat down heavily on a stool next to the jarl. The old warrior was giving him a stern appraisal. Ordulf was too drunk to feel cowed as he normally would, and took the chance to stare right back.

Ragnvald had an air of authority about him, something that you felt rather than saw. It reminded him strongly of Count Adolf, who had been so different, so casual, but yet held that same aura of leadership. The confidence of his movements and gestures, a look in his eye. He might be ageing and silver-haired, but strength and purpose radiated from him, from his scarred and muscled forearms to his sun darkened face. He kept his silvering beard neatly tied, as many of the warriors did, and his hair combed back behind his head. He looked every inch the lord of war and men that he was.

'Ordulf. We have matters to settle,' the jarl said, waking Ordulf from his assessment. Many of those warriors and women still conscious had stopped talking to listen to the exchange. The jarl was smiling; there was no malice in his tone.

'It is my duty as jarl to dispense justice fairly and according to the laws and customs of our land. I have been thinking about the events of today and have come to my judgement.' He paused and raised his voice to help the others hear.

'You saved my life from these attackers today.' He paused and nodded sagely. 'I was about to walk out in front of them; they would have overwhelmed us.' The hall was now silent. 'You could have run, you could have stayed quiet. Instead, you, a slave and unarmed, attacked them and ran through them to warn me. This act prevented my death at grave risk of your own. The act of a brave man indeed.'

Men around the hall pounded their tables and grunted their assent.

'Do you disagree?' the jarl asked, as he saw Ordulf lowering his eyes, embarrassed.

Ordulf saw that it was too late to change direction. 'Lord, you have mistaken my actions. I saw the men and by the time I decided whether I could pass them or not, it was too late to turn around. I had no choice but to go through them. I shouted, as much hoping that you would save me as to warn you.' He lowered his head, ashamed.

The jarl looked stunned and then roared with laughter. 'My word, boy! You are an honest and brave man indeed to say that after I just praised you in front of everyone.' He wiped a tear of mirth from his eye. 'Well, your actions saved my life, and honour demands recompense. It seems that I have settled that well, as I saved you after you saved me.'

'Yes, Lord, and I am most grateful that you did.' Ordulf looked earnestly into the jarl's blue eyes.

'Excellent!' the jarl exclaimed. 'We have done right by each other in front of the gods and my men. Now I must address a second issue, one of law. You first defended yourself against a warrior sworn to a different lord, a man who was trying to kill you without cause. A man who had no right to take you, my property, from my service. Self-defence in this situation is allowable even for a slave, and requires no punishment. The second matter; you also took up a sword to defend Leif from his enemies, a brave but illegal act.' The jarl turned his stern gaze down into the massed benches in front of him.

'Leif,' the jarl called down to the table where the man was sitting. 'What would have happened if Ordulf had not driven off the man sitting down there?' He pointed to the man with the ruined nose, who was sitting on a box at the side of the room, watching intently. He had removed the woollen tufts, his broken nose re-set by the healer and bleeding long since stopped.

'He would have killed me while I grappled with the other man, Lord. And then the two of them would have attacked you before you were finished with your own enemy or before the others could help you. You would surely have been slain.'

The jarl nodded in agreement. 'That is also my view.' He turned to Ordulf, his face once again serious. 'By the laws of our land, as your jarl and owner, I sentence you to death for the crime of taking up a sword against a free Norseman, who was acting in accordance with the law and posing no threat to you. You had no legal right to attack him, no right to intervene in a fight between freemen that was not your concern. Such a crime by a slave can only be met with death, and as a slave you have no right to defend your actions in front of the lawgiver. The transgressions of a slave are the responsibility of their owner, such is our law.' The room fell into a deathly silence, men watching gasped or shook their heads, but the jarl stilled them and continued. 'However, as a reward for saving my life again, I spare you from this punishment and declare you free of the stain of this crime. A life for a life once more; such is our way, such is my right as your lord.'

Ordulf was so drunk and confused he didn't even have time to be scared before he was relieved. There was a rousing chorus of assent and table slapping around the room.

'You,' the jarl asked, looking at the man with the ruined nose in the corner. 'You were wronged by this slave who attacked you without just cause. You are a free man of this land who has committed no crime. Do you disagree with my judgement in the matter, do you assent that my slave be absolved of his crime against you? Speak disagreement and his life is yours, for the offence he committed against you.'

The man nodded his head immediately. 'I agree with your

judgement, lord. The slave was brave and acted out of loyalty to his master. He deserves no punishment.'

'Good man. There are no others with standing to object, so the matter is settled. What is your name?'

'Bjorn Lendirsson, lord.' The man stood and walked towards the dais, stopping a respectful distance away. He looked up at the great jarl, unafraid, all eyes upon him, more than a couple of men reaching for the hilts of their weapons. 'I have a question to ask you, Jarl Ragnvald.'

The room fell to silence once more and the jarl waved his hand in assent.

'I have seen that you are an honourable and fair lord, who acts in the best interest of his people and dispenses the law correctly. You are worthy of respect. I have fulfilled my oath to my past jarl's family and am free of any obligations. I declare, here in front of you and your people, that I am oathsworn to no one.' He paused and looked around the room, his gaze level, ensuring his words were heard and understood. 'You lost a good warrior tonight, a loyal man, and I hope that you would accept an offer of my oath to you, to become your hirdman in his place, sworn to you until you release me through words, or fate releases me through death.' Bjorn stood, proud and silent, as murmurs of appreciation rolled around the room and the jarl considered the offer. It was a great gesture, and well spoken. Fine words well said often meant as much as sword skill to the Norse in their judgement of a man.

Ragnvald nodded slowly.

He retrieved his scabbarded dragon sword from where it rested against the side of his chair. He stood and, with his hands around the scabbard, offered Drekitunga, hilt first, to Bjorn. The sword hung between them like a hawk ready to stoop. If he chose to, Bjorn, who just that evening had fought against the jarl and laid the edge of a blade upon him, could take it up and strike Ragnvald down before anyone in the room could stop him. Everyone watching knew it, and there was a deathly, tense silence.

'Say the words and let it be so,' Ragnvald said into the void.

Bjorn stepped up onto the dais and knelt before the jarl. He placed his hand on the hilt above the jarl's hand, with his thumb resting on the pommel, eyes up, meeting the jarl's gaze.

'I am Bjorn, son of Lendir, free man of Svealand. I was a huscarl of Jarl Harnsted and served him loyally until his death, and after it. I have fought in many battles and never shown my back to an enemy. I killed Lothki Ironfoot Stensson, the champion of Jarl Upbard, in single combat in defence of my jarl's honour, and many lesser foes besides. I pledge my service to you, Jarl Ragnvald, in peace and in war, until the gods take me, or you release me. The next blade that comes for you will have to pass through me. Your enemies are my enemies, your friends are my friends, my honour is my bond or may the gods curse my name.' His words rang around the now silent hall proud and strong. Some men nodded and rubbed their amulets at the invocation of his deeds. The jarl let the silence linger for just a moment before he replied.

'Bjorn Lendirsson, I accept your oath of service. If you are false, may you be cursed and rendered an outlaw. If you are true, I will clothe you, feed you, arm you and fight alongside you, and give you protection under the law and under the shield of my house. I welcome you into my hall, and into my hird.'

Bjorn stood and the two men embraced. The other members of the hird in the room broke their silence and let out a ragged cheer. Bjorn stepped down off the dais and went to join them like he was an old friend, men slapping his back and offering his horns of ale to celebrate.

The jarl sat again and looked at Ordulf, whose face was clouded. 'You are confused?'

'That man tried to kill you this evening, and now he is your sworn man?'

'Yes, why not?' the jarl shrugged. 'He proved himself a brave man. He could have run, but he chose to try to complete his duty of killing me, even though it meant losing his axe and then probably his life. What better man could I want? You worry that he will not be loyal to me?'

'Yes. He was sent to kill you. Surely he will do so now that he will be allowed close to you, armed?'

The jarl snorted in derision. 'You still know nothing of our ways. To break such an oath as he just gave and try to kill me would curse him utterly in the eyes of both gods and men. You cannot imagine the shame of such an action on a Norseman. You have seen yourself that he was willing to die for his last jarl, even after that man's death, when it is not even required. A man of that honour would never betray such an oath. It is impossible. That oath is now an iron bond between us, forged of his honour, and only I or the gods can strike it away.'

Ordulf nodded and looked again at Bjorn, who was now arm-wrestling with another drunken warrior – and winning easily, he noted.

'But you offered him your sword, before he was sworn to you, could he not have done it then?' Ordulf said

'True, he could have, it would have been deceitful but not illegal.' The jarl thought for a moment, watching his new hirdsman. 'Sometimes, to truly trust a man, you must give him the opportunity to betray you. I looked into his eyes and I judged him worthy of that trust.' Ragnvald shrugged, as if trusting a stranger who had just tried to kill you was a small thing. 'Listen, Christian. In the North a man is nothing but his *wyrd* and his word. His fate and his honour. The gods decide the path of a man's life and its destination, but he alone decides how he walks it.' He gestured at his new warrior. 'This man walks in the path of honour, and it is plain to see for a fellow traveller on that road.' He nodded to himself in satisfaction, and those hooded blue eyes met Ordulf's once again.

'I have satisfied our business in the eyes of the law and of my men. I commend you for your actions. Do not worry that they were not as brave as they seemed. All men are not as brave as they or others believe them to be.' He smiled at Ordulf wickedly. 'Now, I have heard the rumours that you are terrified of women,' he said, with mirth on his face, 'but there are a couple of very attractive young serving slaves who live in the back of this hall. Perhaps I might send one of them back with you as a reward?'

Ordulf laughed nervously. 'Lord, I risk adding to my reputation but I really desire only to sleep. I can barely even sit on this stool.' It was the truth, but also Ordulf was deeply uncomfortable at the idea of being 'given' a woman as if she were his own slave.

'I understand. My wife Halla will be equally ignored when I retire to bed, if she is not already asleep herself. It is my experience that killing and feasting drains a man like nothing else.'

'I didn't kill anyone,' said Ordulf, shaking his head.

The jarl set his face in a serious expression.

'Yes, you did. The man who took your hammer in his face died before the boar was served.'

Ordulf sat up straight and looked over to the side of the room. The man was gone, and blood stained the bench and the dusty ground beneath it. He was shocked to his core. He had killed a man?

'A man's first kill is a momentous thing. For it to be in battle against an armed and trained foe is no small achievement. You have honoured yourself with this tonight, a man who has killed a wolf in the wild, and a warrior in single combat, an *Ulfdrengr.*' The jarl reached out to Ordulf's neck, hooking the leather thong and pulling the wolf's tooth from underneath his tunic. 'To be a wolf warrior is a mark of honour that many men yearn for, and yet you are just a slave, unable to carry the title, nor wear the pelt in battle.'

Ragnvald let the tooth fall, and it hung on his chest over his tunic while the slave sat deep in thought and avoided Ragnvald's gaze.

After a moment of silence, the jarl chuckled, slapped Ordulf on the back and dismissed him. Ordulf stumbled around the small band of remaining warriors who were picking out sleeping spots or just passing out on tables and headed for his bed. *He had killed a man.* The thought still shocked him, but it also made him feel… powerful. That man had tried to kill him and he had killed the man instead and not been punished for it. The wolf had been different, he had felt nothing but fear, and then relief to escape, no pride in the killing. But this time, to have killed a warrior, and to have the recognition of the roomful of Norsemen. The power of that feeling, it was… intoxicating.

When he returned to the slaves' longhouse, he was barraged with questions. He had forgotten that the slaves, who had been confined to the longhouse all day, had no idea what had happened. He did his best to tell the story, unable to conceal his pride at the way the jarl had spoken of him. He showed his injured arm and tried to catch Brunhild's eye, but she looked at him scornfully and turned to go to her bed. He joked loudly about the gift that the jarl had offered him, of a slave to warm his bed for the night but that he was too tired, and as Brunhild walked away, jested that perhaps he should go back and accept the offer. A pathetic attempt to make her jealous. He saw Otto scowl at him and the mood in the room darkened, but Ordulf, still drunk and flush from his victory, didn't notice.

It had been a long day and for the first time in a year, between the realisation of the kill and the recognition of the jarl and his men, he felt like he was not just a slave. Maybe he was not a warrior, an *Ulfdrengr*, but he was not powerless anymore. For the first time since he left Hamburg, Ordulf felt like a man in charge of his own destiny.

CHAPTER 5

THE CUT AND THRUST OF IT

THE NEXT MORNING, Ordulf's head was sore and his arm was burning so much under the linen wraps that he could barely move it.

When he rose, everyone else was gone and the fire was merely embers, the morning meal cooling in the pot. He grunted and rolled out of bed, trying to avoid using his injured arm. He stood and was surprised to find himself completely naked. He did not remember undressing. He did not know where everyone had gone, and he was content to rest and try to ignore the waves of pain coming from his arm. He spent much of the short day like that, nursing his head and his arm, and pondering the events of the day before, but eventually Otto appeared.

'So, you are alive,' said Otto, with a tone almost of disappointment.

'Where is everyone?' asked Ordulf, ignoring the odd tone.

'Preparing for the funeral.'

'What, whose?' he asked, confused.

Otto looked at him in exasperation. 'Harald! The huscarl who died? You were there, do you remember anything?'

'Oh, yes, Harald,' mumbled Ordulf.

'Get dressed, the preparations are complete. You must go soon and join them.'

'Oh, we have to go to the funeral?' said Ordulf.

'No, just you,' said Otto with barely concealed spite. 'The jarl says you are to go with them. You fought with Harald at his last, so you must witness his funeral.'

Ordulf dragged himself into the yard as the sun was just starting to dip down over the roof of the hall, casting shadows on the yard and its silent occupants. The doors to the hall were open and fully armed and armoured men were lining the space from the door to the cart, unlit torches in their hands, solemn and still in the early evening light. Ordulf stood at the side of the yard, out of the way. Many of the freemen and women gathered around outside the line of warriors.

After a time, the jarl appeared in the entryway to the hall. He was dressed in all his finery and full war gear, fur cloak clasped with a gilded chain at his neck over decorated maille, and high, fine leather boots trimmed with fur over heavy embroidered trousers. His arms sported a dozen shining rings of various metals, gold and silver and bronze glinting in the dying sunlight. He held his dragon sword at his side and his helmet in his hand.

He stepped slowly along the path between the watching warriors. At the end closest to the hall, two men lit their torches and passed the flame down the line, torch to torch, matching the speed of and lighting the path of the men who followed the jarl. Four men, chests and arms painted with blue patterns and runes and wearing nothing but wolfskin cloaks and short linen trousers, bore Harald on a litter. Four huscarls, his closest companions, carrying him on his last journey.

The tiny procession was completed by a woman Ordulf had

not seen before. She was dressed all in black, loose cloak trimmed with gold braid, a coat of feathers around her shoulders, a head-dress of woven fabric supporting black feather wings on her head. She carried a gnarled staff that was taller than her and she was chanting softly. With her heavy, odd clothes, headdress and heavily painted face, Ordulf found it impossible to guess how old she was.

The procession walked out of the yard, past the cart, and headed towards the gate. The warriors with the torches followed in two files either side, lighting the way. The cart followed behind the litter, and finally the rest of the household and women in a solemn crowd joined at the end. A warrior beckoned Ordulf to follow, so he did, walking awkwardly and alone at the very tail of the column.

The procession wound its way out of the city, between the fields and pastures. As they walked, the sun set behind the low hills to their left and the sky went from dull blue to black until the only light came from the torches and the moon. They walked until they reached a small woodland block, and within it, a hidden, treeless dell. In the centre of the dell was an oval of standing stones, half the height of a man. Within the oval was a bed of stacked wood and cut grasses.

When they arrived at the bowl in the woods, the torchbearers spread out, some standing between the stones in an inner circle, some standing around the lip of the bowl in an outer circle, all of them facing inwards. The jarl stood by as the four litter bearers carefully placed Harald's body on the bed of wood and grass and began arranging the items from the cart around him. The shield they put over his chest. An axe was put in his hand. Valuables were placed around his legs, and a roll of soft felt was placed under his head. When it was done, the four men took up torches of their own and stood by the four corners of the pyre, as Ordulf now recognised it to be.

The woman in the feather cloak had been chanting the whole time and now she strode towards the pyre, chant rising in volume, thumping her stick into the ground in time to the chant; slow, loud and mournful.

A slave followed her with a jug, head bowed. The black-clad woman, who must have been a priestess, Ordulf supposed, danced slowly around the inside edge of the circle of stones. Her chants were strange and hard to follow. She implored various gods to accept the body of Harald as tribute and to give him honour in the afterlife. She thanked the Norns for allowing him a worthy life, praised his virtues, and blessed the ground. She referred to the body as being in a ship, and Ordulf finally realised the oval of stones was in the shape of a longship like the one he had been brought to the city in after his capture. Finally, she took the jug from the slave and poured its contents over Harald from head to toe.

She ripped some feathers from her cloak and laid them on Harald's face, muttering an incantation; an offering to the Valkyr, thanking them if they had taken Harald to Odin's shining hall. Then she turned and swept from the circle. Everyone stood there in silence for a short time and then the jarl nodded to the four wolfskin-clad men around the pyre. They dropped their torches into the base of the wood and it burst into flames. The flames spread rapidly from the corners, moving like the wind until they met and leapt up into the air, scattering dry grass and embers in the uprush. Soon the body was covered in a curtain of flame reaching fifteen feet into the night sky.

Ordulf had expected singing, cheering, grunting, speeches – anything similar to the feast the night before – but no one moved. No one spoke, no one made a noise. The whole party stood, bathed in the light and heat of the flames that consumed their comrade until the pyre collapsed in on itself and the flames died down into embers and the torches burned out, leaving them all standing like a field of statues by the light of the moon.

When Ordulf returned to the hall, he found Otto sitting by the fire, eating. He sat down next to the man as he often did, but Otto ignored him. After getting his own food, he gave Otto a confused look and nudged him with his elbow, his irritation clear in his voice. 'What's the problem, have I done something else I'm not aware of?'

'You aren't aware of anything you do,' Otto snapped back, still not looking at Ordulf.

'What? What is the problem now?'

Otto turned and gave the bigger man a withering glare. 'You. You are the problem, Ordulf.'

'Why?' he exclaimed. Banging his bowl down on the bench.

'Why? Because you think you are better than us, Ragnvald's golden boy. Invited into the hall to feast, repeatedly given clemency by our master, strutting and boasting of your deeds. Wearing that stupid tooth around your neck like a warrior.' Otto shook his head in disgust.

Ordulf looked at him with an open mouth, his anger rising like bubbling water in a pot. 'Jealousy? Really, Otto, is that it? You tiny little man, jealous because I saved our jarl and got rewarded? Makes you feel inadequate, does it? Tough. I didn't do anything wrong, I just did what I had to do, it's not my fault if the jarl rewards me for it.'

Otto shook his head, almost sadly. 'There it is, you really do think yourself better than us.'

'Maybe I am,' sneered Ordulf. 'You are just sore because now that you have taught me how to speak Norse I don't need you anymore.'

Otto carefully placed his spoon in his bowl and stood, looking down at Ordulf with pity. The whole room was silent, half the slaves watching, Ordulf hadn't realised, but it was too late to back down and he ignored their scolding looks. 'You don't need us anymore then, Ordulf?'

'No,' Ordulf leered back at him. 'I never needed you.' His pride was running rampant now and he let it take over, enjoyed the rush of its power.

'Look at you, killer of wolves and men, friend of the jarl, sitting there in all your childish pride.' Otto shook his head bitterly. 'You think you don't need us, but how will you live here with people who know you think you are too good for them? You say you never needed me, but how many times have I saved you, when you lay in the dust with a sword at your throat, begging for your life?' Ordulf flushed bright red, the shame of the memory washing over him. 'I showed you how to survive in this world, I taught you its ways, how to deal with us, how to live in the group. Name one person here who is your friend?'

Ordulf swung his eyes around the hall, the truth of the words biting. Otto was the only slave he could remotely call a friend.

'I thought so. Ordulf the brave, who had to be cared for like a child, who has no one who would speak for him. Well, I hope the jarl really is your friend now that you think you are above us, but let me teach you one last lesson, Ordulf. *He* still thinks you are below him. Now you will be trapped between us, with no one to turn to. Now you are going to find out if you are right, if you truly don't need any of us. Good luck.' Otto gave him one last look of pity and walked away.

Brunhild walked back over, and for a moment Ordulf gave her a desperate smile, thinking she would sympathise. That thought was crushed by the scorn in her eyes.

'You know that slave girl you joked about being given as a gift?' she said in a calm voice.

Ordulf sagged, panicking as he realised where this was leading.

'That girl you joked about claiming is my friend, one of us, a slave. But you spoke about her like you didn't care, like she was a reward you could just use. You spoke about her like a free Norseman would speak about her, like she was nothing.' Ordulf gaped and shook his head, desperately trying to find the words to explain herself.

'Tell me,' said Brunhild, stepping in close to him, tilting her head back, raising her lips right up towards his ear to whisper, her hip carelessly grinding into his groin and her breast gently resting in the crook of his ribcage. 'Is that how you think of me? I'm a slave, if I was offered to you, would you take me? Would you like to use my body as a gift?' Horrified, Ordulf felt his loins stir, the reaction only shaming him more, knowing Brunhild knew it too. He hung his head and couldn't summon a denial.

'It was just a joke,' he said, lamely, shuddering as Brunhild continued to slowly rub her hip against his groin, a hand gently caressing his thigh.

'Well, no one found it funny,' she hissed, stepping back and walking away, leaving Ordulf standing there, humiliated, aroused and alone, in a circle of disgusted slaves.

Returning to the smithy the next day, Ordulf once again threw himself into the sword project, trying to forget the damage he had caused in the slaves' longhouse with his foolish pride. The other smiths were working flat out making simple weapons of many different types. He asked Dengir who they were all for.

'The army, next year. The Leidang will be called, the jarl told us so. They will require all the weapons we can make. Not you, though,' the smith said, poking his finger into Ordulf's chest. 'You are to make your special pointy sword with me.' His tone made it clear that the smith still thought it a waste of time.

The blades Ordulf had made so far, using the purely Christian style, had not satisfied him. He had a new idea, mixing some aspects of Norse sword design with the ones he was used to. Dengir snorted at that, and said he would make his own, and they would see which was better.

Ordulf spent several days forging and modifying his simple iron sword, the metal so soft and simple to form that he could work it entirely alone, without the need for a hammer team. After two days of adjustments and finishing to give it a vaguely sharp edge, he was done. The master smith had finished the previous day. They attached basic wooden handles and solid iron pommels and guards on the swords and a pair of the jarl's warriors were sent down to test the blades.

The warriors used them both to hack and thrust at each other while using captured Crusader shields fixed to their arms. The blades' edges quickly dulled and one of them bent during a heavy parry, but the warrior fixed it in a moment by flexing it under his leg against the ground. Then they practised thrusting at a sack of straw with multiple layers of linen wrapped around it and a piece of ragged old mail on top. Ordulf laughed to himself at the similarity with the test that Sir Hans had performed on his thrusting sword at Hamburg. The warriors finished testing the blades and came over to Ordulf and Dengir.

'This one,' one of them said, holding up Dengir's blade, 'is fine – it's not as good as a normal sword against a shield, but it thrusts better. There is nothing wrong with it, I would carry it into battle, but it doesn't seem to be much different from what I am used to.'

The other warrior nodded. 'This sword,' the first warrior continued, holding up Ordulf's shorter, thicker, more tapered blade, 'is alien to me. It is very different to control – it feels heavier in the hand and lighter to turn. But it moves well, it cuts nearly as well as a normal sword and it is much better in the thrust. It does not bend so much, and I find it easier to move and aim well. I think, with practice, I could use this well.'

The second warrior came over and took both swords. He held them up one at a time, balancing them horizontally across one finger. He showed that Ordulf's sword balanced with the finger closer to the hilt.

'This is why it feels quicker in the hand, despite being heavier.' He looked at it again, flexing the tip in his hand. 'I like that it is stronger than the other but doesn't feel much heavier. I would like to try this in good steel.'

The warriors left. Ordulf eyed his sword thoughtfully, wondering how he could increase its length without ruining the balance or making it too heavy. Dengir was swinging his sword around, considering the warrior's words. He grunted and threw it to the ground in a corner.

'I am no swordsman. I don't know how to gauge the worth of the blade other than by what I am told is good. This is all new to me. Maybe I am too old for new things, eh? It's time you made a real blade, boy. Come, we shall prepare the steel together.'

The next blade took Ordulf a full ten days. It was made with a central bar of twisted steel and two bars of folded steel around it at the edges, the outer bars longer at the tip, so that they formed a sort of fish-mouth shape around the inner bar. The outer bars were heated to blazing hot in the forge hammered together at the tip overlapping the inside bar, so that the tip would be the harder and more rigid steel or the outer parts, not the softer twisted pattern of the core.

Again, they put minimum effort into the hilting of the sword, just making it strong and functional. This time the jarl came down with his two warriors, bringing with them a cart containing something straight out of a nightmare. Ordulf stared at it for a while as it lay in the cart to be sure he had seen it correctly.

It was a small boar carcass, dressed in a thick woollen tunic with an old maille shirt over the top. The whole thing was lashed firmly to a post on a wide base. The boar's wide dead eyes stared blankly out of the sides of its head and its tongue was swollen and grotesque. The jarl laughed at the wide eyes of Ordulf and the other smiths.

'We wanted the test to be as real as possible. None of my men volunteered for the job, so here is our man,' he said, patting the horrific pig soldier thing and smiling at them. 'So, where is the sword?'

Ordulf handed it over without ceremony. It had no scabbard and they had not wasted effort with polishing or finely finishing the surfaces. But it was strong, straight, and razor sharp. A war blade. Frankly, Ordulf was embarrassed to hand over such a rough thing, but time was limited and all their efforts had been spent in the forging. This sword had a deeper fuller than the iron test blade, much deeper than a normal Norse blade, and it was thicker in the rim. It was slightly longer than his previous attempt but still as stiff, thanks to its thickness in the ridges on either side of the fuller. Ordulf knew its weight was slightly increased despite the reduced core, but believed it was not enough to matter. At the tip it had a spear-like point, and a faint ridge linked the end of the fuller to the tip where the two edges met in the spear point.

The jarl took the sword and made some simple cuts with it in the air. Then he rolled it around in his wrist and aimed some thrusts. He nodded to himself and swapped to his own serpent blade, repeating the process, and then repeated it again with the Minden sword.

'This is good. It feels much better in the hand than the Christian sword, and it flows into a thrust better than my sword. Let's try it on a shield.'

One of the warriors took up one of the Christian shields and

Dengir's soft iron test sword. The jarl then sparred with him with his serpent blade and Ordulf's new sword, trying to bully his shield out of the way, get past its rim or force the man into a mistake and get past his iron blade. After a fair amount of time spent sparring, Ordulf could see the new sword was working better. He understood little of the technique, but he could read the fight, see that the jarl was dominating more easily. The jarl's serpent blade swung faster and cut better, but could not dominate the iron sword as easily when they met and could not push the opponent's shield back as hard, since it was more flexible.

Finally, he stopped battering his weary hirdman and came over to the smiths. He smiled and thumped Dengir on the shoulder. 'This sword feels alive in my hand. It goes in and out of a thrust like a spear but I can still cut with it. I think this will be a fine battle weapon in the shieldwall.'

Dengir smiled. 'I am glad to hear it. I was not convinced myself, but your slave is persuasive.'

'So, Ordulf, shall we test it on the boarman? Will your sword work against an armoured foe as well as against a sword and shield?' asked the jarl.

'I hope so, my lord, I can't think what else to try if it doesn't.'

The jarl took the Minden blade first and dropped into his stance in front of the boar on the pole. He carried a Norse round shield in his left hand, not up and covering his shoulder as they did in single combat, but in front, close into the body, head just behind the rim, as they did in the shield wall.

He stepped sharply forward with his left foot and snapped forwards with the sword. It punched into the maille over the boar's side and the padding underneath and he withdrew it. There was dark tacky blood on the blade. He repeated this again with the serpent blade and the maille caught the blade, which flexed and bent. Then he tried Ordulf's new sword, and Ordulf watched nervously as the jarl slammed it forwards into the target, and breathed a sigh of pure relief when it split the rings and sank into the boar.

After he was done, they stripped the armour off the boar and inspected the wounds. The Minden blade had sunk a handspan or more into the pig's ribs on the thrust, going through the ribs entirely and into the cavity behind. The serpent blade had damaged the maille but not broken through. The new blade had slammed through the maille and into a rib, breaking it but stopping. Ragnvald looked impressed.

Finally, the jarl used all three blades to deliver a huge blow to the now unarmoured pig. The Minden blade did the least damage, lacerating the skin and the muscle beneath deeply and lodging in the ribs. The new blade made a deep slice in the belly that penetrated through into the abdominal cavity and into the spine, leaving the lowest part of the pig hanging. The serpent blade flowed through the body of the pig, its much thinner blade went through the spine and stuck, more than halfway through the carcass. Ordulf winced as he saw the wound that blade had caused to the muscular pig. It would have cut a man in half.

The jarl spent long enough discussing the results in a huddle with his warriors that Ordulf had time to go and relieve himself and fetch some water for the group. A while after he returned, the jarl broke from the huddle and came over with the three swords.

'That was very interesting. I think this new blade will work significantly better against the armoured Christian soldiers.' The jarl nodded to himself and wiped the sweat from his brow. He had spent a long time sparring with the swords and even the fittest man would be tired from the exertion. 'But it will still work in an open fight. Well done, I am pleased. Now we need more.'

He signalled to one of his men, who brought a heavy leather bag and handed it to Dengir. 'This is to buy the materials and start making swords. I will give you more later, and whatever else you require.'

Dengir nodded his head in agreement and the jarl clasped his arm, then released it and turned to leave. His warriors picked up their gear and stripped the armour from the boarman and followed.

Over his shoulder, the Jarl called, 'You may share the meat around your people – it is a gift for your work.'

The boys and younger smiths around the yard whooped and chatted excitedly. For families like theirs, getting a big cut meat like that was a significant event, even if it was a day old. Ordulf forced himself not to break into a smug smile as the old master regarded him thoughtfully, weighing the bag of silver in one hand absentmindedly.

Then he tossed the purse to Ordulf, who scrambled to catch it, feeling its weight with a low whistle. 'We better go and see the traders about buying some more charcoal and ore,' said Dengir with a grin.

'How much?' asked Ordulf, bouncing the bag of treasure in his hands.

'All of it.'

Ordulf looked up and returned the grin. It was going to be another long winter forging swords.

PART 2

Sir Hans Mettel, Knight of Lower Saxony and the Northern Crusades

CHAPTER 6

THE SINEWS OF WAR

Crusader camp at Aarhus. Spring 1117.

SIR HANS RATTLED along the wooden boards that lined the path at a jog, the soles of his riding shoes echoing dully in the quiet air between the rows of tents. The success of the first Crusade in capturing Denmark had spurred the Pope to once more rally the armies of Christendom to the cross in an effort to scour the Norse from their northern homelands.

The second Crusade had taken nine months to plan and organise, but now the time was upon them. A great fleet was preparing to leave French and German ports to assemble in Denmark and the faithful and ambitious were coming from all corners of the Christian lands to answer the call to conquest. The new Crusade would push across the islands in the narrow sea and into Skania, then clear the Norse lowlands and coastal areas all the way to capturing Uppsala. Twice the size of the first Crusade, this force would be unstoppable.

Sir Hans had made a name for himself in the first Crusade, and the dawning of the second saw him once again in command of the knights of Lower Saxony. Many of his men had taken to outfitting themselves in the same green surcoat that he had become known for. The green-clad knights of Saxony were now one of the most recognisable contingents. Their leader's once unique steel-faced helm was now known across the army and others were starting to commission their own versions.

Despite being a quiet and reserved man by nature, Sir Hans quietly revelled in the fame his exploits had earned him, and tried to conceal his vanity towards his image with a carefully crafted air of nonchalance. But those who knew him noticed with amusement how often he seemed to have the famous faceless helm with him, even when it was in no danger of it being required.

He found the building that housed his lord and was shown in by a liveried page. Adolf, Count of Schauenburg, Lord of Holstein and Stormarn, and now Governor of the new Crusader province of Jutland, was sitting at a stout old wooden table that must have been taken from a fine Danish hall, judging from its decorative runic carvings, eating a meal of some sort of roasted bird and reading a stack of reports. Adolf was still a young man, at least for a lord of his power. In his thirty-seventh year, he was no longer a fighting man in his prime, but still a vigorous and capable battlefield commander.

Sir Hans noted that a dash of grey streaked the Saxon lord's hair, streaks that had not been evident when they left on Crusade. The weight of command and the years were pressing down hard on his liege lord, not that he would ever let that show in any way he could control.

Seeing Sir Hans arrive, Adolf smiled and set the papers to one side, indicating the seat opposite him and then snapping orders at the page for more food and some wine.

'Sir Hans, my man, how are you? By God, the roads must be in a good state for you to be here already. How did you get our contingent here so soon?'

Sir Hans shook his head. 'I left the main body outside Hamburg and came here with a dozen men riding, travelling light. I wanted to check the route and ensure things here are ready for them when they arrive. Should be about another five or six days.'

Adolf nodded. 'Excellent, a good decision, I am sure. How are things back at home? I regret that I have not been back for so long. How is my son?'

'The lands fare well, my lord. It was a great harvest last year and the returning men were most welcome. Your son is not the boy you will remember. He is nearly a man fully grown now and full of ambition. He has been ruling in your stead with the help of your stewards, and quite effectively at that.'

'Really? It's been just over a year that I have been away. How much can he have changed? By god, they grow like weeds at that age!' The count smiled and chuckled. 'And ambitious you say, and taken to command in my name? Well, he is my son. I shouldn't have expected him to be content with less. It's a great sadness to me that I shall have to wait so long to see him again.'

Sir Hans shifted nervously in his seat.

'My lord, you will not have to wait long at all. He will be arriving with the main body – he insisted on coming on the Crusade as a squire and no force would dissuade him.'

'What?' The count looked up with a mixture of happiness and alarm. 'Hartung is coming on the Crusade without my instruction? I shall be glad to see him, but damn his arrogance for coming unsummoned. He left my wife alone to govern?'

'Your wife was more than coping with the task while Hartung studied and trained,' replied Hans.

'Hildewa, yes, I suppose she would have done, a fine woman. But nonetheless, ruling such a large area with so many ambitious vassals?' He looked concerned.

'Your reputation and stewards will keep any troublemakers

in line; your wife was most insistent. Although she also opposed Hartung coming here, he would not be refused, even by her.' Sir Hans shrugged. The disagreements of his lord's family were out of his control.

'Fine, I will discuss it with him myself when he arrives. Perhaps I will assign him to some minor role away from the main fighting, he is as yet my only adult heir.' He chewed his lip as he thought about it for a while. 'Oh, damn him for being his father's son. Such a lowly appointment will only insult him and make him resent me.' The count sighed and cut himself some more meat. 'I will think on it later. Let us talk of other matters.'

He ate a mouthful of still-warm bird and continued.

'Are you aware of the general situation of the Crusade and its preparations?' he asked.

'I have heard rumours that our lord Duke Lothair has been removed from his command, to allow the French king to appoint a commander for the Crusade.'

'Yes, but no,' the count said sternly, gesturing with his knife. 'Yes, the emperor gave the king of France the right to choose the commander in exchange for a much larger French contingent being committed. We will need it because the emperor is busy with half his banners messing around in Italy fighting some unruly cousin or other.' He took another slice. 'But also no, that is not the official story, which is that our lord duke, fresh from his great success in the first Crusade, has returned home to allow another to earn God's glory.'

Sir Hans smiled wryly. 'Of course.'

'The fact of it is that the duke isn't all that disappointed. He has secured his position and being removed allows him to go and politic for position with the emperor and the other princes of the Empire.' Count Adolf had been serving Duke Lothair closely since they were an impoverished knight and minor count respectively.

The men had worked together to rise rapidly through the ranks of the Saxon nobility, using Lothair's political nous, and Adolf's military prowess, to propel them both far beyond their inheritance, helping the emperor gain his throne and being rewarded with titles and lands that made Lothair the wealthiest and most powerful of all the German lords, some said above the emperor himself.

And where Lothair's star had risen, he had rewarded his friend Adolf equally. Giving him counties and incomes, land and lavish gifts. Sir Hans knew that Adolf would be privy to every detail of Lothair's plans and ambitions, and following his instructions carefully in turn.

'So who will command the German contingent?' asked Sir Hans.

'Duke Welfard of Bavaria,' said the count through a mouthful of bird. 'Although he has indicated to me that his command will be in name only. He is a governor, not a military man. I will command the German troops in practice. The duke will deal with the politics and represent the emperor's interests.'

Sir Hans nodded approvingly and thanked the page, who had set a goblet of wine before him and brought in another roast bird, steaming gently on a wooden platter.

'And which Frenchman will grace us with his command?'

'Don't know for sure yet; I hear it will be the Count of Flanders, but that may not be true. We will find out soon enough. The French contingents will start arriving next month.'

'The Count of Flanders, is that the son of Robert the Crusader?'

'Yes, although the title over-sold the man's abilities, and his son is an arrogant little prick by all accounts. Hopefully he has grown into a better man since that judgement. I don't hold my breath for it, though.'

'So our commander will be a man of what, twenty-five years? God help us,' sighed Sir Hans.

'Yes, and he comes on Crusade with a massive reputation to build and the arm of St George in his baggage, which his father brought from Jerusalem.' The count shook his head in frustration. 'We shall have to hope he listens to the council of older, wiser men. Otherwise we are in for a much tougher campaign.' Adolf stopped to wipe the grease from his fingers. 'Anyway, whoever our commander turns out to be, we are two months from launching the Crusade and have more preparations and planning to do yet. Your early arrival is a boon. I'm drowning in work the other lords see as below them.' The count gestured irritably at the pile of papers. 'I have been getting as much information about the islands between us and the mainland as possible and it is clear to me we will have to take the larger ones. Every town and village on those islands can crew a raider's ship so we can't ignore them and leave them in our rear. We will secure the first major island, Fyn, as soon as sufficient forces arrive. Then we only have Sjælland left in our path and some minor islands that we can mostly ignore.'

He stood up and paced the room behind the table, stretching after his meal. Hans noted with amusement that the count's belly was significantly more prominent. A year of good eating and administration clearly had not kept him in fighting shape. 'I hope that whoever turns up to command accepts these plans; I have been preparing for months. Hopefully the first island will be secured before he even arrives with the French fleet. That will save some of the time that would have been spent asserting authority. The passage to get to the island of Fyn is only one mile wide, which we can cross with barges, and my scouts report that the island is partly deserted. Many people fled to Sjælland last autumn.'

Sir Hans raised an eyebrow. 'Will having started the Crusade before the commander arrives not risk angering him?'

'Possibly, but the Crusade is tasked to take the mainland and there was no explicit mention of the islands. I am merely doing him a favour by securing good logistical bases for his glorious victory. Or something like that; we will dress it up well.'

Sir Hans tilted his head and thought about it. 'That might work.'

'I need to stay here, to manage the rest of the Crusade, and to prepare for our commander's arrival. I need you to command the attack on Fyn.' Adolf looked up as he sensed Sir Hans stiffen.

'Surely there is someone of a higher rank suitable. I have no experience commanding such a force.'

'No. I do not trust any of the other lords to simply do what I say, and do it quickly and efficiently. It will be a simple invasion, the logistics and supply will be organised in advance, all you must do is conduct the crossing and secure the main town. I expect you will not be greatly resisted. And it would not be your first command.'

Sir Hands looked at the back of his hand as he contemplated it. 'I will do as you ask, of course.'

'That is exactly why I have chosen you,' said Adolf with a reassuring smile. 'You will do well, you have proved yourself ever more capable.'

The two men ate the rest of the meal in companionable silence before the count wiped his fingers on an embroidered cloth and said, 'We have never spoken of your last command, the battle at the ford and the capture or Aalborg.'

Sir Hans tensed and his face fell into a grimace. 'That battle was my one great failure as a knight, I will never live free of its stain.'

The count snorted in surprise. 'What nonsense. I heard reports from half a dozen of the men at that ford. I wanted to know if you had failed in your duties and I was completely convinced that you did not.'

He leaned in across the table, fixing Sir Hans with an intense stare. 'Why do you think it was a failure?'

Sir Hans gritted his teeth. 'It was the only time I ever fled from an enemy. I left twenty men, *my* men, dead on that bank and I *ran.*' He spat the last word like it was poison. 'My duty was to look after those men and I failed them.' He hung his head, unable to meet the count's gaze.

'Nonsense. Your duty was to complete the task I gave you, which you did admirably. Men die in war. You did not abandon your men – at least, that is not what I heard. Hans, no commander – not even an experienced one – wins every fight. Your crossing of the ford was correct and well managed; you were simply outmatched by an ambush you could not expect.' He sat up and clasped his hands together on the table. 'Now, it is true, some commanders in that situation choose to die with their men rather than face the shame of defeat.' Sir Hans's head dropped another measure. 'But those men are fools. You had a task to accomplish and the rest of your men to lead. Your death would have achieved nothing. Every man I spoke to said you fought to the last moment and could not have done more. Your companion told me he had to *beg* you to leave.'

Sir Hans looked up suddenly with a flash of anger in his eyes. 'I did not run because someone begged me to, no matter what my men might say.' The flash of anger passed, to be replaced with sadness. 'I left because the only man left alive was the smith, Ordulf, and I could not save him. Perhaps I should have tried,' he trailed off.

'Nonsense!' exclaimed Adolf with a half laugh. 'You, sacrifice yourself for a commoner? A tradesman. Don't be ridiculous. You did the right thing. Ordulf was a likely enough young lad, but a mere smith nonetheless. We are fighting a war, and you are worth ten of him, fifty maybe. Don't let this nonsense trouble you. Why do you even still think of it?'

Hans grimaced in distaste. 'I made myself watch him die, and

I cannot put the image from my mind.' He was tapping his foot rapidly on the floor now, staring down at the tabletop. 'I didn't see it as I crossed the ford, but apparently he took two men down with his hammer, before I saw them subdue him and execute him.' He paused, not meeting the other man's eye. 'He was part of my charge and I left him. After I left, he, an unarmed, untrained boy, put two of the enemy in the dirt while I ran. It shames me.' His voice was still bitter.

'It is of no consequence, we found another smith in the city, a Dane, yes, but probably a more experienced craftsman. Anyway, put it from your mind. Tomorrow we must discuss the details of your invasion of Fyn. I intend to capture the town of Odense. It is the only major town on the island and will be useful for the supporting of the invasion of Sjælland. Now, go and find Orbert, he will have quarters ready for you already, I am sure. You are early, but he always is too.'

Sir Hans nodded. 'Thank you for the food and your kind words, my lord.' He smiled stiffly and bowed his head before leaving to find Orbert, the Saxon contingent's efficient, bizarre, list-obsessed camp master.

Five days later, the lower Saxon contingent, marching in fine order with banners raised and dressed for war, arrived in the camp. Adolf and Hans were there waiting for them as they trooped by into the central square, tired and with mud from the road splattering each man from shoes to waist, but nonetheless with their chins up and equipment in fine condition.

Sir Hans saw Adolf greet each rank of marching men, praising their form or calling out to men he knew in welcome, a smile beaming on his face. After the briefest of inspections and a short speech, he dismissed them to clean and rest. Hot food was already being prepared for them over a dozen firepits.

Only once the men had been dismissed did Adolf stride over to where his son Hartung sat on a fine bay gelding and embrace him as he dismounted. Hartung was fifteen years old now. He had grown by a handspan since Adolf had last seen him and was fuller, more muscled, the first wisps of a beard carefully cultivated on his chin with clearly absurd pride.

'I am pleased to see you, Hartung, even if I did order you to stay at home and help your mother. Who are you squiring for?'

'Sir Dietmar of Eresburg, father,' said Hartung, trying to extract himself stiffly from his father's public embrace.

'Never heard of him, who does he serve?'

'Duke Welfard.'

'Ah, excellent, that is a good contingent to be in, all under my command anyway. Well, I look forward to meeting him.' Adolf beamed at his son as he looked him up and down. 'What a man you are growing into, my son, I am filled with pride to see you so. I am sure you will be an excellent squire.'

Hartung shuffled uncomfortably on the spot, looking vaguely resentful. 'Thank you, father, may I go and see to my horse?'

Adolf was taken aback but consented. 'Of course, that's important. Off you go.' Hartung bowed curtly and walked off, leaving the count confused watching him leave.

'He was not even slightly glad to see me, he resented my merest touch!' Adolf mused bitterly to Hans.

'He is a boy growing into a man, he is filled with pride and desire to be seen as his own man. He will settle, I am sure,' Sir Hans tried to mollify his lord.

'I see, perhaps I should not have embraced him in front of the men. Hmmm. I shall instruct this Sir Dietmar to report back to me often and go easy on him.'

Sir Hans shuffled his foot and made a non-committal grunting.

'What? You disagree? Oh, spit it out, man.' Adolf looked

exasperated and then sighed. 'I shouldn't ask his knight for special favours, should I?'

'Well, it's none of my business, lord, but would you have wanted them? When you squired for the Count of Brunswick?'

'No, you are right, damn you, I would have hated that. Fine, I will leave him alone. When do fine children become such surly men?'

'When they come into their first beard, my lord, I find that is always the case. All the pride and arrogance comes with it. He will grow out of it, I am sure, if he has time and opportunity to prove himself.'

'That sounds like what my wife would say. When did you become so wise, Hans? You have no grown sons?'

'Three younger brothers, my lord, which, given that my father had a string of increasingly young wives and mistresses and drank himself to death, came to much the same thing. My youngest brother is younger than Hartung, and I raised him myself while my father drank and whored.'

Adolf snorted and nodded. 'Ah yes, your father, an amusing man.'

'A useless heap of shit, my lord, begging your pardon for disagreeing, but he taught me one very important lesson.'

Adolf turned to face him, brows raised. 'And what was that?'

'Not to be a useless heap of shit.'

A month later, before spring was fully taking hold, and the mornings were still arriving with a white coating of frost, ten barges ferried the men of Lower Saxony, and a few other mixed German contingents, across the icy narrow channel between the peninsula and the island of Lunen in three waves. The force, some two thousand strong, crossed ready for war, but were not met with a single enemy. Scouts sent across during the days before met them on the beach and reported no armed men for ten miles around. Some villages were deserted, the fields were un-sowed and most livestock were either dead or gone. The remaining people were scattered, in small farms and remote villages, hunkering down and trying not to be noticed.

Sir Hans was not surprised. It had been eight months since the Crusaders took Aarhus, just up the coast. They would have been able to see the smoke on the horizon from here as the city burned, and would have been well aware of what was coming.

Once all the men, draft animals and supplies were unloaded, it was past midday. He ordered a short march to a camp some five miles inland. Moving fast along a good road and carrying only supplies for ten days, the small army made excellent time. They made camp before dusk a half-day's march from Odense.

They were being watched now. The few mounted scouts they had with them reported small groups of armed men shadowing them. The camp was made small and tightly packed, with double watches and a ring of sentry fires to guard against a surprise attack.

None came. In the morning, camp was broken and they resumed their march to the city. A small force of Norsemen tried to stop them, at a river so small it didn't even need a ford to cross – it was more of a stream. Sir Hans arrayed the vanguard of Bavarians and Saxons across his side of the stream and stared at the blocking force in confusion. Perhaps two hundred men, not very well armed, and not very well organised, were trying to stop an army of two thousand at a position that could at best be described as mediocre. Although, he admitted to himself, this land did not lend itself to defence and this was the most defensible location they had seen so far.

He sent heavy scouting parties to the flanks and rear, checking for any trap or pincer movement and then sent the vanguard – five hundred men – to cross the ford under cover of archery. The short fight was a massacre. The German attack rolled across the river and right over the thin Norse line, which broke and fled. Only sixty or so were left dead and Sir Hans did not have spare cavalry to pursue the survivors. He was utterly perplexed. No other attack came, no trap was sprung.

He decided to continue the advance to Odense; there was probably still time in the day to reach the city, which, scouts told him, was not walled. The reason for the desperate blocking attempt was revealed when they came into sight of the town. The settlement was a hive of activity. A line of ships were streaming out of the harbour, evacuating people, food, valuables and other supplies. More ships were still coming to the docks and loading whatever they could, as fast as they could. Sir Hans smiled. They had caught the Danes off guard by invading so early in the season.

With the evacuation unfinished, they had desperately tried to slow the Crusaders down enough to give them an extra day. Sir Hans mused to himself that it had nearly worked and then ordered his vanguard to form a wide battle line and advance into the city.

The town was captured almost intact. Some Norse did try to set fires and some did fight but resistance was completely disorganised and they fought only when trapped or for their own lives. A freed and desperately grateful German slave told them that most of the warriors had left the previous season or in the last two days.

The Crusaders even captured four ships that were too slow to leave the docks, and found them piled with smoked and salted meat from slaughtered livestock, boxes of tools and other valuables and weapons. The ships that had escaped at the last moments watched from a safe distance and then rowed away down the fjord leading away from the town. The whole island of Lunen was captured at the cost of only seventeen Crusader soldiers and enough food and supplies were captured to feed the entire Crusade for a month.

It was an easy victory that belied the campaign to come. Even as Sir Hans celebrated in the great hall of Odense with his men, in the west and the east, storm clouds were brewing that would threaten to consume them all.

Baldwin, the young Count of Flanders, was worse than Adolf could have imagined. He swept into Aarhus at the head of a French fleet with the ceremony of a conquering hero. Adolf was worried that the new commander was going to reject his plans and disagree with his preparations. It never occurred to him that the young man, the French king's hand-picked commander, would simply ignore him.

The young noble set up his own command and started holding meetings and issuing orders as if none had come before. Adolf sent a messenger to ask for a meeting and his steward was rudely rejected. Adolf went himself, and was made to wait for hours before being told that the commander was too busy with the affairs of the Crusade to attend to Adolf's problems. The French herald told the furious Saxon count that his master was sure that Adolf would be able to solve his own problems by himself and that the count would discuss command only with his equal, the Duke of Bavaria, who was, rather inconveniently, still in Bavaria.

Thirteen days passed while nothing happened before Adolf was finally summoned to a meeting to report. He dressed in his finest cote and went to the fantastically elaborate command tent that the French count had set up, to report as commanded, his bemusement turning to deep sadness when he saw that the tent they were meeting in was practically a palace. It alone must take an entire wagon train to move about.

The French guardsman at the entrance asked for his sword. Count Adolf was stunned.

'I am Adolf, Count of Schauenburg and governor of Jutland,

where we currently stand. On whose authority do you demand my sword?'

The guardsman blanched and ducked inside the tent, calling in French to someone. A moment later, the same herald who had dismissed him before came out, looking completely at ease, perhaps even a little annoyed to be interrupted, in the way a man might react to a merchant calling at his door uninvited.

'Count Adolf, my lord is most pleased that you have arrived. Please, leave your sword with the guardpost and come inside.'

Adolf gritted his teeth and stepped up to the herald, who maintained his bored look. 'I am the lawful lord of these lands and no one bars me entrance from anywhere, nor dictates where I can wear my sword. Now stand aside before I have you flogged for your impudence.'

The herald took a half step back, shocked at the aggression; he was clearly used to acquiescence.

'My lord will be most displeased if you come before him so armed.'

'I don't care if your lord shits himself and runs to his mother. He is in flagrant violation of protocol for not coming to see me when he arrived in my lands. Now move before you find out what it is to cross the legal governor of the land you stand in.'

Adolf stepped again into the herald's face so their noses almost touched and the man visibly quailed.

'What is going on here? My lord, is there a problem?'

Another Frenchman, a lord by his manner and dress, had arrived in the entrance and was regarding the scene with disdain.

'I am Adolf, Count of Schauenburg and the governor of this province. This overdressed flounce has informed me that your count insists I surrender my sword before I come in. He must be mistaken; no great lord of France could be so ignorant nor foolish as to think that he can disarm a lord in his own lands by anything other than violence. Perhaps it is this incompetent fool who failed to inform his master that I am the lawful governor of these lands and that it was required by custom that he come to meet me?' He turned from the herald and glared at the French lord. 'Now, am I to be granted entry or shall I have to ask your master to leave my lands at once?'

The knight bristled but held his temper. 'It is a misunderstanding, I am sure. The count did indeed order that all foreigners are to disarm before entering, but I am sure he did not mean to include you.' He managed to imply in his tone that the enraged German lord definitely was included by intent. He stepped to one side and held up his arm to indicate the entrance, the way a page might indicate the way a cupbearer should go. Adolf's blood boiled in his veins but he gritted his teeth and swept in with his small party, consisting of one of his senior knights and some pages carrying documents, following behind him.

The 'meeting' turned out to be a farce. It became apparent that, in the thirteen days since Count Baldwin's arrival, no real planning or preparation had been done. Baldwin treated Adolf with the sort of disdain usually reserved for children or incompetent servants. When Adolf presented his plan for the conquest of Sjælland and the invasion of the mainland, the young Frenchman bristled and rejected the entire thing root and stem.

'Why did you presume to make my plans for me, my Lord Adolf? Did you not realise I would have my own campaign set out already? My commanders have this all in hand. As to this business with me being in *your* land, I am on Crusade, directed by God, and no mortal may stand in my way without being subjected to his wrath, through his instrument: me. I have a Papal warrant instructing all Christian men on pain of excommunication to grant me passage, aid and succour such as I require, so grant me that you shall.' He waved Adolf's concerns away like a tray of unwanted food.

'And I have not refused you aid, passage or succour, I have merely asked to be afforded my due rights and respect, and to not be accosted and disarmed by low-born guardsmen in my own land.' Using his last vestige of control and patience, Adolf dropped the argument and added in a more conciliatory tone. 'In any case, lord count, could you direct me to your scoutmaster, your commanders of your army and fleet, so that I may organise with them the involvement of my men in the coming campaign to capture Sjælland, and hear the details of the plans you have drawn up?'

The Count of Flanders frowned and, for the first time, looked flustered. 'Why would we have need of some windswept island? I am not troubled with it. No, we will be bold, not overly cautious. We will strike hard for the heathen capital Uppsala. We will capture it and the whole northern lands will bow down before us and before the glory of God. I hear it is their sacred city? So once we have it, they will know the supremacy of our faith and will have no choice but to submit to us. This is how my father captured the holy land and subdued the Saracen heathens, striking for the capital, the heart of the enemy, and so it will be here for the northern heathens.' The count looked exceedingly pleased with himself. 'We will do this in the summer; I expect it will take a month at most. You will be informed of the plans at the appropriate time by your duke, I am sure.'

Adolf looked on in open-mouthed amazement, beyond the ability to speak. This man had not the faintest understanding of how a campaign worked, nor the enemy they fought. Looking around the room, he tried to find evidence that anyone understood the stupidity of what the French count had just said. He saw many faces filled with disinterest or contempt for his complaints; those were the faces of other equally overdressed and young lords and courtiers. He did note a few older men, presumably men with experience, perhaps even of the great Crusade, who looked embarrassed or sympathetic.

Just as he was about to explode and educate the upstart about how supply lines worked and that the Norse wouldn't suddenly bow down in submission at the loss of just one city and nor did the Saracens, from whom the Crusaders had meticulously taken a whole chain of mutually supporting fortresses before marching on Jerusalem, a hand gently gripped his arm and someone leaned in and whispered in his ear, 'My lord count, I beseech you, not now, this exchange is lost to you. Please retire and speak to me in private.'

Adolf bit his tongue and turned, sweeping from the room without another word, with the stranger striding after him. Outside the tent, he turned and fixed his furious gaze on the guard, who desperately tried to pretend he wasn't intimidated and failed.

The stranger appeared at the flap. He was a slightly built man, wearing a simple belted tunic, cote and riding boots, much as Adolf was. Campaigning clothes.

'My lord count, I am Sir Hugues, brother of Folmar, Count of Metz, and the leader of the contingent of the Duke of Lorraine.' He inclined his head. 'I beg a word with you that may help to… explain the situation in there. Please, let us go where we will not be overheard.' He looked behind him at the nervous guard.

Adolf nodded and set off down the wide avenue between tents that led back towards the Saxon camp. Once they were out of earshot he grunted to the young baron, who he guessed must be in his early thirties, 'So, what is the meaning of that absurd display in there? Who is this child that has been sent to command us?'

Sir Hugues pursed his lips and set himself. 'My lord Count Baldwin is… inexperienced in the ways of war, and has been raised on stories of his father's glory in the first Crusade.'

'Presumably those stories involved no telling of how his father actually achieved his success?' said Adolf, acid dripping from his voice.

'Well, quite. So it seems. Nonetheless, he is the chosen man of King Louis and—'

Adolf waved his hand agitatedly. 'Sir, please cut to the chase and spare me the pleasantries. You said you would explain what was going on – do so succinctly as I care not for the politics of it. I don't believe for one second that King Louis, who is reputed as an intelligent man and a great military leader, thought this puppy a good choice to lead the Crusade. So explain to me why he is here.'

'Very well. To the point, then. The situation in the kingdom of France is very delicate. Many of the great lords who led the great Crusade to Jerusalem and gained great power there are old or dead. Most of their successors are young, arrogant, ambitious and unruly.' He gently inclined his head back towards the tent they had left to show what sort of man he meant.

'The new Count of Toulouse is still a child and the Duke of Aquitaine – the only capable great lord of France remaining from the Jerusalem Crusaders – is aiming to obtain the county of Toulouse, which would make him a lord of equal power to the king. Thus, he refused to send a contingent to this Crusade, claiming that he has already done enough for God. The Duke of Burgundy is more interested in scripture than war and has no male heir, so the vultures are circling there. The Duke of Normandy is more focused on holding onto his tenuous claims in England fighting King Harold's heirs in the North than helping the French king. Thus the loyal lords of France have more potential enemies within than they do without.' He stopped and smiled thinly.

Adolf thought through all he had just heard. He knew some of the political struggles in France, but not all. 'So the French king sends his young troublemakers here and leaves his cooler heads at home to contain his problems.'

'Well, that is certainly part of it, yes, although not the extent of the move, perhaps.'

'What do you mean?'

'Well, before the first Crusade into Denmark the Empire was also beset with chaos, was it not? A potential civil war and a conflict between the Pope and the emperor were brewing over the investiture crisis?'

Adolf nodded. 'Yes, trouble was brewing, but the success of the Crusades and the successful joint effort between the emperor and the pope certainly smoothed relations between them. They have somewhat resolved their differences.'

Sir Hugues smiled thinly again and opened his hands. 'So the king of France is understandably... nervous... about the situation. With the hugely powerful regions of Burgundy and Toulouse potentially up for grabs on the edge of his kingdom, and a newly united and powerful Holy Roman empire on their far borders, he, well... I have not met or spoken to him, but I suspect that he regards the potential conquest of the Norse lands by the Emperor as... strategically inconvenient.'

Adolf's eyes widened and then he closed them and cursed, long and fluently. 'So he is sabotaging the Crusade!' He put his hand to his face and paced back and forth. 'He jostles for position to secure the right to select the leader and promises to replace empire contingents with his own, just so that he can ensure it fails? How can he think to get away with this!'

Sir Hugues looked around them in alarm and, leaning in close, said with an urgent voice, 'My lord, I said nothing of the sort. Such conclusions are not mine, of course, you understand. The king has made his orders clear to everyone: they are to do their utmost to ensure victory for the Crusade. It's just that, perhaps by some error, he has sent inferior contingents and commanders to complete the task. A... mistake, I am sure.' The baron shrugged knowingly.

Adolf fumed and looked at him suspiciously. 'So what leads

you not to share with me this theory that you don't have? You are not a vassal of the king of France – why don't you inform our liege lord the Emperor Henry of the deception?'

'It is true that we are not a vassal of France, but we are also not truly part of the Empire. Our people are more inclined towards France than the Holy Roman Empire. Lorraine is within the old boundaries of the kingdom of France. Both kingdom and empire find the Duchy of Lorraine and the Duchy of Lower Lorraine somewhat convenient as a buffer to prevent conflict between them. Given the, ah, problems currently being experienced in Lower Lorraine and my lord's claims on that title, we need to maintain a certain neutrality in disputes. The Count of Flanders also has designs on the Duchy of Lower Lorraine, or so I hear.' He let his voice drift off in overly forced nonchalance.

Adolf sighed. 'So the King of France needs the Crusade to fail, preferably losing some of his troublesome lords and their men in the process, so that he can then regain control over all of the Kingdom of France. The emperor wants it to succeed so that he has the power to exert influence over – or even take – the border counties such as Burgundy, Toulouse and Lorraine. Either eventuality is bad for your lord, who wants to consolidate power by re-joining the two halves of Lorraine back under your independent control.'

'I didn't say any of that,' Hugues said, smiling.

Adolf rolled his eyes. 'Curse my luck to be stuck here trying to conduct a campaign in the midst of all this politics.' He jabbed his finger into the baron's chest. 'This isn't politics to my men. They live and die on the success of this Crusade. I'm not letting their lives be thrown away to satisfy someone's powerplay.'

Hugues raised his hands. 'I am counting on it, my lord. I also do not wish to waste my men on a hopeless expedition, and like you I cannot simply withdraw without great shame and loss of standing. I suggest that we make sure that the Crusade succeeds. After all, that "puppy", as you call him, wants nothing more than for it to succeed. All we need to do is find a way to help him not...'

He waved his hand in the air, searching for the right term.

'Fuck it up?' Adolf interjected.

'Well, yes. I suppose that is one way of putting it.'

'So, what do you want in return for helping me? If the Crusade is successful, you fear losing your semi-independence to the emperor, do you not?'

'Well exactly, my lord count. And who, do you think, is most likely to become emperor if Henry dies?' Hugues inquired innocently.

Adolf nodded, the final piece of the puzzle falling into place. 'My lord Lothair, the Duke of Saxony.'

'Quite so,' Hugues said, smiling. 'So I think we have an understanding, do we not?'

Adolf finally smiled wryly, the whole scheme laid out before him. 'Yes. I suppose we do. You help me unfuck this Crusade and I persuade my lord to look favourably on his loyal subjects of Lorraine in their case for maintaining their independent position and their claims in Lower Lorraine, if he becomes Emperor.'

Hugues winced. 'I do wish you wouldn't put it so plainly, it is not the normal way of politicking, but yes, that is what I am broadly suggesting.'

'But this must remain a secret, otherwise the King of France might retaliate against you for exposing or ruining his schemes,' said Adolf pointedly.

Hugues winced even more painfully. 'Please do not speak in such a way about it. My lands are ten miles from the French border of Champagne, land owned by one of the king's most loyal men. Subtlety is essential here. I am not, in any way, scheming against the king of France, I am supporting his stated orders to make this campaign a success. I am trusting you deeply in the hope that our goals are mutual. The only reason I can even be seen talking to you is that none of those children in there have any clue about these matters and will suspect nothing. I will return and claim that I persuaded you to submit to Baldwin's authority, earning his favour and allaying any suspicions. I would appreciate it if you did not contradict that claim.'

Adolf nodded thoughtfully.

'I accept.' He looked away and stood staring at the sky, hands on hips. 'I thought I was just coming here to conquer some more heathen lands. I am a soldier, always have been. I won my titles through war and I care nothing for this scheming of foreign lords.'

Hugues shrugged again. 'And I have never seen combat. All my family power is gained and maintained by subtle moves and careful relationships. I think if we combine forces, our different skills will see us through to success.' He smiled at the brooding German count.

'Fine. So, what do you suggest we do about the pup? We must start the campaign and we must start soon.'

'Well, all the German and Italian contingents will follow your lead, I think? You are here representing the Duke of Bavaria and thus wield his power? The contingent of Lorraine will likewise follow your lead.' He inclined his head slightly.

Adolf nodded.

'So, that is enough to conquer Sjælland?' Hugues asked.

'Yes, but we have no fleet to carry us there. Most of the ships are French.'

'Well, Count Baldwin already said that his objective is Uppsala. I suggest we present Sjælland as a fairly irrelevant side-note, not worthy of his attention. Play to his arrogance. Say you understand his reasoning and perhaps he will let you take care of this minor affair for him before the Crusade starts. Emphasise how unimportant it is, rather than how essential.'

Adolf sighed. 'I'm going to need you and your scheming mind around a lot this year, aren't I?'

Hugues smiled. 'I suspect so, my lord, I suspect so.'

Adolf mustered his entire force and the rest of the Holy Roman Empire contingent, broke camp and moved everything to Odense over the next two weeks as the final Crusader forces arrived. His second meeting with the Count of Flanders had been utterly humiliating. The only thing that got him through it was the remembrance that it was all to save his men and to do his duty. He had been forced to apologise to that pup in front of all of the French lackeys and admit that he had been wrong about the strategy. The count had been so thrilled by his public victory that he had not even bothered to contest the idea that Adolf be allowed to secure Sjælland with over half of the army and fleet, on the basis that it was 'good experience for the lesser Germanic soldiers and their Italian allies'. The idea that his untested French troops needed no practice of warfare against the Norse seemed to make perfect sense to the Count of Flanders, despite the obvious logical flaw in that opinion. Adolf had even laid the groundwork for bringing forward the invasion of the mainland to late spring, by saying it was in order to have nicer weather for the victory celebrations afterwards. The dolt had actually agreed with that reasoning. Adolf could not believe the previous Count of Flanders, hero of the first Crusade, had sired such a useless whelp.

One crisis had been resolved to his rear. Unknown to him, another, even greater challenge was brewing to his front.

CHAPTER 7

THE KING AND
THE DÍSABLÓT

Uppsala, Early March 1117

FOR ALL OF that long winter of 1116 and 1117, Ordulf made swords. He slept, he ate and he made more swords. He was at least warm during the day, due to the heat of the forge, and it ended up being a mild winter by Norse standards, or so they told him, much to his disbelief.

The other junior smiths made the steel for the swords with Ordulf. When the material they had was variable, they twisted and folded it into basic patterned bars – nothing fancy, just enough to make it reliable. When the steel was better quality or they had enough of the right kind, they made blades from unfolded bars in the way Ordulf was used to back in Minden. These took half the time to make but steel good enough for them was rarer. These were simple but tough weapons for battle, not the beautifully crafted blades made for jarls and great heroes from the sagas. Still, the Norse smiths spent the little spare time they had available making simple yet beautiful runic decorations in the hilts, and sculpted, lobed pommels. This seemed to be something they just wouldn't go without.

Over that winter, the forge made twenty-seven swords. Given that this was a much smaller operation than his old company in Minden, and had far fewer smiths and resources, Ordulf didn't think this a bad result. Swords were much rarer here than in the Christian lands, so to have this many at once in one smithy was impressive indeed. The swords were also, he was proud to admit, of higher quality than the Minden blades, and he refined and improved the design as they went.

Still, twenty-seven wasn't nearly enough. The jarl took nearly half for his men and persuaded half a dozen other jarls in the city to buy and try out a handful each – no small investment, as the swords were not cheap, even though Dengir accepted little more than the cost of producing them. The Norse had not had a raiding season for three years and all the lords were running short of silver. Hoards were being dug up, family treasures cut up for hacksilver or sold in the market. In their preparations for war, the lords of the land were bleeding silver like a dying boar bleeds from half a dozen spear wounds.

The King of Norway arrived with a small army of lords, followers, merchants and household warriors in the seventh week of the new year, just before the Dísablót celebrations commenced. Ordulf was in the courtyard repairing his leather apron when he saw the King and his procession walk through the city into the main square. Uppsala was crowded with visitors for the Dísablót, camps sprawled outside the city. It seemed everyone crowded into the square and the street leading to it to see the king arrive.

The Norwegian king surprised the assembled people, and his hosts, by announcing that he would go straight to the temple, and bade the crowd follow him. As they walked through the city, more joined all the time, wanting to see what was happening at the temple. The temple at Uppsala was the largest building in all the North, dwarfing even the king's hall. It had stood long enough that no one knew when it was built and the wooden walls were blackened with age, strange carvings of serpents and monsters adorned the doorways and indecipherable ancient runes were inscribed on the doors themselves in scripts lost to history. Their meaning was known only to the servants of the temple whose secrets they kept.

The building was three levels high, each level smaller around than the one below, leaving a stepped look with a great wooden tiled roof at the pinnacle. Across the front of the great building, four times the height of a man from the ground, a great carved wooden chain covered with beaten gold was hung. From a distance, it looked like an impossible weight of solid gold surrounded the temple like a necklace, shining in the sun. From close up, it still looked like the riches of an entire kingdom for a year, and probably was.

The king led the crowd, now numbering in the thousands, out of the city and to the steps of the temple where he stood with the high priestess at his side and faced the assembled crowd, including most of the lords of Scandinavia. He made a great speech calling for unity in the face of the Crusaders and for the Norse to fight as one people to protect Odin's lands. He spoke of the end times and the age of heroes past, saying that now was the time to make their own legends.

During the speech, a messenger arrived. He told of the fall of Odense, news which spread through the gathered crowd and caused such a stir that the king stopped speaking, unable to be heard over the commotion. One of his men ran up onto the stage and spoke urgently into his ear. The king nodded solemnly and then held up his hands for silence. A dozen of his blue cloaked huscarls banged their axe or spear hafts on the floor to get the crowd's attention.

'People of the northlands, grim news has arrived,' he shouted.

Those still talking slowly stopped and turned to listen to him and the spear hammering ceased. 'Our enemy has struck again, much sooner than we expected. Fyn has fallen, soon they will move across the cold sea and come to Sjælland, or to Skania.' There was a ripple of anger and shouts of protest in the crowd.

The king swept his gaze across the crowd, his face stern and hands on hips. He was a huge man, tall and broad. The high priestess at his side looked a child by comparison. His long red-brown hair was swept back and unbound, his beard wild and bushy. He wore a blue woollen cloak trimmed with fur around his shoulders. He looked like a god of war and the crowd could feel the anger coming off him in waves, like a living thing.

'The time has come for the people of the North to unite, to join together to face this threat, to set our petty differences aside and fight as one people, or fall one by one, like Jutland and Fyn.' There were calls of support from the crowd. 'I am here to ask you for the throne of Sweden!' he called. A low silence fell on the crowd. Rumours had of course spread as to his intent, but to hear him say it, on the steps of the temple, where the kings of the Svear and then Sweden had been crowned for ten lifetimes of men, shocked the crowd of proud Swedish men and women.

'I come not as a conqueror but as a friend. I come not to force my claim on the throne, but to ask you for it. Nor,' he said, raising his voice to a roar so that even at the back all would hear it, 'do I come as a foreign king.' He took the golden chain, the symbol of the kings of Norway, from his neck with a single tug, splitting a shining ring that clattered to the ground. He held up the sundered chain in front of the crowd, and then threw it to the ground at his feet. 'I renounce my title as the King of Norway, and I abolish it. Let no man ever claim the right again.' There were mutterings of protest from the assembled contingent of Norwegian lords, confusion in the mass of Swedish onlookers.

'I renounce my claim to be King of Sweden, let no man claim that title again. I am here, at this sacred place, to claim the kingship of all the North, of all the people of Odin, all the lands from the great fjords of the east to the forests and farmlands of the west, of Gotland and Skania and the wild forests and mountains of the interior, wherever man has set foot or where our gods still hold sway.' True silence fell on the assembled crowd at the enormity of the claim. Never in history had the peoples had one ruler. The ambition of it was breathtaking. Above the crowd, a single white-tailed eagle circled, beak pointed downwards, eyes searching for prey. The priestess snapped her head up to watch it, one hand shielding her eyes against the sun.

The king let the silence drag, gauging the reaction of the crowd. 'If you grant me this request at the Thing, make me the *Norðrikonungr*, the king of all the people of the northlands, I swear that I will have one purpose only.' He paused and held out a clenched fist to the crowd. 'To fight the Crusaders, until they are driven from our lands, or the life is driven from my body.' He swept the crowd with his eyes again and then dropped his hand to his side before he started to walk down the steps.

Behind him the high priestess was muttering to herself. She looked at the eagle, and then down at the broken chain of the kings of Norway, abandoned at the head of the steps. Then up to the great golden chain that hung from the front wall of the temple. 'Wait, Sigurd Magnusson,' she called, stooping gracefully to pick up the chain, turning it over to examine it. Sigurd paused and turned in surprise, halfway down the temple steps.

'The gods teach us to read their intent through signs. This morning I saw two ravens come to the morning scraps, but they did not eat. A sure sign that Odin is watching us. Now, an eagle circles, watching, but it does not watch for prey, it is watching you, Sigurd. A portent of battle to come.' She reached out a hand to

Sigurd, beckoning him up to join her. 'You came here to call for unity in the face of a threat from our enemy, and news came that the threat has already arrived.'

Sigurd reached the top of the steps and let the priestess take his hand. Her touch was light, her eyes so alluring that Sigurd was captured by them as she spoke. She applied a slight pressure, twisting his wrist downwards, just enough to signal intent. The huge man, easily twice the size of the slight woman, let his legs weaken and he dropped to his knees in front of the high priestess, who looked down at him lovingly, like a mother would look at a child. Then she turned again to the crowd.

'It is not for the people to decide if one man can lead us all. It is for the gods, for they would not let a false man stand here in their presence and swear a false oath.' She continued to twist Sigurd's wrist, bending his finger back towards him, giving him no choice but to be seen to resist, or to be forced lower to the ground. He stooped until he was half bowing in front of her, and she gently held him there, caressing his rough skin between her slim fingers like a lover.

'I say that this foreign man has been led here by the gods, to lead their people in these dark times. He has arrived in humility and taken an oath to serve them, and they have not rejected it. Does any man dare oppose it?' She looked out at the crowd. No one spoke. She stood there, the huge man kneeling before her, palm upraised and stretched out towards her, and she smiled at him. 'The gods thank you for your offering,' she said, hefting the gold chain, before casually casting it through the open portal of the temple beside her without a backwards glance. She used her now free hand to pull a small knife from her robes, a knife she used to kill sacrificial animals. She passed it over Sigurd's upraised palm with a quick slash and he grunted and tried to remain still as blood started trickling from the shallow cut. She bent down and, meeting his eyes, she put her lips to the cut and kissed it.

Raising her eyes to his, his blood bright on her lips, she spoke so that only he could hear. 'You have made a blood oath with the gods, King Sigurd, be sure you remember it, for they surely will.'

The priestess released her grip on his hand and stood back, giving him room to rise. Sigurd pulled himself to his feet, ignoring the ache in his knees from kneeling on the hard wooden steps, and stood to face the uncertain crowd. 'We cannot name you *Norðrikonungr*, Lord Sigurd,' the priestess said, loud enough so that the people could hear her. 'Because you already are.'

A thump sounded from the steps, a huscarl thumping his spear butt onto the steps in slow rhythm. Then another joined him, and more. Then a chorus as the Norwegian contingent joined in, thumping their hands on their chests or their feet on the hard ground. Some of the Swedish jarls voiced their support loudly, encouraging their people to join in. Soon most of the crowd was hammering and shouting their support. The king looked over the crowd, standing there and watching as the tension broke and the first of his men climbed the steps to embrace him and kneel before him to give his oath to the *Norðrikonungr*, the first king of all the northlands. As Sigurd stood there, taking the renewed oaths of his men, and the support of the crowd, he felt nothing but apprehension and the cold, slim fingers of dread.

After a while, the priestess declared the Dísablót would commence the next morning and the gathering broke up, the crowd starting to head back to the city. Sigurd went inside the temple alone, his men remaining outside, talking and laughing. Ragnvald had watched the unexpected events with his brother-in-law Jarl Frode, and when they were over Jarl Gustav had come over to join them, a sour expression on his face. Before he could voice his concern, Jarl Steinar approached them, smiling, and greeted them warmly. 'Brothers, my king would like to thank you for your support.'

'Our king, not just yours apparently,' grunted Gustav.

'Quite, I apologise, just a habit, I meant no offence.' Steinar thumped Gustav's back awkwardly.

'Well, tell our king when you see him his gratitude isn't necessary, we didn't do this for him, we did it for our people. I hope he remembers that,' Gustav chided the Norwegian jarl, his clawed hand pointing disconcertingly at the temple behind them where the king had gone.

'He does, and you may tell him what you think yourself, he has asked for your council,' Steinar replied, seemingly unaffected by the rebuke of the older man.

'Now?' asked Ragnvald.

'If you would?'

Frode looked around the group. 'If our king commands it, of course we will come.'

'He invites you,' corrected Steinar.

'Whatever you call it,' said Gustav, tucking his hands into his furs against a sudden biting gust of wind. 'It's warmer in there, I'm happy to see what he wants.'

Steinar looked perplexed. 'You invited him here to become your king. We all know what we did to clear the way, you did so willingly. Why do you now seem hostile to him?'

Gustav turned his weathered face on the young Norwegian jarl. The oldest jarl in the Svealands had had decades to perfect a withering look, and he turned its full force now on the young Norwegian. 'I invited him because it was the best thing for my people. Doesn't mean I like it. What you said was true. He is your king, not ours. And now he is standing in our temple, on our land, telling us what to do. He was supposed to be voted in at the Thing of all Swedes, our sacred meeting. Instead he sidestepped us with that little trick. He abolished our crown and named himself *Norðrikonungr*?' Gustav shook his head. 'I'm old enough to remember when our peoples were enemies, and now one of you is king of my lands, something I fought against my whole youth, and he took it without following our customs, without respect for our laws. I'll do what he asks, I'll follow him, but I don't have to like it. Any other questions?'

Steinar shook his head sadly at the rebuke. 'No, just give him a chance.'

'We've given him more than that already, we've given him our country. Now, let's go and speak to him before I get any older or any colder. I can afford neither.' Gustav turned and walked towards the temple doorway with its runic border, even older and more gnarled than he was. Ragnvald smiled at the other two men knowingly and followed, Frode close behind him.

When the three lords entered the temple, Sigurd was standing in front of the statue of Odin, alone in the dim light of the temple. Faint light shone through windows on the second level windows, and a fire was lit in the hearth in the centre of the building. Ragnvald gazed around and tried to adjust his eyes to the darkness. The outer edges of the interior were full of huge carved pillars that supported the upper levels.

In the centre was an open space of wooden boards, and at the back of that open space, the raised platform with the three stylised statues. Odin the wise, the traveller and guidestar to kings, sat in the centre in a cloak of wood with his spear Gungnir in one hand and his one eye watching all. Thor, the mighty god of thunder, sat on the right with furrowed brow and sculpted muscles, his hammer Mjölnir resting at his feet. On the left sat Freyr, the god most loved by the Svear, the bringer of the harvest and all the pleasures of life. He was sitting there with what Ragnvald always thought was a smug smile, although he thought anyone sitting down with such a huge erection that it almost reached his chin would be smug.

Freyr's carved wooden member was the size of a tall man but other than that, he was unarmed and unadorned, content to sit there, bathing those before in his peace and serenity, and envy at his manhood.

Sigurd turned and smiled at the three men as they walked out onto the floor. Ragnvald had never met Sigurd up close before. He was a huge man, deceptively normal looking against the backdrop of the enormous statues, but now that they were face to face, Ragnvald saw that Sigurd was a half head taller than even him, and broader, much more muscled. He looked like Thor come to earth. He was unarmed, as they all were, weapons were not allowed in the temple.

'I came here when I was a child,' said Sigurd, an easy smile on his bearded face. 'I remember thinking this temple must be Valhalla itself. And then staring at these statues and being unable to decide if I wanted Odin's spear, Thor's hammer or Freyr's...' He grinned at the Swedish jarls and stepped down to meet them, leaving the joke hanging. He clasped hands with each of them in turn, his grip like a blacksmith's vice.

'So, I wanted to meet with you alone before I left, the three men who brought me to this place, to apologise for the manner of my arrival.'

Gustav folded his arms over his chest. 'Aye, and what are you sorry for, Lord Sigurd?'

'That I forced that little event on you.'

'Why?'

'Why am I sorry? Well, I know it wasn't what yo...'

'No,' interrupted Gustav. 'Not why are you sorry, I couldn't care less. Why did you do it?'

'Ah.' Sigurd let the rudeness of interrupting him slide. 'We received word of the fall of Fyn while we were on the road. I decided I had to get here before the news, or risk arriving under a dark omen, of the whole thing being overtaken by that loss. So we rode half the night, went straight to the temple, and arranged for the messenger to arrive at the end of my speech.' He clasped his hands together at his waist. 'I had to decide quickly and decided it was the best way to use the news, to warn of the threat and then be proven right, not to arrive after the news and bawl about how sad it was. I hope it did not lose me your confidence.'

The three Swedish jarls looked at each other thoughtfully. 'How did you get the high priestess to go along with it?' said Ragnvald.

'Oh, I didn't. I had no idea she would crown me.'

'What? You were crowned accidentally?'

Sigurd's scratched his beard awkwardly. 'Yes.'

Ragnvald laughed ruefully. 'Some of us yearned for the crown of Sweden all our lives, and you got it accidentally.' Even Gustav let out a gruff chuckle.

'It is not how I intended this. I didn't intend any of this, last year I was just the son and cousin of kings. but here we are, at the whim of the gods.'

'Here we are,' agreed Ragnvald.

Sigurd's face turned serious for the first time. 'Will you be able to follow me, Ragnvald, you who could have been king? I will need your support, your council. All of you.'

'Yes, Lord Sigurd. I would swear my oath to you now, but…' He gestured to the king's empty sword belt. 'There will be time later, at the king's hall.'

Sigurd took Ragnvald by the arm and clasped his hands. 'There is no need for you men to swear to me. I know what you did to bring me here, what sacrifices you made. No, you will never have to kneel to me.'

'We wouldn't do it if we had to,' snorted Gustav. 'We will do it because we choose to. And we need to be seen to do it, and not here, Ragnvald. Not witnessed only by the gods, it will be done in front of all the people. You first, and the rest of us to follow. Let them see you kneel, let them hear your words, let them know your loyalty.

There was some bad blood in that crowd, they need to be assured there is none between us.' Gustav's tone did not allow dissent.

Ragnvald stiffened at the thought of kneeling to a foreign king in his own city for all to see. He stared at Gustav then reluctantly nodded. 'The old man is right, as usual.'

'With age comes wisdom, boy.'

'A gain of wisdom and a loss of body parts,' Ragnvald quipped, gesturing at Gustav's crippled, splayed hand. The hand that gave him his name, 'Gustav the Raven's Claw'.

'Aye, but look where you are and learn.' He gestured to the platform with its three silent watchers. 'The young bucks like Lord Sigurd come in here and can't decide if they want Gungnir or Mjölnir or whatever Freyr calls his ridiculous prick.' He looked at Sigurd, who cocked his head and looked back at the statues. 'But what you should want is Odin's missing eye. For he lost an eye and gained all the wisdom of the world.' Gustav stretched his famous Raven's Claw towards Ragnvald and gestured to it. 'Losing this finger saved my life, made me look at the world a new way, the ridiculousness of my pride and ambition. You will all need to do that on the road we are travelling. We won't get there through strength of arms alone, but by using this.' He tapped the side of his head.

'A wise man indeed, who recognises the wisdom of the gods for what it is,' a new voice said from behind the three Svear lords. They turned in confusion. A figure in a long dark tunic and a furled hood was standing in the shadow of one of the great carved wooden pillars.

'Who are you to interrupt this meeting?' snapped Gustav with outrage in his voice, his fingers closing unthinkingly at his empty scabbard.

The figure was unperturbed by the anger, and stepped out into the dim light. He was a slight man of middle age, and his appearance instantly removed the atmosphere of threat or betrayal from the three lords. He was unarmed, his clothes were old and patched, and he had no air of violence or threat about him, but more disturbingly, no fear, despite the power and anger of the lords now facing him.

'Apologies my lords, I didn't mean to...'

'Tormund, leave us!' boomed the king with an irritated sigh.

The man bowed without a hint of annoyance, turned and disappeared back into the shadows. They heard a door open and then close again, and Gustav turned to the king in confusion. 'Who is that man who sneaks up behind us when we believe we are alone, discussing matters of import? I have killed men for much less.'

'My apologies, friends, that is Tormund, who men call five-bones. He was my father's seer and he has strange habits, he does not think or behave like other men, but he is quite trustworthy, I assure you.'

'You keep a seer?' asked Ragnvald, visibly unsure of what to make of it. Seers were few and far between, and few placed much stock in their babblings anymore.

'Yes, I think it befits a king, especially in these times. And he is useful.' The king twisted a few strands of his prodigious beard with his fingers. 'It's hard to explain, but he sometimes knows things when it should not be possible, and before other men do, and claims to have the Odinsight. My father found him useful.'

Ragnvald looked back again at where the man had disappeared with a thoughtful expression. 'Perhaps he knows too much because he sneaks around listening where he is not supposed to be.' He suspected the man had not left, merely opened and closed the door and still lurked in the shadows, but he decided not to embarrass the king by discovering it.

'That is undoubtedly true, at least in part. But...' The king shrugged and a look of pure pain crossed his bearded face. 'He came to me and told me my brother was dead, before the message boat even arrived ashore, two days before. He saw it in his dreams. He told me I would be the king, and to prepare myself.' The king looked at the men with a sad shrug. 'I cannot explain how he knew that, but prepare myself I did, and I am thankful that I listened. It saved a great deal of trouble over the succession.' Ragnvald looked down and nodded, uncomfortable at the king's raw emotion and his unnerving gaze.

'Do you not trust in the gods, and believe they guide us, Lord Ragnvald?' asked Sigurd. Standing as he was beneath the high roof of the temple, in front of the statues of the gods themselves, it felt like a very pointed question.

Ragnvald looked back up at the king and considered his answer carefully. 'I do, but I do not trust in every man who claims to know their minds, nor claims to know the future.' Truthfully, he did not believe any man had the Odinsight, the ability to see what Odin planned, or to know the future. Many a drunken wanderer would claim to possess it, and want to share that gift for a meal or a coin.

Sigurd laughed his short, booming laugh, reverberating in that high space. 'A wise man you are too, Lord Ragnvald,' said Sigurd, turning to stare at the statues. 'We cannot just put our faith in what we believe or are told the gods want for us, we must make our own path, no matter how hard it may be. And that is why I will need you with me, I will need all of you with me.' The three jarls said nothing, he already had them.

CHAPTER 8

THE PAIN OF PRIDE

FTER THE MEETING with the three jarls and a blessing from the priestess, King Sigurd went to the great hall for the feast that followed. The feast was huge, only the most important sat in the great hall, the rest spilling out into the square on tables and benches brought from surrounding buildings, and lit by a dozen temporary firepits as the people crowded around them in the fading light and the sharp chill of the spring evening.

When the men had eaten their fill, and the drinking was roaring into full swing, King Sigurd stood on the dais, his scabbarded sword unbelted and carried in his right hand, and took the oaths of the lords of the North. Ragnvald went first, as silence fell on the raucous hall. He looked up at Sigurd, who whose face was impassive behind his big beard, but whose eyes roved the hall intently, trying to read the mood, and search out any who might oppose this moment.

'Lord Ragnvald,' he boomed as the hush fell to a deathly silence, his voice carrying even to those in the depths of the firelit square. 'I thank you and your people for the welcome you have given me here in your city. I am filled with joy to have an ally such as you for this war against the Christians, for your reputation alone is worth a dozen longships of warriors. Men will come from all over the North to fight alongside you, and together, we shall lead them to victory, and a glorious future.'

Ragnvald inclined his head in thanks. 'King Sigurd, I have come before you today to pledge my allegiance to you as *Norðrikonungr*, to bring my lands and my people into your realm, if you would take me as your vassal.' A moment of awkward silence passed between the two men while Sigurd fiddled with the hilt of his sword with his left hand. Then he held it out, hilt first, the hilt balancing on his left hand as he held it out with his right.

For the first time in twenty years, Ragnvald knelt before another man. He put his hand on the foreign king's sword, and gave his oath. The rest of the lords of Sweden present followed him to a man. The oaths went on into the darkening night, and when they were finished the lords of the new kingdom drank together until they were insensible.

Ordulf lay in the longhouse and listened. He would be staying in Uppsala while his fate was decided elsewhere. He did not exactly want to go through the rigours of another campaign, but as a slave it was a moot issue, it was not his choice. He would stay and make swords and axes and wait for news. As he lay there, staring at the starlight filtering through the smoke hole in the roof, another body walked over and slipped into the furs next to him.

'Can't sleep either?' the figure asked in a soft voice.

It was Brunhild. It had been months since she had really talked to him, even looked at him. He stirred and looked towards her, nothing more than a dark shape in the even darker room, words of shamed apology trying to form on his lips. Behind them the sounds of the feast roared to a crescendo as some game or other came to conclusion. He opened his mouth to speak to her, but warm lips pressed over his and a soft thigh pushed between his legs. 'Now is not the time for that,' she whispered.

He forgot both what he had wanted to say and the noise of the party as a familiar but long-absent hand trailed slowly down his chest to the even darker darkness between their entwined bodies. The raucous noise of the celebrations across the yard disguised the scuffles and gasps as Ordulf rolled his unexpected companion onto her back and pushed her willing legs apart with his.

The celebrations of the Dísablót commenced the next morning, an early start for a town of thumping heads and bleary eyes. A huge number of animals were sacrificed and the high priestess shocked the assembled lords by stripping her tunic and dancing and writhing naked and in ecstasy at the foot of the statue of Frey – an unheard of act, even for the raucous Dísablót. It was an offering of passion to the god of love to ask for his blessings in the coming season. Two days passed after the priestess declared the Dísablót concluded and the great assembly was formally called.

The first Thing of all Norse was held in the open on benches, as the hall could not hold so many leaders gathered from so many Norse lands. It was the greatest gathering of power in the history of the northlands. For two full days, the plans for fighting the Crusaders were discussed, debated, detailed and agreed. Each jarl and lesser chief declared what forces he would bring, and where and when they would gather. Every town and area committed supplies and support.

There was only one hotly debated topic: the defence of Sjælland. Many of the lords present, particularly the Norwegian and Swedish jarls, wanted to abandon Sjælland as they had abandoned Fyn. The Danish jarls argued that Sjælland must be defended, it was their last vestige of their kingdom outside Scania and in their traditional homeland. They had abandoned Fyn because it was impossible to defend; it was broad, round, flat and too close to the Jutland peninsula to hold. Sjælland, they argued, was across a treacherous strait full of shallows and reefs. It was a forested and rolling island, larger and more defensible than Fyn. Other jarls, including Jarl Rangvald, also said that it should be defended. They argued that it was essential to slow the Crusaders down there and thus reduce the time they would have to invade the mainland before autumn storms would close the cold sea.

Eventually, after an entire afternoon of debate, Sigurd made his ruling. Sjælland would be both evacuated and defended. They would help whoever wanted leave to do so, and they would fight the Crusaders on the island to sap their strength, perhaps to delay them for a season or even defeat them, keeping the war away from the mainland for months or a year.

With the plans for the season decided, the assembly was dissolved, and the lords of the North went back to their homes to assemble their forces and prepare for war. The scale of the preparations for war was unprecedented. Coastal towns and villages readied their ships and crews; inland communities prepared to march to the coast. The lords of the North had pledged nearly six hundred crews to the campaign – a previously unimaginable force for the Norse, nearly 17,000 men for the main army, thousands others were to defend towns, raid supply lines and patrol coasts.

The core of the army were the hirds of each lord, the true warriors of the Norse, experienced, well-armed and trained. The rest of the army was made up of a large tithe of the best karls and other freemen, the Leidang, who would bring their own weapons and shields and would be lightly armoured, probably with nothing more than thick wool or perhaps a padded linen jacket. Some rich ones would have swords but most would fight with spears or axes.

Some would bring hunting or war bows and a hand axe or seax and fight as skirmishers.

Some ships, over a hundred, would be sent to Sjælland to help evacuate it. The remainder of the army were to be gathered later in spring and go to Lund, on the Skanian coast, after the crops were in the ground, in order to reduce the burden of supplying an army of such an unheard of size in the field. If the Crusaders invaded the mainland before taking Sjælland, the local forces would quickly gather to slow them while the main army gathered and the fleet cut off the Crusaders' supplies from its base in Jutland.

The machinations of power and the debating of the great lords did not much penetrate the world of Ordulf's slavehouse, or the people who lived in it. The preparations for campaign merely meant fetching more of different items to different places, the weaving of different clothes, the preparing of more salted meat. For Ordulf it meant a rush of weapons that needed repairing or re-hilting ready for battle, and the clearing out of every usable weapon Dengir could provide.

Eventually there was nothing left to do at the forge, and Ordulf was no longer able to ignore matters at home, where he was still very much alone, and where Brunhild was once again treating him with disdain and contempt. On one quiet day, while Brunhild was alone preparing a meal, he summoned the courage to ask her, clumsily, to share his bed again that night.

'No,' she replied, bluntly.

'Why?' Ordulf asked, with a hint of a whine.

Brunhild sighed and her shoulders slumped. 'Because of this.'

'What, what have I done wrong now?'

'You think I will be with you when you want,' she said bluntly, resuming her chopping.

'What's wrong with that?'

Brunhild dropped the rough knife on the board and turned towards him with an impatient frown. 'Because you don't care about anyone but yourself. You have not learned, you have not apologised, and I have nothing else I want from you. What, you expect me to just rut whenever you want?'

Ordulf stuttered. It was pretty much exactly what he wanted. 'No? I just, well…' He swallowed and looked to one side, trying to keep his face blank to hide his hurt. 'Why not? What would be wrong with that?'

'Because you want to own me. As soon as I let you lie with me whenever you want, you will just want me to be yours. I read it in your eyes every day.' Ordulf had a pained look on his face. 'Tell me it's not true, tell me you don't want me to be yours.'

Ordulf was left flapping his mouth like a landed fish, trying to find the words, and trying to work out what he even thought.

'Exactly,' Brunhild said. Folding her arms across her chest. 'Listen to me, Ordulf. No one will ever own me. You understand?'

He couldn't help himself. He knew before he even said it what a mistake it was, but he said it anyway. 'But you are a slave, Ragnvald owns you.'

She blanched with fury and advanced on him, sticking a finger in his chest with surprising force. Ordulf recoiled and leaned back under the pressure of that lancing finger, trying not to show it was hurting him.

'Horse shit. You don't understand. You have no idea what it means for a woman to be owned by a man.' Brunhild was seething now, her face strained and eyes blazing. Ordulf felt genuine fear. 'Listen, boy. I was born a slave, my father was some passing trader I never met and my mother was a farm slave who died when I was young. The old karl who owned me was killed by another man and he took me as his slave. I was in my twelfth summer. He thought he was kind to me, he never hit me, he fed me well and clothed me and looked after me and did not make me work in the fields. But he was very clear about what he expected in return.'

Ordulf's mouth opened and then hung there stupidly.

'That man thought I liked him, I made sure he thought I liked him, because it kept me safe. I was trapped in a prison of my own body, and I was owned by him like that, body and mind.' She finally withdrew the finger but the stare was only more piercing.

Ordulf tried to apologise but she just talked right over him. 'Then he grew tired of me and sold me to his jarl. I expected more of the same, I knew nothing else, but Jarl Ragnvald wanted me simply as a worker, and although he has owned my service, he has never touched me, he never gave me to anyone for their use, and he doesn't own my mind. I don't have to pretend to like him, I don't have to share his furs. My mind is my own, my body touches only what I choose. I swear to you my body and my mind will ever be owned or controlled by a man ever again, I will die before it happens.'

Ordulf nodded dumbly. 'I'm sorry, I understand.'

'No you don't, stop pretending you know anything, you may have seen the world beyond this land but you walked through it with your eyes closed. I know men like you, Ordulf, as soon as I let you put your prick in me whenever you want you will think you own me. You may treat me well, you will think you love me, but really you will just want to own me.' Ordulf stared in confusion and shame at his hand, pretending to pick at a fingernail.

'Now, tell me again how you want me to be available to you for rutting at your convenience? Tell me how you want me to be yours?' she asked, eyes wide and searching.

'But then why were you with Geir?' asked Ordulf, lamely, wincing at the invocation of the recently dead man.

'Because he understood. He never tried to control me. He never complained when I didn't go to him and he didn't care when

I went to others. Most of all, he never looked at me like a puppy who has been left behind for the day when its master is out of the house; that look you have been giving me all these months.' She folded her arms across her chest again and just stood, waiting for the anguished Ordulf to continue. He finally managed to look up and hold her gaze.

'Then why did you come to me the other night?'

Brunhild snorted with laughter. 'You truly understand nothing.' She shook her head and looked at him with amused pity, her anger swept away. 'You have the mind of a child,' she said, tapping her head in emphasis. But then she slowly swept her eyes up his body, her gaze caressing him like a lover. 'But you have the body of a man.'

Ordulf flushed bright red under her gaze and she laughed at his embarrassment. Brunhild turned back to her work, still laughing to herself and shaking her head, leaving the confused and ashamed smith standing there nursing his ego and trying to summon the courage to turn and slink away. Brunhild spoke again without looking around. 'I have nothing else to say to you, Ordulf.'

Chastened and blazing with frustration and embarrassment, Ordulf finally slunk away.

Days passed, and Ordulf worked in the forge when there was work to do and tried to avoid the other slaves in the longhouse for the rest of the time, particularly Brunhild. He realised he had never considered her past, how she had become a slave, what that might mean, how her life would have been. The whole concept was incomprehensible to him. To learn how she had been used, to feel the lash of her anger at him had been something he had struggled to bear.

One evening, after eating some stale bread and dried meat, he went outside and found Brunhild feeding the goats that were living in the low outhouse along the back of the compound.

He, stopped, and, summoning his courage, he walked over to her, only to be met with stony silence and the accustomed lack of recognition.

'What is wrong?' he asked with disappointment laced in his voice.

'The same thing that was always wrong,' she replied, without looking at him.

Ordulf felt the familiar blush of anger. 'Well, I came to apologise to you, for what I said, after the fight.'

That got Brunhild to turn around, scorn written across her face. 'Really? Now, after all this time, now you want to apologise for that.'

'Yes.'

'Why now, Ordulf, what took you so long? You came to me to tell me you wanted me, but never came to me to apologise.'

'What? I just…'

'You just what? You just couldn't apologise before for some reason?'

'Well, you weren't talking to me!' protested Ordulf, surprised to have been met with such scorn. Once again, the conversation was rapidly spiralling out of control. To make matters worse, at that moment Otto walked out of the longhouse and came across them.

'What's going on?' he asked, seeing the situation and stopping with a stern look.

'Ordulf was just explaining why he hasn't apologised to me yet,' Brunhild said. 'Has he apologised to you?'

'What do you think?' replied Otto sarcastically.

Ordulf ground his teeth together and closed his eyes, trying to calm himself under the onslaught. 'I just…'

'Just what?' goaded Brunhild.

'Would you let me speak!'

'You've had months to speak, and done nothing about it,' said

Otto. 'All you had before was words, opinions on everything, but then so long with nothing.'

'Stop! Why are you so upset about something I said when I was drunk?' he shouted, instantly regretting his outburst.

'Why?' asked Otto. 'Let me see. You behaved like you were better than us. Then you said you were better than us. Then you joked about having one of us as a sexual reward, then you told us you didn't need us anymore, told me you didn't need me and that you never had.'

Ordulf pouted but did not reply.

'Oh, and you were selfish, when you have received nothing from us but generosity.'

'What?' Ordulf blurted.

'What? You were offered a reward by the jarl. You could have asked for something for all of us. You could have thought of your fellows, who fed you and guided you and lay with you and taught you and helped you survive in this world. Instead, you sought something only for yourself. And then you couldn't even apologise to us and instead left your foul attitude and sulking darkening the hall for weeks.' Otto shook his head. 'Enough, I waited but I don't care anymore.'

'I wanted to apologise,' Ordulf replied pleadingly. 'But I didn't get the chance.'

'Didn't get the chance? We have all been sleeping in the same room as you, for months.'

'Yes, but,' Ordulf gestured limply at the longhouse. 'That's in there, I wanted a private conversation.'

'Ah, so you wouldn't have the embarrassment of a public apology,' Otto sneered. 'How touching.'

'Okay, yes, I didn't want to do this with everyone around.'

'So, in wanting to apologise for being selfish, you chose to do it selfishly.'

Ordulf's shoulders slumped. 'Well, maybe, but...'

Otto held up his hand. 'Stop, I'm not interested. Why can't you just stop defending yourself and admit you were wrong?'

'I would, but...'

'Don't bother, you had your chance.' Otto turned and walked away, leaving Ordulf standing dejected. He turned to Brunhild, hoping for sympathy, and found none in her steely gaze.

'Well?' she asked.

Ordulf's teeth grated with anger at the combined attack, but he unclamped them and choked out a reply. 'I'm sorry, Brunhild, I didn't want to upset you.'

'That's it?' she asked, incredulous.

'What do you want?' he said, spreading his arms out in frustration.

'For you to grow up and understand how the world works and where you are in it! To control your stupid temper and have courage of the mind, not just courage of the body. To apologise like a man, and not make excuses like a child.'

'What would be the point! You all clearly hate me!' Ordulf suddenly felt himself close to tears and felt a burst of shame.

'I don't hate you, you idiot. I am just so disappointed.' She shook her head and picked up her basket. 'Well, Otto hates you. But that is because he envies you and wants an excuse to hate you, one you have amply provided. You have no future with him, that thread is cut. Me? I would forgive you if you could apologise and mean it. Show me you know you aren't above me, that I'm not just a potential reward or a soft set of thighs to you, something you want to own and use. Show me that you know you are one of us and not one of them. I'll give you another couple of months to think about it.'

'Another couple of months!'

'I suggest next time you try to apologise, you know what

you are going to say first, and think about why we are so angry,' Brunhild said over her shoulder as she walked away. Ordulf was left standing there helpless, as alone as he had ever been in his life.

CHAPTER 9

A FAREWELL TO FRIENDS

April 1117

A MONTH LATER, JARL Ragnvald gathered the warriors of his hird and the men of his Leidang to Uppsala, to set out to war in their ten longships, every large ship his people owned. Four hundred men, most of the experienced fighting men in his lands, the most he had ever gathered, packed into the great hall and spilled into the yard, feasting and laughing through the night.

The jarl and his men left for Sjælland on a glorious day. Many of their children and wives were there to see them off. The mood was tense. This was no common raid they were going to. This was a war the like of which the Norse had not seen in their history. Jarl Gustav was there to see Ragnvald off, a large group of his men going with the younger jarl in their own ships. Gustav was too old for the campaign and he knew it. He would remain behind and help organise the preparations on the mainland. The Raven's Claw gave Ragnvald a firm embrace and some parting words of jest and then stood on the dock, talking to his men as they prepared to leave. Thralls helped to load the longships and then, with the blowing of horns and half-hearted cheering, the boats were away, rowing down the narrow river to join the rest of the local fleet at the main docks before heading out to sea.

The ships rowed down the rivers and lakes leading to the cold sea, where they would meet with all the ships of eastern Sweden. Sixty-two longships were due – a huge force at any time, but just a tithe of the overall strength of this great army that would be gathered. Some of these were smaller boats from local villages, crewed by freemen who were otherwise farmers, fishermen, or woodsmen. Some of them were large longships suited for long raids to the isles of Alba north of France, filled with the veteran hirds of other great warlords. Jarl Ragnvald was in command of this fleet. They set sail across the cold sea for Sjælland, to land an army and evacuate those they could get away in time. Once the Crusaders arrived, the army would march to meet them.

Five days' rowing and sailing saw them to the shores of Sjælland at the town of København. The weather was cold, but good. A fresh breeze from the south would allow them to cross from København to Lund on the mainland and back in a single day. With one return voyage a day, this fleet could take nearly a thousand people and their possessions or the weight of one-and-a-half thousand men in supplies a day. København was a new town, but prosperous, and perhaps ten thousand people still lived in the area. If they were willing and organised, they and their possessions and the needed supplies of food, tools, materials and other important assets could be removed in twenty days. Perhaps. Ragnvald doubted it was possible and doubted they had that much time, but every load of people, supplies and equipment saved strengthened the people on the mainland. There was more than enough room for more settlement inland in Scania.

Much of the Norwegian and western Swedish fleet was likewise evacuating Roskilde, the only other large town on the islands. That town might have twenty thousand people still in its area and the fjord leading to it was long and winding; it would take much longer to evacuate there. Given the near certainty of not completing in time, they would have hard choices to make.

On the nineteenth day of the evacuation, when they arrived in København for another return voyage, a messenger was waiting on the dock for the jarl, agitated and nervous.

'Lord Ragnvald, the Crusaders sailed in a huge fleet from Odense yesterday, and landed near Trelleborg on the west coast; the town and fortress there is now under siege and is calling for help.'

'What force do they have?' he replied.

'They landed with forty large ships, perhaps six thousand men, and hundreds of horses. When we left, the fleet was returning to Odense; we saw more men still encamped there than went onto the ships. They will probably return full again today.'

The jarl nodded thoughtfully. They could be facing well over ten thousand men with a significant mounted force.

'Did any other ships see forces gathering elsewhere, on the mainland?'

'I don't know, lord. We were always outside Odense.'

The jarl nodded and said, 'Thank you for your message.' The man turned and ran off down the dock towards his small ship, a light boat with eight oars a side.

The plan was for the army to assemble at Roskilde when the Crusaders landed. The majority of the people who wanted to leave Sjælland had already left. The rest simply refused to leave or couldn't. Most of the fighting men of the island had remained to fight for it. Along with over a hundred crews from the mainland, the army on the island, commanded by King Sigurd himself, would number over six thousand men. Five hundred more were in the fortress at Trelleborg.

Jarl Ragnvald left his ships at København, under guard by a hundred men with strict instructions not to let the ships be taken back to the mainland, as they might be required at any time. Another seventeen local Danish ships were also left there at anchor. His force set out for the march to Roskilde. It was already midday when they started; it would be a hard march in order to arrive by nightfall.

The men formed up on the road leading inland, armed, armoured and carrying most of their gear on their backs but little else. They would travel light and move fast, getting supplies from stores left along the route. Rangvald walked in the middle of the column, his huscarls around him, their maille whispering and gear rattling from the brisk pace.

For the rest of the day, almost until darkness, they kept up the pace, stopping once to refill water skins at a river. Just after nightfall, they arrived at Roskilde in time to eat and fall to exhausted sleep in the longhouses of a section of the half-abandoned town. The king had left the town the previous day, and left instructions for any that arrived later to follow him as fast as possible to Trelleborg.

The morning brought rain and misery on the road. Nearly five hundred extra men joined Ragnvald's small army on the march to Trelleborg, along a single track that quickly turned to a muddy morass. They intended to reach Haraldsted that day, a town between two lakes in the centre of the island. All day the men tramped, cursed and slogged through the slippery mud of the single road. They made a rough camp and slaughtered and feasted on a small herd of sheep they had found wandering abandoned there.

The next day, by the time they caught up with the king's army, the light was just starting to fade. The two armies merged joyfully; men clasped hands and the new arrivals were welcomed around the fires. Sentries were put out in force. Just two miles away, across a gentle valley, the Crusader camp could be seen outside the Trelleborg fortress. It was *massive*. It looked like half the world was camping over there. The smoke from their orderly lines of fires blurred the horizon.

With a group of Swedish jarls in tow, Ragnvald went to report to the king, who was sitting on a tree stump looking out towards the Crusader camp, eating a joint of fresh cooked meat with a group of his Norwegian jarls around him, deep in conversation. Ragnvald approached the group, few of whom he knew well, but he recognised several from the Thing of all Norse. Several men recognised him and one clasped arms and welcomed him enthusiastically. Others in his group were greeted warmly, one by one, these former rivals, foes and enemies breaking nothing but smiles.

'Jarl Ragnvald! By Thor, we are glad to see you here!' A big Norwegian slapped Ragnvald on the back and continued, 'The Crusaders were getting noisy today, looking like they might attack. Your arrival gave them pause. Quivering over there in their tents they are now!' the big jarl guffawed.

Ragnvald smiled. 'I remember you from the assembly, but I do not know your name.'

'I am Jarl Kjartan. My hall is near Sarpsborg.' Jarl Kjartan was a tall, jovial man. A prominent scar across the top of his forehead and right eyelid left his left eye half closed, as if he was squinting. He was not a good-looking man anyway, with a lumpen, oft-broken nose and ears like sails, but the scar made it considerably worse.

'Kjartan, I am pleased to meet you. I am glad to be here before you had time to kill all our enemies. How many lives did they bring for us to take?' Ragnvald jested, nodding across the gentle valley.

'We think fifteen thousand. Perhaps a little more. They have a thousand horsemen but no siege engines. I don't think they were expecting this fortress.' The big man chuckled.

The king had stood up and was walking over. Ragnvald had forgotten in the month since he had last seen him just what a presence the man was, especially now armed and clothed for war. Ragnvald offered his arm to the big man, only to be surprised with a full embrace that felt like being attacked by a bear. By the gods, this man was strong.

'Ragnvald, you brought your army.'

'Lord, it is your army,' said Ragnvald, his mouth filling with fur from the king's cloak in the process.

'I am glad to hear you say it, but you brought these men here from Sweden, so I think we can call it your army.'

Ragnvald blushed and smiled. He was so happy to be praised so warmly by the king that he suddenly felt like a child again, thrilled to be praised by a demanding father.

The king released the smiling jarl and said 'So, given that this is your army, do you mind if I borrow it for a while?'

Ragnvald laughed with the men around them and nodded his assent. Men slapped him on the back and the king gestured to the stump. 'Come, sit, you have had a long march. I know, I did the same thing yesterday.'

Ragnvald wouldn't sit while everyone else, including the king, remained standing, so he merely raised one foot and rested it on the stump, stretching his sore legs in the process. Sigurd nodded approvingly. 'So, the Christians have their main body in front of the fortress and another few thousand on the other side of the river, blocking escape. The rest are roaming the countryside and causing trouble and guarding things, and whatever else it is that Christian soldiers do. They really are an active bunch, very well organised; even their tents stand in neat rows.' Sigurd turned to look at Ragnvald. 'Have you ever seen the fortress at Trelleborg? No? Neither had I until today. My local men drew me a likeness in the dirt.' He gestured to the ground in front of the stump, where Ragnvald saw that there were indeed some lines scratched.

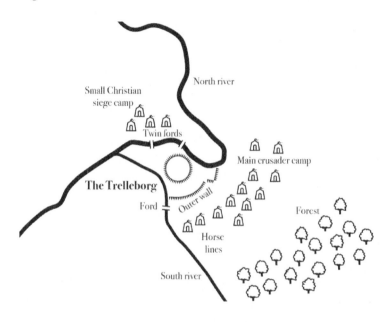

'So, the fortress is in the joint between two rivers. The rivers are not particularly broad or deep, but deep enough that a man cannot easily walk across, nor can a ladder span it.' He indicated two wiggly lines that joined on the far side. 'Other than two deep fords that are waist high and guarded with earthworks and a wall, it is impassable without barges. The fortress itself is a palisade on top of earth banks and twenty feet tall in total.' He pointed at the rough circle in the centre of the markings. 'Then there is an outer wall that runs across the gap between the two rivers. That is what the Crusaders assaulted yesterday and were repulsed. It was not a heavy attack, just a test.'

He stopped and turned to the man next to him. 'I got that

right?' The man nodded. 'See, this is why I'm the king, eh?' the king said with a self-deprecating grin.

His face turned serious and he gestured to the group. 'So the problem we were discussing here is that of our men are inside that fortress. Their only roles here were to force the Crusaders to besiege it while we gathered, and to waste their time, to prevent them moving on quickly inland and facing us before we were ready. Now that has been achieved, and we need to decide how to act. The Crusaders have enough men gathered now to attack us; it seems they were about to this afternoon until you arrived and they were dissuaded. I think now they will assess our new strength and maybe attack tomorrow. They can't have us behind them if they assault the walls or risk being crushed between us and the fortress.' The king paused, looking around the council to see if anyone disagreed. No one did.

'We cannot attack their camp over the open ground, not with their numbers and the horsemen they have. Nor can we defend this hill for long before being surrounded and cut off. We all agree we cannot leave without trying to save the garrison, but no one has a good idea how.' The king stopped and shrugged. 'We appear to have no good options. This is the problem we were discussing when you arrived. What do you think?' he asked Ragnvald and the Swedish jarls.

Ragnvald exhaled deeply and nodded. 'That is indeed a problem. We cannot attack, cannot defend, nor can we leave, without losing something in each case. The least bad option is to leave – but then why come here at all? We must gain something from this fortress and the loss of five hundred men, other than a few days of time.'

The king nodded in agreement. 'That much most of us agree on. We must act to help them, but to do what is the question.'

Ragnvald thought about it for a while, staring down at the

camp. 'Why are we forced to stay together and not free to manoeuvre? We should be able to move around freely, strike at will, avoid decisive combat. That has always been our way as warbands; it should be our way as this army.'

'Their horsemen are why,' said Jarl Kjartan, to nods of agreement.

'We have all heard what they did at the ridge near Ribe, when the Christian knights caught an army in the open,' said another man.

'Yes, indeed, their horsemen are the problem. Without their threat we could strike at will and force them to either break the siege or turn on us, yes?' Ragnvald said.

There were nods and murmurs of agreement in the group.

'How do we defeat their knights? We cannot simply force them to fight on our terms. Nor could we easily defeat them, even if we did,' said Kjartan.

'No, indeed,' agreed Ragnvald, smiling wickedly. 'But we do not need to defeat their knights, we only need to remove the use of their horses. Even for a day. See here, beyond the fortress where two fords lead into its rear. You say there are a thousand or more Christians here?'

'Yes,' said Kjartan.

'So why don't we move around there and trap those men against the river, kill them and evacuate the fortress there?'

'Because that land is terrible for us. It is open and flat for many miles. If we crossed the river upstream to attack the blocking force from the rear, their main army would move north-east on our flank and have us against the sea. We would trap ourselves by crossing that river – in fact they may be hoping for us to do this. Then we would have to face them in flat fields with no cover and no retreat. It would be a disaster.'

'I understand,' Ragnvald nodded. 'How long would we need in order to make the attack and then get clear?'

Sigurd started to smile as he watched the conversation. 'Half a day,' he said, 'maybe slightly more. Then we can make the attack and have time to retreat to where the river turns inland and get into the hills and woods there, where we can defend ourselves.'

Ragnvald smiled. 'We need to stop thinking like soldiers and start thinking like Vikings. Have any of you ever tried to round up a thousand panicked horses at night before?'

Men around him looked confused and Jarl Frode laughed at the idea. 'No, of course not, but it sounds awful!' he said.

Ragnvald nodded, an evil smile on his face. 'It might be awful, mightn't it? Shall we make the Christians find out?'

'Come on, you smug bastard, tell us your plan,' said Sigurd, rubbing his hands together in glee.

So Ragnvald told them.

CHAPTER 10

FORTRESS AND FORTITUDE

May 1117

SIR HANS WAS frustrated. All day, he and his men had scouted the Norse army in its woodline, trying to ascertain its strength and positions. But they had moved around like smoke, ambushing his contingents if they came too close, attacking and withdrawing. Then, towards the end of the afternoon, as he finally thought he had their measure, another large force arrived, and it became too late in the day to mount a full attack. Now he still did not know how many they faced, or where they were camping. All he knew was they were not behaving like a normal army.

'So what do you suggest?' said Count Adolf, casually picking at his nails as the two men sat in his tent.

'They have an army nearly as large as ours up there – attacking them while maintaining our siege of the ring fort would be difficult.'

'But they cannot hope to attack us down here either, not in the open ground.'

'No.'

'So, we continue the siege until it is successful, and then drive them back?'

'And risk more of their forces arriving? Who knows how many more are coming, and we have only half the army. No, I think we must try and take the fort quickly, and move against their army with our full strength,' Sir Hans said, clenching and unclenching his hand, stiff and sore from a day holding a shield.

'Good,' said Adolf sharply and sat up. 'I agree, but I wanted to hear your thoughts. I want you to lead an escalade in the morning, attack while it is still dark, and keep the preparations hidden. Let us try surprise instead of brute force. Most of the army will remain in camp. Perhaps, if we are lucky, we can carry the attack successfully before the enemy can react and counter us. We have built dozens of ladders, I will give you a thousand men, ours and some of the Bavarians, for the assault.'

He looked at Sir Hans. 'Any problems?'

Sir Hans shook his head. 'No, that might work, I will make the arrangements.'

'Good man.' Count Adolf went back to cleaning his nails.

The next morning, while it was still deep in darkness, as the Crusaders quietly moved their ladders into position, the Norse army split into two. The majority, around six thousand men, moved north through the woods. Aggressive patrols of skirmishers had driven the Christian scouts back from the edge of the woods all through the evening and thus cleared the path north. The remaining force of around eight hundred men were lightly armed. Skirmishers, spearman and bowmen, mostly local men of Sjælland.

While the main army moved quietly north in the night, the skirmishers moved south and hooked around through the scrub and woods along the flank of the Crusader encampment into bow-shot range. With the first hints of dawn still not visible on the horizon, they struck. A dozen carefully hidden fires were lit and bowmen with arrows wrapped in oil-soaked cloth stood by them. A line of skirmishers ran forward and swarmed the Christian picket line, rushing and cutting down startled sentries. The alarm was sounded in the camp, but the Norse didn't attack in force; most of them melted back into the woods as the first wave of fire arrows soared over their heads from the woods, and down into the horse lines.

A few brave volunteers from the men who had overrun the picket line ran for the fence and guard posts surrounding the horse lines, darkness and confusion hiding their approach as most of the sentries focused on the chaos just behind them. Inside, hundreds of panicked horses were jostling and whinnying as the fire arrows rained down. Some horses were hit and screamed as burning oil ran down their flanks, cauterising their wounds and driving them mad with pain.

Seeing no attack and focusing on the panicking horses, most of the guards didn't notice the few men sprinting towards them, low to the ground and wearing dark clothes with mud-darkened faces. The fence around the horse lines was intended to spoil an attack by a battle line, not stop a few unarmoured men climbing it. Some attackers were cut down by alerted sentries but a dozen or so broke through in the chaos, by climbing the fence and bypassing or killing the confused guards.

Those dozen started cutting ropes and stabbing horses.

It was utter chaos inside the horse lines. Ropes snapped, stakes holding the lines were pulled from the ground, and wounded, thrashing and panicked horses broke free, charging around and knocking into each other and any men foolish enough to get in their way. In the tumult, no one noticed until it was too late the two men who went to unbar the rough gate in the fence leading out of the wall and swung it open. The men died with arrows in their backs, but some horses had spotted the opening that they could use to escape the terror, and they fled. Others saw it, and dozens and then hundreds of panicked animals were funnelling through the gap in the fence in an unstoppable torrent of terrified horseflesh.

On the other side of the horse lines, a wounded horse had fallen and tangled with the fence that separated the horse lines from the main camp. A section of fence fell and dozens of horses poured through it into the main camp, spreading out and running through groups of horrified men who had been wrenched from their preparations to respond to an attack. Instead, galloping horses, some with flaming arrows still stuck in them, were rampaging through the camp. Tents were torn down, men bowled over, and the chaos spread. By the time the horse lines were empty of everything except the dead, the wounded, and those horses that had been too well tied down to escape, the Norse archers and skirmishers had fled, cutting inland at a jog to avoid a pursuit that now couldn't happen.

To the north of the camp, Ragnvald stood in his full battle regalia, dragon-crested helm on his head with its maille coif, Drekitunga sheathed at his waist. He was watching the skyline intently. He looked up as saw the fire arrows rise into the sky, and the sounds of alarm drifting over, and smiled. In front of him, crouched in the low ground, several thousand Norse warriors stood up and started running across the open field towards the Christian blocking positions by the river. The sentries there had turned to look at the chaos behind them, as men will tend to do, and the attackers were halfway across the field before one of the Christians, more diligent than the others, turned back and saw the onrushing Norse and shouted in warning. The line of silent running Norsemen burst into war cries as they reached the low earthwork defending the small Crusader camp. Christian soldiers poured out of tents at the sound; most had slept in their armour or had not been sleeping at all. The commander of this camp was no fool and had been prepared for such an attack.

Jarl Kjartan was with his men in the front wave. He took two running steps up the rough earth band and sank his spear into a terrified sentry, who was watching wide-eyed as the wave of steel-tipped death swept towards him out of the darkness. The Norse went through the sentries like a spear through cloth, and Kjartan was down in the camp, running into the tent lines with dozens of his men. A Crusader came around a tent in front of him and turned to swing at the jarl, but a long axe crunched into the back of his head and he went down.

Kjartan saw more and more armed Christians pouring from their tents as they were overrun, retreating, gathering into larger and larger groups and starting to resist the Norse attack. He growled and looked around him, seeing the fierce fighting erupt-ing as his disorganised men stalled in their attempts to push deeper into the camp. 'SKJALDBORG!' he shouted, pointing with his spear to show men where to form it. His men shook out into a rough line, and began their attack deeper into the camp in earnest.

However, that assault was only a diversion. One of the fords was on the extreme left of the camp, near the outer wall. A group of Ragnvald's warriors, about fifty strong with Leif at their lead, ignored the main battleline which had pushed to the right with Jarl Kjartan, and ran straight for the barricades the Christians had erected across the head of the ford, killing the small group of sol-diers there and starting to tear down the barricade. Leif shouted across the narrow river to their Danish comrades manning the fortress wall on the other side.

'EVACUATE, EVACUATE THE FORTRESS! BRING NOTHING BUT YOUR WEAPONS!' One man ran through the shallow water to the far side to take the message directly. As he climbed the bank, the rough gate was hauled aside for him and he went through.

For perhaps as long as it takes a man to wash, nothing happened at the gate to the fortress. On the near side, the surviving Christians had formed a solid line about halfway across the camp and were defending themselves effectively, even as some of their comrades were still hunted through the overrun tents where they fought or tried to hide. From his perch on the captured wall, Ragnvald could see Norse warriors dead on the ground amongst the Crusaders. Some of the Norse were trying to work their way around the flank of the outnumbered Christians but the Crusaders were using the camp wall on that side to safeguard their left flank and the river to safeguard the right and rear. Their position was now a strong one.

Then, just as Ragnvald was starting to get impatient, a double line of men started pouring through the gate of the fortress and splashing into the ford. Ragnvald knew they had to evacuate the fortress before the main Crusader camp understood what was happening and responded. Ragnvald's fear was realised when a man shouted from the wall of the fortress. 'THEY ARE ATTACKING THE FORTRESS, LADDERS AT THE WALL!' Ragnvald cursed, it seemed impossible how quickly the Christians had attacked. Without men left to defend its walls, the Christians would be over the main fortress wall and opening the gate in moments; they could pursue the fleeing garrison across the ford and harry his army as it retreated. He couldn't break away easily as the men in the camp this side were still not defeated. His men were gaining ground and pushing around their flanks, but at significant cost. The plan could still unravel.

He grabbed the man next to him, Bjorn, and pointed at the ford. 'Find the fortress commander and tell him to hold that ford after his men are safely across it. He is to retreat when the main force attacking the camp does.' Bjorn nodded and ran down the edge of the field towards the huddled groups of erstwhile defenders, who were gathering behind the fighting, shivering in their wet clothes as more of their fellows splashed across the ford.

Suddenly the sound of combat could be heard across the ford; men screaming and metal clashing. Ragnvald looked at the camp and saw that the Christian shieldwall was still holding firm. It would not break in time, not without great cost. He pointed at another man. 'Go to Jarl Kjartan, tell him to stop attacking the Christians in the camp and instead to hold them there until we need to withdraw.' The man nodded and hared off across the field towards the fighting.

As Ragnvald looked back towards the ford, he could see men from the garrison forming up this side of the barricade. Then there was a commotion at the gate on the far side. Men of the garrison were jumping down off the wall to escape as others rushed through the gate. They were running down the bank and splashing across the ford as the last of them desperately fought in the gateway against unseen foes. A few arrows started zipping down from the fortress wall and men started to fall in the waist-deep water. Ragnvald watched, helpless, as the stragglers from the garrison were dying on the far side of the ford.

The last of the defenders in the far gateway were cut down and suddenly the ford was clear. The Christians did not immediately try to cross; a few Norse bowmen from the evicted garrison began trading shots with the Christian archers and the two sides hunkered down behind their barriers on each side of the river. The fortress was lost, and much faster than he had hoped.

The fighting in the camp had died down. The two tired and

battered lines disengaged by the length of about two spears and watched each other over raised shields. For a moment, Ragnvald was unsure of what to do. If he retreated now, the Christians could start to pour across the ford and the survivors from the camp might attack, forcing him to defend until he was overrun. He could wait until the battle in the camp was won, but the casualties would be horrendous.

He could not see a way to escape this situation unscathed, but every moment made it worse. He took a deep breath and gave his orders to rest of his men waiting below him.

'Tell Leif at the ford that the bowmen and a few others from the garrison are to hold the barricade at the ford to the last second – they must stop the Christians until the main force retreats.' He pointed at another man. 'Sebbi, tell Jarl Kjartan to withdraw slowly, facing the enemy, until he gets here. When we are all together, we will break formation and retreat back to the king as fast as possible. If the Christians press us during the retreat, we will give ground and retreat the shield wall steadily. Understood?' Men nodded in the dim light. 'Go!'

He watched for sixty heartbeats as his men spread out and passed the orders before finally the force in the camp started retreating, marching backwards in formation, maintaining their shieldwall as they moved. The Norse practised this manoeuvre often in smaller groups but it was working well even with over a thousand men in the line.

As his men retreated, a line of archers appeared on the Christian side of the ford and started pouring arrows towards the Norse side. The outnumbered Norse archers on the barricade were swept away or forced to hide. The gate at the far side disgorged a triple column of men into the ford, shields up, formation tight. They splashed into the river at a run, screaming their war cry. The garrison survivors had formed into a rough shield wall just behind the river barricade.

Ragvald cursed at them under his breath and willed them to run before they were cut off. Just as he was about to sprint down the field and shout at them to retreat, the main group turned and started running back down the field towards the retreating main body as the first Crusader soldiers reached the barricade and started climbing it, hacking at the few remaining defenders. The men there held them for a few moments until one of them also shouted to run.

It was too late. Christians from the camp cut them off and there was a brief and chaotic melee in the field as a dozen running survivors of the garrison tried to hack their way through double their number of Christians, with more bearing down on their backs. Only a handful made it through, outpacing the exhausted enemy.

With his surviving force now formed up, the wounded being helped along behind the main line, and the Christians not yet able to follow and force combat, Ragnvald signalled the retreat. The entire body of men turned and jogged down the field, melting from view of the assembling Crusader forces into the darkness beyond the reach of the sentry fires, even as the first light of dawn started appearing on the horizon.

King Sigurd and his men were waiting at the bend in the river that would take them inland. When the tired assault force filtered into their lines, carrying their injured comrades and heads hanging low due to the fight followed by a mile-long run in armour, they were greeted with glee as word of the success passed through the waiting men.

Sigurd himself came down to greet Ragnvald at the rear of his column with another almighty bearhug. 'By the gods, you did it.' He released the tired jarl and stood back, hands on Ragnvald's shoulders. 'I see how many injured we have; it was a hard fight?'

Ragnvald nodded. 'It was, we were unable to clear the near bank. The camp garrison were well prepared and organised, and larger than we expected.' He was breathing hard. 'But we managed to push them back far enough to clear one ford and the garrison got out. Well, most of them got out, anyway. The Crusaders saw what was happening and assaulted the empty fortress walls behind them, chased our garrison right out of the fortress and into the ford. Some of them were lost. I don't know how many.' Ragnvald shook his head. 'The Crusaders are better than I expected, and I knew they were good.'

Sigurd nodded sagely. 'We will discuss it fully later; for now we have three miles to go before we can make camp in relative safety. Can your men march three miles at speed?'

Ragnvald shrugged. 'We have injured men, it will be hard and the men are exhausted, but we have little choice.'

Sigurd nodded. 'Take your men and be the lead, set a pace you can keep up. The rest will follow and fight off whatever force follows us.'

Count Adolf stood staring at the dead horse in the dawn light. He was inside the charnel house that had been the horse lines. It was his personal warhorse whose body he stood over. The magnificent mare had been hit with a fire arrow in her chest. The arrow, at the end of its maximum range, had not pierced her deeply, but the oily rag had burned on her, flames licking up her chest and burning her neck and half of her face and setting her mane alight. The terrified horse, running around in agony, had broken a leg trying to escape the enclosure and thrashed around on the ground until someone had cut her throat to end her misery. A small mercy in a horribly cruel death. Adolf in many ways felt worse for the innocent creature than the dead men that were piled over beside the wall.

'My lord?'

Adolf realised that someone had been talking to him. 'What, what is it?' He didn't look up. It was one of his runners, a dour Bavarian squire.

'My lord, I have the reports from all the contingents for you.'

Adolf tore his eyes away from his poor horse and looked at the man. 'Hmmm, right. Give me the summary.'

'Yes. There are around eighty horses either dead or so injured that they will have to be killed. A mixture of heavy chargers and riding horses and such. Another two hundred have injuries of some kind but will recover if we treat them and leave them here under care. We have rounded up around four hundred otherwise healthy horses and more are coming in all the time. Some three hundred are yet to be found.'

Adolf closed his eyes in anger. At least three hundred horses he couldn't use, either soon or ever, including many of the priceless heavy warhorses of the knights. On its own it was not a disaster, but it was certainly a setback. Not being able to ride after and trap the Norse army immediately was the disaster. He had lost the men of the camp over the river for nothing. The Norse had outmanoeuvred him, forced him into inaction and helplessness, and he felt sick to his stomach.

'And of the men?' he asked, dreading the answer.

'The detachments of the Austrian and Lombard contingents on the far side of the river numbered sixteen hundred before the battle. They mustered a little under eight hundred fit to fight this morning, although their captain points out that they could use a rest before they do so, and many of them have minor injuries. Of another three hundred with various more serious injuries, perhaps half will recover to fight again, although not many in this campaign.'

Adolf nodded bitterly. Five hundred men dead, many of them Austrians. The Austrian contingent was small, just over a thousand men. They would have lost nearly half their number in the first battle. He hoped the remainder did not go home.

'In the main camp: of sentries, men killed by horses, arrows and by infiltrators, we lost fifty-four dead and one hundred and thirteen injured, from various contingents. In the capture of the fortress and ford we lost twelve men of the Lower Saxon contingent.'

'And of the enemy?'

'We recovered the bodies of several dozen enemy from the attack on the main camp horse lines, no prisoners.'

Adolf sighed; the men were appalled by the attack on the horses. He had personally seen one wounded enemy being brutally dispatched by three furious squires. It was a shame; he would have liked to question the man.

'In the fortress we found over one hundred enemy dead, some laid out neatly in the yard who must have died in yesterday's attack. The rest were either stragglers killed in the storm of the fortress or those who died trying to cross the ford. In the camp on the far side, there were over two hundred dead enemy from the attack there, and a few very badly injured, none of whom survived the morning,' the squire continued.

Adolf cursed. 'Not a single prisoner?'

'I'm afraid not, my lord, the enemy took most of their wounded with them as they retreated.'

Adolf thanked the man and dismissed him. He stared down at his horse again. Nearly nine hundred dead or badly wounded and hundreds of precious horses lost and the enemy escaped. It was a bitter failure. The morale in the camp was low that morning. The army had been bloodied and, despite the capture of the fortress, they all felt the pangs of defeat.

He turned from his blackened horse to go and find Sir Hans. He wanted every recovered horse mounted and a force sent to hunt the raiders and to shadow their main army to make sure it could not escape. He had underestimated the opposition and would not do so again. This was a much more organised force than the army they had faced at Aarhus and they had made a fool of him.

Ragnvald was relieved that there was no follow-on force from the ford. Nor did a mounted force come from the main camp; the raid there must have been successful. Dawn came and went and the sun was well up before the tired Norse army made it to their pre-pared camp without any resistance or sightings of the enemy. Men dropped down and slept wherever they could find space. Water was passed around, cold food eaten and the injured seen to by the healers. A dozen or more had died on the short march and their bodies had been left by the wayside where they fell by comrades too tired to carry them and without enough time to bury them.

Sigurd told his commanders to allow less than half a morning's sleep and then they would march further inland to a better camp-site. The army had barely slept for two days, had marched through the night and half of them had fought a battle. The men would not put up much of a fight if they were caught by the Crusaders.

That short rest passed in what seemed like moments and the men were roused again and set to marching. Men who had not been involved in the battle had gone ahead to make camp and cook, something that helped raise spirits in the still-weary war-riors. Jarl Kjartan came back down the line to find Ragnvald and fell into step beside him.

'Reports came in from our scouts while you slept,' the jarl said. 'The enemy are not pursuing us from the ford. They broke their camp, cleared their dead and crossed back to join the main army.' Ragnvald nodded; this was good news. They would have almost a day's march on the Crusaders now.

'Our light forces aren't back yet. They had much further to march so they should be joining us today. Our scouts watching the raid from the ridge this side say that the raid was a total success. The Christians were still rounding up horses when they left to report this morning and dozens of dead horses could be seen in the lines. No large contingent had left the camp to pursue us, only large scouting forces on recovered horses.'

He smiled warmly at Ragnvald. 'It was a superb raid and a great victory. You have earned quite a reputation as a trickster. Men are whispering that you are guided by Loki himself.'

Ragnvald shrugged. 'It does not feel like a great victory, it feels merely like an escape. We lost what, four hundred men? Five hundred?'

'Around that, yes. But I think we surely slew over a thousand enemy, so it is a great victory in any case.'

Ragnvald nodded. 'I fear it is only a portent of things to come. I expected the river camp to fall entirely to such a surprise attack and I never expected them to storm the fortress so quickly. Their army is superbly trained and well organised. They will not fall for that kind of trick again; they must have some very capable commanders over there.' His voice was tired and low. 'We must not get overconfident.'

Kjartan nodded. 'I admit, they reacted surprisingly well, but still, they have not pursued and they are too cautious, we will use this to our advantage again. Keep your head up, Jarl Ragnvald, the men think you are a hero, it is important not to let them think they are wrong.' The younger jarl slapped him hard on the shoulder, causing Ragnvald to almost stumble, and then he was gone down the line, calling out encouragement and cracking jokes with his men, who laughed with him as he passed them. The men were indeed in high spirits and their self-confidence after the victory was absolute; Ragnvald could see that and hoped it would carry them through the tough days ahead.

He admitted to himself that the battle had gone well, despite the fierce resistance, but deep in his heart he started to doubt that such men as these Crusaders could be defeated entirely. They were too many and too good. He quashed that thought and smiled at the men as he walked, trying to retain his image of the great warlord as his insides churned.

CHAPTER 11

THE ROAD TO SALVATION

Southern Sjælland: A week after the fall of the Trelleborg

S IR HANS DROPPED wearily off his horse, handing the reins to a waiting page. He beckoned to Hartung to follow him and headed off through the evening gloom to find Count Adolf.

'How did it go today, Hans?' asked the equally weary count.

'Same situation as yesterday. We poked at their rearguard ineffectively all day, we couldn't get around them to slow them down, we couldn't get enough force close to them to make them stand and fight.' Sir Hans dropped onto a stool, exhausted and mud-spattered. Layers of new filth ground into layers of old filth in his once green surcoat.

'I don't know how much longer we can do this. The men are exhausted, fighting poorly, demoralised, making mistakes. I am losing men every day to stupid little errors, theirs and mine.' Sir Hans looked utterly dejected. 'Perhaps it is time you tried a different captain,' he added.

'Nonsense, you are doing well under the circumstances. Stop

bleating and get on with it, war isn't supposed to be easy. But yes, we need to change our strategy. I had hoped to force them into battle. It is clear they intend to merely waste our time and wear us down. So, I have a new plan, one that will require you to be awake and functioning. So go and get a good night's sleep, tomorrow night it will be our turn to deceive them in the darkness.'

Ragnvald leaned back, resting his head on the flat stones at the back of the spring. The cool water soothed his sore muscles and stung in the cuts and scrapes on his body. He rubbed a week's worth of grime from himself and sighed in pure relief. He was enjoying himself too much to even feel guilty that most of the men of the army would be bathing in the nearby lake rather than this beautiful and crystal-clear spring.

A few other lords were in the pool with him. Soon he would get cold and have to get out. He would go and see the king and others would take his place. But not yet. Now he closed his eyes and let his body soak in the soothing water, let the feel of it be drawn down into his very bones.

The spring at Køge was famous in the area. The now deserted town was full of the tired and ragged army, as were the fields around it. For nearly two weeks they had toyed with the Crusader army, skirmishing with its scouts, using woods and valleys and local guides to avoid encirclement by its cavalry. The rearguard had clashed with the Christian forces half a dozen times but always the smaller and faster Norse army had been able to escape, often using its priceless local knowledge to guide them down the fastest routes and hidden paths on this rugged land. A raid on their camp during the last night of the chase had caught them off guard. Fifty warriors were lost and the raid had nearly led to disaster, but had been repelled in the end.

But now that game was over. The Norse army had risen the

morning after the chaos of the raid, tired, wet and ready to march again despite the lost night's sleep. But they found the Crusader army had abandoned its pursuit. The raid had been a diversion to cover their night march in the opposite direction. In the woods east of Næstved, their army had turned suddenly towards Roskilde and København, gaining nearly a full day's lead before the Norse became aware of the deception.

It had been a well conducted ruse. The Norse army had been left in dire straits. If the Crusaders reached Roskilde and København first, the fleet there would be forced to leave or, worse, be captured, and the army would be severely hampered, or perhaps even be trapped on the island.

The exhausted Norse had marched for nearly a whole day and night through rough country without rest to reach the abandoned town of Køge. They were now resting for a few hours in the remains of the darkness before they would set out again at first light for København and the waiting fleet, in a desperate race to get there first.

A small number of longships were moored off the shore near their camp, having arrived in the evening to exchange messages and deliver supplies. They had brought good news: the fleet at Roskilde had left safely. The Christian fleet had been spotted working its way around the north of the island towards the mouth of the fjord leading to the city. Warned of this, the Norse ships had left the city, with all the men they could find to crew the ships, before they could be trapped. They had sailed for København and Sigurd had ordered that the army was to march with all speed to meet there and embark for return to the mainland. With no hope of defeating the much larger Crusader army in open battle, the king had decided to abandon the island before they were trapped there.

The primary concern was that there were no up-to-date reports on the Crusader army. There were ten miles between the two roads that the rival armies were using to march east – too far for dismounted scouts to report back with accurate news quickly, and the army had precious few horses, just those they had found abandoned or captured from the enemy.

To make matters worse, the Christians had thrown up a thick screen of cavalry patrols between the two armies; no scouts had yet penetrated it and returned with any useful news at all. So King Sigurd was blind; he estimated that the Crusaders would not yet be in Roskilde, but he could not be sure. The Norse had to reach København first; there was nowhere else to embark such a large army on this coast both safely and quickly. If they were trapped against the sea, much of the army would be destroyed.

Ragnvald shivered and levered himself out of the spring. He dried himself in front of the roaring fire next to it, naked but for a fur cloak on his back, steaming in the darkness. When he was dry and warm, he dressed and hobbled off on sore feet to see the king before snatching what little sleep he could for the remainder of the night. He would have a couple of precious hours and then he would have to put his ruined shoes on again to resume the march. He was glad the marching was nearly over; he was fairly sure that one more day would see him walking barefoot like some of his men already were. He was getting too old for all-day marches anyway.

The morning saw nearly six thousand tired men pack up what little gear they had left, drink and eat whatever food was available (which was thankfully enough, due to the ships still floating off-shore), and start the march. The most seriously sick and lame in the army were loaded into the waiting ships to sail to Lund, a welcome boon that would allow the army to march faster. The flush of the early victory over the Crusaders had worn off. The whole army wanted to get off this island and stop the ceaseless marching. Only the contingent of Danes was still willing to fight for it, and even they recognised that the cause was lost.

Sir Dietmar spurred his horse down the narrow path beside the trees. Somewhere ahead and to his left, other men were whooping and calling to each other. Enemy scouts had been spotted and he was racing to cut off their retreat from the woodblock on his left. They would have to cross this path to escape, and he would have to get in front of them.

His horse pounded down the muddy trail, hooves kicking up clods of wet earth, breath steaming like smoke. It was a fine horse, his second of the campaign; he had ridden the first one to lameness. It was surefooted and agile, threading the trees with ease under the directions he gave with his knees. Behind him, more horsemen followed; his squire, Hartung, was with them, following Sir Dietmar.

Suddenly, ahead and to his left, he saw flitting shapes in the trees. Men, running towards the path. Wearing the distinctive tunics and wool hats of the Norse.

Sir Dietmar called out his sighting and tucked his spear under his arm, aiming to ride down the leading man. The enemy scout saw him coming and panicked, turning to run away alongside the path, rather than attempting to get across it in time.

Dietmar nudged his horse a little to the left, almost brushing the trees on that side of the path and judged the movement of the horse with the running of the Viking. He put his spear across the neck of his horse and stood in his stirrups when the moment arrived. As the horse's head drew level with the running man he lunged with his spear, in a gap between two trees, feeling it thump home into the running man and hearing his squeal. He let go of the haft as the man went down and it struck a tree, avoiding being thrown from his horse. He sawed on the reins, turning and bringing it to a halt.

He jumped down from his horse, drawing his sword. His victim had only been stuck in the shoulder and was on his feet again, the nasty wound bleeding freely. The man rushed Dietmar with a long seax, unarmoured and unshielded, and Dietmar parried a determined slash at his face, then took another harmlessly on his maille hauberk. He thrust forwards, the scout barely twisting out of the way before attacking again. The scout was slashing wildly, cuts coming so fast Dietmar couldn't see or block them all. But that was what armour was for, the light blade too fast to track, but too light to damage him with a cut. He blocked a thrust with his left arm and punched forwards with the sword, the blade hitting the scout horizontally across the face, scoring deeply across his cheek and the ridge of his nose.

The Norseman reeled back with a cry of pain and Dietmar stepped forward and slammed his blade into the man's chest and he went down.

Dietmar looked around; another enemy was down on the road, horsemen milling about. Hartung was trotting over to his knight, blade drawn and red.

'Hartung! You got one of them, eh? Good lad.' He reached up to pat the neck of his squire's nervous horse.

'I did, rode him down in the bushes, got him with an overhead cut to the neck. He won't get far,' the boy said, proudly.

Dietmar frowned. 'Won't get far? You mean he isn't dead? You didn't see him fall?'

Hartung recoiled. 'No, he was diving into a bush as I got him, but like I said, he won't get far, it was a murderous blow.' He was still prideful, but now there was a hint of uncertainty in his voice.

'We must chase him down and find the body. Come, on foot, you three, with us!'

The Norse army marched along the coast, the long golden beach of east Sjælland rolling along their right side. It was a melancholy sight; that beautiful shore was likely feeling its last march of an army of Norsemen for a generation, if not eternity. No one talked, no one sang or joked. Each man stared at the back of the man in front, ignored his tiredness and battered feet, and marched. The army laboured on to the sorrowful sound of the wheeling gulls and the gentle roar of the breaking waves.

At midday, a muddy, bleeding and exhausted scout reached the front of the column and Jarl Erling, leading the vanguard, called a halt. The man had a nasty wound to the top of his left shoulder, down to the bone. His arm was hanging uselessly, as he gulped down water and spilled his story. He and two fellows had gone the previous night to the hill overlooking Roskilde, which was only seven miles inland from where the Norse army stood, to watch over it. In the morning the scouts had seen the Christian vanguard approaching the town, no more than two miles to its south-west. The scouts had run from that hill to get back and report, but in their haste had run into a patrol in the woods. The other two men were cut down and the surviving man took a sword slash to the shoulder from a horseman, before he escaped by jumping a small stream and disappearing into thick underbrush on the far side. He had run most of the way back, but it had taken him a significant amount of time. The Christians would be past Roskilde by now and only half a day's march from København.

King Sigurd was troubled by the news. He called a hasty meeting of his commanders.

'The Christians are about as far from København as we are; they must have left their supplies and support behind and pushed on with the fastest men, travelling light.' He looked around at the men. 'We have no choice but to race them there or call the fleet to us and hope they can evacuate us before we are found. Agreed?'

The faces around him, haggard and tired, all nodded.

'So, do we race them to the docks in the town when, if we lose the race, we will be destroyed? Or do we send a ship to call the fleet and try to evacuate from this beach?' He looked around at the group. 'We must decide within moments.'

One of the Danish jarls spoke up. 'This beach is only four miles from the road they will take. Their cavalry will surely see us waiting here and report. Even if we are already being evacuated, it is likely their army will arrive before it is complete. There is nowhere around here to defend where they cannot outflank us. It will be a nasty fight on the beach and we will probably lose half our army, maybe more.' The man shook his head in rejection of the thought.

Another jarl spoke up. 'Is it better to save half than risk losing all?' There was a murmur of disagreement. Another commander spoke up. 'I will not watch from the safety of my ship as my comrades are killed. We should all fight together and win our way out, or die in the shieldwall together. I would not see us repeat the shame of the fall of Aarhus.'

The king nodded. 'I understand. My father must have felt the same when he decided to stay and fight there.'

The men fell silent and nodded. Some touched their hammers and offered blessings to the dead king and his noble sacrifice.

The king looked around the group a final time. Fresh fire and determination were on their faces. He made his decision. 'We march to København. Be ready to stand and fight if we have to.'

Sir Hans listened to the report from one of his cavalry scouts and nodded, dismissing the man and trotting up to where Count Adolf was in the column. The main body of the army was just passing Roskilde, which the vanguard had found abandoned and desolate.

'Update me, Sir Hans, what is happening?' Adolf asked when he saw the man approaching.

'My lord, we have spotted the enemy army on the coast, seven miles south of where we are. They are marching for København, and they are closer to it than us.'

'Closer! How in hell did they get so close so quickly? Damn them! I thought we had them.' Adolf slapped his saddle in frustration, startling his horse.

'They must have marched all night, my lord, and their road is shorter. We have been screening their scouts from seeing our position, ours are mounted and theirs mostly aren't, so we have a huge advantage, but it is only a matter of time before one manages to report our movements, if they have not already.'

Adolf nodded. 'Then we must assume the game is up and they know where we are. It's a straight race now. Sir Hans, call in the scouting screen and gather all available mounted men, we must move to block them or slow them down. What can you currently muster?'

'Around six hundred mounted men, my lord. That is all the horses we have left fit for battle. Around half of those are just riding horses and light men, scouts and lightly armoured riders. Not enough to stop their army alone.'

'And are our foot soldiers too far away to cut them off in time? Damn. Gather what you can and go to the enemy, slow them down by whatever means necessary but do not lose your force. I will take whatever men are still able to march hard and go for the town. The army is near exhaustion, but I should be able to get there with enough men, if you win me the time.'

Sir Hans nodded and spurred his horse away from the column, shouting orders to his companions, who peeled off in all directions to recall the widely dispersed cavalry.

'Win me that time!' shouted Adolf after the retreating figure. *Do that, Hans, and we shall have them.*

After a mile of marching along the beach, the Norse army started to see cavalry scouts on the horizon inland of them. As the miles passed at exhausting pace, those patrols grew in size to a column of horsemen perhaps several hundred strong. Ragnvald jogged up to the king and gestured to the enemy horsemen.

'They will try to slow us down, force us into a solid formation that cannot move fast, and then hold us like that.'

Sigurd nodded. 'It is too late to send for the ships. What do you suggest?'

'We keep the pace up, as close together as possible. We only react to fend them off if they commit to a charge. We might lose men if they do charge, but they cannot defeat us with so few. It is more important that we keep moving.' The king sucked in a breath and nodded. He passed his orders to his jarls.

The game of cat and mouse began. The enemy cavalry force grew in size and started to include more heavy horsemen, mounted knights in their head-to-toe maille, helmets shining and long spears lancing the sky. Soon, just after the army had crossed a narrow stream into an area of flat ground half a mile long, the horsemen broke up into two groups and quickly moved towards the front and rear of the marching Norse army.

'Bows, make ready!' called Ragnvald to the men on his flank. The army slowed its pace to a slow walk and tightened up the ranks, but did not stop. Tense spearmen on the flank watched the cavalry over the rim of their shields. Bowmen checked that their strings were taut and that arrows were ready to hand.

There was the sound of a horn from the leading group of horsemen and one hundred or so peeled off and broke into a trot, angling towards the front of the column, forming a shallow and broad wedge as they moved. As they were about to enter good bowshot range, the Norse jarls called a halt all up and down the line and the army crashed to a stop and raised their shields and weapons, forming a solid shieldwall in moments.

Bowmen nocked and raised their bows to loose their arrows. Another horn blew and the cavalry sawed on their reins, turning and scattering. The bowmen loosed a volley but no more than a couple of horsemen were hit due to their sudden change in direction and the long range.

The leaders along the ranks called to move again and the second line of horsemen broke into a trot aiming at the army. Ragnvald looked nervously at Sigurd.

'It is as you said,' the king nodded. 'We will not stop again until they commit to a charge. It will lessen the effect of our bowmen but we cannot be stopped by these feints.'

Ragnvald nodded and orders were again shouted up and down the moving column. As the next wave of cavalry swept in, the Norse did not slow much. Men naturally raised their shields and shuffled a bit into closer formation with their fellows. This did cause a drop in the pace and a slight bowing and disorganisation of the line but, true to expectation, the cavalry pulled their charge before striking home.

There was a pause and a different horn signal sounded from the Crusader cavalry. A second group of horsemen from each contingent trotted forward into a line. The Norse were nearly halfway across the open area now. The gathering horsemen were fully armoured – big men on big horses, long spears in hand and big kite shields covering their sides. They spread into a deep V and angled towards the Norse vanguard.

Ragnvald watched them for a few moments. The spacings of the horsemen were wrong, they were too far apart for a charge: this was a feint. 'KEEP MOVING!' he roared. Others repeated it up and down the line. The horsemen kept riding in, past the point where the light horse had turned. *Was he wrong? Would they charge?* The section of the column where the charge was aimed slowed and edged to the right, fouling the men behind.

Just as he prepared to call a halt, the heavy horsemen broke off, peeling from the wings, each horsemen turning left or right only fifty paces from the Norse line, and then they trotted back out of range. Ragnvald saw a small party of horsemen up the field watching, keeping pace with the column. One of them waved a flag above his head.

'Damn!' said Sir Hans, watching the manoeuvres. 'I thought that would work. Not stopping the march in the face of a charge of knights? These are brave men indeed.'

'They will reach the broken ground soon, we must try them with a real charge, hope they don't stop to face it,' said one of his companions.

'Indeed, signal the attack, get our reserves ready to go in there and cover them when they need to retreat. Let's see what these Norsemen are made of.'

'Lord Sigurd!' Ragnvald called, pointing at the waving flag. 'This one will surely be real – we are almost off the best ground.'

Sigurd nodded and orders were again shouted up the column of nervous warriors. Many of these men had never faced a cavalry charge before. Now they had already stared down three, and nerves were wearing thin.

The two groups of horsemen moved again. The heavy knights formed their lines again and started down the slight slope. The lighter horses followed two hundred paces behind them and the whole mass increased their speed. The knights dropped their spears down in front of them again and moved into a gallop. This time they were closer together, the formation narrower.

'HALT! BOWMEN LOOSE!' he roared at the contingent near them. The second cavalry force was headed straight for them; the first was angling for the head of the army. The whole contingent slammed clumsily to a halt. Men bumped into each other and cursed, the shields went up but the line was ragged, the shieldwall not fully formed, indecision and confusion over the mock attacks crippling the response.

The enemy knights were *flowing* across the firm and open ground, moving shockingly fast to the men forming in the Norse lines. Ragnvald felt the rare grip of real, deep fear as the enemy swept down the gentle slope, spears held still and level, seemingly pointing straight at him, shields covering them from their chins to their left feet. Norse bowmen fired a ragged volley at the wave of horsemen. A handful of horses shied or pulled up as they were hit and a couple of men were thrown or fell from their saddles, but most of the well protected men were unharmed, arrows stuck in shields, stopped by armour, or deflected by helmets. The wave kept coming, Ragnvald saw that the bowmen would only get one more volley.

Ragnvald stood three paces behind the shieldwall, in the fourth rank, Drekitunga in hand. two axemen stood to his front with the big two-handed axes over their shoulders. They were braced against the men in front. The front of the wall consisted of two close-pressed ranks of men with shields, spears, swords and handaxes, still jostling into position in an uneven line. He couldn't see most of his huscarls, they were somewhere else in the line, there hadn't been time to organise into their normal formation, men simply got into the wall where they stood. He keenly missed the solid dependability of his best shield brothers at his side.

Ragnvald felt the sweaty grip of his palm on the hilt of his sword. His dragon-crested helmet was slightly crooked, obscuring part of his vision on the left, but it was too late to adjust it. He braced his shield on his shoulder and watched the leading rank of cavalry arrive in the last moments of their charge, so close he could see the flared nostrils of the horses, the narrowed eyes of their riders under their steel helms as they swept in for the kill, and he felt a shiver of fear. He fought down the instinct to turn and run. Everything was wrong, unfamiliar, unnerving. He struggled to maintain his composure.

The ground thundered beneath the thousands of hooves that pounded down the slight slope. The drumbeat of death and destruction thundering down onto the fragile Norse line. Christian knights stood in their saddles and leaned forward into their spears as the wave rose to break over the defenders.

Some of the bowmen let off another ragged volley only a heartbeat or two before the wave of horseflesh and steel-clad men hit the still-imperfect wall. At that range and with the horsemen standing in their stirrups, a few more were hit, but it made no difference, in fact it made the charge worse. Falling armoured men and uncontrolled horses smashed into the line, tearing gaps in it. Alongside those falling horses, men who were still in their saddles, leaning into their spears, hit the weak points in the wall.

The physical, chest-pounding impact of a large horse smashing in between two men to his front stunned Ragnvald for a moment. The knight on the horse put his spear through the chest of the axeman ahead of him, even as the great axe swung forward and sliced into the side of the horse's neck. The horse tangled its legs in the dying axeman and tried to pull itself away from the metal in its neck. It fell, hooves flailing, catching a Swedish warrior in the head and felling him like a tree. The rear hooves flashed past Ragnvald's face with a handspan to spare as he stood rooted to the spot in shock.

Five men were down, either dying or stunned, and a hole was open in the wall to his front. The second wave of horsemen were angling for it, horses were naturally tugging and moving towards gaps or weaker areas of the line like this. The unhorsed knight had rolled free of his dying mount, kicking his feet from his stirrups. He sprang to his feet and rammed his sword into the spine of the Norse warrior next to him, who was still in the wall facing outwards. It was a vicious blow and the warrior folded awkwardly over his hips and fell to the ground, screaming. A Norse sword scored across the knight's back but did nothing to his thick maille armour. The knight pulled his sword from his first victim and threw a lightning reverse cut back into the shoulder of the warrior behind him, who caught it on his padded arm and pulled back, shouting in pain from the blow.

Ragnvald snapped out of his shock. He stepped forward and thrust hard at the knight, who twisted and parried his blow to his outside then pushed down on Ragnvald's blade and used the leverage to clear space for a blistering return blow towards Ragnvald's body. Ragnvald dropped his shield down to cover the blow only just in time and the knight pulled his sword back and retreated two steps, shield and sword raised, four Norsemen following him. *By Odin, that man was good.*

The second line of horsemen, lightly armoured men on small, stout horses, arrived. Two of them pushed into the gap in front of Ragnvald and forced men back with flailing hooves and swinging swords.

The unhorsed knight turned and ran out through the gap in the wall, the first horseman following him. The second wheeled his horse, its rear hooves kicking as it turned and he dug his spurs into its side. The horse leapt forwards out of the Norse warriors, almost avoiding a spear thrust that scored a line in its haunches, and then the horsemen were gone.

Warriors moved around Ragnvald to fill the hole in the wall. It had happened so fast and with such astonishing violence that Ragnvald had barely had time to do more than exchange a single blow with the knight who had fallen, almost at his feet, before he was gone.

Ragnvald finally had time to look around from his tiny patch of awareness and saw that all along the line, the horsemen were retreating. Some unhorsed men were running back on foot, some were holding onto the saddles of mounted men and being half carried. A couple of horsemen who had penetrated too deeply into gaps to retreat were being pulled down and slaughtered.

Sir Hans watched grimly as the column repulsed the attack, saw the retreating force diminished, unhorsed men and riderless horses returning among the unharmed. He saw a man he knew pulled down off his horse and disappear into the Norse ranks. 'These bastards are tough. We will have one more go at them. Everyone. Form up everyone, no tricks, we go for the head of the column with everything.'

The last Christian alive in the column was dispatched and the contingent collectively shook itself back into order. Men were wild-eyed and breathing hard, standing around, looking at comrades on the ground, helping those merely knocked down back to their feet. Ragnvald didn't hear his name being called. A hand thumped onto his shoulder.

'We must continue the march. Now! Let's move.' It was the king, his helmet askew and blood on the side of his head. His eyes were tight, focused; his hand was steady on Ragnvald's shoulder.

The calm he exuded spread to Ragnvald, who nodded and then shouted out orders to the men around. Men who could be carried were carried. The badly injured and dead were moved to the side and left. Ragnvald saw one man put his seax into the heart of a friend who was whimpering on the side of the road, guts spilling from a belly ripped open by a spear, sparing him a slow agonising death by the roadside.

It took precious time to reform the march and continue. They had to go around dead horses and shake shocked men back into line. The Crusaders had also reformed and were once again threatening a charge. Ragnvald looked on in horror at the thought of facing down another wave of those hard men in their coats of steel rings, on their huge horses. The Norse vanguard was only two hundred paces from the broken and scrub-covered ground to their front where they would be relatively protected and free to run to the town of København.

The Crusader horsemen made one last attempt to stop the column. Their whole force attacked this time. To Ragnvald's great relief, the charge did not again fall on his contingent. To his horror, both enemy formations hit the already-mauled vanguard from the front and side simultaneously. Still reeling from the first strike and more of a gaggle than a formed unit, the front and side of the vanguard crumpled like a rotten tree stump to an axe blow. The cavalry, in two tight wedges, went deep into the wavering ranks and overwhelmed the Norse warriors with the sheer weight and fury of their charge. Within moments, Ragnvald could see that it had descended into a chaotic melee. The cavalry did not turn and run this time. The knights, both the mounted men and those who had been unhorsed, were trying to clear space and join together in groups, fighting the survivors of the vanguard who were desperately defending themselves in disorganised clumps. The second waves of lighter cavalry forced themselves into the fight as every Christian still mounted was committed to the attack. A mass of several hundred horsemen moved forward together, swords rising and falling, swarming and cutting down those Norse who were left behind or mixed in with the enemy.

Within a short time, a line of sorts had formed between the two sides. Half the Norse vanguard was gone; the rest were being joined by the contingent behind and were finally forming into some order again, giving ground slowly to the now-stalled horsemen. Ragnvald was too far back to do more than watch and worry. A jarl near the front was shouting orders and pointing his sword over the heads of his men, left and right. The next two contingents in the column set off at a run towards the flanks of the growing melee, aiming to get around the sides and close in on the Christians. Outnumbered and with the momentum of their attack gone, they would have to retreat or be surrounded.

Sir Hans hacked desperately at a warrior below him, his sword bouncing off the man's shield. Then another horseman speared the man in the back and he went down. There was a chaotic press in front of him. Riders and dismounted men hacking wildly at the rough shieldwall forming in front of them, trying to get the enemy to break, trying to get some openings to exploit. Losing on both counts.

He saw a knight pulled from his horse by a Norse warrior, the horse going down with its rider. An axe opened the horse's neck as the rider struggled to rise. As he got to his feet, the warrior hit him in the chest with a hand axe, a vicious blow even through the armour, and he staggered back against his dying horse. The knight desperately thrust his sword forwards as the axeman lunged in for the kill. Both men struck simultaneously, the axe smashing into the knight's face even as his sword punched into the warrior's guts, and both men went down.

Sir Hans looked around, he saw enemy shields appearing on the left and right of his men. They were being surrounded. He turned wildly, looking for his signaller – the man was dead or missing.

'RETREAT!' he shouted instead. Repeating it over and over as he rode behind the tangled lines, finally his signaller heard the message and blew his horn, relief surging through Sir Hans as, all along the line, his men responded.

Ragnvald punched his sword hilt into his shield in excitement – someone up there was thinking on their feet and making smart decisions. The two flanking contingents were rapidly getting around the sides of the melee.

However, the same could be said of the Crusaders. Before they could be flanked, a long double horn sounded and the dismounted men pulled back and broke into a jog. Those still mounted cleared a space and held back the Norse warriors until the men on foot were fifty paces clear and then the whole mass dissolved and ran, urging their horses on, a desultory shower of arrows chasing them and picking a few men from their saddles.

The short but vicious battle was over. As the front contingents reorganised, finished off stranded enemy and tended to the wounded, the units behind them in the column passed by the mess on both flanks, urged on by their jarls to move into the safer ground of the scrubland.

Ragnvald caught up to the scene of the fighting and found the king already there. He was talking to a bloodied man who Ragnvald did not recognise. The vanguard had been a Swedish contingent led by Jarl Erling. 'Where is Jarl Erling?' he called, looking around. The man talking to the king looked around.

'He is dead. I am his brother,' the man said flatly.

Ragnvald touched his chest over his hammer amulet and put his arm on the man's shoulder. 'I am sorry, he was a great man and a fine warrior.' Jarl Erling had been against the bringing of a Norwegian king to rule Sweden via treachery against Jarl Harnsted, and Ragnvald had thought he too might become an enemy to their cause. But the man had accepted the ruling of his peers and supported them in the fight, laying their differences aside in service of his people. And now he was gone. Ragnvald felt the loss bitterly.

'Do not be sorry,' the brother said with a strained smile. 'His death was glorious. He killed one of their knights – near cut him in half with his long axe before he was brought down by two others, and he stuck one of them in the groin with his seax before he died. I wager no other man here killed two knights in this battle.'

Ragnvald smiled a smile he did not feel and nodded. 'Glorious indeed. We will drink to him tonight.'

He surveyed the carnage on the ground. There was a scattering of dead horses, some dead Crusaders and an appalling number of Norse warriors on the ground. Many were clearly dead, others only stunned, the rest bearing a range of hideous injuries. He could see that many of the badly injured and dead had been trampled by the iron-shod hooves of the heavy horses as they churned in the melee.

Just past their group, a large horse was lying dead on the ground. Propped up against its belly was a knight in a sitting position, arms and legs splayed. His head was tilted back over his spine and a hand axe was buried in the front of his open-faced helmet. Over his legs was sprawled a warrior with the knight's sword deep in his belly, barely alive and clutching the hilt of his seax as he drew ragged breaths. In the scale of the carnage, he had been passed unnoticed.

Ragnvald looked around to find someone to tend to him, but when he looked back the man was stilled, hand still wrapped around the hilt of his knife. He said a short prayer for the brave man's soul and hoped he would be noticed by the Valkyries.

Erling's brother was still talking to the king and a couple of other jarls.

'If we move now to run to the town, we will have to leave almost all the wounded behind.' The brother was gesturing around him at the carnage.

The king looked sternly on and shook his head. 'If we don't run now, we will lose an army. Look, the cavalry is disengaging.' He gestured up the slope. 'They still have the force for another attack but aren't moving to do it. They think they have done enough. It must mean the Christian army is close to the town, perhaps even ahead of us by now. If we don't leave, everyone here will die, they have delayed us too long already.' He clasped the man's shoulder. 'I am sorry, but there is no choice. We must take those who can run and leave the rest behind. We will call in the two boats out there and see if we can load some of the wounded. Perhaps the Christians will interfere; perhaps they will be too busy. It is the best we can do for the badly injured.'

The brother nodded and lowered his head in acceptance. He looked downcast. 'I will stay with my men. I cannot leave this place with so many wounded and so many abandoned.' He clasped hands with the king.

The king pulled him into an embrace, forehead to forehead. 'Go well, brother. I will see you in Lund or Valhalla, and I hope for one before the other.'

The last of the army was passing the site of the short battle when the king called to those of his men around him and they set off after the rearguard of Danish warriors. A dozen or so men stayed with Jarl Earling's brother to help the wounded who were too badly hurt to leave with the army. Those from the battered former vanguard who were able to leave said goodbye to their fellows and followed the rest of the army.

As the battlefield receded behind them, Ragnvald saw the two ships arrive and crews run up the beach to help with the wounded. The move did not go unnoticed by the Christians; a detachment broke off and started trotting down the slope. Before more than a few dozen wounded had been helped into the longships, there were shouts of alarm and the crews ran back down the beach to the ships, which were being held in the shallows of the mercifully calm water. The brother of Jarl Erling and a few of his men picked up spears and axes and spread out to get in the way of the oncoming horsemen and buy the ships time to escape.

For a moment, the cavalry stopped their rush and spread out

into a proper formation. Then they swept down on the loose line of Norsemen. The brother and his men were overrun in a flurry of horses and sweeping swords. A few horses went down and Ragnvald lost sight of the warriors in the swirl of combat. After a short time, the commotion stopped and the cavalry carried on down to the beach, but they were too late – the ships were already pushing off from the shallows. Ragnvald saw nothing moving at the scene of the short fight, which was now six or seven hundred paces away, just a collection of misshapen dark lumps on the sandy ground. He shook his head and carried on with the run, realising that he hadn't even learned the brave brother's name to offer a prayer to Odin for the man's soul.

'Could we have done more?' asked Hartung, sitting on his horse next to Sir Dietmar.

'No, lad, the horses are blown and we are too few. We did what we could. You fought well today, I will ensure your father hears of it.' The boy visibly swelled with pride under his steel helm.

'Thank you, sir, I was pleased to do my duty.'

Sir Hans trotted over and stood with them as they watched the Norse army disappear into the scrubland.

'It wasn't enough,' he said simply, his voice dejected.

'You are sure?' asked Sir Dietmar.

'Yes, they will reach the city first. But perhaps Count Adolf will catch them there and destroy them as they embark, we can only pray now.'

'God is with us,' said Hartung, nodding confidently. 'My father won't let them escape.'

'If only it were that simple, lad.'

Hartung snorted and flared his nostrils at the captain. 'Which do you doubt? God or my father?' and he walked his horse away in derision, leaving Sir Hans annoyed and perplexed.

'The arrogance of youth, eh?' said Sir Dietmar. 'He is a good lad, he will learn.' Sir Hans nodded reluctantly.

'I hope so. Anyway, we are done, the horses are blown. It's out of our hands now. Perhaps the boy is right.'

CHAPTER 12

THE FATE OF SJÆLLAND

RAGNVALD MANAGED TO get up about halfway along the column by the time the new vanguard reached the outskirts of København. He saw, with a huge sigh of relief, that the town was empty and the Norse fleet was packed onto the long dock front or waiting in the calm waters behind.

The leading elements of the army ran straight to the docks and started loading into boats. The jarls there didn't let men organise into their own boats or crews; instead, they filled each ship as quickly as possible and pushed off the docks to make space for another. The unfamiliar crews would work it out for themselves on the short journey to Lund.

Even with this method, loading the army was painfully slow. The ships had mostly been left with crews of six or eight men, barely enough to manage them and move them around.

Ragnvald gathered with some of the other jarls in the small central square in front of the docks. He was gasping and sucking in air. He felt that his strength was spent; he wasn't even sure he would be able to pull an oar. There was an atmosphere of relief in the group as the army was finally getting into the ships.

A sudden commotion from behind them drew their attention. A man was in the watchtower at the outskirts of town. There was no complete wall around this town, although one was in the later stages of being built. Some earthworks and palisades were in place, leaving only two or three large gaps. The man in the watchtower was shouting at someone on the ground, his words lost over the distance, but they all knew it could only mean one thing: the Crusaders were here.

A man sprinted down the street towards them, yelling at waiting warriors to get out of the way. He ran straight to the king's group and blurted out, 'Enemy spotted on the road out of town, about one mile away and marching hard.'

Sigurd nodded. 'How many?'

'The column is just coming over a rise in the road; it goes out of sight – impossible to say, but a lot.' The man shrugged helplessly.

'Thank you.' Sigurd looked at the gathered jarls. 'One mile? That is it, then. They will be here before the ships are all loaded and gone.' He sounded resigned. It was the first time Ragnvald had seen the irrepressible man sounding so disheartened and it hit him hard. The men around him were also quieted.

There was no talking or discussion in the group. Men stared down the street at the unseen road or just at the ground. One of the jarls stepped forward and broke the stony silence.

'Lord, this is my town. Over there,' he pointed at the big hall behind them, 'is my home. I was born there; my father died there. I am minded to defend it. I'm sure my men will agree.' He nodded his head down the street. 'We were building that wall all winter and I think we should put it to use. I think we can hold those gaps long enough for the army to embark. If we can't, we can hold the narrow streets and set the town aflame to slow them. No man can attack down a street between burning buildings.' He forced a strained smile onto his face. 'In any case, I like this town, I didn't want to leave it and now that we are back here, I want to stay.'

The king nodded at him, sadness in his every feature. 'You would have me do what I promised not to do; abandon part of my army and leave?'

'No, lord, you are not abandoning part of your army. We are men of Denmark; we never held an assembly to make you our king, so we are merely allies.' He put an arm on the king's shoulder. 'And friends – good friends, I think.'

The king nodded sharply and grunted his assent, unable to say more.

The Danish jarl removed his arm and flexed his shoulders. 'You came to help us defend our lands and now that you are leaving, we thank you for your help. In any case, we were in the rearguard and missed all the fighting on the road today, now we will have our share. I will not let you stay here and selfishly hog it all.'

The king forced a smile and clasped hands with the Danish lord. He would be the last jarl of the kingdom of Denmark still free and armed in their ancestral lands, a fate worthy of a great saga. The king promised himself he would ensure it was written. 'Then it is decided. Go well, brother, and if you change your mind and don't like your new guests, we will be waiting here with our ships to carry you away.' He managed to say this without his voice cracking.

The Danish jarl bowed his head to the king, a rare thing indeed for a Norseman to a foreign ruler, and the king bowed his head in return, a thing unheard of in any situation. The Danish jarl quickly clasped hands with the other jarls, wishing them well on their journey and sharing short jests, and then turned and strode over to the street where the men of København were assembled in defiant ranks. He gave a short speech and the men cheered him before turning and running back down the streets to the walls.

Ragnvald watched them go, shaking his head. Sigurd was next to him.

'How can we afford to lose men such as that?' he asked his king, a catch in his voice.

'We can't,' Sigurd replied solemnly. 'We could just fire the town now and block the Crusaders?' the king suggested, desperation in his voice.

'No. Not with this wind. The fire would be upon us before we had loaded into the ships and the army would be taken by the flames.' He pointed at the columns of men still winding through the buildings, waiting in patient lines. 'We need more time.'

The two men stood together in silence as all around them the dock still bustled with activity as more and more ships filled and departed.

'That fight at the beach, that troubled me deeply,' Ragnvald said after a while. 'I don't know how we can defeat such men in open battle,' he added. 'I have never fought any enemy like that before and fear we will not survive a full army with them in it.'

Sigurd shook his head in solemn agreement. 'They were like gods come to earth. We cannot fight them in the open. We must use the land to help us, we must stop their horses, or kill them, or starve them. But no, we can never face those horsemen over an open field with foot soldiers in support and hope for victory. We were fortunate that they did not have more men to attempt to block us. Can you imagine if they had had two hundred more heavy horsemen, with a thousand foot soldiers to follow them? They would have carved half our army up and stopped us dead.' Sigurd sounded awed. 'We can never let them charge us over open ground like that again. We lost ten for every one of theirs who fell.'

Ragnvald was about to reply when the first sounds of battle erupted from beyond the buildings ahead of them. Horns sounded and war cries filled the air over the clash of steel – the song of battle that would draw the attention of the gods and have the Valkyries stirring. He looked back and saw that more than half of the ships were loaded and away from the docks. *They might still be able to leave in time.*

Sigurd looked close to despair. 'We cannot do this again either – split our army and leave some to die. We must choose our battles more carefully. Perhaps we were wrong to come and fight them here.'

'No!' Ragnvald turned on his king, shocked by the king's black mood. 'We learned so much about them from this fighting. That was invaluable. We slowed them and we bloodied them and we made sure they know that it will not be easy. We have shown our people that we will fight and these men have not died in vain.' He jabbed the ruler of the North in his mailled chest as he growled out the words.

Sigurd stiffened his back and grunted. 'You are right, I am grieving for men who are not even dead yet.' He barked at himself and thumped his chest. 'I have shamed myself with my fear. I have broken my oath to never leave my men to die again. That brave jarl, that *drengskapr*, just offered me an excuse to avoid keeping my oath and I took it like a drowning man grasping for a rope.' He was red in the face now. Tears of shame forming in his eyes as he turned away from his men. 'I don't even remember the man's name and yet he went to die for me! The gods will never forgive me this.' He raked a hand through his thick, swept-back hair and raised his eyes to the sky.

'Lord, you only do what you must for your people. Jarl Halsted is making himself a fine end and giving this army the chance to fight again. We must not waste it,' Ragnvald urged him, keeping his voice low.

Sigurd nodded violently. 'Yes, Halsted, I remember now. No, we will not waste his death gift. When the Crusaders arrive on the mainland, we will raise the whole North against them. We will fight them on the shores and bury them in the forests. We will never again run out of land or be trapped by the sea. We will harry them like wolves harry a stag and we will bleed them!' He pounded his fist into his shield. 'We will avenge these brave men a hundred times.' He was raising his voice as he beat his shield, head up again and eyes blazing. Men around him, shuffling to the boats in lines, looked up, trying to catch the king's words as his voice carried, ever louder, across the open docks.

'We are not beaten; we have not even shown these bastards what a real fight is!' He drew his sword and started hammering it on his shield boss. 'If these flea-ridden sons of whores come to Odin's country, we will decorate our homes with their skulls!' Men began drawing their own swords and hammering their shields and shouting in reply. 'I *swear* to you that I will stand here again at the head of an army!' Men on the dock and the boats had stopped now, tired eyes on the king, tired hands on weapons, tired voices growling or shouting in agreement. 'Let's make those Christ-whores hear us and know fear, let our brothers fighting them know who they fight for and that we are not beaten. Let Thor be woken from his slumber by the sound of our defiance!' The men were roaring now, a sea of noise that crashed around the open square by the docks. 'Let their nailed god quiver on his cross at the sound of our anger!'

The men packed into that square burst into thunderous cheers and the crashing of weapons; Ragnvald's ears rang and his chest vibrated. He looked into the king's face and saw the fearless lord of war that he had known before returning. He saw the battle mad-ness etched into the king's face as he roared at his men. Then he saw the king's eye swivel to the direction of the wall and his mouth close into a snarl.

Oh, shit. He realised what was about to happen. He moved to stop Sigurd, but it was too late. He might as well have tried to stop the tide rushing in.

'I WILL NOT leave my brothers here to die,' the king snarled past Ragnvald. 'I will not stand here idle while good Norsemen fight and die for me. I made an oath to the gods and I will keep it. You men!' He turned and pointed at the men nearest the docks. 'Keep loading the boats. You!' He pointed at the rearmost group of several hundred men of Norway, including his own warband, his household warriors. 'Bring torches! Set fire to the buildings and let's go bring our brothers home.'

Men all around the square snapped out of their trance and sprang into action. The men on the docks got into boats and pushed off to make room for the last wave. Others ran into buildings, found torches and lit them, passing them around. A few hundred formed up in the streets leading to the walls and waited, looking at the king, whose famed blue cloaked huscarls were gathering around him, adjusting their equipment and readying weapons. Sigurd grabbed Ragnvald roughly by the arm. 'Stay here and keep loading boats until the docks are clear and then get the remaining boats alongside. We will be coming back in a hurry. Set the fires in these streets when you see us coming; we burn the rest of the town now.'

Sigurd released Ragnvald, protest at the risk the king was taking dying in the jarl's throat, and turned to the men of Norway assembled in the streets. He raised his sword into the air and roared at the crowd of warriors. 'This is OUR land. These are OUR people. We are NOT defeated AND WE NEVER WILL BE!' He pumped his sword at the sky and screamed at the assembled warriors, face red and spittle spraying down his wild beard. 'FUCK THE CHRISTIANS!'

'FUCK THE CHRISTIANS!' his men roared back at him, wildly pumping their weapons in the air or banging their shields. The two roaring columns set off at a run to the two gaps in the walls, the king and his cloaked huscarls leading them out. Other men ran off to set fires in the buildings to the left and right, leaving the main streets clear. The king and his men disappeared down the streets and the sounds of battle cries and combat at the wall soon intensified.

Ragnvald stood helplessly for as long as it takes a man to eat a good meal, listening, waiting to see who would come back. He turned to look behind him and saw that the last of the main body of the army was loading, ships pushing off from the dock.

The sounds of battle were growing nearer. Suddenly, men were running down the streets towards him, bloodied and injured. Norsemen. They streamed past him to the dock. One Danish warrior, with a half-severed forearm hanging uselessly by his side, ran up to Ragnvald. 'Fire the buildings, they are coming now!' he shouted, and then carried on past Ragnvald to the boats, trailing blood in his wake.

Ragnvald shouted at the men waiting with torches and they began running the torches along the line of the thatch on the buildings in those two main streets. Flames quickly rose into the air. Ragnvald could see the backs of the king's men now, who were still fighting as they retreated down the broad passages with the remainder of the Danes. Retreating in step, maintaining the wall, keeping their faces to the enemy. The disciplined shield wall along with their superb maille armour and swordcraft was keeping them and the retreating Danes alive as they gave ground. Dozens of warriors filed past him at a jog, then hundreds, running to the boats.

Ragnvald's chest felt like it would burst with pride for the king and his magnificent household warriors, even afraid as he was. Injured men in blue cloaks were pulling back from the line and running or stumbling down the street back to the ships.

Thirty paces now separated him and the backs of the last few dozen fighting men holding the narrow street. The fire was starting to rage, burning through the thatched and wooden buildings on both sides of the passage. The heat was starting to steam the sweat on his skin, his dragon-crested steel helmet starting to cook his head.

He raised a hand to shield his eyes and stared at the king's men. The heat was starting to become unbearable. Those men had to run now or they would be trapped. They wouldn't hear him shout over the sounds of battle. Just as he was about to go to them, he saw the rear ranks of the Norwegian and Danish warriors turn and run. They pounded down the street, herding into the centre to pass through the flames. More from the thinning line broke and ran, and then finally the last of them. Some were hauled back or cut down by the surging Crusaders, but most escaped. Ragnvald saw one burly axeman, wearing the blue cloak of the king's household warriors, swinging his long axe in a huge arc, driving the Crusaders back for a few moments to buy time for his fellows to escape, before a spear took him in the side and he went down.

The last of the men in the right-hand street burst through the gap between the flames and reformed to ward off any chase. None came. The Christians baulked at the wall of heat and burning buildings.

The last Norsemen in the left-hand street did not get so lucky. The flames were more fierce and the buildings closer together. The last groups had to actually run through flames to get back and some were trapped on the other side with the Christians, unwilling to run the hellish gauntlet to escape. Mercifully, Ragnvald did not have to see their end, shrouded as it was by the smoke and flames.

Seeing that the Crusaders were not immediately giving chase, and all the buildings surrounding the square were well aflame, the surviving men retreated to the dock, away from the heat, and wearily started loading. Men were slumping into the boats or dipping burned arms or faces into the water. More than a few had to be carried to the ships. Ragnvald scanned the crowd of warriors, desperately looking for the king. He couldn't see the big man any-where in the retreating groups. His heart sank and a cold grip took hold of his guts. Sigurd had a brother but no adult sons; losing him would be a desperate blow to the new Norse confederation, and to this army.

As he scanned the dwindling number of warriors moving past to get into the boats, a voice said in his ear, 'Who are you look-ing for?'

Ragnvald turned to find himself staring into the grinning face of his king. He shouted in relief and threw his arms around the slightly smoking ruler of the North. 'I didn't see you come back down the street!' he exclaimed as he released the big man, who was still grinning like a child. A huscarl was standing next to him, watching the walls of flames for signs of a chase, and others were piling into a boat behind.

'I got cut off by the fire; me and my lads had to come back through a burning building and hack through a wall while those bastards chased us,' replied the king, as if these were minor matters. His shield had battle marks and soot on it; his beard was heavily singed and his face was glowing red. But he was alive and unhurt.

'Bastard,' Ragnvald said. 'How long did you watch me looking for you?'

'Long enough to calm down and get my breath back,' he replied, grinning ear to ear, a surreal expression in the flame-driven winds and chaos around them.

'You took a foolish risk, Lord Sigurd,' Rangvald said with a wry smile on his face, arm still around the king's neck. 'But the gods must love you.'

'Bah! The gods love bravery and foolish men, do they not? But they like watching them die even more. No, it wasn't the gods that saved me, it was Gunnar here.' He indicated the huscarl beside him. 'The champion of my hall. Not the first time he has pulled my dumb arse out of the fire, and it won't be the last!' The king slapped his champion on the back and laughed heartily at his own play on words. Rangvald looked the king's champion up and down, surprised. Gunnar was an unremarkable-looking man, the first signs of grey in his twin-braided beard, of middling height, old scars on his arms and a jagged one on his cheek which gave him a grim expression. A dozen rings of various sizes on his arm were the only indication of the fearsome abilities that had brought him to be the champion of the Norwegian king's huscarls.

'Come now, the boats are almost done loading. Let us go, eh?' the king said, snapping Ragnvald out of his appraisal. 'We brought about half the Danes back, I think, although Jarl Halsted remains; he fell somewhere on the wall.' The king maintained his smile. 'I think he wanted it that way.'

Ragnvald and Gunnar turned and stepped into the last ship behind them, leaving the king alone. King Sigurd Magnusson, the first king of all the Norse, stared at the few Crusaders visible through the curtain of fire and smoke, eyeing them nonchalantly, alone on the dock, the last free Norseman in Sjælland. Then he turned to get into the ship. He followed his battered army out of the narrow passage, away from the burning town and towards home. Beard still smoking, hand on his sword hilt, gold arm rings glinting in the sun, he stood in the bow and turned his back on the burning town, an image of all the power and glory of the warlords of the North made flesh. His eyes, and his mind, were already focused on what lay ahead.

On the shore, standing in the watch tower as his men pulled back and the flames encroached, Adolf, Count of Schauenburg, Lord of Holstein and Stormarn, governor of Jutland and soldier of Christ, watched impassively and pondered on what could have been. He watched the last ship slipping out of the harbour until the view was obscured by swirling smoke, and then turned to climb down and leave the burning town.

Sjælland had fallen, but the war for the North had only just begun.

Sigurd Magnusson, Norðrikonungr, leaves burning København behind

PART 3

CHAPTER 13

SHAME AND SERVICE

Mid-summer 1117

ORDULF PASSED THE early summer of 1117 in dejected and reflective isolation. At first he had been angry, believing he did not deserve the treatment he had received. Then he had been ashamed, for he knew that he did. He had chafed against the instruction to hold his attempt at reconciliation with Brunhild, but as time passed, and he became more and more aware of how he had behaved, and of how much he needed the other slaves, of how wretchedly he had treated them, he was glad of the time. He stopped trying to feel sorry for himself and justifying it to himself in the quiet hours of sleepless nights. In the self-imposed isolation of the crowded house, he finally realised what he needed to say; simply the truth. He realised how he needed to say it; without seeking sympathy for himself, without expecting anything in return.

He approached Brunhild as she was cooking vegetables in the longhouse. Alda, the old slave who he had once made a fleeting kinship with over making stew, was there with her. She saw him coming and nudged Brunhild.

'What do you want, blockhead?' She didn't even look up to meet his gaze.

Ordulf smiled, the attempt to rile him breezing past. 'You were right.'

'I know I was right, but do you know I was right?' she said, finally turning to face him.

'I do,' he said as she waited expectantly. 'I did believe I was better, that I was above you, because I was not in my heart a slave. I longed to join the warriors, and have their approval, and be free. So I told myself anyone who didn't was less than me.' He smiled mirthlessly.

'So, you have truly dropped your belief that you are not one of us?' Brunhild asked. Ordulf hesitated. Alda sidled away with a wink, giving the two of them space. She and half a dozen others were still listening keenly, though, the house having come to a quiet halt.

'No, I have not. I am not one of you. I do not accept being a slave, I never will.'

Brunhild's brows furrowed. 'You still think you are better than us? You are truly shit at apologies.'

'Wait,' said Ordulf, putting a placating hand out. 'I thought that it made me better, refusing to accept my fate, stronger than those who do. And then you showed me that it was a weakness, not a strength. I'm sorry I didn't see that, I'm sorry I treated you as less than me. All of you. I don't reject slavery because I am better, I reject it because I am stubborn and proud. I will not be one of you because I am not strong enough to be one of you. Otto told me once I had to accept my fate or it would destroy me.'

Brunhild eyed him with genuine surprise on her face. 'Well, I believed you were a stupid angry child. Now I think you are just a scared, angry child.' She smirked. 'It's an improvement.' Someone behind him laughed, but he let it wash over him. Brunhild gave him the first hint of a smile, to take the barb out of her words.

'I accept your apology,' she said, with the smile twisting the corner of her mouth up and Ordulf beamed with uncontrolled glee which he quickly tried to stifle.

'Thanks,' was all he could manage in return.

'Well, do you need something from me? Or are you just going to stand there grinning like an idiot?'

'Yes, there is something I need from you,' he said.

'Oh, really? Be careful what you say, remember what I told you about coming to me with your needs.' She waved the knife at Ordulf's groin with a wicked smile.

'No, it's not that,' Ordulf said, backing up a step with his hands out.

'What, then?'

Ordulf cleared his throat, now feeling the dozen eyes on him acutely. 'I need your help,' he finally blurted out.

'Oh, really?' Brunhild said, with wide eyes. 'With what.?'

'With... everything,' Ordulf admitted sheepishly, unable to look Brunhild in the eye anymore.

Brunhild looked genuinely surprised and half-choked in shock, looking round the rest of the slaves in delight. 'The mighty Ordulf, the legendary smith, the slayer of wolves and warriors, needs our help!' The whole room laughed and Ordulf suddenly found himself bombarded with jests and jeering offers of assistance with wiping his arse and carrying his ego about. Brunhild dismissed him with a haughty and exaggerated wave and he meekly walked back to his bed area, enduring the good-natured taunts and back slaps.

It felt wonderful.

With the army away, there was not much work at the forge, and Dengir often had nothing to for him to do. Many of the other smiths were away helping with the spring sowing, or hunting or helping with livestock. Eventually, Dengir sent Ordulf away and told him not to return for a month. Halla had quickly noticed the big smith idling around the compound during the day.

'You. Ordulf, is it?' she had called to him as he sat watching some of the women in the courtyard making new clothes for the summer. He stood up and nodded. 'Yes, mistress.'

'Why aren't you working?' Halla asked, annoyed.

'Dengir sent me away, he has no work for me, not for a month.'

Halla stared at him for a moment incredulously. 'And you thought you would do nothing for that time? You big oaf.'

Ordulf tried to protest but she silenced him with a curt hand gesture. 'Not interested in your excuses. Help the girls until I find you something to do.' With that, Halla turned and walked back into the hall, pausing to give a curt instruction to one of the girls weaving. Ordulf kicked the ground in frustration. *How am I always getting into trouble?*

Ordulf reluctantly slouched over to the group of women spinning yarn and weaving it on looms in the spring sunlight and looked around awkwardly, waiting. Brunhild and Alda two other thralls were there, and two of the free women. Brunhild gave him a wink but carried on with her work.

He was unsure who to talk to, so he just stood there uncomfortably. Then one of the freewomen looked up. 'Stop standing there just blocking my light. Go and fetch more wool.' Ordulf stepped to the side and mumbled an apology but half turned to leave and stopped.

'From where?' he asked.

The woman looked up at him and frowned. 'From the barn stores. Where else?' Ordulf looked at her blankly. 'You don't know where that is?'

'No,' he replied.

She shook her head in exasperation and snapped her fingers at Brunhild. 'Go with him, show him where the stores are, bring back enough for the next few days. The sheep have just been shorn so there is plenty of it.'

Ordulf winced internally as Brunhild stood up and fixed him with a bemused look. 'Well, come on, blockhead.' She turned and walked out of the courtyard, and Ordulf followed along behind with a fresh spring in his step.

The barn was perhaps a mile outside the city, one of a series of low buildings forming one of the many outlying farms that surrounded Uppsala on the fertile farmland around it. The sheep were gone, off to their summer pastures, and Ordulf and Brunhild filled three woven baskets with clean wool and she shoved two in his direction wordlessly and left with the third.

Ordulf picked up his two baskets, which were awkward if not overly heavy, designed to be carried on the back one at a time. He suspected this was more than they needed, and that Brunhild was just playing with him, but he decided to accept it in silence. One basket slung uncomfortably over each shoulder, he trotted to catch up with her.

He drew level with her and slowed to a walk, smiling to himself. He saw her note his smile and give him a scornful look. 'I told you not to follow me around.'

Ordulf made an unseen shrug under the baskets. 'Can't help it, I was ordered to come here,' he said pleasantly.

'No one ordered you to walk with me, you know the way back now,' she said.

Ordulf refused to let this upset him and smiled even more broadly. 'True!' he replied, and upped the pace to a fast walk, saying over his shoulder, 'I'll go and drop these off, do you want me to come back and help you with yours?'

Brunhild swore at him, made some suggestions about what he should do to himself that he chose not to agree with, and he set off without looking back, a broad grin on his face.

By the time he arrived at the city, he was flushed with sweat and his arms ached from the awkward load. He slowed to a walk through the gate and looked around before setting off for the compound. He heard a panting noise behind him and someone shoved into one of his baskets, almost knocking it to the ground.

'You horse's arse. Now I'm sweating like a ploughman.' Brunhild's angry voice came from behind him as she staggered to a halt beside him.

'Sorry!' said Ordulf, as he tried not to show how out of breath he was. 'You didn't want me to walk with you,' he replied innocently.

'I expected you to follow me.'

'I thought that was what you wanted me to stop doing,' Ordulf said indignantly, but still wearing his foolish grin. Brunhild glared at him for a moment and then set off down the street. Ordulf stood there and watched her leave. After a few steps, she stopped and turned around with a scolding look.

'What? You told me not to follow you,' Ordulf said with a laugh. Brunhild did not look amused, tossing her head in the direction of the compound as she held her basket.

'Fine. But this is very confusing.' He walked over to catch up again.

He followed her to the courtyard, neither saying another word, and arrived to find a curious scene. A well-dressed woman was just arriving in the central courtyard. Trailing her were two warriors and three thralls, with a cart piled with belongings. She was standing there impatiently, looking at the house. Brunhild and Ordulf walked around the odd group and put their baskets down beside the other slave women weaving in the yard, who had stopped their work and were watching the new arrivals with confused looks, whispering to each other.

'What is it, who are they?' Brunhild asked one of the other thralls.

'She announced herself as Jarl Birkir's wife,' said the woman, with eyes wide.

Brunhild looked back again at the woman in shock. They all knew what had happened to Jarl Birkir.

'What is she doing here?' Brunhild asked in a low voice, nervous of the two strange warriors who were eyeing everything in distaste.

'I don't know, she just asked for our mistress and stood there waiting.'

At that moment, the door to the hall opened and Halla walked out, dressed in fine furs and with golden bracelets around her wrists, none of which she had not been wearing earlier as she had worked in a plain linen shift and woollen tunic.

'Tora Hansdottir?' she asked, looking around the woman and her group.

'Yes, and you are Halla, wife of Jarl Ragnvald?' the woman replied with quiet dignity.

'I am. What are you doing here?' Halla asked with uncertainty in her voice. Two armed men had followed her out of the hall and were eyeing the new arrivals with undisguised hostility.

'I have come to ask for shelter and protection.'

This took Halla completely by surprise. 'Why?' she asked, perplexed.

'I no longer have a husband to protect me.' Halla stiffened at the pointed barb, delivered so politely. 'The new jarl of my lands married another, and banished me with nothing but my family, a few possessions and a few loyal men,' she said, maintaining her dignity, but lip quivering and a tear in her eye.

Halla's hostility sagged slightly and she looked around the small group with renewed sympathy. 'Where are your children?' she asked.

Tora looked away with a pained face. 'I did not know if they would be safe here, so I had to leave them behind with some family.'

'They would be in no danger here,' said Halla sadly. 'You have no enemies here.'

Tora fixed her with a withering gaze. 'So my husband believed, before yours cut him down outside his own hall.'

Halla blanched at the retort and flicked nervously at her fur cloak. 'I am sorry, Tora, but I hold no grudge against you. If you hold none against me, you are welcome here. It is not our responsibility, what happens between our husbands.'

Tora nodded and cuffed away a tear. 'I know, thank you, but I still could not trust that before I came.'

'Then why are you here?'

'Because I had nowhere else to go and no one else who owed me a debt, except you,' Tora said quietly. 'Our husbands swore they would always be welcome in each other's halls, and I am here to see if you will honour that promise for me.'

Halla's composure broke and she walked forward to embrace the surprised woman. 'Come, come into our hall, we have plenty of space. You are welcome here.'

People watching in the courtyard looked at each other in consternation, but Halla was a whirlwind, setting everyone to the task of getting the new guests settled in. The weaving was abandoned as people were sent for sheets, straw mattresses, clean clothes, food and water. The cart was unloaded and the people ushered into the great hall. Ordulf shook his head and returned to his longhouse, his troubles with Brunhild temporarily forgotten.

In the great hall, Halla sat nervously with her guests and a few of her men. She had felt bound to welcome them, given it was her family who had caused them to be dispossessed, but now she had no idea what to do next. Since her husband had left, she had managed his lands, as she always had when he was away, and often when he was there. She had dealt with grumbling karls who perceived Ragnvald's absence as a good time to voice complaints, she had organised the spring planting of their farm and the bringing of the livestock to pasture. She had negotiated with merchants for supplies and discussed matters of the law with the city's law giver when one of Ragnvald's remaining men had killed another in a drunken fight.

Everything she had managed without concern, but on this matter she was unsure. She had a grieving and vulnerable widow in her hall, a potential enemy in her midst, and no idea how long that might be for.

As they sat making awkward conversation and eating some broth, Sten watched them with curiosity from the side of the hall. Where Halla saw a problem, Sten saw an opportunity. Sten was the older brother of Fenrir, the warrior who had died in an honour duel against Leif. A conflict sparked by the capture of Ordulf, when Fenrir had wanted to kill him, and Leif had shoved him to the ground to save the Christian's live. That Ragnvald had given the order to spare the smith had not saved Fenrir's pride, nor quenched his anger.

That anger had led to more confrontations, and finally to the Holmgang, the fight for honour, where Leif had ended Fenrir's quest for revenge by ending his life. Sten had watched and roared and writhed in fury as Leif put his sword through Fenrir's chest. The older, more experienced warrior shocked by the piercing steel and the defeat, the surviving brother left destitute and alone.

Sten had all the viciousness, cunning and spite of his younger brother, but little of his skill. He was also a cripple. One foot had been badly injured during a minor skirmish by a spear thrust that had left it to heal crooked and half useless, rendering him incapable of moving properly, or standing in the shieldwall. As an honoured man now incapable of going on raids but having been wounded in service to the jarl, he had lived a comfortable life in his service, performing guard duties, helping around the hall and other easy tasks. All winter he had been sent to an outlying farm, ostensibly to manage it, but no management was needed and he knew the jarl had sent him away out of shame, because he could not bear to look upon Sten and remember his betrayal.

He had loved his younger brother more than anything, despite his jealousy, and when Rangvald had allowed Leif to kill him over a nithing, a slave, a Christian slave at that, Sten had burned with rage.

He had been plotting his revenge ever since, his heart holding nothing but anger for his brother's murder, and what he saw as his jarl's betrayal of a loyal man. But murdering the jarl, even if he had succeeded, would have meant nothing more than his own swift death. And above all, he was a coward. So he had dithered until it was too late and the jarl was gone, perhaps never to return. And he had stewed, and fumed, and howled inwardly at his own reticence.

Until now. He had been called back to the city when the warband left, to help guard Ragnvald's property while he was gone. Now, the opportunity for revenge presented itself to him, and for the first time in a long time, Sten grinned to himself and felt once more the surge of pleasure that he got from the idea of finally having his vengeance.

Two days later, as evening was falling, Ordulf wandered back into the longhouse, aiming to go through to the pits behind in their rough wooden shelter for a piss. As he went into the house, he saw that Brunhild was heading into the pits too. He sighed in frustration. There was room for two people to do their business there, and men and women did use them together, but given everything that had happened he didn't think it was a good moment to follow her in.

He stood there for a moment in annoyance, realising that it might be a while before Brunhild left, and his need was great. *It's nearly dark, I'll just go behind the outbuilding.* They weren't allowed to piss against the back of the outbuilding that adjoined the great hall, but people sometimes did, especially warriors who had been drinking in the hall and needed a convenient place away from the aromatic delight that was the great hall's outhouse after a whole day's feasting.

Ordulf made his way around the building and opened his trousers. As he was about to start, he heard muffled voices coming from the other side of the wall to his right, one that separated the great hall's outhouse from the rest of the compound. It was two men who had just started talking in low voices. Slaves were not allowed to use that outhouse, so it was probably two of the warriors talking. He cursed inwardly, they might hear him pissing and come to find out who it was. As he stood there deciding if he would risk it, he heard what one of the men was saying, and shocked, trousers hanging open, he slipped towards the end of the wall and strained his ear to listen.

'Why would I believe you?' said the first man.

'Why would I be lying?' said the second.

'To trick my mistress into betraying her host, give her an excuse to kill her too, send her to join my old jarl, her husband.'

'Fuck excuses, we could just kill you all and say you attacked us. Everyone would believe us.'

'Is that a threat?'

'No. Look, Ragnvald betrayed my brother, got him killed. I

have no loyalty for the scum, nor for his haughty wife. Bitch won't even look at me, thinks she is too good to talk to the likes of me.'

'If he killed your brother, he betrayed his oath to his men, go to the lawgiver, do it properly.'

'Lawgiver?' there was a low chuckle. 'Are you serious? Yes, he betrayed his fucking oath, but do you think the lawgiver will rule against him? No, Ragnvald will wriggle out of it, and I will be left out in the cold, me, with one good foot and no name. Fuck that.'

'So, what do you want? You can't kill her, you will be gutted for it.'

'Exactly, but your mistress can.'

'What? You want my mistress to do your dirty work? You are insane. Fuck this, I'm going back in.'

'Wait!' There was a thump as a man was shoved against the far side of the wall, just a handspan from where Ordulf stood still like a stone.

'Get your hand off me, cripple, before you lose it.'

'Look, calm down. Of course I don't want your mistress to actually do it. I'll do it myself, your mistress just needs to say she did it, or got you to do it, and claim lawful revenge.'

There was a pause. 'You've lost me.'

'Look, it's simple. Your mistress has a legal right to revenge for her husband, she can use it as a reason to kill Hela.'

'So, why would she? Then we would be out on our ear again. Why the fuck would we do that?'

'Because you wouldn't be out on your ear, would you?'

'Why?'

'Because I would let you stay!'

'How?'

'I'm the most experienced and most senior of the men left here. My brother was a famous huscarl and I'm sure if we take care of a couple of potential troublemakers and grease the palms of a few others with women and silver, I can name myself the next jarl. There is no one left in this town who would stop us. This world is for the strong to take what they can.'

'Hmmm.' There was a pause. 'Even if I believe you, what is in it for us? We just end up the same as when we started. How is this good for us?'

'Of course it's good for you! Your mistress needs a husband, a powerful jarl, so she can live well and have a home. I want to be a powerful jarl. How obvious do I need to make this?'

'You want to marry my mistress?' said the first man, spluttering in surprise.

'Is that so insane?'

'But what if she doesn't want to marry you? A cripple, of no name.'

'Oi, fuck you, don't you talk to me like that. Listen to me, before I lose my patience. She doesn't have to fuck me or anything, you know, if she doesn't want to.' Ordulf heard the man snigger. 'She just has to marry me. I'll be a jarl with a proper wife, she will be safe, we both have our revenge. It's fucking perfect!'

'And when the real jarl comes back?'

'Pah, he probably won't come back. They went off to fight these Christians, who raped the whole of Denmark in a month and killed all its warriors, those Christians will smash Sigurd's army flat. Ragnvald will die out there.'

'And if he doesn't?'

'Then we deal with that when it happens. We will have time to gather men and get ready. Your mistress can be a jarl's wife, and you, you can be the head of my huscarls.' There was silence as the second man let that offer sink in. 'What is your other option? Wait here till she makes you leave and be beggars again?' he continued.

There was silence for a while. 'Yeah, fuck that. But how would we do this?'

'I need to talk to your mistress and you first. Make a plan.'

'She can't come to the pits with us, what do you expect? She is with Halla right now. We can't all sneak away! Anyway, I would need to talk to her first, bring her round.'

'Fine, do it quickly. Will she do what you suggest? She seems like a weak little thing to me.'

'I can make her see it my way. She tried to have Ragnvald killed once already, and she hasn't given up on revenge. If I show her a way, she'll do it.'

'Fine, then when Halla has gone to her room, talk to her, convince her. Then we will talk. I should be able to get a couple of others to join us.'

'And if she agrees to do this?'

'Then we will do it right away.'

'Why are you in such a hurry?'

'You won't change your mind by having more time to think about it, besides, we expect a hunting party back tomorrow or the next day, four warriors, too many to overcome. So, tonight is the night.'

'Fine. I'm off, need to go in before people get suspicious. You better not fuck us, I will rip your guts out.' There was a thump of footsteps up the steps into the hall and then only one man was left the other side of the wall. Ordulf heard the man pissing, something which made him remember how badly he needed to, and then he heard the man chuckling contentedly to himself. 'I've got you, bitch.'

Then the second man turned to go up the steps and Ordulf heard the door close.

Despite the fear and shock coursing through his veins, he finally relieved himself on the wall, in utter panic that one of the men would return and hear him, and then quietly slunk back to the longhouse.

Arriving there, he saw Otto and Brunhild and a few others sitting around the fire. He walked over to them and leaned in between the two. 'I need to speak to you, right now, outside.'

'What? No, get lost,' mumbled Otto.

Ordulf tried to keep his voice calm. 'Trust me, right now, don't make a fuss.'

Otto sighed and put down his bowl. 'What now? Can't you keep me out of it?' But he grumbled and stood up nonetheless, and the three walked out. Ordulf led them away until he was sure no one could hear what he would say.

'Screwed something up again, have you, Ordulf? Come on, what is it?' Brunhild said with a mischievous grin.

'Please talk quietly. This is important.'

'Ordulf, just get on with it,' said Otto.

'Fine! look, you must hear me out, and don't tell anyone else,' said Ordulf earnestly as Brunhild rolled her eyes. And then he relayed what he had heard.

Brunhild's face went from mischievous grin to concern to total horror. Otto listened grim-faced and stony right to the end.

'Shit,' said Brunhild when he was done.

'Sten,' said Otto, stroking his stubby beard.

'How do you know?' said Ordulf.

'He is the only man here who has lost a brother, and it just sounds like him.'

'Yeah, he does seem like an evil prick,' said Brunhild in agreement.

'So, what do we do?' said Ordulf desperately, looking at Otto.

'I need to think.'

'Think?' said Ordulf. 'We need to warn Halla! We don't know how much time there is. Halla might already be in bed, they might already be organising this. We need to do something!'

'Do what?' said Otto. 'They sleep in the hall, we can't just walk into her bedroom, we aren't allowed in there uncommanded. What do we do on our way through the plotters in the hall? Just say, "Sorry, we are off to warn our mistress that you are about to kill her"?' said Otto, gesticulating wildly.

'You are suggesting we do nothing then?' said Ordulf in horror.

'Yes, maybe.'

'We can warn one of the warriors. Get them a message, it must be possible.'

'Which one? You heard Sten saying he could get some of them to support him. He has had time to talk to them, which one do we talk to? The wrong one and he kills us!'

'So you really think we do nothing?' said Ordulf in disbelief.

'Yes. Look, Sten is right. This is legal. Tora can kill Halla and cite revenge, it would be legal. And Sten can seize the jarl's lands and marry her. It might not be legal to do that part but it's the way it's done. The sword is a law unto itself. What is certain is that we are slaves, we have no right to interfere in this. We should let the Norse settle their own affairs. We just do what we are told by whoever is left in charge.'

Ordulf gaped at Otto and shook his head. 'You would let Ragnvald's wife die.'

'Why not?' snapped Otto, looking around nervously.

'He is your jarl!' gasped Ordulf.

'So? How things have changed, Ordulf. Not so long ago you hated him. Now you are talking about loyalty to him?' Otto stared at Ordulf, eyes wide and fearful. 'Ragnvald enslaved me, he killed my friends and kept me forever from returning to my family.' Otto held his hand up and waved it in Ordulf's face. 'He cut off my finger to discipline me and took away my entire life. Why would I risk my life to help him? I don't care who owns me, him or some other Norseman. Why do you? Ragnvald was nice to you once, because he needs you to be compliant, and you are suddenly willing to risk your life for him? You don't owe him that.'

Ordulf recoiled, there was heavy truth in Otto's words, but he had never heard the man express any of it before. Ordulf had never really considered Otto's past life or feelings, so wrapped up was he in his own. Once again, he felt sheepish about his ignorance. But he shook his head angrily. 'Halla never did anything wrong to us, we can't just let her die.'

Otto groaned and clasped his hands to his face, scrunching up his forehead. 'Well, I'm not having any part of it. You want to risk yourself to rescue her? Fine, but leave me out of it.' He turned to go away, but suddenly doubled over in pain as a knee slammed into his stones. Then Brunhild's arm snaked around his neck, cutting off his cries. Ordulf looked on in shock.

'Ordulf, he is a fucking coward. He would probably go and warn Tora, he might tell them we know if he thought it kept him safe!' she said as quietly as she could. She was struggling now, as Otto regained his breath and started to try to wrestle free, squeaking and groaning.

'Why do you care?' hissed Ordulf, grabbing both of Otto's forearms and clamping them still in his meaty hands. The smaller man groaned and gasped as Brunhild's arm kept its lock on his throat.

'Remember what I told you!' she growled. 'I will never be owned by another man. Sten is a fucking animal. I will not be a slave to him, you know what he would do, death is better.' She grabbed him with her other arm, pulling him closer so that their faces touched and Otto's gasping mouth was pushed into Ordulf's shoulder. 'Ordulf, I will not let Sten have me. Do you hear me? Help me. Help me do this, you asked for my help and now I need yours. I will not be Sten's slave.' Ordulf looked back into those eyes, he saw the resolve in them, and heard the steel in her voice.

'Fuck, I'll do it.' He stood back and then watched in mild shock as Brunhild used her other arm to completely lock around Otto's neck, choking him until he passed out. Finally, the man stopped moving, but Brunhild did not let go. Ordulf looked at her in confusion.

'Enough,' he said. She shook her head.

'Enough!'

He let go of Otto's arms and prised Brunhild's away from the unconscious man's neck and she sneered at him, snatching her arms back. 'We don't need to kill him.'

'You are weak, Ordulf, too weak for this world. Too weak for what we need to do now. Can I count on you? If you can't even kill a man who threatens your life?'

Ordulf bristled and balled his fists. 'I've killed before.'

'Oh, yeah? Was it deliberate?' Ordulf jutted his chin out and said nothing. 'I thought so. Now we might have to fight. We will probably have to kill, are you ready?'

Ordulf relaxed his fists and nodded with confidence he did not feel. 'Yes.' He looked down at Otto. 'But you can't just kill anyone, only if we have to.' Brunhild snorted and turned to look at the great hall.

'Okay, this is what we need to do,' she said.

Halla snapped awake, unsure why she had woken. There was a noise outside in the hall, a muffled cry. She sat up and looked at the wall separating the bedroom from the great hall in alarm. She ripped the furs aside and tried to go for the large seax that was hanging on the wall near the bed, but then the door to her room opened and Sten sauntered in, closing the door behind him. Sten had blood on his bare chest, a longseax in his hand, and a wolfish grin on his face.

'Hello, Halla.'

'Sten? What is happening?' she asked, for a precious moment not linking the available facts together until suddenly she understood. She opened her eyes wide with shock and lunged for the seax. She was too slow, Sten launched himself across the room, landing awkwardly on his crippled foot but knocking her back onto the bed.

She tried to cry out in pain but Sten was onto her, he shoved his hand onto her face and leered down at her. She wriggled and he put the knife to her throat. Stilling her.

'You're wondering why? Because your husband betrayed my brother and let him be killed, that's why,' he said, saliva dripping onto her face as he spat the words at her. 'But that is why I'm going to kill you. The other thing I'm going to do?' He leaned down until his mouth was next to her ear. 'That's just because I have always wanted to.'

She started wriggling and struggling again and Sten laughed, holding her down with one hand while he fumbled his trousers down with the other. She heard the door open and Sten cursed and called over his shoulder. 'I haven't finished here yet, go and wait outside!'

When he got no response, he turned and started to angrily shout, 'Fuck off!' but his jaw slackened and his eyes widened as a slave girl jumped onto the bed and stabbed a knife deep into his side, screaming like a banshee while she did it. Sten tried to bring his own knife around to defend himself but Halla grabbed his knife arm and sank her teeth into his wrist, biting and wrenching her head from side to side, ripping at the soft skin and delicate internals of his wrist. Sten roared in pain and lashed out with his elbow, hitting the slave girl in the chest. She was knocked backwards with an 'ooof' of exhaled breath, but she had already plunged the knife into his side three or four times and blood washed out of him in pulses. He weakened and stopped struggling, even as Halla ripped the knife from his nerveless hand and held it, pointed like a spear at his chest.

Two figures crashed through the open door as Halla watched Sten's eyes begin to unfocus. Tora's warrior, Gorm, was on his back, wrestling and kicking as a huge slave pummelled his face. The warrior's struggles became weaker and weaker as Halla watched, until finally Gorm sagged back and the big slave stood and crushed his throat with a sickening stamp.

The room stilled as the two slaves looked at her. She looked back at Sten with pure rage in her eyes and he gaped back at her in open mouthed confusion and agony. Halla screamed and lunged forwards, stabbing the seax into Sten's chest, knocking him back and scrambling onto his chest as he lay helpless on the bed, as she had lain helpless beneath him just moments before. She pulled the Seax from his body and stabbed him again, screaming her fury into his dying eyes, violating his body with steel as the life slipped from his features until there was no movement left at all other than the shuddering of his body beneath the blows.

Ordulf stood, panting, as he watched Halla finish off the dying man. Halla screamed at the dead man's face for a few moments after she finished stabbing him, and then let go of the seax handle as Brunhild gently pulled her away while she broke down in sobs. Brunhild looked at Ordulf and pointed with her chin, telling him to get out of the room, leaving her with the jarl's shocked wife.

Ordulf went out into the main hall. The room was thick with the smell of blood, bodies slumped on the floor. He and Brunhild had come with one of Ragnvald's warriors, Ebbe, who had been in the long house, and who Brunhild had decided was trustworthy to tell. They had heard the sound of fighting start before they reached the hall and rushed inside. They found that Sten and Tora's warriors were slaughtering two of Ragnvald's men; they had clearly refused to turn traitor. Ordulf and Ebbe had attacked Tora's two companions as their backs were turned and while Brunhild made for the room at the end of the hall.

Ordulf walked over to where Ebbe was sitting on Tora, holding her down while he held his hand to a nasty wound in his side. Ordulf looked down at him with pity in his eyes. The man was dying, and they both knew it. He had taken a seax in the side from Gorm, before Ordulf had tackled the man and driven him into Halla's room.

'Better take over,' he said, his breath ragged.

'I'm sorry,' said Ordulf lamely.

'Did you save her. Halla?' the warrior asked, hope in his eyes.

'Yes, she is alive.'

'And...' the man was breathing heavily now. 'Did you save her honour?'

Ordulf nodded curtly. 'Yes, she is... Sten didn't do anything.'

The man smiled a pained smile and nodded. 'Then all is well, I have no regrets.' He gripped Ordulf's arm with his hand. 'Tell the jarl what I did. Tell him none of us betrayed him. Tell him we died well.'

'Don't worry, I will.'

'Thank you.' The man grimaced and groaned as he levered himself to the side and sat heavily against the wall. 'And keep that fucking bitch alive for him. He will want her.'

Ordulf mumbled his agreement and reached down to lift the cowering Tora to her feet. She was terrified. Eyes flicking nervously from side to side. 'I didn't want to! I swear, it was all Sten, and my man, Gorm, they forced me! They forced me. You have to believe me!' she pleaded with him, sobbing freely. 'I just wanted to be safe, I just wanted to be safe.'

Ordulf hesitated but kept his grip on her, unsure what to do. 'I'll deal with this, thank you, Ordulf.' Ordulf looked around and saw Halla standing there, dishevelled and covered with blood, but somehow having collected her wits and composure. Brunhild was standing behind her, her face emotionless and set.

Ordulf let Tora go and she reached out hesitantly to Halla. 'Halla, I swear, I came here in peace,' she pleaded, moving forwards, arms wide, going to nervously embrace Halla. 'I'm so sorry, my men, they forced me to do what Sten said. They forced me. They wanted your lands. I had no choice.'

'It's fine, Tora. It's fine.' Halla opened her arms and accepted the embrace. Tora burst into wild sobs, her face buried in Halla's shoulder. 'I know you had no choice. For you are a coward, and you could do nothing against those men.'

Tora pulled her face away and looked at Halla with horror. Halla's grip around her was unyielding. 'I am not a coward!! And I...'

'And you came here, hoping for pity and shelter, and then plotted to murder me, as my guest.' Halla's voice was ice and silk swirling together.

'And your husband plotted the death of mine! And you didn't stop him!' Tora wailed, anger seeping into her voice.

Halla tutted and shook her head sadly. 'Tora, my dear Tora. No, I did not.' Halla drew Tora back into her embrace and hugged her close, pushing her head back into her blood sodden shoulder. 'There is something you need to know about me and Ragnvald, we are together in all things. I didn't stop him, I convinced him. He told me that he would not be able to kill Birkir, and I told him that he had to.' Tora choked in anger and shock and pulled desperately back from the embrace.

Halla plucked the bloody seax from her belt and plunged it into Tora's side. The woman spasmed and arched her back, eyes wide in horror and mouth pinned open in a silent scream. She hung for a moment and then collapsed back onto the ground. Ordulf looked on in total shock, immobile.

Halla surveyed the carnage of the hall for a moment, she looked at Ebbe, but he was slumped, sightless eyes staring at his own knees. She sighed and then turned to the two slaves.

'Does anyone else know about this plot?' she asked pointedly.

Ordulf gave Brunhild a firm look and then shook his head. 'No, it's just us.'

'Good. Then we are the only people alive who know what happened.' She looked at them sternly. 'And it must stay that way. People will arrive any moment, the screams would have been heard. No one must know any of Ragnvald's men betrayed him. No one must know what happened in my room. Do you understand me?' She snapped the last words at the two slaves. They both nodded submissively.

'If anyone hears that one of his men betrayed him, or worse, that that man forced himself into my bed and onto me, Ragnvald and his reputation will never recover.' She hammered the words home with her eyes.

'But he didn't...' said Ordulf.

'He didn't what? He didn't have time to force himself into me? Says who? Two of my slaves? Who will believe you? There will be whispers that he did. Whispers that he violated his oath to his jarl by violating me most foully, and they will spread and it will bring shame and ridicule on me and on Ragnvald and I will *not* allow that. Do you understand it? Convince me!' She brought the seax around to face them.

Brunhild nodded vigorously. 'I understand, mistress, we will tell people what you want us to tell.'

'You'd better. And this man? He is yours? You can make sure he sticks to the story?' Halla indicated the still overwhelmed Ordulf.

Brunhild gave a thin smile and looked at Ordulf and then back to Halla. 'Yes, he is mine. I will make sure he knows what to do and that he does it.'

Ordulf stifled a protest but then nodded curtly. 'Good,' Halla said. There were shouts in the courtyard and Halla pursed her lips as she looked around. 'Here is what happened. Our guests betrayed us and all Ragnvald's men died defending me, killing both of Tora's men in the process. You two were not involved. There will be no awkward questions as to why two slaves were armed and killing free Norsemen in my hall. You both arrived after the fighting and helped the wounded, including Sten, who we laid on my bed to tend to his wounds, which is why I am covered in his blood. Tora was killed in the fighting, we don't know by who.'

Ordulf gaped at Halla in horror. 'But…'

'You have a problem with not being the hero this time? Tough. You have had your moment of glory and saving the jarl's life. Now you must merely be a slave, a witness to events above you. Understood?' She softened her face and smiled at him. 'But you have my thanks, and my promise you will both be protected for the rest of your time here and, if possible, freed when your service is over.' Brunhild put her hand to her mouth and held back an exclamation of pure glee. 'And Ordulf, I'm sorry I called you a big oaf.' Halla smiled at him warmly. 'Sometimes a big loyal oaf is just what is needed.' As she finished, someone hammered on the barred main door, shouting to be let in.

Halla turned towards the door and shouted to the man that she would let them in and that she was the lady of the house. Then she walked over to the door and unbarred it. The door opened violently and three armed men burst through, stopping and staring around in the half lit room, trying to take stock of what they saw, searching for threats and seeing none. Halla held her arms out and started explaining.

More men arrived, and more, drawn from all over town by the commotion. Halla's story was accepted and the slaves ignored other than being ordered to help clear away the bodies, the intruders to be dumped in the refuse pits outside the city, the dead household warriors to be prepared for burial.

Men from other houses volunteered to stand guard over Halla that night, until more of her own could be brought in, which she gratefully accepted. Eventually the rest left the hall, and Halla shooed Brunhild and Ordulf out into the yard with the rest of the slaves who had been called in to help.

Ordulf, still trying to process what had happened, looked at the open door of their longhouse and saw Otto's face framed in it, a look of pure hatred on his features. Then Otto turned and walked away and disappeared into the darkened interior.

'You will regret not letting me kill him, or not telling Halla he knew about the plot and letting her kill him. Somewhere, somehow, that is going to come back and bite you,' said Brunhild.

Ordulf stood there, exhaustion finally overcoming his shock and excitement, still clenching and unclenching one fist and picking absentmindedly at the dried blood that still clung to the side of his face. He was going over the events again and again in his head. As he stood there, forgetting he was not alone, a hand gently took hold of the one he had left dangling by his side and he turned to see Brunhild smiling up at him in the gloom.

'For all your faults, she is right, you know.'

'Right about what?' he asked, curling his fingers gently around hers.

'Sometimes a big loyal oaf is just what you need,' she said with a cheeky smirk.

'What? Oh! Now? Seriously? After what just happened? I mean, sure, I guess if I washed and calmed down and... do you really want to?' Ordulf stared back at her in amazement.

Brunhild snatched her hand back and gave him a chiding look. 'Well not now that you suggested it! But yes, I'm happy to be alive and it makes me... want things. But I told you never to come to me with that in mind so now it's not happening.' She patted his arm and started walking away with a laugh.

'But... what? It wasn't my idea!' Ordulf protested, hands waving in frustration.

'You'll learn how it works, my big oaf. You'll have to, I own you now; the mistress said so.' She wagged a finger over her shoulder at him as she walked away into the darkness. And Ordulf was left shaking his head and trying to let the stress and shock flow out of him. He was exhausted, exasperated and confused. He didn't understand the Norse, or women. Combined in the mercurial form of Brunhild, the result was utterly perplexing to him.

'Well, are you coming or not?' Brunhild called.

Ordulf looked up, and saw Brunhild outlined in the moonlight, standing in the doorway, holding her hand out towards him. He smiled and jogged over like a pup seeing its master coming home from the fields. 'But I thought...'

'Stop thinking,' said Brunhild, grabbing him with her outstretched hand and pulling him into a passionate embrace. His lips met hers and they kissed, Ordulf felt pure joy flow through his veins as she grabbed a handful of the hair on the back of his head and pressed her mouth into his. She pushed him against the doorframe and her hip ground up against his groin and he groaned uncontrollably.

Then suddenly the pressure and the mouth were gone, and Brunhild was smiling ferociously at him. For a moment he thought he was being teased again, but then Brunhild slowly half turned away and took a step into the shadows of the longhouse, a single hand trailing out behind her in a gesture of invitation and promise. He took the hand and allowed himself to be led, grinning, into the darkness.

For a week of pure, unrestrained joy, Ordulf spent his days sharing chores with Brunhild, and his nights sharing the furs with her. The events in the longhouse had shocked the city, and people came and went as they met with Halla, expressed their outrage, and promised their protection and loyalty. Armed men patrolled the compound day and night, and all movement in and out of the city was closely watched.

But for the household slaves it meant little. Their days were spent working as at any other time, fixing and making clothes, chopping and stacking firewood and a hundred other chores. With the army away, and no swords to make, Ordulf was used to helping them, and someone seemed to be ensuring it was always Brunhild he was helping, a mystery that was solved when he saw Halla giving him a warm smile and a nod of the head when he was sent out with her one day to fetch more wool from a farm.

The walk back together along the riverbank on a glorious summer day took a little longer than strictly necessary, and Ordulf arrived back more tired, more dishevelled and more pleased with himself than any slave sent to gather wool had a right to be.

It was the first truly happy time in his young life, and all he wished was for it to continue forever. How the gods laugh at the wishes of men.

CHAPTER 14

RESPONSE AND RESPONSIBILITY

Crusade headquarters at Aarhus, 27ᵗʰ June 1117

'ORDER, ORDER!' SHOUTED the French lord, gesturing to the standing and seated nobles and commanders of the Crusade. The raucous room stilled to quietness as Baldwin, Count of Flanders, watched impatiently.

When the room was still, he removed the hand from his chin and spoke. 'We are here today to discuss the failure of Count Adolf's mission to Sjælland, and what future actions we will take against the Norse.'

Adolf gaped in outrage, unable to speak, as he stood to one side of the room. He had come to make his report, fresh from the capture of Sjælland, and Baldwin had asked him to come the next day to present it to a meeting of commanders. Instead, when he arrived, it seemed every nobleman in the entire army was here, and now the purpose was clear. To witness his humiliation.

Baldwin continued in a stern tone. 'Count Adolf, I have had

it reported to me that you allowed the Norse army on the island to escape? That you lost a major battle, and that most of the supplies, people and food were removed from the island, you having failed to secure it.' There was stone silence in the room. 'So? Explain yourself!' Baldwin leant back and all eyes fixed on the stunned German count.

Sir Hugues was standing behind Adolf, unseen eyes begging him to control his response, not to play into Baldwin's hands by exploding and making a fool of himself. Adolf closed his mouth and ground his teeth together, face a mask of fury. He considered simply storming from the room, and nearly did, but that would reek of cowardice, or him accepting the accusations as fact.

He gradually composed himself to speak. 'Well, what do you have to say for yourself?' added the French count, holding his hand in the air, a mock quizzical expression on his face.

'You have been misinformed, Count Baldwin, which you would be aware of, if you allowed me to present my report, instead of taking it from other men,' Adolf retorted. 'You sent me to capture Sjælland, and I did. The Norse army did not defeat me, not once, although there were many engagements and we did suffer casualties, we won the field every time, the Norse merely escaped, ran, survived.' He glared around the room defiantly.

'Not only that,' he continued, 'but the enemy had already evacuated the island before the campaign even began, taking their people, supplies and equipment with them. If I had attacked straight away after the capture of Fyn, we would have secured a season's worth of food, mirroring the success at Odense. I could not secure that which no longer existed, because wiser men advocated waiting,' he said curtly, fixing Baldwin with a pointed stare.

Baldwin flared his nostrils and sat forward in his ridiculous chair, hands gripping the ends of the armrests tightly. 'Do not lay your failures at the hands of others! You were defeated at Trelleborg.

Your horse lines were destroyed, the enemy army escaped and many of your men were lost, were they not? What excuse do you offer to cover for this?'

Adolf feigned confusion. 'You cannot mean the siege of Trelleborg fortress, which we captured after just three days, resisting a midnight attack on both camps even while we assaulted the fortress, forcing the survivors of the garrison to swim a river and flee with the army? If that is a defeat, my lord, I do not understand how a victory works. Perhaps you could explain it? From your broad experience of battle?'

Sir Hugues gripped Adolf's arm tightly and whispered fiercely in his ear. 'Enough! You must accept some measure of humiliation here or make such an enemy of him that the Crusade implodes! Think of the consequences, you must be able to still work with him. Insult him no more, accept some fault.'

Adolf stiffened at the instruction from the young French noble but nodded discreetly. On the platform, Baldwin was speaking heatedly with an aide, his face red with anger, his composure gone. The French commander dismissed his man with a wave and jabbed a finger at Adolf. 'You had superior forces and you failed, after three weeks, to bring the enemy to a decisive battle. Perhaps you never actually ran from the field in defeat, but you did not press a significant victory. Do you acknowledge this or do you have some weasel words, some pithy saying to absolve yourself?'

Adolf winced at the truth in the words and drew his lips into a tight line before replying in a more measured tone. 'It is true that we did not have the degree of success I would have liked. The enemy was much better prepared, much better led. I was more cautious than I could have been. I valued the certainty of success more highly than risking failure of the campaign for greater victory.'

His words, his admission, hung in the air. Some men snorted in derision, others nodded slowly at the sense of it.

'So you admit your failings, then?' asked Baldwin, clearly relieved.

'Yes, I do, a commander only improves by acknowledging his failures and learning from them. But was the campaign a failure? No. We set out to secure the island as a base to invade the mainland, with enough time to do it this year. We succeeded on both fronts, despite the unexpected tenacity and competency of the enemy.'

Baldwin frowned and swept his eyes around the room. The German count's words had clearly resonated with many of the commanders, and despite his loyal supporters doing their best to make noises and gestures of contempt, they were not carrying the atmosphere in the room. He realised his attempt to humiliate the man had failed, the limited but honest admission had won the opinion of the crowd. He returned his eyes to Adolf and glared at him.

'Be assured that we shall learn from your failures, Count Adolf. And I shall learn from my mistake of assigning such an important task to such a cautious and tentative leader. Wars are not won by tiptoeing around, allowing the enemy to do as they wish. We will strike and be decisive, when the enemy gives ground we shall pursue them relentlessly, we shall not be tricked or deceived or frightened by shadows in the night!'

Adolf set his tongue to reply but the firm hand was back on his arm. 'Enough!' the voice whispered in his ear. And Adolf clamped down on his reply.

'Fortunately, we shall not have need of your command again. Duke Welfard will arrive any day, to take over command of the German contingent, who will now support the French forces as we invade the Norse mainland.' With that, Baldwin stopped looking at Adolf and started a conversation with one of his aides. And with that, the 'meeting' was apparently dismissed.

'That could have gone much worse, I think,' said Hugues in a forced tone as the two men walked away from the meeting.

'How?' Adolf growled.

'Well, he didn't dismiss you from the army.'

'That's it? That's the only way it could have gone worse?'

Hugues shrugged. 'Well, that was what I was expecting to happen. Now, you are still here and we have a base to attack Scania. All is well with the Crusade.'

'All is very far from well. I was humiliated by that ignorant brat and now he will be taking command of his forces as they invade, a task he is utterly unprepared for. He didn't even get my scouting reports, notes on the enemy tactics, weapons or equipment. Vital information he needs in order to defeat the Norse.' Adolf shook his head in despair.

'Hmm, give me all those reports you speak of, I will divert them through various other channels and make sure they reach the Count's commanders. That way, the right men will hear them and they will not be rejected.'

'You will what?' asked Adolf in disgust. 'You will make my hard work look like it has come from other sources?'

'Yes, it will be rejected if it comes from you,' Hugues said, as if this was obvious.

'But then, if he uses this information and succeeds, he will think himself the military genius and be able to claim I was the idiot who could not understand these matters!'

'Yes, probably,' Hugues replied, without emotion. 'But the key there is that he will succeed. I thought that was the aim, not personal pride.'

'Of course it is!' Adolf snapped. 'I had just hoped to do it without destroying my reputation!'

'I'm sure we can find a way to salvage that. Perhaps Duke Welfard will prove sympathetic.'

'I've never met the man, he owes me nothing.'

'Perhaps, but I have dealt with him on several occasions and have his ear on some matters of state. I will talk to him, explain the delicacy of the situation.' Hugues nodded to himself as he spoke.

Adolf shook his head and strode away, leaving the scheming baron to his plans, wishing for a simpler time. Duke Welfard of Bavaria, commonly known as Welf the Fat, was due to arrive any day, and Adolf did not know what to expect but he had heard that the man was lazy, distant from Holy Roman Empire politics, heirless and not a military man. Adolf suspected Welfard had not volunteered for this Crusade, but how he had been leveraged into the position, he did not know. He hoped his relationship would prove to be easier with the German duke when he arrived. He wouldn't have long to wait.

A day later, and Adolf sat in the tent of the newly arrived duke while Welfard nodded rapidly, his prodigious chin wobbling in agreement with his face. He didn't care what people called him. He was fat because he was rich, and he was the Duke of Bavaria, so those who insulted him were invariably smaller men, in every sense. Duke Welf cared for one thing and one thing only at this stage of his life. Enjoyment. And to enjoy the waning years of his life he needed peace and a lack of responsibilities, something being sent to lead a Crusade was interfering with to an unacceptable degree.

He had been young and full of vigour once. He had tried his hand at the great game of power. He had married the ferocious Matilda di Cannossa, a childless Italian widow with enormous power and lands. He had gone to war with the previous emperor alongside her, even won that war, only to see everyone credit Matilda with the victory, making him seem weak and subservient. Matilda had opened her bedchamber and her skirts to him but once, to formalise the marriage, and then never again. She had controlled him to the extent of personally selecting his mistresses, and 'dissuaded' any other from getting close to him. She had pledged her lands to the Pope when she died, so Welfard would get nothing from the marriage.

He had been duped into a marriage for her political gain, he was the subordinate in the relationship in all but genitalia, and he knew it. Worse, everyone else knew it. Unable to bear the embarrassment, and unable to divorce her as the Pope was her staunch ally and would not grant one, he had returned home and settled into a life of gluttony and pleasures of the flesh. He had sired a dozen bastards, that he knew of, but no legitimate heirs, her last wound to him. He would have no dynasty, she had extinguished his line.

He found himself, so many years later, admiring her ruthlessness. If she had been born a man, she would have been the emperor of the Holy Roman Empire, or perhaps the world. It hadn't even been personal, she didn't hate him, she didn't even dislike him; she *nothinged* him. He was so far below her capability he was simply a step to stand on for her, nothing more, nothing less.

He had dissociated himself from the politics of the Holy Roman Empire, agreeing with the new emperor Henry to support him in all things, in exchange for protection and freedom to do as he liked in Bavaria. But now Henry had called in a favour, and so Welfard found himself sitting across from Count Adolf of somewhere, tired from the road, bored stiff, and apparently now the actual co-commander of a Crusade. Something that might have amused him at another distant time.

'So, let me be clear, Count Adolf. I will deal with this French pup, I will relay your suggestions as if they are my own, and we will get this whole mess over by new year so I can go home?'

'Yes,' nodded the count.

'Good. I don't need to know more. You see to everything and send me written lists of what orders I need to give.'

Adolf was taken aback at the utter disinterest the Duke of Bavaria showed in his command, or the Crusade in general. He had heard rumours and had letters expressing the duke's support for whatever course of action he saw fit, but this detachment was beyond his experience.

'Don't look at me like that, Adolf. I'm nearly fifty years old and not in good health. I may live another five or maybe ten years and all I want is to do that in comfort and peace. I have no sons, no legacy to cement, no military career to build, I frankly couldn't give a shit about this Crusade, other than to see it successfully concluded as soon as possible so that I can go home. You have pissed off this French prick, so I will deal with him and pretend to agree with him that you are useless, while secretly leaving you in charge. You think I am decrepit and lazy and I think you are all fools for wanting to invade some godforsaken land in the frozen North in search of glory you won't find here. Let's leave that disagreement aside and get this nonsense over with,' Welfard said with obvious distaste. 'But be careful, Count Adolf, for unambitious I may be, but I'm just as smart as you and ten times as powerful. So abuse this arrangement at your extreme peril. Are we clear?'

Adolf nodded speechlessly as the rotund duke levered himself out of the chair and walked out of the room without any further words.

Astonished, and apparently dismissed, Adolf stood up and left the room. He went to his own tent to start writing the orders that the duke would give, thinking that the situation couldn't be more bizarre or, frankly, more perfect.

The other side of the cold sea, Sigurd was also holding court, in the great hall at Lund. Well, that is not entirely true. Sigurd was near blind drunk, half-naked, and swapping stories with a group of Swedish warriors around a table, not holding court in a way any Christian lord would understand.

The Hall was in its third night of feasting. It had simply been impossible to throw a feast for five thousand men of the returning army of Sjælland in one night, so the king had declared five straight nights of feasting, each to serve one thousand men, some in the hall, most on rough tables around fires in the square outside it.

Many of the jarls had ridiculed the idea of hosting a feast for the entire army, stating it would be impossible. Sigurd had insisted that not only would they do it, but he would host all five nights himself, and try to celebrate with every single warrior who had come back with him.

Sigurd, as usual, got his way.

'So, I was standing there in someone's room… bedroom?' Sigurd suddenly stopped and looked confused. 'No, there was no bed, it was just a small hall. Uh, what was I saying?'

'Your beard was on fire!' three men shouted simultaneously, roaring with laughter.

'Yes! My beard was on fire! So, one of my men was poking Christians with his spear through the doorway, and I was beating my own face with my shield, trying to put out the fire!' He stood unsteadily on the bench, ale-horn in one hand, gesturing with the other. Getting his hands mixed up, he mimed beating his beard with the hand holding the ale-horn instead of his empty one, sloshing ale all over his face and huge bare torso, causing the warriors to erupt into laughter once again.

'So, while I'm beating my own face with my shield, Gunnar is hacking through the burning wall with an axe…' Sigurd carried on with the story to repeated peals of laughter.

Across the hall, Ragnvald watched with Jarl Kjartan. He was nursing a horn of ale he had barely touched, the effects of the last two nights weighing him down like an anchor stone. He could barely look at the ale, let alone drink any of it. 'How does he do that?' he asked, shaking his head in disbelief.

'Youth, and practice,' answered Kjartan, who was not even bothering to pretend to drink anymore. He had been outside twice already to empty his stomach.

'No, not that, how does he gain the love and respect of the men so easily, no matter who they are? Everyone loves him.'

'He was born to it. I have known Sigurd his entire life, and he has always been that way,' said Kjartan solemnly. 'Some men are simply blessed with the adoration of others. It must be Odin given. The Allfather is also blessed with the love of all men.'

'Perhaps, although I try to avoid just allocating everything I don't understand to the gods,' replied Ragnvald. 'Oh well, here I go again. He is about to reach my part of the story.'

'RAGNVALD!' roared Sigurd, looking unsteadily around from his audience of rowdy warriors, 'RAGNVALD, where are you when I need to mock you!'

'Here, Lord Sigurd!' said Ragnvald, sneaking around the edge of the room and stepping up to shout in the king's ear from behind. Sigurd nearly fell off the bench in drunken surprise and saved himself by grabbing a handful of Ragnvald's tunic, ripping it in the process.

'Ha! Ragnvald, tell them… tell them how I sneaked up on you on the dock, how you greeted me like a woman greets her husband after a whole season of raiding and worrying.' The men roared in mirth at the Swedish jarl, who rolled his eyes and started dramatically recreating the moment, hugging his giggling king with one arm as they stood on the bench.

Sigurd did not turn up for the gathering of the senior jarls the second day after the feasts ended. The jarls shared their lessons and experiences, captured equipment was examined, analysis of Crusader tactics swapped. But without their king, no future plans could be discussed. Late in the day, the king finally arrived in the hall, looking like he had fought all night with… well, with someone his own size.

The king slumped over and sank down into the throne on the dais, which was vast and comfortable, and promptly started falling asleep.

'So he is not invincible, then,' Ragnvald noted to jarl Kjartan, smiling wolfishly.

'He drank enough to kill a jotun, I couldn't even attend the last two nights I was so ill. But he did it, he did it every night, he turned a defeat into a great story of victory, and there isn't a man in the army who wouldn't have walked through that fire in København for him now.'

Ragnvald nodded, still smiling. 'He is a smart man, he will need that love in the months to come.' Kjarten nodded sagely as the king started snoring heavily, head tilted back, mouth open, the very picture of nobility.

One of the Norwegian jarls approached the dais and prodded the king gently. Sigurd snapped back to awareness with a snort and looked blearily around him. He struggled to sit upright and waved vaguely in the direction of Ragnvald, who took this as instruction to start the discussion.

'So,' said the king some time later, after the jarls had all had their say, his chin still resting on his hand, but eyes now clear and alert. 'We expect the Crusaders to come soon, before the season is over. We all agree they will come to the coast of Scania, we cannot agree where, but probably somewhere from the area around Helsingborg in the North, to the area of Trelleborgen in the south. It's a four- or five-day march between the edges of those two areas, between places they might land.'

Sigurd drummed his fingers slowly on his bearded chin. 'We cannot defend the entire coast. If we gamble and defend one end, we will not reach the other in time to contest their landing. To me, it seems the best choice is simply to gather the army at Lund and wait. When we receive news the Crusader fleet has been sighted, we move to where it is landing and hope to crush them before they land their entire force. It pains me to suggest we do nothing until they arrive, but I see no better course.'

There was silence around the room as the other jarls contemplated the choices. Ragnvald spoke up. 'We don't do nothing, Lord Sigurd. We set up supply caches and camps at half-day intervals between the north and south. We have ships ready to harass the enemy fleet, and scout ships out observing them from when they leave to when they land. We set up a network of watchers on the coast, sentinels with a dozen men and some horses, to report any landing when it happens. We garrison each of the three fortresses, and the coastal towns, with enough men to resist for a few days. Everything rests on knowing the landing location as fast as possible, having the local defenders hold out for a few days, and getting the army concentrated there before the entire Christian army lands.'

Sigurd nodded. 'I agree. Make the preparations, gather the army, we must expect the attack at any time. The men of Norway will garrison the northern fortress, the men of Denmark the centre, the men of Sweden the southern. One thousand men in each, it will not be a long siege in any case, so fill those forts to the brim with warriors and stay alive until the army comes.'

With that, Sigurd dragged himself wearily to his feet and walked out of the hall, his jarls following him and dispersing into the cool afternoon air outside.

CHAPTER 15

THE GUARDIANS
ON THE SHORE

At sea approaching the Eyrarsund, Skania, Kingdom of Denmark
July 1117

THE ROUND SHIP wallowed. There was really no other word for it. It did not glide, it did not cut through the waters. It lurched from trough to trough, stirring the stomachs of the miserable soldiers below decks like a maid churning butter.

The smell that emanated from that dark hold was like nothing Adolf had ever experienced before. He had never been on a long voyage in bad weather. Especially with a hold full of seasick soldiers.

He was in that moment never more grateful for his rank. Not for the power or wealth or position or respect it gave him. No, he was grateful because it allowed him to be on deck, away from the stink of men losing their control of more bodily functions than he cared to think about. The glory of God's war could not have been further from his mind in that rough sea, not that it was ever something he really believed in at the best of times.

The Count of Flanders had driven the last enthusiasm for this campaign from him. Welfard had argued, on Adolf's suggestion, that they should make several landings, to feint and distract and confuse the enemy. That way, preventing them from concentrating their forces. That a single landing, a single port, was too fragile a position. Of course, Baldwin, Count of Flanders, understood none of this, he merely revelled in the chance to level criticism on subjects he wanted to appear to understand. Although he was still invited to command meetings, Adolf did not bother to speak except to provide Welfard with details and reports, to burnish the idea it was Welfard who made the decisions. Sir Hugues also continued to redirect Adolf's advice and reports through others in the various contingents. So that Adolf had the impression that he was commanding the entire Crusade in secret, via suggestion, an absurd and inefficient way to do things.

Eventually, Baldwin had been convinced that a feint landing was his idea and, enthused by it, he had ordered the fleet to sail to the south of Scania, near the fortress of Trelleborgen. There, the fleet had abruptly turned around and sailed north, arriving in the north of Scania the next day and landing at the port outside Helsingborg. He hoped the distraction was worth the extra two days aboard the ship.

As he was fuming at the rail, his son staggered over and slammed into the rail next to him, gripping it with white knuckles and wide eyes. Hartung had acquitted himself well in the Sjælland campaign under Sir Dietmar's close supervision. During the failed attempt to halt the Norse army on the road to København, he had been in the thick of both of the charges of heavy cavalry and lost his horse from under him on the second. The lad had fought his way clear and back to safety with not a scratch on him. Sir Dietmar had reported that two Norsemen had fallen to his spear and sword.

His son was one of the only bright spots in this whole rotten business for Adolf. His pride in the slim and hawk-nosed young man obscured his offspring's ill temper and fragile ego from him. The son worshipped the father in an oddly unfriendly way, seeking approval without trying to appear friendly and taking any criticism or jest with poor humour. It was an odd dynamic that Adolf ignored without a care, pleased as he was to have his son by his side and earning a fine reputation for skill at arms.

Hartung gasped and shook at the rail, turning to shout at his father, 'Captain says we will have to ride out the storm at sea! We can't make an unfamiliar port in this weather!'

Adolf nodded, already having steeled himself to another night at sea. The Crusader fleet, some one hundred and forty ships strong and carrying over eighteen thousand men, had been so large it had launched from four ports and was scattered over fifteen miles of water. His portion had left from Odense. The remaining Crusader forces had come from the Danish peninsular and spent an extra day at sea. He could only imagine how bad things were for them, facing another night afloat. Another night at sea on top of the one already suffered would be unpleasant for his force but not fatal. His men would simply have to suffer it. He hoped they would not have to fight after landing. He suspected they would be weak as kittens for days. Another 10,000 men and horses with all their extra siege equipment, camp followers and three weeks' supplies waited for the second return trip of the fleet.

He patted his unsteady looking son on the back and wobbled back to the small cabin they shared with the captain at the stern.

Sigurd fumed at the messenger. 'They didn't land?'

'No, my lord, the fleet turned around and sailed north in the morning. There was a storm, we thought perhaps they were forced to head out to sea, to safety, but then they were gone.'

Sigurd cursed the weather and the gods, making men touch their hammer amulets around him.

Ragnvald was standing deep in thought. They were nearly a day south of Lund with the entire Norse army, over fifteen thousand men, only a day's march from Trelleborgen, but four days' march from Helsingborg. The Crusaders would have time to land and establish themselves, perhaps even land a second wave of men.

'We must assume we will face their entire army, should we still offer battle?' he asked, to himself as much as to the king.

'Yes, we must fight them now, they will only get stronger. Give the orders, in the morning we march north. I cannot hold an army this size together for long in the field, we either use it now or lose it forever. We must strike, and weaken the Christians, try and save that fortress.'

Ragnvald nodded. He knew the fortress at Helsingborg contained men the king knew well, loyal vassals. He would not leave them alone. Battle was inevitable. The men dispersed, shouting orders and sending messengers scurrying around the vast army, setting about the task of turning it around on the road, and starting the four-day march back north.

'UP! Up the ladders!' Sir Hans screamed at the men around him. Men were struggling in the muddy, body-choked ditch, holding shields over their heads, struggling to climb the rain slicked rungs of the ladders. Forcing themselves up into the storm of war above them. The fortress was full of Norsemen. More than Sir Hans could believe. In the rain, the besiegers could not pour crossbow bolts into the battlements, could not use fire arrows or try to burn the gate. The assault had degenerated into a vicious and one-sided brawl, several thousand Crusader soldiers trying to get up a few dozen ladders, with a rain of rocks and arrows hammering down on them. For those who did make it to the top, long spears and wicked broad axe blades waited.

It was hopeless. He saw a man refuse to go up a ladder, trapped in horror at the base as the man in front of him fell with a spear wound in the throat. Sir Hans stepped forward to take the man's place himself, to gather them for one last effort, and then the horn to retreat sounded. Relieved, he jumped back down into the muddy morass and waved at the men to withdraw, missiles and jeers following them until they were out of range.

'How many of our men did we lose?' asked Adolf.

'Forty-two men from our contingent, my lord,' Sir Hans reported glumly. 'Around five hundred men of the Crusade in total. It was utterly impossible, the enemy is two deep on the entire wall, with enough missiles to drown an army.' He shrugged. 'I don't think we could take that wall with two hundred ladders of men, we need to lay a proper siege.'

'We don't have time, we have what, three days at most before the Norse army arrives? Maybe only two. If we don't secure that fortress, our position is greatly weakened.'

Sir Hans spread his hands in frustration. 'We will break our army on that wall if we try again the same way. We must wait for trebuchets, they will open it like a rotten barrel.'

'The trebuchets won't be set up for another day at least.'

'Then we must find another way. You cannot take that fortress by escalade, not in the rain, not while they are so well prepared.'

The next morning, the ladders went up again. Adolf watched helplessly as four thousand Frenchmen assaulted the fortress. The rain had subsided from the storm the previous day, but the ground in front of the walls was a quagmire of knee-deep mud, obstacles, bloating bodies and a chest-deep ditch filled with water and spikes.

The French infantry had advanced gamely enough, then they reached the mud and their formation started to slow and disorganise. The defenders on the wall merely watched, jeering and hooting, their disdain audible even from the low rise where Hans and Adolf stood. When the first French, now totally exhausted and disorganised, finally reached the wall, then the missiles started falling, picking off the first men, the bravest and the fastest.

The whole mass of muddy, helpless attackers, struggling under the weight of nearly fifty ladders, stalled at the flooded ditch and wall base and died by the dozen. Ladders did start going up, but jubilant defenders simply pushed them down one by one, the French unable to get enough purchase in the muddy ground to keep them steady. Not a single Crusader made the top of the wall.

Sir Hans was horrified watching the carnage. 'Why did they attack again? What did they expect?'

Adolf shook his head sadly. 'Our wise commander said the last attack failed because the German contingent was insufficiently determined, and that the superior French troops would be able to carry the walls. I told them it was impossible, I fear that merely made him more determined to try.'

'What an appalling waste of men, we will regret that sorely when the Norse arrive.'

Adolf nodded. 'Two days, or so our scouts tell us, and then they will be here. Our reinforcements about the same.'

'What will happen if the Norse arrive before our men?' Sir Hans asked.

'Nothing. This ground is terrible for a battle, there is no room to manoeuvre, it will be an easy place to defend. We have dug defensive ditches and ramparts across the whole right flank. We could hold this area with half this number against all the armies of the world and we have the fleet at our back to supply us. Let them come and fester in that muddy farmland, much good it will do them.'

Hans smiled and looked back once more at the retreating French. 'So some good news, then.'

'Not really, we will have the same problems getting out as they will have getting in. we will have to slog across that same sodden farmland, no hope of using cavalry, no flank to turn, only woods and marsh beyond. It will be horrific. We will be trapped here if they decide to block us in. This damn storm has sunk us like a rotten ship.'

'I had no conception of how hard it would be to move so many men about in our own land,' said Sigurd, standing sodden by the rough road as the army continued to go past. 'We are still a day from the Crusader lines, and the army is almost ruined. Seven days, marching back and forth in this mud and filth.'

Jark Kjartan looked on grimly as the miserable army slowly wound past them. There were no jokes or cheers as the men passed their king, most probably didn't notice he was standing there. 'We have never made war like this before, not in our whole history. The Christians do this all the time. Big armies, long marches, bad weather. The bastards love it. I bet they are sitting in that port thinking this is fine campaigning weather. I have no idea how the gods could curse us with this unseasonal storm. I can't remember the like of it before.'

Sigurd grunted in agreement. 'It seems a poor fate that has been laid out for us. At least they haven't captured the fortress yet, the rain has done something for us as it curses us with this misery. My scouts tell us two full assaults and a night-time surprise attack have been repelled. But the Christians nearly have their siege engines ready. When they are done, it's only a matter of time.'

'We must give battle tomorrow, then, and try and push through to the fortress.'

'Yes, tomorrow we will repay them for this wet hell.'

Rangvald stood behind his men, half the morning they had been waiting for orders or news from the rest of the army. He could see the Christian line ahead, a rough mud and stick rampart with a line of shields and helmets visible at the top, perhaps five hundred paces across the fields in front of him.

The Norse had watched, helpless, as the Christian fleet arrived in the harbour below them and disgorged another ten thousand men and a huge number of horses, just as they themselves had arrived the previous day.

It had been too late for them to organise an attack that evening, and the army was exhausted. Instead, they waited for the next day and prepared to attempt to relieve the fortress. They could see the fortress now from the rise where King Sigurd had placed his tent. There were two gaping holes in the wall, hastily and roughly barricaded by the defenders. The two trebuchets were about to be joined by two more, the only thing preventing them from flattening the thin wooden walls atop the fortress rampart being a lack of suitable stone in the small Christian-controlled strip of land. But the new ships had brought more in their ballast and, even now, Ragnvald could hear the occasional thump or crunch as a missile hit home a short distance to his front, beyond a small wood that obscured his view of most of the battlefield.

'Where the fuck is the messenger?' he shouted for the fourth or fifth time. The orders for the attempt to relieve the fortress had been very simple: Ragnvald was in charge of the left flank, and was not to attack until the main assault on the right was ready, otherwise it would be wasted. 'Await the messenger,' Sigurd had emphasised. Now, half the morning gone, his men standing bored in their lines in the still soggy fields, no message had come. Due to the lie of the gently undulating land, Ragnvald couldn't even see the rest of the army. Small patches of woodland, rolling fields, small rises and areas of marsh littered the entire stretch of land. It was, he thought, utterly hopeless ground to fight on.

As the sun reached its zenith in the sky, his men sitting on their haunches or even lying on shields trying to catch some sleep, a man on a stout pony finally slogged his way across the churned-up ground to the rear and made a beeline for Ragnvald.

'Lord Ragnvald, you are to attack when you hear horns on your right flank.'

'Fucking fantastic, what took so long?'

The messenger waved back the way he had come. 'The ground is flooded and marshy all across the front, the right has barely got into position, and the centre is almost impassable.'

'So, how long until the horn will blow?'

'I don't know, King Sigurd knew it would take me a long time to get here, you are the furthest from his position, but didn't know how long to allow.' The scout shook his head. 'This earth is cursed with water, each contingent cannot see the next, passing messages takes too long.'

'Okay, so we attack on the horn. When do we stop attacking?'

The messenger gaped dumbly. 'Uh, I wasn't told.'

'So, we can't see the rest of the army, I've got thousands of men here scratching their arses and getting wet and bored, we attack when we hear a horn blown by men we can't see, and then we just… what? Make up the rest for ourselves? Do we attack until we are all dead or do we pull back not knowing if it is too early?' Ragnvald was beside himself now, shouting at the hapless messenger, who just shook his head apologetically.

'The king was extremely busy, nothing was going according to plan, I'm sorry, he didn't give any more instructions.'

Ragnvald kicked the ground in frustration, only succeeding in splattering mud halfway up his leg. He waved the messenger away furiously and turned away from the poor man, looking at the back of his lines again in near despair. Leif trudged out from the line towards him.

'Any message for the king?' asked the harried messenger as he turned his horse to leave.

'Hurry the fuck up! No, don't tell him that. Shit, there is no point passing a message, it won't get to him before the battle is over.'

The messenger nodded and he heard the horse squelching away behind him.

Leif arrived at his side, eyes asking the question his mouth repeated. 'What is going on?'

'That message was that we are to wait for the signal to attack, which is when we hear horns.'

'That's it?'

'That's it.'

'This is madness. We have lost half the day.'

'This is war, as I am increasingly learning. It's nothing like raiding or fighting small warbands. It's utterly shit. I want to go and fight just to be done with the waiting. But we wait for the horn, and hope someone knows when to blow it, or in fact that we will even hear it from here.'

Ragnvald stood, hands on hips, staring at the Christian line, so close he could have shouted at them, if he could be bothered.

'I think I realise now that we are good fighters, but I think we are shit at making war. The king is in command, but can't see half his army, messages take so long to pass that half the day is wasted. We should have local commanders for each part of the army who make their own decisions. It's simply too big to have a single plan and a single commander. I bet the Christians do this better.'

'They are still not attacking?' asked Adolf, walking over to where Sir Hans stood, behind the wall on the right of the Crusader positions.

'No, they just stand there. It must be a distraction. The attack must be elsewhere.'

'Well, they only just arrived opposite our positions on the left, there is nowhere else to attack. I suspect they are just struggling in the mud.'

'We are sure they cannot attack in the centre?'

'Absolutely, it's a bog, with no way through. We actually lost a man scouting it, drowned in the mud right in front of his fellows. It's appalling, no army can pass there. We have a division covering it anyway, we have more men than we can use.'

Sir Hans screwed his brows up. 'So what are they doing?

'That is the question, Hans, that is the question,' Adolf said with his arms crossed on his chest as he stared at the stationary Norse ranks.

'Ragnvald, the horn!'

Ragnvald was deep in thought, staring at his half-sunken shoes, trying to work out how the army could improve its planning and communication. He snapped out of it and looked up. He couldn't hear anything, other than the grumbling and chatting of his men.

'Are you sure? I hear nothing,' he shouted back at Leif.

'Certain, it blew twice.' Other men around Leif nodded in agreement.

Shit. I didn't hear anything. What if it was just a man blowing a horn, not THE horn signal we were waiting for? Doubt and frustration boiled over in his mind and he snapped to a decision.

'Fuck it, let's attack, I'm done waiting anyway.' He turned to the man behind him. 'Blow the horn, signal shield wall. When it's formed, we will signal the attack.' The man nodded and put the big war horn to his lips and blew it, a single long note followed by three short blasts.

All over the fields, men stood, shook cramped limbs awake and spread out into line. Commanders started shouting at their men, cajoling and encouraging. The four thousand men under Ragnvald's command were mostly Swedish, split into three blocks, The heavily armed warriors to the fore were forming into a wall six hundred men across, four ranks deep, lighter armed men and skirmishers on the flanks, archers behind, all together the force covering five hundred paces of front. Ahead of them, the Crusaders saw the movement, heard the horn and got back into their line on the rough hip-height wall.

The men of the main shieldwall were ready now, in one solid line of lindenwood shields topped with protruding helmets, weapons and resting on a forest of cloth and wool wrapped legs. A burly axeman stepped out from the line and raised his long axe at the Christian lines, shouting incomprehensible insults at them. Somewhere in the line, the shield song started. Men hammering their pommels or axe heads against their shields in time. A slow, steady beat that gained in volume as more and more joined in.

The shield song reached its crescendo and Ragnvald nodded to the horn blower: the men were ready. The man raised his horn and blew the attack. A long blast and a short one, repeated over and over, the timing of a shield wall advancing in lock step. It served as a signal, and also a way of getting the wall to set off and maintain order as they got into the rhythm of the advance.

The whole line started moving forwards across the flat, muddy ground. The line of shields to the fore held at an angle so as not to foul each other, waiting for the first missiles to fly before they would raise them.

'Here they come!' shouted a man on the wall. Sir Hans heard the horn, he had started to think they might not attack that day, but now, in the early afternoon, the assault was finally happening. He could hear horns to his left as well, faint and distant further down the line.

'MAN THE WALL!' he roared at the men sitting behind it or resting with their backs to the earthen barricade. All along the line, men scrambled to their feet, picked up their weapons and strapped helmets on heads. He had let them sit and rest to keep them fresh, now they reformed in moments, to present a solid topping of steel and flesh on the barricade they stood behind. Behind them, cross-bowmen readied their weapons, putting their feet into the stirrups on the front of their bows and hauling back on the string to cock them. Archers carefully arranged handfuls of arrows in the earth in front of them, fletchings separate and spread out, for easy access.

The Norse line was halfway across the field now, two hundred or so paces distant. Sir Hans raised his hand and held it there. At a hundred paces, he judged the moment and brought his hand down. The crossbows cracked and the bows hummed and a thousand missiles passed over and around his head and shot out towards the Norse line.

'SHIELDS!' roared Ragnvald and other men up and down the line. The first rank dropped to their knees mid-pace and stuck the bottom edges of their shields into the ground, kneeling behind them, heads tucked in. the men in the second rank held their shields flat, above and behind the front rank, so that only a few feet and heads were visible from the front. A hail of bolts and arrows struck the line, most missing entirely or hitting shields. Some did find their mark and men screamed in pain or fell back to the ground.

'ARCHERS!' shouted Ragnvald, but they were already

moving, they knew their business. The line of archers ran up to the rear rank of the shield wall, even as a second volley of arrows hit it, and raised their bows. They started firing, not timed together, but in a continuous stream as each man aimed and loosed as fast as he could. They did not drop their shafts onto the front line of the Christians, but behind it, at where the unseen enemy archers fired from. Their arrows crossed with a third Christian volley mid-flight, and from then on each side was firing as fast as they could load. The Christians more numerous, the Norse better protected behind the shield wall.

The incoming volleys reduced in intensity and became more ragged as Christian archers were hit or slowed down, dodging shafts or looking for cover. Ragnvald nodded to the horn blower again. 'Sound the rapid advance.'

He blew the horn, rapid staccato blasts this time. The front rank stood and started jogging down the field, shields held out in front, the rest of the ranks following at intervals, leaving a sparse line of dead and wounded behind them on the field. The archers remained where they were, emptying their quivers at the hidden Christian archers to cover the advance.

The Norsemen ran down the field until they were just thirty paces from the wall and then the horn blew again. A single long note: the halt. The front rank stopped and reformed, almost spit-ting distance from the wall, too close to it for the enemy archers to hit them, too far away for thrown spears to be dangerous. The next three ranks reformed behind them in moments and the final horn signal blew, the advance again. The front rank locked shields and stamped forwards together, moving as one, spears reaching out above joined shields, axes held waiting over the rims, swords lurking, waiting to stab or slash over the top.

'Steady!' shouted sergeants up and down the Christian line. Sir Hans was impressed and disappointed. His archers had been much less effective than he expected. Caught out by the deployment of the double shield wall and then the return fire, they had quickly lost effectiveness and their aim became wild. When the Norse charged to close the distance, they had been too slow to adjust their aim, missiles falling mostly behind the enemy, until they could not fire for fear of hitting their own men.

He could see perhaps fifty Norsemen lying out in the field in shapeless bundles, more limping or crawling to the rear; more of his own archers, unarmoured and defenceless, lay in the mud around him, shafts feathering the ground and their bodies.

The Norse line was pounding on towards contact, deliberate and menacing and imposing. Warriors shouting insults and curses over their shields, Crusader soldiers shouting back and readying their weapons.

The Norse line suddenly shuddered ten paces from the wall and gaps appeared as men stepped up to throw spears and small axes. The unexpected shower of heavy missiles from spitting distance tore a number of holes in the defenders as spears punched past shields or axes thumped into faces or tore arms. Screaming men fell back from the low wall and then with a great roar the Norse arrived at it, still in one solid mass.

Spears from both sides struck first, stabbing at heads and gaps between shields. The legs of both sides were protected by the wall as the Norse line closed to touching distance. Men fell on both sides, gaps opened in the ranks, to be rapidly closed by men from behind. Then the lines almost locked together over the barricade in a furious cacophony of noise. Over a thousand men in the front ranks, battering at each other with iron and steel, the devil's orchestra of noise and fury.

Norsemen leaned forwards to hack over the barricade with

long axes, Christians covered themselves with their shields or stabbed back with spears. The fight degenerated into a bloody stalemate within moments. The Norse line was unable to step forwards over the wall, any man who tried having to raise his shield to climb up, and instantly being struck down underneath it.

The roar of shouting men and hammering steel was deafening, even to Sir Hans, standing behind the line in his faceless helm.

I know that helmet, thought Ragnvald, looking over the press of furiously hacking men at the Christian knight in the dirty green coat and the steel-faced helm. *He was at the ford in Denmark*. He was certain – he had never seen another Christian with a helm like that. The Christian knight was shouting orders at men, directing reinforcements to weak spots in the line, waving and pointing as Ragnvald's thousands of warriors struggled for an opening, a weak point in the line, oblivious to the stare of the Norse lord opposite him.

'Give me a spear!' he shouted at the rear rank men around him. A light spear was picked up off the ground and passed to him. He stepped back two paces, watching the knight, lining up his shot. It was a long one, the knight was twenty paces away, in full armour, shield held in front but low, mostly covering his groin and legs. His chest was exposed. A small target at twenty paces, throwing while standing in mud.

He waited until the knight was looking away, down the line, until that steel-faced helmet would blind him to the threat from the side. Ragnvald cocked back his arm and threw, grunting with the effort. It was a powerful throw, straight and true, shaft wobbling as it passed a few handspans over the fighting lines and then seemed to pause, floating in the air, before it gracefully swooped down towards the green-coated Crusader knight.

The knight started turning back to his front, body twisting

too late to avoid the spear but preventing it hitting him square in the side. It struck him at an angle just below his left shoulder, the force throwing him to the ground, helm flying off, shield flapping on his left arm, and he was gone from Ragnvald's view.

'Got him!' he shouted in triumph, pumping his fist in the air. Men who had seen the throw snarled and shouted their curses at the enemy over the wall. The Christians nearby wavered, some looking back over their shoulders to see what had happened as cries of alarm sounded from behind their line. Several men rushed to the downed knight and the line on the wall sagged, just half a pace.

'NOW! NOW, MEN OF ODIN!' Ragnvald screamed at the line in front of him. A handful of burly rear-rankers, long axes in hand, shoved men in front of them to the side and threw themselves at the wall, men shielding their flanks as they swung murderous blows at the cowering Christian infantry, forcing them further back, some falling to sickening impacts on helmets or shoulders. Ragnvald saw one helmet split in half, gore and blood spraying from the gap and from under the rim of the helmet of the unfortunate man.

There was a moment where the push stalled, an axeman went down with a spear in his gut and tripped another, both falling back into their fellows, but then there was a rush of warriors into the cleared space and in moments, the wall belonged to the Norse for ten paces in each direction.

The Norse line poured over the low wall and pushed the enemy back almost at a run. The defenders peeled away from the barricade like a strip of bark being torn from a tree, the Christians unable to stay on the wall as they were each flanked in turn. Within fifty heartbeats, a breach one hundred paces wide was formed until the Christians finally stopped the rot by committing reserves onto the ends and front of the bulge.

Ragnvald stepped up onto the wall to look over the fighting, shouting encouragement to his men and, as he stood up and looked beyond the Christian positions, his shout died in his throat.

A hundred paces beyond the fight, a long, deep line of Crusader infantry waited. A thousand paces long, six ranks deep. An overwhelming force. Even as he watched, enemy captains shouted at the line, and it started rumbling forwards.

Sir Hans lay and looked at the sky, confused and in agony. He could hear fighting in front of him, he could not understand what had happened. He had been shouting orders when a huge, piercing blow had hit his chest under his shoulder, fire still burned there under his maille. But something had hit him in the head and it felt... wrong.

He struggled to get to his feet but couldn't, limbs refusing to work, fuzzy and indistinct. Someone was over him, cradling his head, shouting at someone else, he couldn't work out what. Someone else was pouring hot water on his shoulder. That was really weird, why were they doing that? He looked down at his shoulder, begging his eyes to focus.

Oh, no, not hot water; blood. Blood was soaking his shoulder, running down through the maille in rivulets as someone helped him sit up. *Oh, shit*, he thought, and then he passed out.

'Blow the retreat!' shouted Ragnvald desperately, waving at the signaller. The Christian reinforcements had nearly arrived now, the men in the wall in front of him were still pushing forwards, Christians giving ground and bleeding space and lives steadily. Some looked back at him, confused that he was calling a retreat in their moment of victory. But then the horn blew, and the discipline of the warriors slowly won over their battlerage. The line shuffled back and awkwardly clambered over the wall, fending off the half-hearted counter-attack of the relieved Crusader infantry. And then the new division arrived. Unable to charge due to the solid wall of allies to their front, they added their weight to the line and caused it to rapidly push forward, ejecting the last of the Norsemen from their side of the wall and reclaiming the whole line.

There was a moment of relative calm as the Norse line edged backwards from the wall and the Crusaders declined to give chase. The ragged Norse line reformed, ready for a counter-attack, and the two sides stared at each other from twenty paces, exchanging a desultory patter of missiles and insults.

Eventually, with no chance of assaulting the wall again and unable to taunt the Crusaders into leaving its safety to assault across the muddy open ground, Ragnvald reluctantly sounded the retreat and his army turned and walked back across the open fields, the jeers of the enemy burning in their ears.

The mood in the Norse camp that evening was sour as week-old milk. The attack on the right had been repelled too, more by the land than by the Christians. On ground unsuitable for even two thousand men to attack, over five thousand Norse had tried to force their way across against an equal number of defenders. A whole afternoon of pointless pushing at shields had resulted in not much more than a muddy and confusing brawl. The Norse had not made it even halfway to the fortress and had lost a thousand warriors trying.

By the time the whole army had returned to the camp, it was nearly midnight. In the morning, the king called a meeting on the rise overlooking Helsingborg, to decide on a new course of action to relieve the fortress, only for the commanders to sit there and watch it be attacked again, too late and too far away to do anything about it.

The wall of the fortress facing the Crusader camp was a mess, a mire of churned-up earthen berm topped with shattered wooden palisades. In bright sunshine, the lords of the North watched in silence as thick columns of Crusader infantry advanced over the drying ground and forced their way up and into the breeches. Twice, the determined defenders forced them back, horns blowing and jeers floating across the fields as the attackers retreated.

By the third assault, visibly fewer defenders lined the crest. The Crusader archers massed forwards, the arrows flew in both directions, and then the blocks of armoured infantry surged up the slope once again. This time they did not retreat. After a while of vicious fighting, steel flashing even at that distance, the Crusaders pushed over the lip and poured into the fortress. The golden cross was raised over the gatehouse, and it was over.

CHAPTER 16

RETREAT AND REPERCUSSIONS

WATCHING THE FORTRESS fall, helpless to prevent it, took the fire out of the Norse army. The king particularly fell into a black mood. Ragnvald went to stand across from the big man, still sitting on a bench outside his tent, elbows on his knees, silently watching the Crusader camp and the fallen fortress as the sun started to set.

'King Sigurd, we must make plans for tomorrow,' Ragnvald said softly, as behind him a group of jarls watched and waited. 'This is a setback, but we still have our army, and the Crusaders are still contained. We have not lost.'

There was a silence and Ragnvald wondered if the king had even heard him; he stepped forward to speak again, louder, but the king interrupted him.

'My cousin was commanding that fortress,' the king said, his voice blunt and his body still unmoving. 'He was my childhood friend, hunting companion, shield brother. I fought my first fight alongside him, raiding a rebellious jarl's village in the fjordlands.

I took my oath to my father alongside him, I fucked my first girl while he kept watch outside for her parents. The last time I saw him, I swore I would come for him if he needed it.' The king fell silent again, the silence between them stretching.

'You did what you could my lord, your cousin died well and—'

'Stop lying to me, Ragnvald, trying to make me feel better. You least of all can think I need it after what we have been through. I am not sulking, I am thinking. You say we need a plan, I think I should stop making them by holding meetings. My intent gets diluted, and then in the battle no one knows my mind. No,' the king stood up, 'from now on I will form the plan, I will consult some key men I trust on it, and then I will spell it out to the other jarls, make clear the intent and purpose, and then leave them to conduct it according to my instructions.'

Ragnvald paused and straightened. 'I see, I had some thoughts on the problem and I...'

'And I will not hear them, for my mind is made up on the matter.' The king stared at Ragnvald levelly. 'Take no offence, when I need your advice I will ask for it, and it will happen often, but on this matter, I have thought deeply, and my will is iron.'

Ragnvald was concerned. Was this an overreaction?

'From now on, we will dispense with the need to make everyone feel included, the company of friends and equals. In planning I will lead, and everyone else will follow. In battle I will give each commander their instructions, and leave them to command their men until those instructions change or they think of something better. Yesterday was a disaster because I spent too long taking opinions, and then tried to command the entire battle myself according to the muddled ideas and reports of others.'

Ragnvald frowned. 'I am not sure that is entirely correct.'

'It took you half a day to attack on the left, why?' said the king, his expression unreadable.

'Because I was waiting for your order.'

'And when you attacked, did you think it worthwhile? Did it achieve anything?'

Rangvald pursed his lips and considered it before speaking. 'No, I thought the attack pointless, the enemy were held in place by my presence, we had no hope of the attack succeeding, so it was a futile gesture.'

'So why did you commit to a futile attack?'

'Because it was your order.'

'Exactly. You waited half a day, for an order you knew would come, an order that I gave because another jarl suggested it and I thought it reasonable, an order to attack a position I had not seen, that you yourself could see was pointless. We even delayed the main attack to wait for you to get your orders to do the pointless thing. It was supposed to be a distraction, but it was a distraction only to us. You should have had the freedom to attack or not as you saw fit in the wider plan. I should not have waited for my order to reach you to start the main assault. So can you not see that my proposed way is better?'

Ragnvald thought about it again. 'It doesn't matter if I think it is better, if that is what you have decided, that is what we will do.'

'Good answer, because I didn't care what you thought about it.' Sigurd clapped a meaty hand on the jarl's shoulder. 'Again, take no offence, it is merely that this is a new type of war for us, and we must adapt or lose. We are no longer friends, I am your commander and you will follow when I order, and give wise counsel when I ask, or I will replace you with someone who will.' Ragnvald nodded stiffly under Sigurd's flat and emotionless stare, and the man turned to look at the rest of the gathered jarls, gathered at a respectful distance out of earshot.

'They chose you to prompt me into action?'

'Yes.'

'Good, they trust you and look up to you, you are now my second, to take over if I fall. Not the kingship, the command of the army. If I die, there is not to be another king until we win, it is a distraction now, a vanity.'

'As you say, my lord.' Ragnvald was flustered. There were other, more powerful jarls in the army who might object strenuously to his sudden command and status, Jarl Kjartan perhaps. But the king was ploughing on with his instructions, not even looking at him.

'Explain the new way to the rest of them. I am finishing my plan of our next moves, I will explain it shortly, when they have heard from you.' With that, the king walked off towards his tent, leaving the silent group of jarls in his wake looking worriedly at Ragnvald for an explanation. He set his jaw and went over to explain the new way of things.

The jarls gathered later that morning, standing around uneasily, and listened to Sigurd's orders. 'Tomorrow we will retreat from this place.' There was an instant surge of protest from the assembled men.

'But we are undefeated!'

'We will be shamed!'

'We must try again.'

Waves of protest ran around the gathering.

'SILENCE!' roared Sigurd. And the gathering fell to muttering and shock. 'We cannot attack them where they camp. We cannot besiege them, they have limitless supply by sea while we ourselves are running out of food. This army will fall apart into sickness and despair if we just sit in this wet land. The Crusaders don't need to attack to defeat us, they must merely wait.'

He glared around the room. 'This war isn't about our honour, our pride, our self-belief. This war is about our survival. We have lost here, but we still have our strength and we will preserve it for another day.'

There was another round of dismayed protest and Jarl Oddvar, a Norwegian warlord with one of the largest warbands, spoke up. 'My king, if we retreat from this place, how will we find a better place to fight them? There is nothing to the south but farmland between us and the rest of the coastal towns. Nowhere we can better stand and fight than here.'

'Indeed, and we will not fight them there, on the coast. We will fight them inland, when the ground hinders them, and the weather weakens them.'

There was shocked silence. 'You will not defend the coastal towns? You mean to let the Christians take them?' said Jarl Espen, a Danish jarl with lands in the area under threat.

'Yes. We will garrison the strong towns and abandon the weak ones. This army will not fight in the open against the Crusaders.'

'My king! This is madness!' another Danish jarl shouted, voice desperate. 'The army will think this to be cowardice and desert you!' Other men bristled at the word cowardice and a heated argument started. Again, the king shouted for silence. Again, it fell reluctantly. Sigurd waited for calm and continued, firm and unswayed.

'No, they will not desert, for they are dismissed.' The shock and silence that followed this pronouncement was absolute. 'We were mistaken to fight the Crusaders on their terms, in a grand battle, thinking of glory and easy victory. None was possible. They will always have more men, they will always be stronger in the field where they have the experience and the advantage. You think that is cowardice, Jarl Espen?'

The jarl looked around and replied, 'Aye.' The open accusation lay between the older jarl and the young king like a cloud. Men have been executed for less, but the king didn't even bat an eyelid at the dread insult.

'The commanders before the battle outside Ribbe probably thought the same, when someone suggested waiting for the other forces to reach them. "But we will lose another town," some must have said. "It will dishonour us," perhaps others said. But we will never know. Why?'

Sigurd looked around the gathering, his glare sweeping around every man in the space. No one answered.

'Because they are fucking dead,' he said viciously. 'Their towns are burned, their families are slaves, their land is lost. All to the cause of their honour and bravery.' Sigurd blazed on, anger in his voice. 'I will not throw this army away in the first days of this war just to assuage your need for glory or prove that I am not a coward. Let our descendants say I was a coward if they will, I will just be pleased they are alive to say it.'

Jarl Espen visibly deflated and stepped back. Sigurd ignored him as he continued.

'We are not trained in this way of war, our army is weakened by its size, not enhanced. We will not fight them in one quick and glorious battle, we will bleed them. We will slow them. We will make them suffer on the walls of our towns, starve in the ruins of our fields, be picked off on our blades in the night.'

Sigurd stepped forwards and spoke to each of the silent men in turn as he walked through the crowd placing hands on shoulders as he went. 'We will raid and harass and deny them sleep or shelter or food. Our ships will chase theirs away, burn them, sink them, run them aground, until they cannot supply themselves by sea. We will burn our fields and empty our barns in front of them. We will bleed this Crusader army white, let them be tested in the winter snows and THEN... then, when they have been worn down to the spine, then we will gather this great army once again and finish them.'

He stopped and looked around the room. Men were looking

uncomfortably back at him, confusion and inspiration visibly competing for control of their emotions. The moment hung by a thread, rebellion against the king seeming possible.

'Go back to your homes, those of you who are far from them. Gather the harvest, make weapons, train your men over the winter and let them grow strong in home comforts. Bide your time, and when I call for you in the spring, then return. The local men, those whose homes are within marching distance of the enemy, and my own men, will harass and slow the Christians until then.'

The king straightened and swept his stern gaze standing around him. 'The Leidang is disbanded.' For a long moment nobody moved, the shock of the defeat and dissolution of their army rooting them to the spot. Many of the jarls were looking around the group, trying to judge the balance of opinion, some were visibly angry, the moment oozed menace.

Into that moment Ragnvald stepped forwards, the first man to move, he stepped out of the small crowd towards the impassive figure of the king and nodded to him.

'As you command, King Sigurd.'

Ragnvald walked past without looking back and left the hall. And with that, the resistance sagged out of the room, the meeting, and then the next day the army, which dispersed.

Sir Hans couldn't open his eyes, they refused to work. His head was roiling, his body felt detached, almost unknown. He realised he could hear people talking, somewhere in this fuzzy dream-world. 'What happened to him?' the first voice said, somewhere in the darkness.

'He took a spear to the chest, it struck him at an angle, hit a rib and then ripped out under his armpit. He fell and hit his head on a rock, knocked his helmet off and his senses out,' another voice replied, louder and closer.

'Fuck. Will he live?'

'Impossible to say, the wound to the chest will heal with time, if it doesn't turn sour, which it still might. The blow to the head? You never know, some men's brains are broken forever, some wake up suddenly in the following day and are fine. He woke up and spoke after the wound, in my experience that is good news.'

'Do what you can for him, if you need...' The voice shrank and grew quieter in the blackness. Sir Hans reached out to it with invisible hands, he could feel them, but not see them. Then, the voices were gone.

Adolf ducked past the flap leading from the healing tent, still queasy from the carnage that lay within. He had seen a few battle-fields, but he never got used to the aftermath, even in victory. Another thirty or so of his men either lay within the tent or in the burial pits alongside the coast. The army had lost several thousand in the siege and the battle, but his contingent was being hard used. One in five of the men he had brought to the northlands this year were already lost from the battleline.

The queasiness he felt from his visit to the medical tents paled compared to the feeling he had entering the command tent. Count Baldwin of Flanders, the Crusade commander, was engaging in an orgy of self-congratulation. All the Crusade commanders were taking turns to obsequiously pay homage to his victory, for fear of missing out on the spoils and glory of future victory, or worse.

Adolf walked into the tent for the command meeting, hoping that at least some of the meeting would be about future plans. He had arrived still in his armour, sweat from a hot day on horseback cloying his arming shirt and wool chausses underneath the maille, hair plastered to his now bare head. It was the evening of the battle, and since checking on his men, both living and wounded, he had not had time to change.

When the scene inside revealed itself, he ground his teeth in anger. Most of the men present were dressed for dinner. Bathed, clean, relaxed. Judging by the crowded space, he must have been almost the last man to arrive. As he came to a stop and looked around him, he saw the Count of Flanders reclining on his ludicrous throne-like chair and staring at him in undisguised mirth, several of his aides standing by him making snide remarks and laughing to each other. Servants were walking around with jugs of wine and platters of tender food.

'Nice of you to join us, my dear count!' called Baldwin from the throne. 'It's a shame you didn't use that delay to dress appropriately.' The count looked beside himself with glee.

'I came from a battlefield, my lord count, I didn't want to ruin my best clothes by fighting in them.' The counter was weak, but he was furious.

'Well, you are still in time to congratulate me on the victory, so all is well.' Baldwin gestured for men to make way, and a rough path appeared between the two. Adolf stood at the end as if made of stone.

'I surely will congratulate the commander of the assault, when I see him, it was most bravely and steadfastly done.' His tone was getting darker, anger seeping into his voice.

'The commander? Well, how fortunate, that is me,' the count said, mocking Adolf with his eyes, before extending a hand and gesturing him to approach.

'You commanded the assault, did you, Count Baldwin? Tell me, how was it climbing that slope in the face of the enemy, what was the view from the top like once you gained it?' The amused chatterings and whispered remarks died down to a stony silence as the insult landed. Adolf knew at once he had gone too far.

The smug smile died on Baldwin's lips. 'I *command*, Count Adolf, lesser men like you obey my orders. Men who forget how to speak to their betters should not speak at all. If you are so keen to know what it is like to assault a fortress and stand on the brink, I assure you, next time, you and your men will find out.' The French lord leaned forwards, sneering. 'Now, this celebration is for those with the dress and the breeding for it. You have neither, so be gone.'

Adolf went red in the face and was about to snap back a retort when he saw Duke Welf off to one side, vigorously shaking his head and beckoning Adolf to leave. Unfortunately, Baldwin looked around and saw it too. 'Ahh, look, your master dismisses you.' Baldwin started a false and high laugh and looked away towards his companions, slapping his thigh, and his sycophants joined him in a chorus of mirth.

Adolf turned on his heel and stormed from the tent, avoiding the gaze of an embarrassed-looking Bavarian lord as he left.

The next morning, Adolf was still stewing as he ate his morning meal, meat and oatmeal, the same food his men ate. He heard boots approaching and looked up to see it was Sir Hugues. The man looked annoyed. Adolf sighed and put down his bowl.

'Don't start with me,' he said to the approaching man. 'No man can endure what he puts me through.'

'And yet, you must,' the French baron said, stopping in front of Adolf.

Adolf dashed his bowl to the ground and rose, hot anger filling his throat. 'That CHILD argued for four days that we should burst out of our lines and attack! Only through our efforts was he persuaded of the right course of action that led to this victory, and now he claims it as his own! He didn't even put fucking armour on, let alone fight.' Adolf jabbed his finger towards the distant command tent. 'Does he have no shame?'

'Yes, he does. That's why he behaves so.' That stumped Adolf for a moment, blunting the roiling anger that was flowing through every vessel in his body. 'That is why he is so intent on putting you down, humiliating you, because everyone in the army knows you are the real soldier, and he knows everyone knows that, and that your ideas lead the army, and he is ashamed and jealous.'

Adolf lowered his finger and scowled. 'They don't show it.'

'So what? They understand the game. Christ alive, Adolf, you might understand making war, but you have a terrible game of politics. He is winning, you know. Every time he makes you angry, makes you trade insults, he brings you down to his level. He makes you look less.' Hugues was looking disappointed. Adolf recoiled at it. 'Make yourself seem uncaring of his insults, make light jokes, show you are above it but do not mock him. He will make himself look stupid by attacking you to no effect, and thus stop attacking.'

There was silence as Adolf considered that. 'Won't that make him hate me more?'

'He hates you either way. Let me put this in military terms.' Adolf bridled at the patronising tone but said nothing. 'If you are attacking an opponent and you see it is working, what do you do? Continue, yes?' Adolf said nothing for the point was obvious. 'And if you see your attacks are futile and only harm your own forces? You stop? It matters not how much you hate your enemy. You stop attacking if it isn't working. You must show him it isn't working.' Adolf stared at the man in barely restrained fury.

'What is our purpose?' Hugues asked into the awkward silence.

'Victory, and the preservation of our men's lives,' mumbled Adolf through clenched teeth.

'And how will you achieve that if he won't listen to advice and if he sends you and your men to die in a futile attack?'

'We won't.'

'Then go and apologise, be submissive, seize the initiative

before he demands an apology, appear the better man you are, and hope it's not too late to recover the situation.'

'WHAT?' Adolf gaped at the smaller man. 'Never.'

Hugues shrugged and turned to leave. 'Then you have already lost.'

That hurt, that cut Adolf deeply. He *never* lost.

Adolf walked into the command tent with the air of a man going to the executioner's block. He was dressed in a clean, elegant but simple tunic and trousers this time. Not even wearing a sword, which until now he had always done on principle. He went through the door and saw, to his dismay, that the tent was packed and silent, Baldwin had been giving some sort of speech.

Baldwin stopped mid-sentence, gaping at the entrance, and everyone turned to look, leaving Adolf standing in a sea of silent gazes. Then a hint of a smile started forming on Baldwin's lips and he opened his mouth to speak.

Before he could make a noise, Adolf cut in. 'My lord, I am here to apologise for my behaviour last night.' Baldwin let out his breath with a sharp, short squeak, eyes going wide with surprise, the demand that Adolf apologise or leave dead in his throat, its barbs drawn by the statement.

'I had just come from the healing tents, where many of my men lay dead or badly wounded, including my leading vassal, and I forgot myself.' He paused for a moment to nod to himself sadly, eyes averted in not contrived regret. 'You are the commander, and no matter who conducts an action, you make the decisions and deserve the credit. Such is the nature of command. It was a fine victory yesterday and I salute you.'

Adolf bowed. Not a nod of the head, he bent at the waist and lowered a hand so that it nearly touched the ground, he held there for a moment and rose, head still inclined, face a mask of regret.

Around him, other lords and captains were making appreciative noises and comments to each other.

'He lost a lot of men.'

'Poor fellow, all day in that heat and no rest, makes men prone to incivility.'

Before the stunned French commander could reply, he continued. 'I have clearly interrupted an important meeting, so with your permission I shall withdraw.' He waited for Baldwin's response. The French count was about to explode in rage but then he looked around the room, judging the mood. Men were smiling at Adolf, nodding their appreciation for the gesture, one man patted him on the back.

Staring at Adolf with a new expression of appraisal, Baldwin stiffly replied. 'We thank you for your humble apology for your disgrace yesterday, and you may leave.' Adolf bowed deeply again and turned to leave, walking slowly from the room.

'Well, that surprised the shit out of me,' Duke Welfard said through a mouthful of roast pork as they shared dinner later than evening. 'I didn't think you had such humility in you. What on earth led to that display?'

'Oh, some good advice from a friend,' Adolf smiled in reply.

'Well, listen to him more often, he guides you well.' Duke Welf licked some errant grease from his fingers, ignoring the liberal stains on his cuffs, which were flecked with brown. 'Now, your son, he squires for one of my vassals, Sir Dietmar of Eresburg.'

'Yes.'

'A good man, good family stock.'

'So I hear.'

'I want him to join you.'

'To keep an eye on me?' said Adolf in amusement.

'Don't be ridiculous, no, to keep us better in contact, and ensure our forces work closely together.'

'So, to keep an eye on me,' snorted Adolf with a grin.

Welfard gave him a chiding look but conceded. 'Fine, to keep an eye on you, but also to ensure our forces work well together. Is this a problem?'

'No, it is not. I welcome the chance to have my son close to me.'

'I thought you might. Now, on the earlier subject of advice, what should we do next?'

CHAPTER 17

THE COMING OF THE CROSS

17th of July, year of our Lord 1117

Field report, north-west of Lund

Duke Welfard

*We have continued our scouting around the city of Lund. We
still can find no evidence of the main enemy force. We cannot
tell where the enemy army has gone. We have found fields with
crops deliberately set to ruin, abandoned villages and almost no
living soul. Only the city of Lund appears to contain life, we see
smoke from buildings within the town, even at this distance.*

*On our left side as we march the farmlands give way to forested
lowlands, there are paths into the woods but we do not explore
them deeply and to do so would slow us and risk ambush or
failure. We will continue our scouting around towards the south
coast and the reported fortress there. Perhaps the Norse army has
withdrawn to that fastness.*

Your obedient servant, Sir Dietmar

Adolf finished reading and dropped the unwelcome message onto the table. He shook his head in consternation at Duke Welfard, who was sitting across from him. 'Their army has vanished like a morning mist. We have no idea where they went. My scouting parties cannot find them in the south, the French cannot find them in the north, no one dares venture far into the forest in the east, it appears endless. Our fleet reports a large amount of activity of their ships but to no appreciable pattern.'

He tapped his fingers on the table, irritation rising in his chest. 'What the enemy is doing, I cannot discern. I begin to suspect the only answer is that their army has disintegrated or scattered.'

Duke Welfard furrowed his brows, his thick jowls creasing as he regarded Adolf with irritation. 'Disintegrated? Why on earth would they have done that? They retreated in good order after the battle and returned to their camp. Are you suggesting they are beaten after one small battle? That's absurd, Adolf.' The duke reached out for the pile of reports that sat in front of the count, his wide belly straining against the tabletop. He managed to retrieve the small stack and returned to his seat with a wheeze.

'You must be missing something, some subtle indication of the enemy plan.'

'I hope so, my lord, but I cannot think what it is. There is no one direction an army that size could have gone and not been seen or left a trace. They must have split up into many smaller groups.' Adolf scratched his chin as he ruminated over the problem.

'The report says we have not yet reached the south coast, then they must be there?' said Welfard, looking up from the scrap of parchment.

'Not unless they are stupid, the south coast is a trap, if they are there we could pin them against the sea on flat land and destroy them.'

Welfard snorted in derision. 'But you say they have dissolved their army after one battle, leaving the richest part of their lands undefended? Is that not more stupid?'

Adolf made a sour face. 'I just don't know, perhaps they had a splintering of the factions – they are really a dozen armies, not one, perhaps the defeat shattered their fragile alliance? Perhaps someone overthrew their king, perhaps they are in a civil war now… I need more information.'

Welfard struggled to his feet and shook his head. 'I don't know what to say to Count Baldwin, what course of action should I suggest? If the enemy army is dispersed, for whatever reason, should we not equally divide our men and sweep up every settlement and fortress for ten days' march around us?'

Adolf thought about this for some moments before sighing and responding. 'You may have it. That must be the point in dispersing, they hope for us to split up, and then they can pounce and defeat our parts one by one. We still have not scouted the eastern forest, they may be using it to travel around unseen.'

'You know Baldwin will not be persuaded by anything resembling fear, if we are to sway his course of action, we must have good reason.'

Adolf exhaled sharply and leant back. 'I don't even know what course of action to sway him towards, let alone how to do it. Half of me thinks we should be bold, take rapid decisive action, half of me says since the enemy is gone, we should take our time and ensure no trap has been set.' He chewed his fingernail as he thought for a few more moments. 'Perhaps, in this matter, we should simply let the count decide, uninfluenced.'

Duke Welfard let out a short sharp bark of laughter. 'You mean to tell me we should let the commander actually command!'

Adolf shrugged. 'Strange as it seems, yes. Let's save our schemes for when we know the right course of action.'

The light, when it finally came, was much brighter than Sir Hans remembered. The overbearing light became indistinct, fuzzy shapes, the fuzzy shapes grew heads and arms as they leaned over him. One of them stood up and called over its shoulder to something else. As the fog slowly cleared from his mind, he realised he was unbearably thirsty, he tried to open his mouth to ask for water, but the sound that came out was barely a croak, and carried no meaning.

One of the shapes reached down to comfort him, placed one hand under his head and lifted him, child-like, before placing a wooden bowl of some kind to his lips. Despite their cracked and dry state, Hans instantly felt the touch of the water within and opened his mouth desperately, leaden tongue reaching out for the sweet moisture. Too much water spilled into his mouth in his excitement, and his throat refused to swallow it properly. Coughing and spluttering as some reached his lungs with a pang of fire, he spilled most of the rest of the bowl down himself. His left shoulder exploded in pain as he coughed and, miserable, he lay back down on the bed with a groan.

Some hours passed as he slowly regained his senses and use of his body. He was given water at increasingly short intervals, and soon he was able to drink unaided with his good right arm, although the exertion left him feeling as weak as a newborn lamb. The indistinct shapes resolved into his squire and maidservant, the fuzziness around them into his tent.

'The count is coming to see you, sir, he will be most relieved and glad you are awake,' his squire said to him, a beaming smile on his face as he sat at the side of the military cot. 'I myself am very glad you are recovered.'

'I am far from recovered, lad,' Hans managed to whisper.

'What has happened? What of the battle today?' His squire looked confused. 'The battle of Lund? How would you know about it?'

'I think he means the Battle at Helsingborg, lad.' The new voice was Count Adolf, who strode into the room, dressed in full armour, dirty from a day in the field.

'I knew you would come back to us, Hans,' said the count, shooing the squire from his stool and sitting down on it heavily.

'What do you mean, Lund?' asked Hans, trying to lever himself up on one elbow.

'We just took the city of Lund, it was a tough siege. The battle of Helsingborg was two weeks ago.'

Sir Hans's mouth gaped open in shock. 'I have been asleep for two weeks?'

'Mostly, you awake sometimes, incoherent and panicking, but rapidly fall back to your slumber, and we feared it would be forever.' The beaming count took hold of Hans's hand, squeezing it gently. The cold mail of his hauberk sleeve rubbed up against Han's wrist.

'By God, I have not missed the victory, have I? If Lund is taken, we must have defeated their army?' Hans was visibly distraught, his pale face regaining its colour.

'No, the enemy army has dispersed. We still don't know why. Lund was defended only by some of its own people, their army deserted them.'

Hans's consternation only increased. 'They abandoned their city and dispersed? What madness have I fallen to? This cannot be real. I am surely having a night vision.'

Adolf laughed heartily. 'If so, then we all share it. But no, it is very real. The enemy army dispersed after our victory at Helsingborg and we advanced down the coast and have just taken Lund, I was in the assaulting force myself.'

'Why were you in the assault?'

'Because I have upset the commander one too many times, I think he was hoping I would conveniently die. Shame for him, I actually did rather well, not quite too old to swing a sword, eh?' Adolf had a mischievous grin on his face that intrigued Hans.

'Well, I have the time to listen to your story of heroism, if you want to explain,' said Sir Hans, settling down onto the cot and gently investigating his injured arm with his good one.

'I'm so glad you asked!' said Adolf, slapping his thigh with his hand. 'Yes, I will tell you the story of my heroics, but not now. Now you must rest, and I must get out of this stinking armour.' Adolf stood and patted the injured man on his good shoulder before turning and rustling out of the tent.

Two days later, a small convoy of ships arrived at the port near Lund. Work parties were still clearing the streets of debris and bodies which were dumped in the nearby river or burned in piles in the fields. The reek of death and decay was everywhere. The lead ship actually pushed through several small knots of bloated, floating corpses that littered the harbour at the mouth of the river.

On the deck of the largest vessel, a tall, thin man with short cropped hair held a bag of dried flowers to his nose in a vain attempt to block out the stench and looked on in distaste. His clothing was plain but of high quality and obviously clerical. His sandalled feet peered out from the folds of a full-length gown, long, billowing sleeves flapped in the brisk sea breeze. Despite the thick woollen garments and the hot sun, he did not appear to be sweating or uncomfortable.

The ship reached the dock and sailors took down the last sail and ran out a gangway to the shore. The man continued to observe the scene with disdain as sailors started unloading cargo and baggage down the narrow gangway, sure feet and steady hands accounting for the gentle rocking and swaying as if it was not there.

A small party of more austerely dressed priests appeared on deck from below and hurried over to join the man by the rail.

'Bishop Reinhard, your baggage is unloaded, shall we go to the dock?' one of the tonsured clergymen asked, hands clasped in front of him.

'You think we should step ashore without first giving the Lord our thanks for this safe passage?' the bishop snapped.

'No, of course, lord bishop, we await your prayer,' the man mumbled obsequiously, bowing and backing away a step.

'Are you unable to pray without my help? If you cannot intone a simple blessing without me, perhaps I will find more suitable work for you in the priory stables when we return.' The bishop's tone was icy, biting. He did not look at the apologetic priest as he admonished him, did not even take his eyes off the dock.

The bishop had good reason for not moving, for wanting to delay the disembarkation, for not wanting even to say a prayer or turn his head. The combination of the gentle swell and the stench of death had brought him to the very verge of voiding his stomach. He was fighting waves of nausea and pressing the bag desperately to his nose to quell his roiling innards. *I will not show this weakness at the very moment of my arrival*, he said to himself, desperately fighting his body for control.

Behind him, the priest who served as his assistant and secretary, Brother Bertrand, had finished his tedious and mercifully long blessing for their arrival. After gathering his courage and quickly crossing himself, Bishop Reinhard made his way unsteadily down the gangway onto the dock. At the bottom, a small party was waiting for him. Stomach still roiling, he glared at the waiting men and cast his withering eye on the man who was clearly their leader.

'Welcome to Lund, your eminence,' the man said, and he and his party all bowed low to Reinhard. 'I am...'

'I don't care who you are,' interrupted Reinhard, barely

looking at the man. 'Show me to my quarters and arrange for my people and my baggage to follow.' The man stuttered and then bristled briefly, before deciding against objecting to the foul-tempered bishop. He bowed again, the smile gone, and turning to walk towards a waiting wagon that would take them into Lund, he sent two of his companions off to see to the bishop's people and possessions.

Reinhard was not impressed by the lodgings. But then, he was rarely impressed with anything. The building was one of the grandest in the town of Lund, but in his opinion that was like saying one pile of shit in a pigsty was bigger than the others. The building was tall but managed to have only one floor, which was not even stone, but mostly earthen with some areas covered in boards. The building only had three rooms; one large bed chamber in which there was a bizarre bed, low down to the floor, and a number of intricately carved pieces of furniture. The other two rooms were the large main hall, and a hellhole of a privy. The entire building was dark and oppressive to his eyes, just a roof hole and some battered wooden shutters that opened into the street. Strange stone lamps lit the room to help with the little light that penetrated within.

The main room was huge and a mess. There had clearly been a fight, or just a lot of ransacking in this room, and no one had thought to tidy it up. Reinhard snarled with pure anger when he noticed a large blood stain in the earth on one side, near the wooden benches and chests that lined the sides of the room on raised wooden platforms.

The last room was the worst of all. He had expected a privy, instead there was a hole in the ground, a pile of filthy straw and the smell of the gates of hell itself. He was so disgusted, he once again had to force himself not to vomit.

'This will not do. How is a man of God supposed to go about

his business in a filthy, pagan pigsty like this?' he inquired in his icy tone to the man who had brought him here. He did not raise his voice, he never raised his voice, ever. He considered it a discipline, a point of self-control. And discipline was dear to the Lord. So he believed. If there was one thing he disliked above all others, it was men who had no self-control, no discipline. For him, such men had no value. No, when Reinhard was angry, which was most of the time, his voice merely got more chilled, more rasping, more menacing. He found it was stupendously effective at getting his way.

The dolt who had led him to this forsaken place spread his palms in apology. 'I am sorry, your eminence, but this is one of the best houses left in the city, some were destroyed or burned. His Lordship, Count Baldwin, was sure that this would be sufficient for your needs.'

'Don't make excuses or blame your lord, did Count Baldwin instruct you to leave the blood on the floor? To not make the privy usable? To make me, God's representative to his new flock in the North, sleep in a bed carved with the signs of the devil and his fallen demons?'

The man quailed and looked desperate. 'No, my lord bishop, he merely instructed me to bring you here, he said nothing of the conditions of the house, it is not my responsibility to make it suitable, I am merely to guide you here...'

'Ahh, so you expect your commander, who has to manage the entire Crusade, to tell you individually which rooms to clean and prepare? Should he also tell you to provide food, or water, or clothes, or when to wash, or when to relieve yourself? Tell me, fool, what else has the Crusade commander neglected to tell you to do, for I will go to him and tell him of your complaints later?'

The horrified man drained white and flapped his mouth like a landed fish. 'Please, your eminence, there is no need to trouble him... I... I will find a party of men to come and rectify this house immediately, it will be made as you wish it, I promise!' He was almost beside himself with fear by the end. *Good*, thought Reinhard, *exactly as he should be.*

Reinhard stared with disinterest at the man, as if pretending to weigh his options. 'You are fortunate, fool, for I am a servant of the Lord, and our Lord dispenses both punishment and forgiveness. I follow his divine example and in this case I choose to show you forgiveness. Be warned,' he said, his voice gaining a more cutting edge, almost a hiss, 'I never show forgiveness twice.'

'Of course, my lord eminence, bless you for your mercy, I will see to everything at once and you will not have any cause to speak to the commander, I swear it.'

'Stop talking and begone, your presence offends me,' Reinhard said, gesturing to his followers to bring in his possessions, which had just arrived outside, into the building. The unfortunate man bowed and ran away, disappearing into town with his cloak billowing around behind him.

Reinhard allowed himself a small smile, another uncommon event. He did love putting lesser men in their place with a healthy dose of fear. Reinhard led by fear, not love or example. He thought those who led by love were idiots, fear would make men do things they would never do for love or recognition. Love was a passing feeling, easily lost, hard to rekindle. Fear was much more lasting, and could be easily re-applied when it wore off.

Within a matter of hours, a swarm of workmen had descended on the house, and under the bishop's exacting direction, had removed all traces of paganism from the building. Some furniture had the carvings chiselled or cut off, some was simply removed. The main hall was cleared to form a rough chapel and a carpenter installed a bench seat in the privy room, which was cleaned as best as they could manage, and while still disgusting it was at least now usable.

Reinhard dismissed the men with a curt wave when he was satisfied that all that could be done in a day was done, and had one of the priests bring him food and water. Reinhard did not drink wine, wine made men commit sins, but more importantly, it made them lose discipline. And discipline was dear to the Lord.

'Make preparations to visit Count Baldwin in the morning, send a messenger announcing we will be there after breaking our fast and having Terce,' the bishop said to Brother Bertrand, after they had eaten their meal. 'Now, we must consecrate this hall and conduct Compline. It is a momentous event, this will be the first prayer in a consecrated building in this new land that we bring into the Lord's fold.' He crossed himself and his companions followed suit. Consecrating the rough chapel and then conducting Compline would last long into the night and they were all weary from travel, but none would complain, none of them ever did.

'What form of man is this, who would keep a servant of God waiting for this long in the morning?' Bishop Reinhard asked, glowering at the count's aide. They had risen at sunrise, had their meal and then morning prayer before coming to see the commander, yet still he was not ready to receive them.

'I apologise, my lord bishop,' the flustered man said, for about the fourth time. 'My lord Count Baldwin will be with us shortly, I have no doubt.' His nervous smile betrayed the uncertainty in his words.

Reinhard scowled. If there was one thing he disliked above all others, it was being lied to, especially when the liar was so bad at it. There he was, sent at the personal command of the Pope and with the blessing of the emperor to bring the northlands under the sway of the church, and to convert its people to the true faith, and he was being made to wait while the Crusade commander overslept. The disrespect made his eye twitch as he struggled to repress his anger to a mere simmer.

Eventually, when he was on the verge of leaving, and the aide was on the verge of physical distress, the flap to the inner rooms was opened and Reinhard and his party were invited in. After giving the aide a parting glance filled with such bile that he would carry the memory of it to his grave, he swept into the room and laid eyes on the Crusade commander for the first time.

That can't be him. Reinhard knew how old the count was, but he had not come across such a powerful lord who radiated so much youthful angst. Baldwin was sitting on his throne, he had bothered to put on fine clothes, but not taken the care to wear them properly, or shave. He looked fresh from his bed, tired and hungover.

Reinhard was furious, but this was the one person on the Crusade he could not afford to cross, not directly, not yet. 'Good morning, my Lord Baldwin, I am honoured you have received us.' *You repugnant little toad.* He spoke in flawless French, smiling graciously and making the slightest bow.

Baldwin waved the pleasantry away airily. 'The honour is ours, of course,' he replied, with none of the convincing sincerity the bishop had affected. 'What brings you to my presence, Bishop Reinhardt?'

Reinhard grimaced at the mispronunciation; combined with the man's French accent, Baldwin had mangled his name, both incompetent and disrespectful in a meeting of powerful lords. But Reinhard had not climbed to near the top of the German clergy without being a smooth political operator or being able to hide his distaste for lesser but more powerful men.

'How gracious of you, Count Baldwin. I am here on behalf of the church, sent with the humble task of bringing this new province you have so quickly conquered into the fold of Christ.'

Baldwin perked up at the praise directed at him, and gave the first genuine smile of the meeting. *You are as easy to manipulate as a child, it's pathetic.*

'So, you are the choice of the Pope for this task?' Baldwin was interested now.

'I do not pretend to know how the decision was made, I am merely humbled to be given this chance to serve the Lord.' Truthfully the Pope had selected him at the emperor's quiet recommendation, a barter of power for some favour the Pope wanted, but that was not an important detail.

Baldwin looked disappointed. 'So you do not know if the Holy Father has heard of my rapid progress, that he is pleased with its speed?'

Hearing loud and clear the need for recognition, Reinhard shook his head and smiled knowingly. 'Oh, my lord count, all of Christendom celebrates your success as a soldier of Christ. I am certain the Holy Father is fully aware of your achievements and counts you in his prayers.' That seemed to mollify the young man considerably.

'That's wonderful to hear. So, how can I help you in this holy task?'

'That is very kind of you to offer, I could do with a detachment of men, both armed and labourers, to help establish and protect the new church and its clergy. Also, we need the power to requisition the appropriate supplies and equipment from the army stores, for such meagre purposes as we require,' Reinhard said with a hand gesture that made it seem a trifling matter.

Baldwin nodded as if in serious contemplation. 'I shall have to find an appropriate way to process these requests, some deputy of mine, as I am very busy with matters of the army, you understand.'

Being pawned off on some junior, presumably because the count was too lazy to deal with administration himself, was a perfect outcome. Junior staffers were so easy to intimidate into submission. 'Well, of course, I do not wish to inconvenience you.' Reinhard made a much better pretence of serious contemplation. 'It occurs to me that to reduce the burden on you, you could write me a charter, or an order of delegation, that gives me permission to requisition such materials and men under your name, without having to take up your time in each instance.' He nodded sagely to himself as he spoke, hoping he hadn't gone too far. 'We could then review these requisitions at your convenience.' Reinhard waited with genuine nervousness, having asked for standing permission to take whatever he wanted unchecked, something no competent commander would ever allow.

Baldwin smiled broadly and nodded. 'An excellent idea, I know as a man of the cloth that you will not need close supervision.'

How can this be so easy? I should have asked for control of the entire army, I would have got it. 'That is gracious of you, my Lord Baldwin. As a servant of the Lord, we learn to be frugal in all things. Shall I wait outside for you to draft the order?' Reinhard waved in the direction of the antechamber.

Baldwin paused again and Reinhard seized on the opportunity. 'My apologies, that was thoughtless, you have other business to attend to, shall I have my staff draft a document for your review and seal later?'

Baldwin clapped his hand on the chair arm and stood. 'As you say, Bishop Reinhardt, I already feel we understand each other well, we will have a good relationship, I know it.'

You wouldn't understand me if you had two hundred years to study, and I own you after one meeting. 'I am so pleased to hear that, I will get out of your command tent and get that document drawn up.' He smiled warmly at the count and bowed before leaving.

Bertrand was waiting patiently outside. He frowned when he saw the expression on the bishop's face, it was thunder.

'Come,' snapped the bishop, not breaking his stride.

'Did the meeting not go well?' asked Bertrand.

'What? No, it went perfectly, I got everything I need,' the bishop replied.

'Oh, I'm sorry, I thought you looked perturbed. But you were successful?'

'Don't think, Bertrand, you aren't good at it. I was successful but it was too easy. The count is a lazy child. I am disappointed, I wasted my time preparing various strategies and in the end a single compliment sufficed. He is a fool, and if there is one type of man I dislike above all others, it is a fool.'

Bertrand slyly smiled to himself as he followed the bishop, wondering, as he often did, if he should keep a record in his extensive journals of all the things his master disliked the most.

CHAPTER 18

OF HOME AND HOMELAND

RAGNVALD WAS IN a foul mood for most of the voyage home from Lund, despite the blessing of fine weather and a westerly wind that made the passage calm and easy. They passed the sometimes tempestuous channel by Oland without trouble, yet still Ragnvald glowered. As they passed Gotland, unseen over the sparkling horizon, the memory of the old king, Eric, who had ruled from that distant fastness, soured him further.

Eventually they reached the sea of islands that hid the entrance to Lǫgrinn, the inland lake that led deep into the heart of Svealand. For centuries, all the wealth and power of the Svea had flowed in and out of the three entrances to the Lǫgrinn but the islands were so numerous, and the inlets and coastline so jagged and confusing, that it was said a foreign man could spend a lifetime trying to come into the lake from without and yet die disappointed.

It was not a complete exaggeration. The channels into the lake were well disguised and narrow, one of them half blocked and passable only to small fishing boats. Once inside, dead ends and false channels vied with shoals and powerful currents to stymie the unfamiliar seafarer. But for Ulf it was no mystery, these islands and channels were his birthplace and home, he could, and often had, traversed the entire course in the dead of night.

The eastern entrance, the largest, led to the narrow waterway that passed the ancient island of Agnefit, Agne's meadow, where the legendary conqueror had met his end. Ulf led their little fleet past the cursed place without incident, and they made their way up the familiar inlet towards Uppsala.

Only when Uppsala was nearly in sight did Ragnvald's mood temper somewhat, but he was heavy with what the return would hold. He was returning without many of the men he had sailed away with, just two months before. Men who would never return. More of his warriors lost than in all his years as jarl before that. The nights would ring with widows' wailing in the lands around Uppsala for days to come.

Leaving most of the ships at the main dock in the small bay, Ulf steered *Sedemonr* the last few miles to the docks of Uppsala and they set to moor and unload in gruff silence. A man was sent running to town to announce their arrival, and fetch horses and carts to transport their equipment and baggage.

Ragnvald was standing on the low dock wall, absently watching his men unload the ship, when a voice he knew so well spoke in his ear.

'You look very glum, for a man home early from war.' Ragnvald stood hurriedly and turned around, a broad smile breaking across his face that did not spread to his eyes as he embraced his wife. He took a deep breath of her hair and sighed, pulling away from the embrace as she studied him with an odd expression.

'We heard of the loss of Sjælland, and that the invasion was expected, yet you are home, surely only a great victory or great defeat would bring you back so soon, yet you are all too downcast for victors, and too many for defeated.'

Ragnvald nodded wryly. 'You have it exactly, as you always do, my love. We were neither defeated nor victorious. The king declined to force a final battle, the army was sent home.'

Halla looked confused at this, but Ragnvald waved it away. 'It's complex, I will explain later, let us go home, I long for my own hall and my own bed with my wife beside me.' He smiled warmly at her, but she was tight-lipped and he saw instantly that something was troubling her. 'You also do not look like a wife happily reunited early.'

'No.' She shook her head and put her hands into his, gripping them tightly. 'There is something you must know, it cannot wait because you must hear it from me first.'

Ragnvald was taken aback, a dozen fears flashing through his mind, he physically recoiled from her a fraction. 'What, what is it?'

Ragnvald paced in the hall, alone with Halla, one hand to his head, alternating massaging his temple and digging his knuckles into his forehead as his emotions writhed like serpents inside his skull, anger, fear and self-hatred wrestling for dominance. 'I should have known. I should have known this would happen. What a fool I am for leaving you with so few.'

'It is not your fault, husband,' she said again.

'My wife was attacked in my own home and I did nothing to stop it,' he spat. 'It is the deepest failure a man can have.'

'You left men to protect me, and they did that.'

'They all died protecting you, against only two enemies and a woman?' Ragnvald asked, turning towards her and fixing her with his ice blue eyes.

'Yes, Tora's men attacked ours in the hall, after they had been drinking. After becoming our guests, they took them by surprise and broke the guest bond. Our warriors managed to stop them, to kill them, but only two survived, and both died of their wounds soon afterwards.' Halla explained it again, and Ragnvald shook his head and cursed quietly as he stared at the faint blood stains that still marked the wall near the bedroom.

'And none made it to you,' he said, eyeing the faded marks.

'No.' Halla said, pointing at the door. 'Sten killed the last of them as he came through that door, despite grievous wounds. And we put him on the bed to try to save him, but he died within moments.' Halla shook her head sadly, looking at the ground.

Ragnvald sighed. 'And the bitch died too.'

'Yes.'

'So we do not know if she acted alone, if more enemies will come.'

'I am sure they will not, she was desperate, cast out of her home. She sought revenge alone, there would have been more of them if others had been involved in the planning.' Halla put a placating hand on Ragnvald's shoulder. 'It is finished, we have survived, we should be content with that.'

'In my own home!' Ragnvald exclaimed, pointing at the faintly bloodstained floor. 'That you were so close to being killed, what that means.'

Halla remained silent as the jarl muttered and paced again. 'I will leave twice the number of men next time,' he announced. Nodding to himself.

Halla's eyes narrowed. 'Next time? What will be the next time?'

Ragnvald looked up, confused, then realisation dawned. 'Oh, I did not mean that the army had been permanently scattered. It will reform in the spring for a new campaign. In the time between, warbands will harry and pick at the Crusaders, weaken them and bleed them.'

Halla nodded. 'So you will be here until the spring. That is well. There is much to do.'

Ragnvald put a knuckle to his lips and averted his eyes. 'No, I will be returning shortly, to be one of those harrying them.'

'You returned only to leave again!' Halla exclaimed, voice rising in anger. 'Why would you do this to me? Why can't you stay in your lands and rest like other men your age, instead of leaving me once again to await a return that might not happen?' Halla bit her lip and looked away, regretting her outburst.

Ragnvald stepped over and wrapped his arms around her, clasping his hands at her stomach and laying his head on her shoulder. 'I am sorry, Halla. The king asked me to return with my crews.'

'You could refuse him,' she half-whispered.

'I cannot. Truthfully I do not want to. We must stop these Christians before they reach our lands, you cannot imagine what it is like, in the lands they conquer. It is nothing like war with our neighbours, it is the end of our ways, of our people.' Halla squirmed around to face him inside the circle of his arms and looked up at him.

'So why did you return now?'

'To return the men to their homes, for a few weeks, to gather the harvest, to see their wives and families,' he said with a soft smile, their foreheads touching. 'Not all of them will return with me to the king, some will remain here until the spring. I am taking only the best.'

Halla nodded sadly in defeat and pressed her cheek into his. 'Can you bear it, one more time?' he whispered gently in her ear.

She shook her head. 'Do not promise it will be the last time.'

Ragnvald sighed. 'One way or another, I think it will be.' The two of them stood there in a silent embrace in the flickering fire-light before Ragnvald finally let her go to return to the yard. There were a thousand things to organise before he could rest.

Ordulf sat nervously on a large split log at the end of the long day, watching the jarl thank his warriors and disappear into his hall in the dying evening light. The dozens of the men that had returned with him had divided up their gear and possessions and, dismissed by the jarl with his thanks and a meagre handful of silver each, had set off for their homes during the day, leaving only the household warriors behind.

He had helped them clean and sort rusty and damaged equipment all day, and collected a dozen swords to be cleaned, repaired, sharpened and rubbed with tallow for storage over the next few days.

But now, after the day's work was done, he sat on the log and he fretted. Eventually Brunhild came out and poked him in the ribs with her foot, getting a satisfying 'oof' of exhaled breath from the startled smith. 'What's the problem, blockhead?'

Ordulf looked around in annoyance, and Brunhild sat on the log next to him with a smirk. He looked around to make sure no one was nearby before speaking. 'Do you think he will believe it?' he whispered.

'What?' she said nonchalantly.

Ordulf looked at her as if she was simple. 'The story, what Halla will tell him?'

Brunhild shook her head as if he was the simple one. 'Of course, seeing as it is the truth, and there is no reason to doubt it or behave in a way that might make anyone doubt it. Is there?' she said pointedly, jabbing him in the ribs again with an elbow.

'But what if…'

'Shut up, you worry more than Otto.' She shook her head and stood up again. 'Come on, leave them to their business. There is hot food inside, we have pig in the stew today, good fresh meat, a huge sow broke a leg this morning and had to be slaughtered.

There was enough for us to get some of the good stuff. We'll be eating it for a couple of days.'

Ordulf perked up at that thought. Pork was rare for the slaves, especially in summer, and usually it was the bits that the warriors or freemen didn't want, or was old or a bit rank. Brunhild stood to go into the longhouse with calculated indifference, but Ordulf grinned to himself anyway. She was proud and true to her word, refused even the pretence that she was dedicated to him, but Ordulf couldn't help but note that several other slaves were outside the hall, and Brunhild had not gone to tell them about the special meal. It was a small mark of affection, but it warmed him more than the best pork stew ever could.

Not that he wasn't going to go inside and enjoy that too. His worries about Ragnvald pushed aside, he followed Brunhild in at a respectful distance.

The following day, Ordulf was up with the dawn and carrying a tied stack of scabbarded swords that seemed half his own weight to the forge for repairs and sharpening. Dengir gave the stack an unsavoury look when he reached the forge, and the old master smith grunted and nodded to a broad table out in the yard, coming over to inspect the pile. One by one, he unsheathed the swords, carefully inspecting them for warping, edge damage and integrity of the hilt. Two he found to be unacceptably cracked and weakened and set to one side with grunt, another he found the hilt was too damaged to repair, and sent an apprentice to remove it, ready for a replacement to be made. Most of the rest merely required small edge repairs and sharpening.

He picked up the two cracked swords, both of which were Norse patterned blades, and shoved them into Ordulf's hands. 'New ones, same size,' he said, simply. 'Re-use the hilts.'

Ordulf sighed. Re-using the hilts was a pain. Normally you

would make the hilt to fit a sword, not make a sword to fit a hilt. He would have to make the tang slightly larger than needed, and then painstakingly work it down until it was the right fit for the existing slots in the bronze guard and the pommel. The pommel would inevitably be damaged removing it from the steel tang of the blade, and he would have to repair that too, although both were already in worn condition, so extra damage might not be noticed.

'How much?' he asked Dengir, who looked at him, understanding the question of what value of blades to make.

The smith thought for a moment, chewing his lip, then held up four fingers, and walked off. Ordulf nodded. The smith meant four fingers of silver, a measurement unique to that forge, denoted by the stack of small, identical silver bars the size and shape of fingers that Dengir kept next to the simple scales inside. Ordulf had at first struggled to get used to the system, the Norse had no standard coin and used the coins of other nations, or more often hacksilver. So Dengir made swords according to the value of the weight in silver of those small bars. Anyone buying a sword from him would have to weigh out enough coins or hacksilver to match the agreed number of bars.

He now knew instinctively how much work and what sort of iron to put into a four-finger sword. It was a simple blade, with a twisted single bar core of mixed soft irons, and two folded outer bars of steel. A solid, workmanlike blade fit for battle, but nothing special to look at. Simpler blades not only took less time and less charcoal, but used less iron than a ten-finger blade. Each time you folded or twisted the steel, or added new bars, you lost some steel to the flames and the chisel. A ten-finger blade might use half as much metal again compared to a four-finger blade.

He would make it in the new style, almost everything they made now was in the new style, unless someone requested something different. Pleased to be given new swords to make, noting the other junior smiths were being directed to the repairs and sharpening, he smiled to himself and set off to the prodigious store of iron and steel they had accumulated over the winter.

For weeks, Ordulf's life settled into a routine of making swords all day, and spending as much time with Brunhild as she would allow in the evenings. The summer was fine, with warm days and cool nights and only occasional rain, and he sometimes lay alongside Brunhild under the thin furs, when she decided to allow it, staring at the roof in the smoky darkness, feeling the warmth and contentment of his situation, finally, after the months of suffering and turmoil.

Several jarls and rich freemen had come to the forge to pay for him to make swords for them, word of his new swords and the curiosity of a Christian smith drawing them to Dengir's door. He felt his place in the world finally secured again, both in the forge, and at Brunhild's side. The once fanatically independent thrall had softened somewhat to him, and occasionally showed him genuine affection, although as often mocking criticism, or just nonchalance. But none of it bothered him, he understood her need for it and was content for her to make a show of her freedom from him.

On one of the fine days of the late summer, like any other, Ordulf got up and prepared to go the forge soon after dawn. He would spend his day finishing the construction of a new sword, assembling the cast bronze crossguard and leather-bound hilt onto a finished blade. He had been developing his skills in the hilting of swords, something others had normally done, as it was a very distinct skill. He had never had the patience or interest to do the fine inlaying or careful carving required for the work, but it fascinated him and now he was learning, doing some of it himself with the help of another smith.

Soon he would be making swords completely, from pommel

to blade tip, and for the first time be able to call them his own work entirely. His mood was buoyant as he ate his morning meal and prepared for the day's work.

When he went into the yard, he found a number of men gathered there, with weapons and shields, carrying wrapped bundles of equipment, or bulging bags slung over their shoulders. Many of them he recognised as Ragnvald's household warriors, others he did not know.

Then one of the warriors who lived there, Sebbi, walked over to him with a purposeful stride. 'Ordulf, you are needed.'

He nodded. 'What do you need me to carry?'

'No, you mistake me, you are coming with us to the south.'

Ordulf stammered. 'What?'

The warrior frowned. 'Am I not clear? You are coming with us. Do you not understand my words? Where is Otto?'

'I... I understand your words, but are you sure I am needed? What use am I in the south?' He was filled with a sickly horror at the idea of going to war again, and then with a spike of anguish when he realised it would mean leaving Brunhild.

'The jarl has asked for you, you are to bring what tools you need and come. We will need weapons and equipment repaired. Don't argue with me, boy, just fetch your things. We are leaving soon, so be ready.' With that, the warrior turned and left.

Ordulf half stumbled back to the longhouse with a hand on his head. He looked around the half-empty building, not finding the person he sought. 'Where is Brunhild?' he asked old Alda.

'She was sent to a farm for a couple of days with a few others, they left earlier,' the woman replied without looking up. 'I'm sure you will survive without her for a day or two,' she continued with a chuckle.

Ordulf's heart sank. He looked at his small pile of things with confusion, unable to work out what to take as his mind swirled at the thought of having to leave so suddenly. He managed to gather his thoughts and gathered his warmest clothes. He went outside and the warrior beckoned him over.

'I have to get some things from the forge,' he said, wild plans of running to the farm to see Brunhild, to tell her he was leaving, erupting and being extinguished in his head in quick succession.

'Fine, we will pass there on the way to the ship.' The man set off, following the rest of the group, who were already leaving the courtyard, the men newly called in from the town and farms during the day marching in loose order, some hundred strong, chatting and joking with the other hundred men who had returned from the war. Jarl Ragnvald had now appeared, dressed in all his finest clothes, and he was laughing and jesting with the men who had just arrived from outside the city.

Ordulf looked back once more down the road that led out of the city to the north in despair, as if he would see her running towards him, but the road was empty of anything except a man with a mule pulling a cart of vegetables.

'Come, now!' shouted a voice from behind him and, his shoulders slumped in defeat, Ordulf jogged after the band of warriors. For the second time in his short life, Ordulf was going to war, and an uncertain fate.

Behind him, standing in the entrance to the lord's hall, Otto watched, and smirked.

CHAPTER 19

FIRE IN THE MORNING

ORDULF WATCHED THE shore of the lake go past in a blur of shock and misery as *Sedemonr* was rowed down from Uppsala at the head of a fleet of five ships with two hundred men. He had not been in a ship since the days after he was captured, what felt like a lifetime ago. He had not known where to sit, at first he had gone to a bench, thinking he might be asked to help row, but Sebbi had roughly pulled him from the seat.

'A man has to earn his place on the bench of this ship, by standing in the wall with spear and shield. No slave has the honour of pulling an oar with us,' Sebbi had said, shoving him towards the bow, where he wedged himself uncomfortably into a corner between two ribs of the hull, sitting on his bundle of clothes to try to make it passable.

Leif was just across from him on his bench, the ship's bow man, a position of honour even in the elite group of the huscarls.

'A bit different to the last time you passed these shores, eh, Christian?' Leif said with a wry laugh as they passed yet another island in the lake. Ordulf took a moment to realise he was being addressed, but then turned towards the blonde warrior, who was not looking at him as he rowed, his shoulder muscles rippling in time with the oar strokes in the sun. On that fine day all the rowers had stripped down to their trousers as they toiled in the sun to take *Sedemonr* down the long lake to reach the ocean.

'It is,' he said lamely, filling with suppressed shame at his capture and enslavement. 'I don't remember much of the journey,' he lied.

'No, it would have been difficult to see much from the bilge,' mocked Leif. 'But look at you now, a trusted thrall, a killer of men, going Viking with your jarl.'

'He isn't going Viking, Leif, do not disrespect that word,' grumbled Sebbi from the other side of the bow. 'He is just a slave, come to repair weapons and sharpen them while real men rest.'

Ordulf scowled at the older warrior, safe behind Sebbi's back and out of his view, and looked back out of the ship again without a reply. He knew better than to involve himself in the arguments of free Norsemen.

Leif laughed. 'True, he is not himself going Viking, but yet here he is, with us as we set out on a great raid, one for the sagas.'

Sebbi grunted his disapproval, but did not push the matter further. 'These islands we are passing, do you know where we are, Christian?' said Leif, looking over his shoulder and seeing Ordulf watching the world pass by.

'No.'

'This is the heart of our people's lands, the realm of our kings. This has been our home since before your god was nailed to his wood; since before the time of men began, our gods have walked here.'

Ordulf furrowed his eyebrows at the claim. The Norse, as

many men, were prone to boasting, but Leif spoke with the casualness of certainty.

'What do you mean, how do you know?'

'Because we know our own history, boy,' growled Sebbi.

'Old Sebbi is right, our history here is known, as is the history of the Aesir. Behind me, on the right, is the old king's hall of Fornsigtuna, where the Aesir first came to Svealand, where Odin first set foot on our shores.'

Ordulf's curiosity was piqued and he turned around to look, expecting some great hall, or crumbling run, but nothing except reedbanks on the shore and woodland beyond greeted his eyes.

'You cannot see it, the hall is long gone, but the stones and the stories remain,' said Leif, and Ordulf looked away again, disappointed.

'On this lake are a dozen ancient towns, it is the heart of our kingdom, of our people. This is what your Crusaders have come to destroy, but there is ancient power here, this is the land of the Aesir. We have guarded it for them for a thousand years, and we will guard it for a thousand more. No foreign army can sail these waters, not with us and the gods watching over these lands, and on the seas beyond.'

Ordulf could not pretend he did not feel something at the words. The brooding trees with branches overhanging the lakeshore, the deep, dark water beneath them. He imagined he could feel the currents of power hiding beneath the shimmering surface.

'They only come to your lands because you ravage theirs,' Ordulf said, failing to conceal the defiance in his voice.

Sebbi started to growl out a rebuke but Leif talked over him. 'And your Christians do not? I have heard tales from those who travel to the lands of the Rus, and England in the western islands, and the people on the southern shore of the cold sea. All have faced war and raiding from Christian people. Is there not war in the lands you call home? And I have heard stories of these Crusaders and their conquest of far-off lands in the realms of the sand and sun. What crimes did those people commit?' Leif said with a contemptuous laugh.

Ordulf scowled and stared resolutely out into the lake. 'The Crusade to the Holy Land freed it from heathens, and brought the rule of God back to the lands, freeing them from evil,' he said, reciting almost word for word what he had heard in a sermon at the little church in Minden.

Leif laughed heartily, so much he nearly lost his timing on the oar, and the man in front of him cursed as their blades clashed.

'Your Crusaders conquered an entire land, put their people to the sword, because your god told you to? You freed a people by conquering them?'

Ordulf flushed and said nothing. He knew little of the Holy Land, beyond the impassioned stories of heresy and evil that had been told by the Bishop of Minden in his sermons.

'Let me tell you, Christian. Your god may demand you conquer lands for him, ours may revel in war and the test of steel between one man and another, or those may just be stories. But what I know to be true is that the strong always find a reason to take from the weak. It is the way of the world. We take what we need from those who do not have the strength to defend it. It is better than a life spent hacking meagre spoils from the earth and sea in these harsh lands. The great Crusader lords are not here because we raided some villages, such matters are beneath them. They are here to take our lands because they think they can, it is the way of the world.'

Ordulf pursed his lips and did not reply. He remembered what Count Adolf had said, on the training field outside Hamburg when he delivered his new sword, that it was all a game of power, and he felt ashamed for he knew that Leif was right.

'Do you know what is different about my people, Christian?' Leif asked. He did not wait for an answer. 'We are not weak. The people of these northern lands are hardened like steel by living here. The forests, the winter, the cruel sea, they allow only the strong to prosper. Your Crusaders have never seen a winter here, never suffered at the hands of the land and seasons. They will never survive in this place while we hold steel in our hands, this land will be their grave.'

Sebbi grunted his agreement and Ordulf muttered to himself and stared at the passing water again, unable to believe Leif was wrong.

Six days' sailing in fine weather took the small fleet to its destination. The ships had been able to sail much of the way in a light north-westerly breeze, boredom being the primary challenge, and men fished, joked, played games of chance and told tall tales of their past conquests of battle and women.

For Ordulf, largely ignored in the cramped bow, there was no distraction from the tedium. He longed for each evening when they would pull the boats ashore and make camp or stay in one of the many fishing villages that lined the coast in narrow inlets. He would be given all the worst tasks to do, the cleaning and carrying and digging, but he did not care. It was better than sitting uncomfortable and idle in the bow of the longship.

Finally, they reached their destination, and Ordulf saw a large fleet of longships moored in a broad river estuary, with a good-sized settlement of wooden buildings and longhouses on the gentle slope above it. The small fleet found space to tie up alongside other ships, there was not a measure of empty dock left, and began the process of unloading all their gear and supplies across a line of other ships.

Finally, everything was ashore, and the party made its way into town to find somewhere to camp, quickly discovering that all the buildings were packed to the rafters with warriors, and that the king had made a camp for his small army in the fields above and behind the town, a half mile inland.

As they marched through the town to the camp, they passed the village smithy, a simple affair mostly in the open under a lean-to thatched roof, at the road on the edge of the settlement. Ragnvald said something to Leif, who nodded and came back down the column to Ordulf.

'Set yourself up here, find somewhere to sleep, and work out if you need anything.'

'For what?' asked Ordulf, wondering what work he would be required to do.

Leif's eyes narrowed. 'For your job, to fix weapons or make replacements. What is wrong with you? Have you gone simple in the sun? It's a forge, you are a smith, work it out.' The warrior turned to follow the rest of the column, leaving Ordulf sighing and looking at the worst smithy he had ever seen in his life, just as a gangly old man, presumably the smith, appeared out of the nearby building and gave him a suspicious look.

Muttering to himself, Ordulf walked over to the man, wondering how to explain that he, a thrall, was taking over this freeman's forge.

Ragnvald led his hird into the fields above the village and saw that there were at least two thousand men there. As they moved through the haphazard camp, he recognised Danes from the Skanian coast, Islanders from Gotland and Oland, and finally, as they reached the centre of the camp, Norwegians there with the king. The king's large force were the only other men besides his own band who did not come from the local area.

As he was looking around, Sigurd appeared between two tents

with several of his huscarls in tow, and spread his arms in welcome with a cry of joy, something that was both very unkingly, and brought an irrepressible smile to Ragnvald's face. He braced himself for the assault that was the royal bear hug and tried to keep his footing as the *Norðrikonungr* half lifted him from his feet, laughing and slapping him on the back like a father greeting a child.

The king finally put the older jarl down and stood back, content to leave only a meaty hand on Ragnvald's shoulder. 'I am pleased to see you, Jarl Ragnvald.'

'I might not survive your joy at seeing me many more times, Lord Sigurd,' laughed Ragnvald, coughing and clearing his throat as his lungs were finally able to draw breath once more. 'Your mood is much improved from the last time I saw you.'

Sigurd nodded sagely. 'Yes, we are back to a warfare we understand, that we are good at. We raid and harry and hunt the slow Christians and their fat ships from these havens on the coast. If they march to where we are, we get in our ships and move, if they try to sail here, they have no knowledge of this coast and drift about like confused seals.' He laughed his booming laugh. 'We are fighting them in the old ways, cutting them down one root at a time, instead of tackling the trunk when it is too strong to fell.'

Ragnvald nodded sagely. 'And what of the fortresses, and the towns. Do we still hold them?'

Sigurd's smile faded and he shook his head sadly. 'Most are lost, Only the ring fort of Trelleborgen remains, and soon they will arrive to take it. We have removed most of the garrison to join us here, rather than waste them in a futile defence. Only a few brave men remain behind, to keep the enemy busy and delay them while we do our work. The Christians are masters of the siege, better than we feared. Many brave men have died, but many Christians have gone to the next life with them, and we take more every day.

Soon, they will run out of lives to give, and we will take back these lands they have stolen from us.'

Ragnvald smiled a smile he did not feel, thinking of how the Danes, who had suffered so much loss, would have lost so many more in those fallen towns and fortresses.

'Your arrival is fortuitous, Ragnvald, we are preparing to leave on another raid, the largest yet, half this army to come with us. Our spies tell us a Christian fleet is assembling in Aarhus; soon it will sail for Lund, weighed down with supplies and weapons and everything these Crusaders need. We intend to take it from them. Come, I wish for you to join us, to wet your blades alongside us once more,' the king said, with a single confirmatory nod, making clear it was an order, not an invitation.

'Of course, I would be pleased to sail at your side.'

'Good, then it is done. We leave tomorrow at dawn. Gunnar will show you where you can set your camp. Come to my tent at dusk, we have much to drink, and much to discuss.' With that the king gave him a thumping slap on the shoulder and set off through the camp again. Moments later, Ragnvald heard another exclamation of joy as the king came across another newly arrived jarl, and Ragnvald shook his head at the energy of the man, and his ability to make each man feel his friendship.

Gesturing with his head for his men to follow, he set off with the silent Gunnar, a dozen tasks in his head to get his camp set up, and his men ready for battle the next day.

The next day dawned and still the gods smiled on them, a strong north-easterly wind blew, one that would carry them down the coast and into the bay of Lund, where they would hunt for their prey. Ragnvald left a few grumbling men at the camp and took three crews with him, nearly twenty others following Sigurd in his huge longship, *Fate Maker*, a beast of a vessel that carried eighty men and still had room for the king's ego. Its large sail was dyed blue, like his warband's cloaks, a ridiculous expenditure, a flaunting of his status and wealth in a flock of faded red or stained white sails.

Two days' sailing took them yet again to the Öresund, the bay between the island of Sjælland in the west, and the Skanian shore in the east, and Ragnvald could not help but feel disheartened as they passed the ruins of the lost city of København. Through the Öresund all ships arriving in the twin Crusader ports of Lund and Helsingborg would pass, and so it would be their hunting ground.

In the centre of the Öresund was the island of Hven, uninhabited save for the gulls and goats, the two small fishing communities there abandoned when the Crusaders captured Sjælland. The fleet laid up on this island, out of sight of the harbour near Lund, and sent out a single ship as a scout to watch the passage from Aarhus.

Two days and nights they waited there before a lookout called out the return of the scout ship. Ragnvald heard the call, and the lazy camp burst into activity. 'To the ships!' he roared, along with a dozen others. Men grabbed their equipment and whatever few supplies had been unloaded, and ran for the beached ships. Within moments the first were being launched, crews shoving and hauling at the landed wooden beasts, salt spray being churned up by hundreds of feet as each crew strived to be the first launched and underway.

'ULF!' Ragnvald shouted for the shipmaster, but he needn't have bothered, Ulf was already untying the steering oar and sail, readying them for use even as men started to launch the ship underneath him.

It was a scene that resembled chaos, but it was merely excitement and haste. These were all experienced crews, and in less time than it takes a pot to boil over a strong fire, the entire fleet was at sea and red and white sails were springing up like spring flowers surrounding the one deep blue sail of *Fate Maker*.

The scout ship turned around and fell into position next to Sigurd's ship, the jarl aboard having a shouted conversation with Sigurd. Then, the ship fell back, and Sigurd stood in the bow of his ship, reaching down as a man handed him the boat's snarling figurehead, which he fixed into place on the prow. Cheers sounded around the fleet as men saw the beast taking pride of place. Mounting the ship's figurehead could only mean one thing; the hunt was on.

It was not long before the hunters sighted their quarry. A dozen fat Christian round ships, wallowing down the Öresund in a loose gaggle, headed for the harbour near Lund. The longships swept down on them like a flock of ravens coming to pick at a kill. Fast under their sails, loaded with heavily armed but unarmoured men, for only a fool tries to board a ship with a hauberk to weigh him down or a shield to foul his climb.

Panic set in amongst the Christian fleet, bottled up against the coast of Sjælland and with the easterly wind giving them no chance of flight from the smaller, faster longships. Ragnvald watched in sheer joy as some tried in vain to flee, others lowered their sails and prepared to fight, two even turned opposite ways and collided in a tangle of rigging. It was chaos, a sea of prey for the taking.

Two ships, with smarter or more cowardly helmsmen than the others, sailed straight for the shore and beached themselves in the shallows, crew jumping into the water to flee onto land, abandoning their ships to the raiders.

Ragnvald pointed Ulf at one of the ships, which was holding its course, facing the oncoming Norse, a bright red cross emblazoned on its white sail. 'That one is ours,' he shouted, watching the distance as they closed. 'Sail down!' he shouted, when he judged the distance was right, and the speed of the fat round ship was too slow to escape. The crew rushed to untie the lines and swung the sail round to lie along the boat as it was steadily dropped, half a dozen men gathering and folding it as it was lowered, then tying it closely to the boom when it was finished. They were in a hurry, but the ship could not be rowed without the sail well stored and out of the way.

'OARS!' Ragnvald shouted, and men jumped to the benches, pulling the stuffed leather bungs from the oar holes and retrieving their oars from the neat piles along the centre of the boat each side of the mast. Thirty oars were threaded through the holes and Ragnvald watched carefully for the moment the last one was ready. Start too soon, and one oar out of place could foul a side and spin the ship.

'Ready, and pull!' he shouted, both banks of rowers taking their lead from the stern man, the man on each side closest to the steering oar, who would set the rhythm. Soon, the whole crew was into a steady pace, and *Sedemnor* was cutting through the gentle swell, haring after its target. As they closed, he saw another pair of the dragon ships angling towards the same enemy, and saw it was one of the Gotland jarls leading the two crews, a historic rival by nature, and he grinned wolfishly. The other ship was closer to their prey, but he wasn't going to give it up that easily.

'Some Gotland goat fucker is coming to take our kill, lads, will we let them?' he shouted.

'FUCK, NO!' shouted Sebbi, to a wave of laughter.

'Show them our speed.' He ran nimbly along the ship, past the mast, and jumped into the bow, clinging to their own demon figurehead. 'OAR SONG!' he roared. And Sebbi launched into the familiar song with vigour behind him.

'Sea demon! Wave rider! Carry us! Here we come!' began the chant.

Ragnvald looked across at their rivals and saw that they too were bending their oars, being exhorted on by their jarl, who held up his axe in salute to the Svear Jarl. In a previous generation, they would have been enemies, but now they were merely fighting for the right to the spoils.

'Thor, Lord of Thunder, hear our fury, see our rage, here we come!' his crew shouted behind him between strokes. But despite their efforts, Ragnvald could see they were going to be beaten to the kill, and, with a returned salute of his fist, he signalled to the Gotland jarl that he could have this one.

He looked beyond, and saw another Christian ship, this one was turning, trying to flee, and making a mess of it. He waved to Ulf and pointed at the new ship, the shipmaster nodded and leant into the steering oar, guiding them towards the new prey.

Ragnvald looked to his left and right and saw Norse ships catching and boarding others in the fleet, Norse warriors cutting down the few that resisted and clearing the decks, and his smile deepened. These fat supply ships had no chance against these wolves of the sea.

They passed the first ship he had targeted even as the men of Gotland were crashing alongside and grabbing hold. The Christian ship was much higher, and the Norse had to climb more than the height of a man to get onto the deck, but there were many hand-holds to allow this, and the Norsemen started swarming up the sides of the victim.

Ragnvald's wolfish smile started to fade as a Norse warrior reappeared at the rail, backing up and holding his hand to his throat, blood spraying as he was bodily shoved over the side to splash into the sea. Then another dying Norseman was thrown over the side, landing with a sickening thump in the longboat he had just left. But their fellows were not dissuaded, merely angered, and the Norsemen climbed the sides of the enemy ship with renewed vigour and howls of rage, the second longship coming to the aid of the first, and adding its crew of forty to the first, so that a swarm of warriors was boarding the Christian vessel.

But Ragnvald, although too close to the tall ship to see onto its deck, could hear the sounds of battle, and the screams of the wounded. And he felt unsure. 'STOP OARS!' he shouted. At first his men were confused, and continued rowing, they could see the enemy ship trying to flee in front of them and did not understand. 'Stop oars, now,' Ragnvald repeated, and his men finally dug their blades into the water, bringing the ship to a slewing halt. Ragnvald fixed his eyes on the fight, and his men started to do the same. As they were watching, all they could see was flashing weapons, and the backs of shoulders and heads of the Norse warriors as they fought an unseen enemy on the deck.

But then the backs of those men started getting closer to the rail, they were being forced back, and then a trickle of blood started flowing out of the scuppers off the deck of the Christian ship, and that trickle became a stream.

Suddenly the Gotland warriors were being forced back against the railing, desperately defending themselves, although few had shields and helmets and none wore maille. And then their enemy was brought into view and Ragnvald's stomach turned. A solid line of maille-clad men, shields up, helmets on, swords flashing and hacking in the bright sunlight.

The Norsemen were being slaughtered on that armoured wall, and finally they broke. Some turned and either scrambled down the side or simply jumped into the nearest longship. Others were sent screaming and splashing into the water. Towards the bow of the Christian ship, a knot of warriors were still organised and fighting, defending the narrow steps up to the sterncastle. Ragnvald saw their jarl among them. They had some shields, some they had taken with them, some they had taken from the enemy, and they still were putting up a fight.

As Ragnvald watched, rooted in indecision fifty paces away, a man jumping from the deck stove in the bottom of the first longship with a crunch, a timber of the hull finally giving away under the impacts.

Men in Ragnvald's ship swore and cursed at the sight, some began hurriedly unpacking their maille, safety stowed and wrapped beneath the benches. Ragnvald looked at them, and then at the enemy and saw that the jarl was evacuating as many of his men out of the bow as he could, they were climbing down into the second longship.

'Bring us alongside, turn to the right, now!' he shouted, finally coming to a decision. But half his oarsmen were struggling with their equipment, and the response was slow and disorganised as Ragnvald and Ulf swore at them and tried to get the stationary ship moving again. By the time they were, it was too late. Ragnvald watched as the last man to escape the massacre successfully climbed down into his ship, and the jarl and the last of his men were slaughtered by the relentless Christian soldiers.

Less than half of the warriors who had boarded the ship had survived to get back to their own, and they were abandoning the one that was sinking, dragging their wounded and any equipment they could save into the one good ship.

'We can't board them, lord,' said Leif from beside him.

'I know. Fuck.' Ragnvald chewed his lip and stared at the enemy ship, where one of the enemy stood watching him in return. The man was dressed head to toe in maille beneath a steel helm, wearing a white sleeveless tunic over his armour with a red cross emblazoned on it, matching the one on the sail. The man shouted some orders to the others, who moved to man the whole rail of the ship, leaving no spot unguarded, and then put his bloodied sword over his shoulder and rested a hand on the rail, staring Ragnvald down with a look of contempt.

Ragnvald looked around, seeing that none of the other Christian ships had put up such resistance, this was the only one carrying a complement of these mailled men. He made his decision. 'Burn it,' he growled.

'What?' Sebbi said, looking about nervously. He was right to be nervous, trying to set one ship on fire from another was ridiculously dangerous. They were as likely to set their own ship on fire in the effort.

'You heard me, make oiled firebrands, and we will burn them.'

'Lord…' Leif started.

'Have men standing by with water in buckets, but do it,' snapped Ragnvald. His anger at the enemy commander who so mocked him with his stare was burning at him worse than any fire.

His men reluctantly set to work, some collecting water in buckets, others getting lamp oil and tallow and making firebrands with strips of torn clothing and whatever wood they could re-purpose. They rowed up close to the enemy, which fortunately seemed to have no archers on board, and under the cover of shields as they were pelted with Norse axes, swords and spears left behind by their dead brethren, four men started lighting the firebrands and throwing them onto the enemy ship.

The strange battle lasted only a few moments. On one side, Christians hurled rocks from the ballast, discarded weapons, whatever they could find at the Norse below. On the other the Norse hid under shields and threw burning brands into the rigging, onto the deck and tried to set fire to the outside of the hull, the tarred caulking fizzing and flaring as the fire took hold on that dry day.

The battle was decided when a second of Ragnvald's ships arrived to help, and soon a dozen fires were burning on the enemy ship, their crew and soldiers rushing around to try to put them out, but the ones on the outside of the hull, and the ones in the rigging, could not easily be reached, and Ulf and several others with bows were snapping arrows into those that tried.

'Back oars!' Ragnvald shouted, as the fate of the enemy ship appeared sealed. They shoved off from the rapidly combusting ship as flames licked up its sides and fell in clumps from its burning sails, warriors dumping buckets of water on any embers that landed back in the longship. As they did, a pair of Christian soldiers in full armour roared a battle cry and jumped from the rail, swords in hand. Ragnvald froze in shock as the men launched themselves at the longship. One landed just short, thumping into the side of the strake and splashing into the water, disappearing instantly without another sound as his armour took him down.

The other landed in the rowing benches, an unfortunate warrior filling a bucket bore the brunt of the impact, snapping his neck with an audible crack, and the Crusader sprawled across three shocked and unarmed men, as suddenly everyone scrambled for weapons to counter the unexpected threat. The enemy recovered his feet first, and howled a cry of rage, swinging his sword about, catching two men on its edge as they scurried to get away. Then Bjorn got a shield up and shoulder shoved the man back, so that he had a space all his own in the bow for a moment, facing down fifty shocked Norsemen.

That stalemate lasted only a moment, before the man, seeing that it was hopeless, reversed his sword in his hand and made to plunge it down into the hull, to hole the ship.

'NO!' roared Bjorn, throwing himself at the enemy, spoiling his thrust so that the sword only stuck in the hull instead of smashing through it, springing a leak and sticking there as the two men fell into the bow. Then half a dozen men leapt onto the enemy with seaxes and axes in hand, and the Christian howled as he was butchered through his maille.

Ragnvald looked up from the bloody mess even as Leif moved to deal with the split in their hull, wrapping linen tightly and jamming it into the sword hole. He saw that the enemy ship was ablaze from bow to stern now, and even as he watched, a burning, screaming man ran from the ship's interior, and threw himself into the sea.

The Norse jeered and shouted as the enemy ship burned, even as a few still tried to fight the fires on board. Then Ragnvald saw the man in the white tunic with the red cross appear again at the rail, appearing calm in the chaos. Ragnvald could feel the heat from there, a spear throw away, but the enemy knight showed no reaction, despite the fact his armour was smoking, and his tunic was starting to catch fire.

The man simply stared at Ragnvald, and then finally, wincing from the heat as his clothes started blackening and curling, the man made the sign of the cross on his chest and clamped his sword to his breast, the flames rippling around him now, bursting from his tunic and running up the sides of his head. The man gave Ragnvald one last look of contempt, before stepping off the side and dropping like a stone into the sea. With a hiss and curl of steam he was gone, and no Norseman watching jeered him or celebrated. Instead, men touched their amulets or weapon hilts, rooted to the spot or shaking their heads in amazement.

With that final ship destroyed, and the men who had witnessed the fight sobered by the slaughter and the bravery of the defenders, the Norse rowed away south, leaving a sea of debris and bodies and a single, drifting but unburned Christian ship. The men from Sigurd's crew who boarded that enemy met no resistance from either the ship's crew or the oddly dressed and terrified men trying to hide from them below. Sigurd had recognised the men were Christian priests and stopped the slaughter before it was over.

Finding a Norseman who spoke their foreign tongue, he had questioned one of the surviving priests, a man who had not cowered but shouted at and cursed the attackers, waving his crucifix necklace at the laughing boarders as they killed his helpless brethren. The leader of this band of the nailed god's servants, it turned out.

The priest, kneeling on the blood-soaked deck, warned the Norsemen of the coming wrath of God, and promised them all eternal damnation and that all the North would be turned over to the Christian faith, that all unbelievers would be purged.

'How will you achieve this mighty act?' asked the amused king.

'By bringing the word of God.'

'Words? You hope to achieve this with just words?' asked the incredulous Norwegian, taking the meaning literally.

'The word of God is powerful beyond your comprehension,' snarled the priest.

'He says the words are magical, they hold great power,' said the interpreter to the king with a shrug. Some men backed up or touched their amulets. Some still held the dark ways of magic and gods in high regard. The Norwegian king was apparently one of them.

'His power is in his words? Then let us end them, before he speaks any more, then let this weak and harmless man go to his brothers and show how powerless they are in our lands. Kill most of the rest, leave enough crew to sail it to Lund.'

So, with what crew still remained alive, and a weeping and shrieking priest left tongueless and horrified on board, the ship struggled to raise its sails and continue its journey as the Norse hunters left, the dead still clogging its deck, silent witness to the wretched survivors.

CHAPTER 20

FLEETS AND FIGUREHEADS

23rd of August, year of our Lord 1117

Duke Welfard

I am pleased to report that the fortress at Trelleborgen will soon fall. We have been laying siege now for eight days, and our engines continue to do their work, the walls are much reduced and great gaps split them asunder. Tomorrow we will commit to our final assault and I have every hope of success.

With this last fortress taken, we will be clear to move east into the lowlands and towns of Sweden, un-threatened to our rear. I will send news of our victory tomorrow so that you may have the honour of announcing our victory, I have left instructions in case I fall in the attempt.

Your faithful servant

Count Adolf

Adolf stood nervously behind the advance group of the assault-ing force, waiting in their patient ranks for the signal to advance. Overhead, the trebuchets were flinging baskets of fist-sized stones, not to do damage the already breached walls, but to keep the gar-rison cowed and to dissuade them from missile fire. He wasn't sure it worked, but it did give the assaulting troops more confidence. It would take all the confidence they could muster to fight their way up that slick and debris-strewn hill and win the summit. The Crusaders had become very good at capturing these circular forts that the Norse favoured, this was their fourth, but the Norse defended them tenaciously and ingeniously. The slope would be covered in obstacles, spikes, traps and, if they copied the garrison of Borgeby, several weeks' worth of human shit. Nothing took the spirit out of a man while trying to climb a hill of turds than slip-ping face first into it while archers tried to kill him.

'My lord, there is no need for you to join this assault,' Sir Dietmar said from beside him.

'You are quite wrong, Dietmar, the commander bade me personally command the German contingent in these sieges, he thought it a punishment, but I see it as a chance to show him up and make my reputation in this army. If I climb this last breach and survive the day, all the army will know it. Nor am I needed in the command staff, the French baron I left organising the siegeworks is surprisingly competent.'

'And if you don't survive?'

'Then it's not my problem, is it? I have a son who will survive me, and men like you to guide him.' The count turned to give the knight a wild grin. Dietmar pursed his lips with worry.

'Ah, stop worrying, Dietmar, you think I am too old? Too slow? I can still swagger swords and do my part. Did I not prove that at Lund?'

'Yes, lord, no one doubts your bravery or skill, it is merely a matter of risk.'

'Well, then, I have a reputation to seal. I fancy this will be my last assault, and I wish to do well. Be a good man and make sure nobody kills me?' Adolf was putting on a brave show to cover it, but internally he was terrified. He had survived the assault at Lund only through sheer luck, a man who aimed a killing blow at him with a spear taken, in the last moment, by an arrow in the neck, a miracle shot. At Borgeby he had simply not been in the section with the heaviest fighting, and had not traded a single hard blow with an enemy. Here, the breaches were narrow, and the defenders looked numerous, he wanted nothing more than to excuse himself. But he could not, his men were watching, him being there gave them confidence that they had a chance of victory and survival, when they all knew that many of them would die on this slope in the moments ahead. Men will march into the storm of steel, even facing near certain death, if they are well motivated. And few things helped more than seeing the men who give the orders sharing the danger with them.

Dietmar frowned and nodded, looking back towards the fort. They stood there like that in nervous silence, until finally, when Adolf's neck was stiff from the weight of his maille hood and helmet, and his feet aching from standing still in full armour for half the morning, the orders were shouted in the assault party, and it started moving forwards.

The movement quickly became a jog. Adolf saw archers running alongside the column across the open ground, crossbowmen and men carrying large wicker shields behind them. He focused on his breathing, trying to keep it steady, trying not to fall over on the uneven ground. The maille hood made it hard to look down at where he was going.

Arrows started to fall on the column. Well-armoured men

raised their shields as they ran, the arrows having little effect at this range, as always. Adolf idly wondered why the Norse archers bothered, but perhaps they did not know.

The Crusader archers got ahead of the column and started returning a shower of arrows. A Norse shaft hit his shield with a loud crunch and stuck there unseen, the point breaking through the back face so he could see it protruding. A rough point, misshapen, crude.

Then, the ground before him started sloping down. They had reached the ditch. The men in front of him slowed, weaving around obstacles and obstructions. Adolf kept his shield up, limiting his view to the backs of the men in front of him. Dietmar was shouting instructions on his right, hurrying men on, urging them up the hill.

Adolf started doing the same on his left. 'Up the slope! Move!' He waved with his sword, pointing up the slope. He started up it himself, leather shoes struggling for grip on the loose, churned soil. Mercifully, there was no human waste on the slope. The garrisons were isolated, and they were not learning from each other. *Thank God.*

Each footstep up the hill was taxing his already tired and sore body. The maille chausses were grinding away at the inside of his thighs as he struggled up the hill. Sweat was now soaking his forehead and running down past his eyes, tickling and distracting him. His arm ached from holding it above his head with the weight of his hauberk sleeves.

Suddenly, something crashed into him from in front. A man, tumbling down the slope, stone dead with a crushed skull. The body bowled Adolf over, his vision filled with sky and then soil, his open mouth taking in a great mouthful of it until he was dumped bodily into the ditch at the bottom, on top of the unfortunate man who had hit him.

Adolf breathed heavily behind his nosepiece and assessed his body. He felt sore, he didn't think anything was broken or badly damaged. He wriggled about, trying to regain his feet. A hand grabbed his and helped pull him up, an unknown man, face taut with stress. He nodded his thanks to the soldier and started up the slope again, the twenty paces to the top seeming a herculean task.

As he once again neared the summit, a number of Crusader bodies were strewn about, arrows in them, crushed heads from thrown rocks, spears protruding from chests or blood seeping from rents in their maille. *Dear God, can we win through this?* Adolf kept moving, men ahead of him and men behind him, no one with anywhere to go but up. Another missile hit his shield, arm numb from the effort of holding it up. He forced another step, and then another.

Suddenly the man in front of him was standing on the summit of the breach, viciously swiping at an unseen enemy above him. Adolf moved his shield aside so that he could see.

The enemy had created a rough barricade just behind the breach, and men were lining it, striking across and down at the attackers as they reached the top of the earthen ramparts. A couple of dozen Crusaders were crammed into the space before the barricade, suffering under a flurry of Norse missiles and attacks while trying to push them back off their little wall, covering with their shields and stabbing back with sword and spear.

Adolf was carried into the fight, more by the moment of men behind him than by volition, and suddenly he was defending himself from a long axe that arced towards him from above. The axe hit his shield with a ringing blow that shook his entire body, and then it rose and fell again. He couldn't back away, a man pressed into his back and others were on both sides. Adolf screamed in incoherent fear and rage and pushed forwards, trying to get close enough to attack the axeman with his sword.

He slammed against the rough barricade, and blows were

raining down on his shield now. One slipped around the side and slammed into his shoulder, the maille holding, but the shock and pain causing his shield arm to droop; he was saved when the tip of the shield jammed into a gap in the barricade and lodged there, protecting him while his numb arm refused to work.

Gaps, there are gaps in the barricade. He looked at it again. Yes, there were gaps in it, he could see the legs of the defenders through them on their raised platform. He worked his sword into one of the larger gaps and stabbed it through, again and again, searching by feel for a target. Soon, he felt it bite. A man above him screamed and backed away, the rain of blows on his failing shield reduced. He stabbed his sword into a different gap, angling to his left, and soon found another patch of soft flesh with his steel.

The pressure from above slacked right off. 'GAPS!' he shouted at the men next to him, struggling to be heard over the cacophonous din of the battle. 'Get them through the gaps in the barricade!' He didn't know if men heard him, but the attacks on his shield did not resume. He stood there, panting beyond control, resting his face against the barricade, wiggling his sword around in the gaps like a madman, almost all the strength gone from his arms. And then suddenly the barricade shifted and gave way. Adolf almost fell forward but caught himself using his shield as a prop. He raised his eyes to his front and saw a ragged group of Norse facing him.

He felt the men either side of him move forward, a cheer sounding from the Crusaders surging across the captured breach behind him, and he staggered along with them. Down the slope they went, the breath now burning in his lungs, sweat streaming into his eyes and mouth. He picked his man in the disorganised group facing them and brought his sword up for a downwards chop as the Christian wave hit the defenders.

His target was too slow to react and the overhead blow forced through his parry and deep into the man's shield shoulder. The unarmoured Norseman cried out and took a step back to get out of range. He instead tripped and fell, the rush of Crusaders flowing over him and drowning his screams.

It was all over soon after that, the rest of the combat passing in a blur of exhausting chaos. Adolf had hacked and slashed his way into the centre of the fortress, often too tired to keep up with the front line, stepping over and around the knotted bodies of those who died in the vicious fighting, filling gaps where they appeared ahead of him, not objecting when fresh men moved around him to continue the attack. When they reached the central square of the small fortress, Adolf sat slumped against a building, looking for all the world like one of the shocking number of casualties, utterly spent, listening to the sounds of the last defenders fighting in the buildings and being pried from hiding places. He gave a silent prayer for whoever had been watching over him in that bloody and undignified chaos. That reminded him: *Where the fuck is Dietmar?*

'You are alive then, Dietmar.' Adolf had found the German knight when he finally gathered the strength to climb back out of the charnel house of the fortress. Dietmar was sitting on the wall, facing inwards, his legs dangling over the edge of the short drop. One of his maille chausses had been removed, and a man Adolf did not recognise was standing on the ground beneath the wall, tending to a deep gash in Dietmar's leg.

'I am relieved to see the same is true of you, Count Adolf,' the knight replied, with a weary smile. 'I am sorry I got left behind, I took a spear in the leg at the top of the rampart. When you set off down the slope in that mad charge, I was unable to follow.'

'Mad, you say? Was it mad?'

The knight chortled, wincing as the movement caused his leg to protest. 'You don't know? There were about twenty of you, you charged down into at least fifty enemy, with more on either flank. It was the only section of the barricade that was breached. You should have been cut off and cut down.'

Adolf gaped up at the knight. 'There was no one following down beside us? I had no idea. I couldn't see to the sides, I was barely able to see to the front, I was just carried down the slope by the rush,' he added lamely.

'Well, from above it looked very heroic. Either way, you went through the Norse line like water through sand, it was rather wonderful to watch. Then, the whole enemy line on the breach collapsed and our army was through into that melee in the centre.'

Adolf shook his head in disbelief. 'I need to stop joining in on this nonsense. I'm too old to be leading charges. I could barely keep up, let alone fight. Why did you let me do this?'

Dietmar rolled his eyes at the half jest. 'You got what you wanted, by tomorrow the whole army will know the story of how Count Adolf broke the enemy line and stormed the fortress.'

'I did no such thing,' Adolf stammered, embarrassed. 'I laid my sword on maybe one enemy, poked a couple in the legs, and other than that ran around panting like a sick dog.'

'Doesn't matter, that's what everyone will be hearing, make what you want of it.' Dietmar stifled a cry as the man below him started stitching the neat cut in his leg, leaving Adolf to his thoughts for a moment.

Then the man was finished, Dietmar grunted his thanks and the soldier walked along the line of the wall and knelt down next to a man who had broken his leg falling from the wall.

'I hear the assault on the other breach was a disaster, so the men who came past before you arrived were saying,' Dietmar said, gingerly lowering himself down from the short rampart onto his good leg.

'Oh, what happened?'

'I don't know any more, other than that.'

'Well, let's go and find out, can you walk?'

Dietmar tested his wounded leg gingerly, hissing through his teeth as he put weight on it and staggering, holding onto the rampart for support.

'Perhaps if I had help…'

Adolf grinned and went over to take the man's arm over his shoulder. 'Don't you have a squire for this sort of thing?'

'As you know well, my lord, my squire is attending to the horses, a task he does not thank you for. I cannot imagine he will be happy that you made yourself a hero while he curried chargers at your insistence.'

'Well, I care not what he thinks, he is alive to think it. He is barely a man, he has no place in an assault like that.'

'Other men his age were up there,' replied Dietmar, hobbling along beside the count as they made their way out of the fortress through the now open gate, trying to avoid the trickle of men going in and out, and the bodies and debris all around them.

'Other young men his age died up there,' Adolf snapped back, 'and none of them the only sons of powerful counts.'

Dietmar didn't reply, he was focused on staying off his injured leg, which was throbbing and burning under his padded chausses. But his thoughts were troubled. *There are more ways than death to lose a son.*

The command tent of Count Baldwin of Flanders was full again for the first time in many weeks. The sieges of the coastal towns and fortresses had ended eight days before, and only now was the army finally re-gathered to hear the plans for the next phase of the campaign, even as summer faded away around them.

The town of Lund had grown hugely in size, a tented city springing up around its modest and broken walls. All of the Crusader engine of war was here, with all the camp followers, families, households, servants, clergy, supply trains and scroungers that kept the cogs turning. An army of over twenty thousand assembled, a following of the same number. Still thousands of glum, mourning and dispossessed Norse remained within its boundaries. Lund was now the biggest city in all of the North.

And like any good Christian city, the flock needed a shepherd. Reinhard, the freshly ordained Bishop of Lund, the first, and so far only diocese in the new ecclesiastical province of Nordland. In the three weeks since he had arrived, Bishop Reinhard had established an iron grip over the religious and most of the civic functions in Lund, allowed by a Crusade commander only too happy not to have the responsibility. Now the de facto second most powerful man in the city, he was ferocious in defending the position and power of the church, and by extension, his own. He had sent word to the Archbishop of Mainz, his ecclesiastical overlord, that all was ready and prepared to convert the province. They would be sending a party of priests and clergy to establish a church in every town and major village in Scania, and after that, all of the North. All reporting directly to him, all bent to his will, spreading his control over the whole province. The thought made him truly excited, not an emotion he allowed himself very often, close as it was to the sin of pride.

Now, Reinhard stood in the back of the large room, behind and to one side of the throne-like chair that Baldwin so favoured, watching the room like a hawk. This was the first time he had seen all the commanders together and he was there to spot any potential resistance or trouble to his civic rule.

'Order gentlemen, order,' called an aide in a shrill voice. 'Pray be silent for his excellency the bishop.'

Reinhard stepped meekly forwards as the room fell to silence and briefly surveyed the gathering with an appraising look. 'Let us pray,' he intoned, and the crowd all lowered themselves to their knees.

'We gather today to give thanks for our opportunity to serve our Lord in this, his divine will. We pray for his aid in our success, for the redemption of our sins, and for the continued leadership of Count Baldwin, conqueror of Skania and commander of this most holy Crusade. In nomine Patris et Filii et Spiritus Sancti, Amen,' said the bishop, eyes closed, head bowed, making the sign of the cross before his chest.

'Amen,' muttered the audience in return.

The commander in question strode into the tent at that point with a broad smile and was greeted by a wave of applause from the assembled men as they rose to their feet. Reinhard smiled broadly and stood back to one side.

Baldwin rode the wave of adulation all the way to his throne, and, pausing to accept it with graciousness, signalled an end by raising his hand to the crowd.

'Gentlemen,' he said in a loud voice. The applause died down rapidly to silence. 'Gentlemen, I called you here today to celebrate our victory, and to let you hear of our plans for the rest of this holy expedition, to end the weak pagan resistance, once and for all.'

Another wave of applause rolled around the room. Again the count smiled and acknowledged it and again he raised his hand for silence. 'I am pleased to announce that in the name of our Holy Father, and for the betterment of all Christianity, we have completed the conquest of Skania, the last province of the pagan kingdom of Denmark.'

With a flourish, he produced a slim golden crown from his cloak and held it up for the whole room to see, before throwing it down at the foot of the dais triumphantly. 'The fallen crown of the Kings of Denmark! A gift now, for our church, to aid in its holy work here.' The crowd erupted in cheers, some of genuine enthusiasm. Reinhard politely applauded along with them. He knew the crown was not the real crown of the Danish kings, most in the room would know that, but most of those who were not sycophantic to the young count had long since left his inner circle of command. All that were left were those who followed him absolutely, or those who pretended to do so for their own gain.

No, not all, he thought, his eyes landing on a small knot of men who were not celebrating, who stood stony-faced in the back corner of the room. *So, you must be the famous Count Adolf, the man who has cleared half a dozen breaches. Hmmm, older than I imagined.*

The cheering had died down and the count had finished accepting the plaudits for his victory, a victory achieved without him travelling far outside the Crusader camp.

'So, my lords, we must continue this most holy Crusade, into the vile pagan kingdoms of Sweden and Norway. To wherever the pagans live, whatever holes they hide in, whichever forest they cower in.' Men around the room shouted words of encouragement or agreement. 'We go not for our own glory, or for earthly reward, we go because God wills it!'

'Deus vult!' shouted back the audience in response.

'I have consulted with my advisers and prayed on the matter,' said Baldwin, taking a stern tone and nodding at his own words. 'Some have counselled that we continue with our gradual capture of towns and territory, but no, no more.' He wagged his finger at the assembled lords. 'We have established our base, we have cleared the local towns and fortresses, the enemy could not even attempt to come to their aid, they are finished, defeated, scattered before the fury of the cross, and our righteous swords!' He was getting into his stride now, the speech Reinhard knew he had spent three days preparing well underway. Reinhard had to admit, he was quite good at it, he had captivated the gathering.

'Now is the time for bold action, gentlemen, fellow warriors of Christ. We will assemble our whole strength and march on Uppsala, and, as my father captured Jerusalem, so we will storm the capital of these northerners and break their will, bringing their entire lands into the circle of God's kingdom for evermore. Deus vult!' he roared at the crowd until he was red in the face.

Baldwin slumped heavily into his chair as cheers and replies of 'God wills it' rang around the tent. Reinhard wasn't watching them, however; he was watching the furious face of the man he presumed to be Adolf, Count of Holstein. And the bishop wasn't the only one, Baldwin also had been eyeing the angry German lord.

'Do you object, Count Adolf?' Baldwin asked, hissing the word count as if it was a slight. 'Do you, as ever, think I am doing it wrong? Hmm? What does the *hero* of Trelleborgen have to say about my strategy, which has so far been met with nothing but victory?'

Reinhard watched with interest as Adolf stepped forward and stared at the French count, not knowing what reaction to expect. 'I would say you should not abandon a winning strategy, Lord Baldwin. Your commands, as you rightly point out, have led to victory after victory. Continue as we have so far, expand our control, take each town as we pass, secure our flanks and supply routes, post garrisons and control the populace.'

Baldwin smiled at the unexpected praise but dismissed the notion with the wave of a hand. 'There is no place for that fearful caution. I have defeated the enemy, we have no further need to continue those petty skirmishes, the distractions of sending minor forces like yours to secure unimportant towns. No, we will finally be bold, we will, like a good swordsman, make a single decisive blow to the heart of our enemy and be done with it.' Baldwin looked very pleased with himself over this analogy and turned his gaze away from the German count.

Reinhard watched in fascination as Count Adolf visibly wrestled with his control, teetering between backing down and unleashing an outburst. Just as Reinhard thought the count might disappoint him, he saw another lord desperately signalling to Adolf to back down. Reinhard noted the man for later investigation. But Adolf did not see the gesture, or it did not control his anger.

'That is not how a swordsman fights, Count Baldwin,' Adolf barked across the room.

'What? What are you rambling about now, man?' replied Baldwin, irritation bubbling in his voice.

'Making one single, decisive thrust, regardless of position. That is not the art of sword fighting. You are correct, again, we should do as a good swordsman would do. We have already tested our enemies' speed and reaction, we have conducted a feint and then landed a solid blow but merely scored him, not deeply wounded him. We have used this blow to push him back and gained secure footing. These, these were all the actions of a good swordsman.' The whole room was silent now, all eyes on the two bitter rivals. Baldwin was sitting, unsure of himself now, as Adolf continued to praise his actions, but yet conveyed his unwelcome criticism clearly. Adolf continued in his firm and measured tone, like a master instructing an overzealous student, which, Reinhard thought, wasn't far from the truth.

'But the good swordsman, having secured the advantage, and having better speed and strength than his enemy, does not abandon his good footing and make a single huge lunge, one that will be visible in advance. That would be foolish.' The atmosphere in the room hardened another notch at the word, the German count was close to crossing a line, and everyone could feel it.

'No, the good swordsman uses the advantage to press his opponent, to wear him down, to guard against surprise counters to his sides and to weaken and force his enemy into a mistake. Then, when the enemy has no way out, when he cannot avoid, parry or block our strike; then the swordsman conducts the killing blow. That, Count Baldwin, that is what we should do.'

Reinhard revelled in the awkward silence that sat heavy on

the gathering after Adolf finished speaking, delighted in the open hostility as the angry men stood and glared at each other. Baldwin was not a fighter, and Adolf was fresh from reported feats of arms in no less than three sieges. The challenge was there, unspoken but hanging in the open like thick smoke. Would Baldwin strain credulity by disagreeing, and inviting the obvious charge of ignorance, a charge that would be laced with cowardice?

Divisions in other men were what Reinhard loved above all other things. They gave him avenues to power to exploit, factions to play against each other, cover to increase his own grip as others lost theirs. He looked at the two rivals and he gave silent thanks to God for being his instrument in this place.

Baldwin gritted his teeth, caught in the obvious trap which even he discerned. He could acknowledge Count Adolf was correct, and change his policy, publicly ceding power to his rival. He could argue the issue, which would make him look ridiculous, or he could run from it by dismissing the objection, or indeed the man himself, which would make him look a coward, as Count Adolf had spoken plainly and inoffensively and with diplomacy and even praise. There was no good way out, everyone in the room sensed it, every passing moment of indecision made it worse.

It was in that moment, as Reinhard watched in barely concealed amusement, and the command of the Crusade hung undecided in the air, that the tent flap burst open, and a panting and dust-smeared man swept into the room.

The tension shattered as all eyes fixed on the man as he hurried through the crowd, brushing or simply pushing past half the great lords on the Crusade, to reach the dais. Baldwin watched in shock as the man arrived and went to one knee in front of him.

'What is the meaning of this?' he managed to stammer out.

'My Lord Baldwin, I come from the harbour with dire news. A fleet of the Norsemen appeared in the dawn, they...' He paused, nervous in front of the silent room of watching eyes. Being the bearer of bad news was never a pleasant task, especially not with so many to witness your discomfort. Baldwin opened his hand and gestured impatiently at the man to continue.

'Out with it, man.'

'Yes, my lord. A fleet of the Norsemen, they attacked the incoming supply fleet. They captured and burned many of the ships, others were driven ashore or fled. The fleet was utterly lost. Only a single ship made it to harbour, crewed by a few men, carrying no supplies and allowed through only to give us a message.'

The tense silence broke into shards of dismay and outrage. Baldwin's fury drained and his face paled, he sat down heavily and for a long while did nothing to stay the angry lords, some of whom were shouting questions at the messenger as he gazed helplessly around. Finally, Reinhard stepped forward to speak, a pit of worry in his stomach, swallowing the earlier pleasure.

'What ship arrived, what was the message?' The messenger stared up at him, barely hearing through the rising waves of uproar. The man shook his head dumbly.

Finally, Baldwin waved his hand for silence, which achieved nothing. He stood and shouted for silence and the questions and outrage died down. 'Answer him, what ship, with what message?'

'It was a ship carrying a new party of priests.' Reinhard's stomach relaxed half a degree; so, the ship carrying his new subordinates had been spared. But the messenger had paused again, his lip trembling.

'What message did the priests give to you?' asked Reinhard, his voice barely a ragged whisper. 'None spoken, my lord.' The man's voice cracked. 'All but one are dead, and the last one's tongue was cut out.'

CHAPTER 21

SPEAKING IN TONGUES

Early September 1117

REINHARD PACED IN the nave of his repurposed church, right fist clenched to his mouth and his left hand fiddling with the belt on his simple robes. The mutilated and permanently muted priest from the supply fleet had just left, drained and in agony after a slow and extended questioning. Waiting for the man to write his answers had been tedious and frustrating, but Reinhard had needed many, and taxed the still shocked man to his limit.

Bertrand returned to the hall after taking the mute priest to rest in an adjoining house, one used by many of the priests. He waited politely by the side of the room, eyes gazing patiently at the floor, as they so often did when his master was deep in thought.

Reinhard stopped his pacing at the head of the aisle of benches, facing the makeshift altar with its bright tapestry and shining ornaments. *Even those taken back from the heathens, a stolen heathen building, filled with stolen heathen silver. All dedicated to the service of Christ.* He chuckled to himself. The proper set of silver he had requested, and the magnificent altar cross, had been stolen from the maimed priest's ship. But even that loss he refused to mourn, the coming of the mutilated priest had turned the series of disasters into good fortune, he was sure, if only he could find the way to leverage it.

At that moment, the door opened, and a young French baron strode in. 'Ah, Sir Hugues, I am pleased and humbled that you have come to my church.'

Sir Hugues strode over, smiling politely, and stopped to receive the offered blessing, taking it without a moment's hesitation.

'So you are a man of God, Sir Hugues, a true servant, I take it?'

'A humble servant of the Lord and the Crusade, my lord bishop,' Hugues replied knowingly, with a slight bow. 'I am pleased to be granted an audience with you.'

'Nonsense, all are welcome in this house of worship, So, how may I be of service to you?' Reinhard had seen Hugues, and noted his position of influence with Duke Welfard, and the power of his forces. He had marked the man as one to watch with care and interest. *I wonder what you want, and what you have to offer me in return.* 'Nonnes is not for a while yet, if you wish to take it with us?'

Sir Hugues shook his head briskly. 'Alas, I have other duties to attend to that would prevent that honour, perhaps another time. No, I am here to ask if there is anything I can do about the dreadful sacrilege committed against your brothers.'

'That is most gracious of you, Sir Hugues, I am pleased to have a charitable lord like yourself offer your help. We are much injured and reduced by these appalling massacres.' He paused, looking solemn, hands clasped in front of him. 'It is not for my poor brothers I mourn, they are with the Lord now, but for his work that so few of us left behind cannot continue in their absence.'

Hugues nodded sympathetically. 'I am sure that we can

find some way of easing your burden. Perhaps I could send to my brother, he is a devout man and very close to the Archbishop of Metz. Perhaps they could arrange for a party of volunteers to come here, to share the burden. Priests and lay clergy, to be at your disposal.'

Reinhard sucked his front teeth as he pretended to consider the offer. 'That is a very kind suggestion, but I fear our needs are more immediate, and your lands are too far away. If I may be so bold, your offer has given me an idea, perhaps I could ask a favour instead?'

'Of course.' Hugues smiled expansively, as if having given the bishop a way of asking a favour without seeming a beggar had not occurred to him. 'If I can help in any other way you deem sufficient, it will be done.'

'My blessings on you. Well, we have, due to the generosity of our Lord Baldwin, all the materials and steadfast labourers we need to start building a house of God in every town. What we don't have, and we dearly need as this terrible incident has shown us, is men to guard our peaceful brothers in this dangerous land. I have heard of the many raids of the enemy with great sadness and concern, and if we are to minister to these towns, we will need to protect our ministers. There was a party of knights, men of God sworn to protect the church, sailing with the fleet, but I fear they too were lost to the enemy, God rest their souls.' Reinhard made a pained expression and crossed himself.

Sir Hugues clasped his hands together and rubbed them thoughtfully, like a man judging the price of a horse at a market and deciding what to offer for it. 'Well, I am sure I could find some men of my contingent willing to serve on so noble a mission, to defend the servants of our church. Perhaps eighty men, will that do?'

That many? Well, in dire need of a friend are you, Baron Hugues?

'Sir Hugues, that is both generous and magnificent, such a gift will truly advance the work of God's humble servants in this dangerous land.' Reinhard smiled broadly and placed a hand on the Frenchman's shoulder. 'A friend of the church such as you will always be welcome in my fold, should you need guidance or support.'

Hugues, seeing the polite dismissal for what it was, bowed. 'I will send one of my captains around with the men tomorrow for your instructions. My thanks for your time, and the opportunity to serve our Lord more closely.' He emphasised the last part carefully, and with that he left, crossing himself as he passed the altar.

Bertrand sidled over towards Reinhard, confusion written in his face. 'Do we not need more brother priests? More than we need soldiers, surely Count Baldwin would provide us with men if we asked.'

Reinhard sighed and turned on the man, his smile erased. 'If I asked Lord Baldwin for men, I would appear supplicant and owe him gratitude; by allowing Baron Hugues to offer men, I make him the supplicant. It's not complicated, never ask for something that can be freely given.' Bertrand sniffed, the confusion not dissipating.

'But the priests? How can we have churches with no priests to minister them?'

Reinhard scowled at the confused man. 'More priests are already on the way, that was but one small party. Our blessed papal father has sent the call far and wide for men of the cloth to come here and bring new flocks into the fold. Many will come, more than we need in all likelihood. In any case, the fool Norse made martyrs of our fallen brethren, *and left me a heart-breaking cripple I can parade whenever I need support*, and if there is one thing likely to draw bored and devout priests from all over Europe it's the faint chance of being associated with something notable. So it doesn't matter that some unfortunate brothers died, they are with their Lord now and are easily replaced, something you should remember the next time you ask stupid questions.' Bertrand lowered his eyes and mumbled an apology, backing away a step.

'Now, go and prepare Nonnes; tomorrow, we have a new church to found, and a town to show the path to Christ's light.' Bertrand slipped from the room and left Reinhard alone, thinking deeply. *I have the resources, I have the labourers, I have men to guard us and the sympathy of an army. Now we can truly begin.*

To call it a town would be an overstatement, Reinhard thought, as their little column arrived in the small settlement on the coast south-east of Lund, a few miles from the captured fortress of Trelleborgen. Truly it was more like a fishing village, of modest size. *But was our saviour not a friend of the fishermen?*

The village had already been visited by the Crusade and a garrison was in place, guarding the work parties who were building a harbour worthy of the name in place of the old fishing docks. The locals were downcast, the fighting men who had lived there dead or gone, and the whole place had a sullen air of despair and surrender. It rankled in Reinhard's nose, mixing with the very real stink of fish, and of the animals kept in pens on the outskirts.

However modest, this was the nearest significant settlement south of Lund that had not been abandoned or burned and would thus grow quickly, so this is where he would start his personal Crusade, to take the fortresses of the people's hearts, to turn them to the light and make them soldiers of Christ. From his modest settlement, his priests would travel the surrounding farmlands and hamlets, bringing the whole area, and the thousands of its remaining people, into the fold. From that seed, all of southern Skania could be brought to kneel before the one true God. All this under the watchful gaze, and ready swords, of the men provided by Baron Hugues.

Reinhard knew little about soldiers, other than how blasphemous they were. He despised blasphemy; if there was one thing he could not abide, that he hated above all things, it was crude and blasphemous talk, it was unholy and unpleasant. However, he could tell these were men of quality. Their equipment was well kept, their manner calm and restrained, and their discipline obvious. Reinhard could forgive them their blasphemy, for he valued their discipline above all. *Did our saviour not teach forgiveness?*

The column reached the centre of the town and halted in what served as the central square. Reinhard looked around, disappointed. There wasn't a stone building in the entire place. Longhouses of various sizes, all made from wood and cut turf, surrounded them. He pressed his lips into a thin line as he surveyed the spread of inadequacy. None of these buildings would serve as a church he could be proud of; one would have to be built anew. There was no ready stone in this area, so wood would have to do. No matter, he had carpenters. He had anything he wanted.

'Bertrand, find the highest point in this filthy village and mark whatever building stands there for removal. We will found our church there.'

Bertrand nodded without question and turned away to the gaggle of labourers and clergy who stood behind him, leaning in to relay the orders. The captain of the soldiers, a solid looking man called Francois, nodded to half of the twenty men they had brought with them and they trotted off up the slight hill, off to make whoever lived on top of it homeless.

Satisfied with the progress, Reinhard moved on to four more towns in succession, and then back to Lund, leaving parties of labourers, each with a clutch of clergy to direct them and soldiers to guard them, to build the churches and set about converting the populace.

A few weeks later, three such new churches had been founded, covering the whole area around Lund for thirty miles in each direction, a land of rich farms, countless small settlements and a few other towns. Within days, one of those settlements, the one he had visited near Trelleborgen, had been burned, the half-built church destroyed, and the priests and Baron Hugues's men massacred.

Hugues arrived at the converted hall soon after Reinhard received the distressing report.

'Ah, what a pleasant surprise, Sir Hugues, come to pray again in my humble church?' Reinhard said, putting on a calm front despite his anger and frustration.

'I find it is a peaceful place in this heathen town.' Hugues looked angry and troubled.

'True, the house of the Lord is always a place where you can escape the cares of the world, to stand just a little closer to the grace of God.' Reinhard stepped past the Frenchman and knelt before the altar to pray. He stayed there for longer than strictly necessary, long enough to cause the waiting French lord just a hint of annoyance. *No harm in making sure everyone knows who is in control.* Finally, he intoned a blessing and rose to his feet, smiling and gesturing to the French lord to sit. Hugues, to his credit, managed not to look put out by the little game and sat down beside him on the bench.

'So, you have heard the news, of course? What does the army intend to do about these outrages?' he asked.

'Yes, I have heard, and the appropriate course of action is being decided.' Hugues did his best to convey his displeasure at that situation without open criticism.

'I see. Forgive me, I know very little about military matters, but what action should be taken?'

'Well, in my humble opinion, we need to find the nest of vipers wherever they are, and burn them out. Their ships, that is, we should find their harbour, for it cannot be far away, and destroy them there. I don't have the men or the authority to conduct such an attack, far from the army.' He chewed his lip thoughtfully. 'Count Baldwin may allow reprisal raids, if he can be persuaded of their importance, but there is debate if the Crusade should waste time on this matter.'

Reinhard sucked the air through his front teeth, the faint whistling giving way to an apologetic shrug. 'And why is there disagreement on this? It sounds the correct course of action to me, although as I say, I have little understanding of such things.'

'There are certain parties that believe we should ignore this provocation as irrelevant, and press forward with the march on the Norse capital.' Reinhard nodded, knowing that it would be the young Baldwin pressing the unwise path. 'But the loss of the supply ships, and the delay these raids have caused, have made that quite impossible.'

'Tell me, I saw a German lord, Count Adolf, I believe, advocating for securing the surroundings before proceeding. Did he not succeed in arguing the point, especially after the tragic attack on the fleet?' Reinhard had seen Hugues talking to the German count, trying to calm him when Baldwin raged, and wanted to probe the depth of that relationship.

Hugues grimaced and his sharp eyes flicked upwards to meet Reinhards. 'It is true that his is one of the voices advocating that direction, but he... he is not in favour at the moment. I am seeking others who might lend weight to that choice of action.'

Reinhard thought about this, wondering if his relationship with Count Baldwin would suffer from trying to influence matters of strategy. It might, but equally he needed the attacks to end for his network of churches to be built and maintained. 'That is a shame, it seemed to me to be a logical argument, although, who am I, a humble servant of God, to have an opinion on strategy?'

He smiled harmlessly, refusing to be drawn into an outright offer of support.

Hugues continued to hold his gaze, Reinhard saw the frustration on his face, and the intelligence in his eyes, and decided the baron was worth keeping interested. 'I do pray with the count, and offer him spiritual guidance,' he said brightly, as if the thought had come upon him suddenly. 'Perhaps, the next time I see him, I might enquire as to his thoughts on the matter, impress upon him the importance of the threat to the efforts of my church. It would be a small favour for a good friend of the church such as yourself. What do you think would convince him?' asked Reinhard, regarding the baron carefully.

'I don't know. He is unlikely to launch such an expedition, one that would require thousands of men, over the deaths of a few dozen garrison troops and a handful of priests.'

'Indeed. Perhaps he will need more persuasive methods.'

Hugues's eyes flicked up to meet Reinhard's gaze, the Frenchman's expression betraying his nervousness at the discussion, the German's displaying utter calm and control.

'What would you suggest?' the baron said, slowly and deliberately.

Reinhard suppressed a smile at how quickly he had gained control of the situation. 'I suggest we emphasise the nature of this attack on the servants of the church. This Crusade is intended to bring the Lord's light to these lands; to see his humble servants murdered is a crime that any good Christian cannot overlook, and cannot be allowed to happen again. Surely, any good Christian must be outraged, and demand immediate punishment of the offenders. To do else would be a betrayal of our vows? Or at least, that is what we must make the lords of this Crusade think, and then there will be no choice in the action that we must take.'

Hugues smiled, the first time in a while, and put his finger to his lips, staring at the ground. 'Yes, we create such outrage that the decision is made before it even reaches Count Baldwin, but does not look like we made it. Now, may I ask, did any of the commanders ever meet the surviving priest from the fleet, the one with the missing tongue?' He smiled slyly.

Reinhard instantly saw where he was going with that question. *Ach, why didn't I think of that?* 'My dear Hugues, are you suggesting that we allow the men of the Crusade to get the incorrect impression that he is a victim of this latest attack, that this is now a pattern of mutilation of priests, a deliberate strategy of most vile heresy and insult?' Reinhard said, in studied horror.

'I'm suggesting that, if such rumours did happen to arise, fuelled by some unknown source, that we not combat them,' Hugues replied carefully.

'If we are discovered in this intrigue, we would be seen to be undermining the commander of the Crusade,' Reinhard said, probing Hugues's commitment with the challenge. They were on dangerous ground now.

Hugues surprised Reinhard by bursting out laughing, so hard he had to wipe a tear from his eye. 'My dear bishop, how would the truth be discovered? The man can't exactly tell anyone.'

CHAPTER 22

A NEST OF VIPERS

REINHARD FUSSED ABOUT the makeshift church, fighting to control his own impatience. *For patience is a virtue dear to the Lord.* To his not insignificant anger, he heard that another raid had massacred another garrison, this time to the north of Lund. A single priest had been visiting the village and was slain, but a few well-placed rumours in the right ears had turned that into wild stories of a burning church and a half dozen murdered priests, a story he had been too upset to confirm or deny when questioned, being busy in a day long prayer vigil for the martyrs.

The whole Crusade was now aflame with outrage at the attacks, stories of mutilated priests multiplying even without his input. But still, nothing had been done to counter the attacks. *What else must I do?* His thoughts were interrupted by Bertrand arriving in the room.

'You have a visitor, Bishop Reinhard,' said the priest, staring blankly at him.

Reinhard waved at him dismissively. 'Tell them I am at prayer and unfortunately cannot receive them.'

'Certainly, I will tell Count Baldwin you are unavailable.'

'What?' Reinhard spluttered in anger. 'Why didn't you tell me it was Count Baldwin?'

'You didn't ask who it was,' replied the priest, his expression unchanged.

'I didn't… Ach, never mind, I will deal with you later. Show the count in, tell him I am at prayer but will receive him shortly.' *Baldwin rarely leaves the comfort of his command tent, this is either very good or very bad.* The bishop hurried down the aisle and knelt by the altar, attempting to look serene and as if he had been there for hours.

After a few moments, Count Baldwin swept in and Reinhard heard him stride down the aisle before stopping uncertainty behind him. For a while nothing happened as Reinhard was content to let the count stew in indecision over what to do, unsure if he would interrupt, or join in, giving him time to feel like he was the supplicant, and Reinhard in charge.

After a short time, Reinhard heard soft footsteps and a creak of wood off to one side as the count moved to a bench and sat down to wait. Reinhard worked hard to avoid any reaction to this small victory, his iron discipline working in his favour, as it so often did. After a long time, knees starting the familiar burn from his pose, the count conspicuously cleared his throat. Reinhard ignored it for just a few moments longer, as if it had no effect, before finally breaking his motionlessness to cross himself and stiffly rise from his knees.

He spent another moment facing the altar, muttered a few lines of a random psalm out loud, before superfluously crossing himself again and turning as if to walk back down the aisle. He set eyes on Count Baldwin, who was smiling awkwardly, and feigned surprise.

'My lord count… what a pleasant surprise to have you join me in my humble house of worship. Do you wish to pray with me?'

Baldwin shook his head politely. 'No, that won't be necessary.'

Reinhard smiled graciously. 'Whenever is convenient, our doors are always open to men of the Crusade, and of course any other children of God. So, what can I do to serve you today?' Reinhard suddenly frowned. 'My, where are my manners, I hope you were not waiting too long. I was deep in contemplation, you understand, praying for the souls of our brave martyrs.' He crossed himself as he finished speaking.

'Of course, I understand, I was here but a moment,' Baldwin lied smoothly, waving a hand to indicate it was a matter of no consequence. 'I have come seeking your advice.'

'Ahh, the guidance of God's emissary. I understand.' Reinhard sat down next to the count, uncomfortably close, and clasped the man's unwilling left hand between his own, smiling disarmingly at him. 'What spiritual matter concerns you? Perhaps a matter of morality, or maybe a difficult interpretation of scripture?'

Baldwin leant back and looked at the smoke-darkened roof-beams to hide his discomfort with the bishop's closeness. 'Indeed, I do currently struggle with my views on St Paul's first letter to the Romans, and how that should affect our treatment of the pagans, for I believe he teaches that pagans are not damned simply because they are pagans. It troubles me how this means we should deal with them justly, but that is not why I am here today.' Reinhard was temporarily stunned, his face locked into a rictus of a smile. *He is concerned by what?*

For the first time he could remember in recent years, Reinhard was unable to form a reply. He would have been less surprised if the bench had got up and declared an interest in carpentry than he was by discovering the count had complex thoughts on difficult points of scriptural interpretation. But he did recover in time to avoid the count feeling disrespected by his lack of reaction. 'Certainly, my lord, St Paul's teachings about the deliverance of the pagans are interesting, and worthy of much exploration. Indeed, they guide my hand as I am here in the northlands seeking to bring the pagans into his fold.' Reinhard managed to put the winning smile back on his face. 'But also we must consider the teachings of other epistles and indeed our saviour himself, and I would most welcome a further discussion on the matter. But indeed, what is the subject you are here to discuss?'

Baldwin nodded slowly. 'It is a more earthly matter.' He was attempting to gently wiggle his entrapped hand free of Reinhard's clasp, something Reinhard studiously ignored. 'It is the matter of what to do about these raids and desecrations that brings me here.'

Reinhard pursed his lips and sucked air through his teeth in his unique fashion and leaned back, finally releasing the count's hand. 'I am not sure what help I can offer on such matters, I imagine the solution is military, not spiritual?'

'I disagree, I believe the answer is both. I have already consulted with my commanders, and there is much debate on the long-term solution to this crisis, and complete agreement on the first reaction we must take.'

'Indeed? And what action is that?'

'We must find and wipe out this nest of vipers, the place from which these savages launched their unholy raids.'

'That sounds appropriate,' Reinhard replied noncommittally, amused that Baldwin had clearly adopted the term that Hugues had used. 'What is the disagreement on the long-term plan?'

'My intention to capture Uppsala before winter has already been ruined by these raids, and by the delays caused by those inside my army who insist we deal with these raiders first. Well, if we crush one nest, another will later spring up unless we clear the entire land of them. If we commit our entire army to such tasks, the Crusade will fail. On the other hand, if we strike for the pagan holy city directly and leave more of these nests behind us, more massacres could result.' Reinhard nodded politely as the count laid out the obvious arguments as if they were insightful.

'These mutilations and desecrations… they have unnerved the men, and I am pressured on all sides to prevent a recurrence before we start the final campaign; that we cannot allow the servants of God to be murdered in this way, I am sure you would agree.'

Reinhard exhaled and tapped his hand on his thigh. 'I am most pleased to hear that you wish to end these atrocities, it weighs heavily on my every thought and prayer. But isn't the purpose of the army to conquer more pagan land, not to govern that which is already conquered?'

'Precisely, I cannot defend everywhere, nor split off portions to control this land and still hope to advance the campaign. I cannot control such spread out contingents.' He leaned in conspiratorially, lowering his voice. 'I have only a few commanders I can trust, and some I cannot, who I fear work against me, who would betray me if left unsupervised. If I take the trustworthy commanders with me, the others will fail in their tasks to control the countryside. If I send the trustworthy ones out to complete these missions, the others may sabotage me entirely out on the campaign, perhaps even usurp my command.' The count looked dejected and miserable as he confessed the source of his recent paralysis.

Reinhard listened with an expression of deep sympathy, wondering at how out of his depth the count truly was with the command of a complex political and military operation like the Crusade. 'And whichever result comes to pass, as the commander you will be blamed for the failure? If the attacks continue, you will bear responsibility in the eyes of the distant and the ignorant, when really it is the fault of the disloyal?'

'Precisely,' Baldwin whined.

'I know a little of your problems, my lord. I have seen these men who threaten your leadership; a certain Count Adolf, he undermines you at command meetings?'

Baldwin sat upright and slapped his thigh and exclaimed, 'You have it exactly! Count Adolf and his German kin, they conspire against me, whisper in dark corners spreading lies about my competence, I am sure of it, they will engineer disaster and report back to their emperor that it was my doing!' Baldwin suddenly stopped and looked confused for a moment. 'Perhaps it was even they who caused these attacks? Some message to the enemy about where we were weakest.' Baldwin was now sweating, working himself up into a fever pitch.

Are you really stupid enough to believe that? 'I don't know if that is the case, my lord,' Reinhard said, speaking carefully and slowly 'but it sounds plausible.' *The pot is stirred, and now we strike.* 'So what you need, my lord, if I may be so bold, is to be free to take your Crusade to the heart of the enemy, while leaving someone trustworthy, independent and incorruptible to deal with the safety of the conquered lands, and the men of the cloth who work to bring the light of Christ to them.'

Baldwin's eyes blazed and locked with his, like a drowning man seizing a rope. 'Exactly, I knew you would understand.'

Reinhard leaned back and sat, apparently deep in thought, for a long while. *That seems long enough, time to finish this.* 'I think, my lord, that I might have a solution, or at least, the seed of a solution, one that may grow into one with the correct support.' He emphasised those last words unmistakably.

Baldwin leaned forwards, eyes wide and receptive. Reinhard was almost disappointed at how easy this was. 'Are you aware of the newly formed order of knights that defends the pilgrims and holy places in the Holy Land? The knights of the hospital of St John.'

'I am.'

'Well, perhaps a similar solution is needed here? An order of good Christian soldiers, knights and devout followers, who could protect the conquered lands and the good Christian folk that go about them, separate from the army, allowing the army to fulfil its holy task of conquering more pagan lands, of bringing more potential sheep into the saviour's fold?' He leant back to allow Baldwin the time to think over the idea and come around to it. He needn't have bothered.

'That is a fabulous idea! Yes, a holy order, free from the control of my traitorous German commanders, led by good Christian men uncorrupted by political ambition.' He paused, his eyes flicking side to side as he thought. 'And they would be… separate from my command, to avoid… complications.'

'Of course, they would fall under the jurisdiction of the church, as soldiers of Christ.' He smiled at the relieved man and steepled his hands innocently for the coup de grace. 'Of course, you shall have to find a suitable man to lead this brotherhood, perhaps my lord the archbishop would be able to reccom…'

'What?' said Baldwin, aghast again. 'But surely you shall lead the order?'

Well, if you insist. 'Me? Well, my lord, that is a flattering suggestion, but I already have my work, this chapel and my existing duties.'

'It was all your idea, what other man could be more suitable? A replacement would take a month or more to arrive. No, no, it must be you, no other man could be acceptable.'

Stop making this so easy, it's embarrassing. 'Well, if you insist, I suppose, I just haven't had time to think about it. There is so much to consider. I have no military knowledge, so I must have a partner from the commanders, someone to deal with that side of affairs. I really must pray on the matter and seek guidance… but yes, I can see that this would be God's work, and that I am likely to be guided towards it, no matter how difficult it seems. For after all, our saviour teaches us of the piety of suffering and hardship on the path to good deeds.'

'Well, of course.' It was Baldwin who now seized Reinhard's hands. 'I am so pleased I came to you, Sir Hugues was right to suggest it. He has been a most wise adviser these past few months. So much of what he says turns out to be correct.' The count stood up, smiling for the first time during their meeting.

Reinhard pressed his finger to his chin and looked up at the count. 'My lord, I believe that is a perfect solution. Yes, I see it now. Sir Hugues, he would be the perfect partner for me. He is experienced, a commander of men, wise as you say and above all, you can trust him entirely and thus so can I.'

Baldwin's smile faltered and Reinhard worried he had over-reached. 'I know you will miss his guidance, but you have other excellent supporters to counsel you, I am sure, and of course your own wisdom and experience to rely on. You don't rely on any one man to make your decisions.' Reinhard gave the count his most confident and winning smile yet as he rose to stand opposite him.

'Of course,' said Baldwin, pride prickling him to gruffness at the suggestion that he might rely too much on advice. 'You are right, he would be an ideal commander of this new order and I will continue unhindered by his absence.'

'Superb, I am certain this will be a successful solution to your present difficulties. Your confidence in this has inspired me, my lord, I feel God's work flowing through you. I will have to consult with Sir Hugues of course, and discuss how to proceed.'

'Of course, naturally you must have time to make arrangements.'

'Perhaps after your attack on the raiders, perhaps after that victory we will be ready to propose to you our plan, assuming Sir Hugues accepts my suggestion of leading this brotherhood.'

'Hmm, I am sure he will. But I will put in a good word with

him on your behalf just in case. Don't worry, I am sure I will convince him your plan is solid. Thank you for your guidance, bishop.' Baldwin bowed and swept from the room without a backwards glance.

It was all Reinhard could do not to burst out into tears of mirth. *Put in a good word for me, dear lord, whatever next.*

Reinhard's mood had hardly dampened by the time he reached Baron Hugues's tent. He had even skipped admonishing Bertrand for his earlier failing, an omission he thought was exceedingly generous.

He forced his usual neutral expression back onto his face and pushed through the flap of the tent. Sir Hugues was sitting at a small table, talking with two of his captains. All three men looked up to see who had interrupted them. Sir Hugues's eyebrows went up when he saw who it was and he brusquely dismissed the two soldiers, who left, eyeing the bishop with confusion. The tent flap closed behind them and Hugues finally spoke.

'Good afternoon, your eminence, you bring good news, I hope?'

'Indeed. Apparently, someone convinced the commander to come to me for advice on the subject of the raids.' He stared at Hugues with his bland expression cracking just a touch.

'That worked, did it?'

'To an unprecedented degree, I didn't realise how lost that boy is. He didn't just come for advice, he wanted me to solve his entire strategy for him.'

Hugues choked back a laugh and stood up, running a hand through his hair. 'I was hoping he might allow you to present some input, but he simply took your advice on the counter raid? Well, that is good news, I must see to my men and their preparations.' Hugues moved to usher Reinhard out of the tent but the bishop raised a finger to still him.

'There is another matter we discussed.'

'What?'

'Well, if the army moves on, the raids and trouble will continue in the conquered areas.'

'Nonsense, we will simply leave a force behind to prevent that.'

'Baldwin was very much against that idea.'

'Why on earth? It is the common practice of every army.'

'He claims it is because he doesn't trust his commanders, but I suspect it is because he is terrified of losing control. He worries separate commanders will be successful and become heroes, making him look weak by comparison, as Count Adolf did with his string of successful sieges.'

'That's pathetic.'

'Quite, but he is utterly vain and insecure. He wants everyone close, where he can see them and claim the credit for any success, blame them for any failings.'

'So what did you suggest? We cannot leave the conquered areas open and unprotected.'

'Quite. So, I suggested a solution.'

'Get out with it.'

'A military religious order, like the Knights Hospitaller, that will be separate from the army and responsible for the safety of all the conquered lands, the new churches and men of the cloth.'

Hugues was silent for a while as he considered the idea. 'And he wants the two of us to lead it.'

Ahh very good my friend, straight to the crux of the matter. 'Exactly. Two governors, one military, one clerical, to manage the two arms of the order; the brothers militare, and the brothers ecclesiastical.' *That's not exactly what Baldwin said, but it's how I want it.* 'We would recruit both from the Crusade and from our home countries, forming an independent organisation, with the writ of the commander of the Crusade backing us.'

'That sounds like a dangerously powerful organisation. Why would it be allowed?'

'Because Baldwin is desperate and foolish, so he will allow it, and by the time it is established I will have already dedicated it to the Pope himself and sworn our fealty directly to him. He will be thrilled to subvert some power in these new provinces directly to himself from the emperor, and from that point on, who will dare oppose it?'

Hugues regarded Reinhard with motionless eyes for a long moment, weighing the risk and benefit, searching for the trick or trap in the placid bishop's eyes. 'I will not be your lackey or captain, if I am to be part of this dangerous venture, for it will be dangerous. Power brings enemies like honey brings wasps. I will be in control of my own fate. I have seen how you use men like a cook uses dishcloths, to be discarded thoughtlessly when they are used up, that will not happen to me.'

Not at first, no, but it will be most refreshing to have a challenge. 'Of course, I would expect nothing less. The two governors will be of equal partnership, one responsible for the church, one for the military forces, both required to agree on any joint decisions that affect both. It will be written thus in our charter.' He gave his best disarming smile. 'Through this, I will be able to secure this province and spread the light of our saviour throughout this land in safety and security. An achievement which will make me one of the leading clergymen in the empire.' He smiled sadly. 'I hear my lord the archbishop is of failing health, I suspect in a few years a successor will be required.' *And more besides, a cardinal's seat and perhaps even the papacy would be within my reach after that.* 'And for you, of course, you wish to secure the favour of the emperor in your aims in Lorraine. By securing this province for him, and allowing the Crusade to succeed, you will gain his appreciation and trust. Not to mention the raw power and wealth that might be… acquired, in such a position.'

Hugues tapped his finger on the top of the table, heavy ring clacking on the hard wooden boards. Finally, he straightened and nodded. 'I think you are the most profoundly dangerous man I have ever met. However, I agree our aims can co-exist and both be met through this method. I will agree to nothing until we draw up the charter and I inspect its clauses.'

Excellent, you will be a worthwhile partner, and a worthy future adversary should the time come. 'Splendid! Shall we arrange a time to draw up the charter together?'

Chapter 23

Fire in the Evening

THE FORCE AT Åhus had grown to over fifty ships over the last ten days. As September set in and the land was cooling, Sigurd was planning a final huge raid that would target every harbour in Skania at once, to burn the ships, capture the supplies and destroy the docks that kept the Crusader army fed, paid and equipped, to leave them on the verge of winter with nothing to support them as the weather turned. It was to be the death blow of the Crusaders' campaign, which would force them to evacuate most of their forces or face starvation, allowing the Norse army, at full strength, to reclaim their lands in the spring.

Ordulf worked and slept in the village forge, now used by four Norse smiths, repairing weapons and making spearheads. The Norse never seemed to have enough spears. He was hammering a glowing lump of iron on one of the two rough anvils when he realised he was being watched.

He finished his hammering and inspected the cooling wedge of metal that would soon be a repaired axe-head. He nodded to himself, satisfied that the repaired section was looking straight and strong. He looked up to see who had been standing there and was surprised to see it was Jarl Ragnvald.

'Sorry, Lord Ragnvald, I didn't know it was you there.' He noticed that the jarl was holding his left arm close to his side and that it was heavily bandaged.

'Don't worry, lad, I'm not in a hurry. I came here to have you repair my sword. Some clumsy man bent it on a Christian.' Ragnvald gave him a mischievous smile as he handed his sword over to the Christian smith. 'Have a look at it and tell me if you can repair it here, or if you need to take it back to Dengir's forge.'

Ordulf took the offered blade wordlessly, glancing down its length and eyeing the edge. The sword was slightly bent towards the tip, but only slightly. He looked at the bent area and saw that the edge was rolled in that area.

'Must have been a solid Christian, looks like you hit a rock.'

'Well, it might have bounced off a helmet or two, I don't remember, it's all a bit vague after a big fight.'

'It's easy to repair anyway, I will straighten it and sharpen it for you.'

'Excellent, I'll come back tomorrow. We are going on the raid the next day, so I need it ready for that.'

'You are going? What about your arm?'

Ragnvald looked down at his bandaged arm and flexed it, the pain apparent on his face as he did. 'Bah, this will be fine, it's not a bad wound. I've had worse. The last raid was harder than the ones before. Your people are starting to put up a fight.' The concern on his face betrayed the lie of his words. It looked like he could barely move the fingers.

'Of course, lord.' Ordulf smiled and carefully put the sword down by the rough table, waiting to see if there was anything else he was needed for. Ragnvald nodded brusquely and strode off without saying anything else, his arm still motionless by his side.

Ordulf fished around in the pile of tools, looking for the clamps and wedges he would use to straighten the blade and set to work. He had a lot to finish before he slept.

It wasn't the fire or the smoke that woke Ordulf the next morning, it wasn't even the distant sound of shouting, it was the incessant barking of a dog tied up to the building across the street. He groggily opened his eyes and rolled to a sitting position in his blankets, not understanding the onslaught on his senses. He could see the dog now, and it was barking manically, looking down the road towards the coast. Ordulf saw the red glow of dawn from that direction, to the east down the slight hill, but he could also now hear a background sound off to his left, from the direction of the camp. It was a sound he had heard before, but his sleep-ridden mind couldn't remember when.

The realisation hit him just as a loud scream sounded from down the hill. That sound he could hear from the camp was the sound he had heard of the battle at Blood River Ridge, from half a mile behind the fighting.

Ordulf snapped to his feet in a rush, sleep banished in a moment, and he looked towards the main camp. It was hidden by the shape of the land but he could clearly hear the sound of fighting now. Then he looked down the hill. The red glow wasn't the dawn: below him, just two hundred paces down the hill, the docked Norse fleet was burning.

He could see some ships aflame end to end, others just catching hold. Some were drifting into the channel. Out beyond the burning ships, another, larger shape glided by in the darkness. A bigger ship. As he watched it, a speck of light flared on its deck, outlining its rig and shape, a Christian ship, with men crowding the decks. The light grew and was then flung down into an unlit longship. The flaming bundle hit the timbers of the Norse ship and flared rapidly into brightness, fire spewing over the benches and the rolled sail. Within heartbeats, the whole centre of the ship was alight.

He could now see shapes flitting around down on the docks, figures trying to douse the flames of the nearest ships or wrangling others, trying to launch them or separate them from the burning ones. He saw one man, bucket just emptied into the hold of a burning longship, speared by another who had appeared from the gloom. Then another appeared, then a whole wave of dark figures appearing out of the night, swarming the panicked men trying to save the boats.

Ordulf watched, spellbound, not knowing what to do, feeling distant from the action. More Norse were boiling out of the fishing huts and tents now, in various states of dress and arms. Some of the dark figures down by the docks turned and charged up the hill to meet this new threat.

Ordulf was still standing on his blankets, fortunately wearing his clothes, it had been a cold night. The mass of dark figures washed over the scattered and confused Norsemen in a flurry of shouting and clashing of steel and they carried on up the hill towards him. Ordulf's eyes went wide as he realised they would arrive where he stood in moments, and they did not appear to be sparing anyone.

Still veiled in darkness, he scampered across the street, away from the dark forge, and into the bushes on the other side. Just as he was about to run for the main camp, he stopped and swore to himself. His hammer and tools, his only possessions in the world, were sitting on the cold forge, just ten paces away. And next to them, Ragnvald's sword.

He hesitated, unwilling to leave either behind. He hesitated too long. He made a break from the bushes to the forge and grabbed wildly at the toolbelt and the sword, grabbing one in each hand, and turned to run back. As he turned, he saw an armed man facing him, grinning and brandishing a sword in one hand and a burning brand in the other.

'Christian, I'm a Christian slave!' Ordulf stammered out, holding the Norse sword in one hand.

The man paused in confusion and said something back to him. Ordulf didn't understand the language, it was French, or perhaps English. Just his luck. He shook his head mutely.

The man snarled and stepped towards him, sword raised to strike. Ordulf brought Ragnvald's sword and his hammer up to try to ward off the blow as the strike started to fall. He saw the man's eyes, nothing but dark pits behind his nasal helm.

He caught the sword blow in the joint between his crossed sword and hammer, stopping the blow and gasping in relief. Then the man kicked him back with a straight leg to the chest, knocking the wind out of Ordulf, and then swung the blade again, this time horizontal, arcing towards his left side.

Ordulf twisted his body wildly, bringing his sword around to block the blow. Again the sword rang on his, and again the man followed up the swing with another body attack, this time an elbow to the head that stunned Ordulf and drove him to the ground, splayed flat on his arse, his hammer flying from his grip and clanging off into the darkness. The man was already drawing back his arm to aim a thrust down towards Ordulf, Ordulf had no idea how to block it, stunned and sitting down as he was. He wailed and wildly swept his sword towards the oncoming blade, knowing he was too late.

The swords never made contact. Another figure tackled the Christian swordsman from his side, driving him to the ground and stabbing into him furiously with a seax. Ordulf watched in relief and confusion as his would-be killer died under a flurry of blows. The man rose, looking around him, and then turned to reach out a hand to Ordulf. It was Leif.

'Leif!' Ordulf, said in a strangled voice, his breath just returning to his aching body.

'Get the fuck up, now!' hissed Leif in his face, dragging Ordulf to his feet and out of the circle of light from the dying brand on the ground by the body of his attacker. Other figures were moving over the hill now, seemingly all around them. Leif was physically dragging Ordulf across the road, the slave stumbling along behind him, still clinging to the jarl's sword.

A figure came around the side of the building in front of them, helmet on and sword in hand, and Leif cut the man down without a moment's hesitation before Ordulf could tell who the man even was, friend or foe. Leif didn't break his stride, charging into the bushes, letting go of Ordulf's arm to use his hands to break through the cloying branches, turning only to urge Ordulf to follow.

The two men crashed through the bushes, the sounds of chaos and fighting covering their flight. They ran in the near darkness, across the gentle slope and towards the main camp, where the sound of fighting was still clearly heard, growing as they approached.

Finally, they reached the brow of the small hill and the camp became visible beneath them. The view took Ordulf's breath away. The camp was devastated. Bodies littered the ground, both Christian and Norse, individually and in clumps. Men were walking around on the near side of the camp, poking bodies and searching through tents. They were obviously Crusaders.

The fighting was on the far side of the camp. They could see a line of men across the whole width of the camp, locked in fierce combat. The line was moving steadily away from them as the remaining Norsemen were driven back.

Ordulf could see their path to the Norsemen was blocked by the entire Crusader force. Leif kicked the ground in frustration and looked around, finally making his decision.

'We must go, they will be searching the area for survivors. We need to reach our men by morning.'

'Reach them? Haven't they lost?'

'No. They are retreating in good order, they have not lost yet, we need to get around to them, but the Christians are to our left and the river to our right. We will need to cross it. Can you swim?'

'Swim? No, I don't know how to swim.'

'Bugger. Well, you are going to learn quickly. Let's go, now, it's swim or die.'

Ordulf hesitated, looking over his shoulder.

Leif, bristled. 'You are thinking of running to the Christians?'

Ordulf blushed, unseen in the firelight, and shook his head vigorously. It had been exactly what he was thinking. A sudden tension was in the air between the two armed men, standing on the border between their two peoples. Ordulf looked sheepishly at the sword in his hand, feeling Leif tense up. He turned it and offered it to Leif, hilt first.

Leif took the sword and eyed Ordulf thoughtfully.

'Go,' he said, finally. 'Take your chance, return to your people without one of them killing you, if you can.'

Ordulf looked around, misery on his face, and then shook his head. 'No. You saved my life again, I am in your debt.'

'That is our way, not yours. I'm giving you a chance, a choice. I'll tell the jarl you died in the fighting. Your life is yours to start again.'

'Why would you offer me this?' Ordulf looked at the man. 'I'm not yours to free.'

Leif bristled. 'Careful, lad, before I change my mind.' His expression darkened in the firelight, the accusation against his honour hitting home. 'You have made your swords, the war is already won or lost, we just can't see its outcome yet but you have no further part in it. I think you should have the chance of your life back and I have the opportunity to give it to you, with no repercussions. You saved my life once when you didn't need to. I'm here because Ragnvald sent me. It's different.'

'Ragnvald sent you to get me?' Ordulf's eyes widened.

Leif nodded curtly. 'Ragnvald sent me.'

'Then I am decided. Let's go. No one in the Christian camp ever did anything for me,' Ordulf lied.

'You are sure? You may never get another choice. If you come with me, you may die a slave in the North.' Leif crouched, hunched in the long grass, the sound of war and the smoke of the fleet around and above them, and Ordulf considered the path of the rest of his life. A fork in the road, paths brutally diverging, probably never to cross again. To risk the rampaging Crusaders to return to his life as a free smith in Germany, or to risk the river to return to the life of a slave in the cold North with his captors.

His mind screamed at him to return home. To make his way as a journeyman smith, to find Gunther, the master Bavarian sword-smith, and to take him up on his offer of a job. His heart tugged him the other way. No one in the Crusader army cared for him. The only friends he had in the world were in the North. Sir Hans never talked to him with the respect that Jarl Ragnvald or Leif did. Master Gunther might take him in as a journeyman, one amongst many low tradesmen. But with Dengir he was a respected swordsmith in his own right now, and a killer of men and wolves. Then he thought of Brunhild, and of never seeing her again, never feeling the lash of her angered tongue, or the caress of her forgiving lips.

Ordulf smiled at Leif, the weight of the decision evaporating from him like mist from a morning sea. 'You said something about having to swim? I've always wanted to learn to swim.'

'Come on then, you mad Christian.'

They set off across the rough field, skirting the perimeter of the devastated camp by a few hundred paces, staying down and out of sight. They quickly reached the river and started along the bank. The burning fleet and the Crusader ships were further down the river, the last ships burning low now, the sounds of battle at the docks having died away.

The bank was hard going, soft mud and rushes. Soon Leif stopped and turned to Ordulf. 'It's time, we have to swim across and find better ground. I'll take the swords, you just hold onto my tunic and don't panic.'

Ordulf started regretting his decision.

'The key to swimming is not splashing. Don't put your hands above the water, you can't swim in the air and you will sink. Keep your hands down in the water, push down with them like a dog would do.' He paused. 'You ever seen a dog swim?'

'Uh, yes, I think so.'

'Well then, you just do what they do, and don't climb on me, just use me as a guide. Remember,' he said with a pale smile, 'I'm carrying the swords, it will be hard enough as it is.'

The pair started wading into the river. It wasn't particularly broad at this point, or fast flowing, but Ordulf felt his panic rising with the water as it went up his chest and then to his neck. Suddenly, his leading foot didn't touch the bottom, and he felt himself starting to sink. He started thrashing his arms in panicked instinct, immediately losing track of Leif, water splashing over his face and making him splutter.

He sank beneath the surface and his thrashing feet found the bottom, driving him back to the surface. A hand grabbed his tunic and lifted him up. 'Stop thrashing!' a voice spluttered at him. 'A dog! Swim like a damn dog!'

Ordulf forced himself to calm his wild arms, and kicking at the bottom he could barely touch, with his chin underwater, he started churning with his arms under the water. At first, he made no progress; he would go under, then hit the bottom, push off, and come up for a breath. Soon, he realised how to push his hands down flat, and bring them up vertically, his feet stopped touching the bottom and his chin stayed above the surface.

Leif let go of his tunic and started pushing out for the far bank. Ordulf followed, chin thrashing around on the surface while his arms and legs windmilled wildly beneath, only just managing to keep his mouth in the air.

Eventually, and with Ordulf on the verge of exhaustion, they reached the shallows and walked out of the river, Ordulf gasping in exhaustion. 'Told you it was easy, eh?' joked Leif quietly. 'Now come on, we need to move and find our friends.'

The rest of the trip down the bank was uneventful, and to Ordulf's huge relief, they did not have to re-cross the river. The Norse army had retreated across a ford and were holding it in the face of the pursuing Christians. The exhausted pair arrived in the confused Norse ranks without anyone so much as noticing, such was the disarray. They weaved their way through the mess of wounded, half armed and disorganised warriors until Leif spotted some of Ragnvald's men.

'Leif!' one of them exclaimed, wrapping the man in a bear hug. It was Bjorn. 'We thought you were dead.'

'Me? How could you think that? No, I was merely having a swim. Where is Ragnvald?'

The man released the hug and grimaced. 'He is with the king, over there.' He inclined his head in the direction of a huddle of warriors standing around the base of a tree. 'Sigurd is wounded, men are saying it's bad. He charged into the thick of the fighting, stark naked, laying about him with a borrowed axe. I saw it myself. He got stuck a half dozen times before his huscarls dragged him back.' Bjorn shook his head in wonder. 'His champion, Gunnar, fought and beat three men in succession with one hand, while supporting Sigurd with the other as they retreated. Never seen anything like it.'

'Thor's balls,' exclaimed Leif quietly.

'Yes, and we found out today who has those.'

'Well, I must go to Ragnvald.'

'Why?'

'I have his sword.'

'Ah. Well, I'd be careful about disturbing the king.'

Leif nodded and walked off, Ordulf in tow, with nothing better to do. They made their way towards the huddle under the tree. Ordulf saw Ragnvald in deep discussion with a small circle of other jarls. Leif shuffled over and waited outside the circle. Behind them, there was a brief flare of noise as a contingent of Crusaders tried to force the ford. It was rapidly beaten back, the Norse were well embedded on the bank with spears and bows, and the sounds soon receded.

Eventually the circle of jarls broke up and Ragnvald saw Leif. He walked over, unsmiling, and embraced his huscarl, looking over his shoulder at Ordulf. 'Did you succeed? I'm sorry I sent you, I didn't realise how bad it was.' Ordulf's chest tightened at the carelessness of the remark. *I wasn't worth it?* Leif looked over his shoulder at Ordulf, shame written on his features, and then handed over the jarl's sword. Ragnvald smiled and took it, looking it over and placing it back in his scabbard, which had sat empty at his waist.

Ordulf was hit as if by a physical blow. *He didn't send Leif back for me, he sent him back for something far more valuable: his sword.* Leif read his distress on his face and came over to him, Ragnvald having turned to return to the king. Leif tried to put his hand on Ordulf's shoulder, but Ordulf batted the smaller man's arm away with the back of his hand.

'You came for the sword, not me, you lied to me. I chose to come back to this life believing you had come to save me, that it was the honourable thing to do, and you were lying to me. My jarl only wanted his fucking sword. Is that really worth more to him than me? A sword worth more than a swordsmith? A man who can make swords? Am I worth that little to everyone?' Ordulf's voice was rising, men were starting to look around – he didn't care.

Leif hissed at him to be silent and pushed him away from the gathered jarls. 'No, it was both. He wanted his sword and he told me to get you too.'

'Lies! He saw me and *then* asked you if you had been successful.'

'Not now, Ordulf, don't do this here, this isn't the time.'

'I gave up my life, a chance at a future, to come back with you, and I'm not more important to you people than a pretty bar of steel.' Ordulf was almost sobbing now.

'You gave up what?' Ragnvald strode over, anger on his face. 'The king is wounded over there, and we are trying to save the army and thus the whole fucking nation, and you are whining that I didn't worry about you first? That you don't feel important? Get a fucking hold of yourself, slave.' He shoved Ordulf aside, the smith's mouth open in wordless outrage, and he turned on Leif.

'What does he mean, he had the chance to leave? Did he try and run to the Christians? We have a way of dealing with slaves who run.' Ragnvald's voice was grinding like gravel, other jarls were watching now.

'No, lord, he…' Leif started, but Ordulf interrupted.

'RUN? I went back for your sword. I could have escaped, I could have run, but I risked my life, I nearly died, to go back for your sword. Like everyone else, I was stupid enough to value it above my own life.' Ordulf was furious now, incandescent with rage, other men looked on with confusion at the confrontation between jarl and thrall.

'Speak another word and that sword will take your life, thrall,' Ragnvald growled, teeth grating together, staring at Ordulf before turning back to Leif.

'Explain.'

'He speaks the truth, I found him holding the sword, fighting off a Christian soldier with it. Not running. We left together and came here. Let me take him away, I'll shut him up, he won't bother you again.'

Ragnvald looked around at the watching men, the slave trembling with rage, and he made his decision. 'Fine, I have more important things to do than deal with unruly slaves, make him disappear or I will.'

Leif grabbed Ordulf and started forcing him away from the jarl, begging him under his breath to leave. 'You have no idea what I have done for you, what I have sacrificed!' He wanted to scream, but the words wouldn't form, held in his throat by his promise never to tell of what had happened to Halla. Ordulf was too distressed to resist Leif's firm grip on his arm, and allowed himself to be led away, back into the slavery of a man who didn't value him above a bar of twisted steel.

Part 4

CHAPTER 24

INTO THE DARKNESS

FIFTY CREWS, NEARLY two and a half thousand men, had gathered at Åhus to conduct the great raid, full of optimism and confidence. Eighteen hundred exhausted and demoralised men were now trudging northwards along the coast. Some barely had clothes, many were wounded. Food was scarce, limited to what they could forage, buy or find as they passed through the coastal land. Not all the men even had weapons, few had full armour. The wealth of a thousand lifetimes in ships, weapons and equipment had been lost, along with the hundreds of warriors who had died. Ragnvald's crews had been camped by chance at the far side from the attack and had suffered less than most. But the loss of *Sedemonr* and his other five ships was a disaster. Men, weapons and armour could all be replaced more quickly than half a dozen good, seasoned longships.

Ahead of them, the horizon was filled with smoke. The Crusader fleet was moving ahead of them, burning every seaside village, harbour, dock, fishing hut and boat along the way. The erstwhile raiding force could not reach a safe harbour to send ships with messages for help, could not stop to recover due to the lack of food and the pursuing Crusader forces, whose scouts were visible behind them every day. The king was still alive, rumours abounded as to how badly wounded he was, but he was being carried on a litter, a mercy not afforded to most of the rest of the wounded, who walked, or when they could walk no more were left behind with a knife and an intent to use it. There was nothing else that could be done for them.

Ordulf trudged along at the back of Ragnvald's crews, trying to avoid being seen by the jarl and trying to keep his anger and misery in check. For three days, they desperately marched along the coast, following pillars of smoke, finding nothing but devastated coastal communities, scavenging food where they could, never enough. Looting clothes, furs and equipment where they had survived the fires.

On the fourth day, the leaders gave up the coastal march; wounded men were succumbing to the brutal pace every day and they would never get ahead of the Crusader fleet as they marched around the wide bay of Åhus. Their situation was deteriorating with no end in sight. Every day they were fewer and weaker. It would take weeks for a large enough Norse fleet to gather and fight their way through to rescue them, even if anyone knew they needed rescuing, which they likely did not. Not a single ship had escaped the burning of the fleet. By the point any rescue came, most or all of them would be dead anyway from hunger, or more likely the swords of the Crusaders.

Ordulf sat in sullen silence, watching as the group of jarls bickered about what action to take. He looked around at the way they had come, seeing the Christian horsemen watching from the previous ridge, ever patient and vigilant, a shadow that never left them. For the tenth time that march, he considered running, going to those horsemen, throwing himself on their mercy. For the tenth time, he shook the thought away. He was being watched, he was sure of it. He would never make it that far.

So, he watched the jarls bickering while the men slept or tended their wounds as best they could. Two men who had died in the night were being laid out to be burned on a simple pyre. Wood was just about the only thing they had plenty of. Suddenly there was a commotion over by the huddled leaders. Ordulf craned his neck to see what was happening. Sigurd had appeared, staggering, one arm tied to his bare chest, his champion supporting him as he painfully and slowly stumbled over to the now stilled meeting.

Awareness of what was going on spread, and silence fell over the small field. All eyes on the king, waiting to see if they could hear his words. Sigurd reached the group and spoke for a while, his voice weak and not carrying to where Ordulf sat. Before he had finished, one jarl stood up and shouted angrily at whatever Sigurd had said. He waved towards the coast angrily and then pointed at Sigurd. There was a ripple of consternation around the circle and men angrily gestured at the shouting jarl to back down.

One of them stood and put his hand on the man's shoulder and tried to force him away from the king. The furious jarl shoved the other man away and drew his sword, starting to point it at the king, gesturing and shouting. 'You are not MY king! Some fucking Norwegian who thinks you can come here and waste Danish lives! I'll not follow you any further in this madness. There is nothing inland from here. NOTHING!'

Unseen by the furious man, a royal huscarl had worked his way behind him, and stood there waiting, hand on his scabbarded sword. Ordulf watched in rapt attention as the oblivious man continued his rage at the motionless king.

'The nearest town inland is Jönköping. It's a hundred miles away. A hundred miles!' He was frothing now, shouting himself hoarse. 'Half these men will die before we get there. It's just forest and marsh and tiny villages all the way from here to there. The paths are narrow or non-existent. You will lead everyone to their deaths. NO! Enough. I would rather die facing the Christians than take another step in the wake of your madness.'

The man finished his shouting, still pointing his sword. A deathly silence fell over the field. The king spoke, the first movement of any kind he had made since the shouting began. 'Are you finished?'

The man was taken aback, the sword wavered, his arm tiring. 'Yes, I am finished… now I will leave…'

The king nodded and the huscarl drew his sword in a flash of polished metal and beheaded the angry jarl where he stood, before the man even knew what was happening. The body, sword still in hand, fell to the ground with a thud, spraying the closest men with bright arcs of blood.

The silence around the field deepened in the shocked silence that followed. No one protested the act. Everyone had known the man was dead the second he drew his sword at the king. Sigurd pushed himself away from Gunnar to stand unaided, white with the effort, left leg shaking. He looked around at the tattered force and spoke again, voice scratchy and strained, but loud enough to carry.

'If we follow the coast, we will all die. So we will march to Jönköping. The journey will be hard, but we will make it there. Six days, six days of suffering. We are Norsemen, we will survive it. I need volunteers to go down the coast to Norkoping, to Kalmar and to Uppsala and the surrounding towns, also to go west through the forests to find a ship to take them to Ánslo and my Norwegian jarls. Those men will take a message, that we are alive, that we are at Jönköping, that the Crusaders are following us and have started a march into the forests with winter approaching. We need food, we need weapons, we need clothes and equipment. We need warriors to join us there to defend it.

'I need fifty men to take this message, unwounded, healthy men who know the land, how to survive off it. Spread out across the kingdoms and speak it to whoever will listen. We have lost access to our ships, to the whale road that carries them. So, we will move through the forests like wolves, and this huge herd that follows us will blunder about, swiping at us in vain. We will bleed them, we will frustrate them, we will take them into the darkness and we will consume them. This I swear.' The king wheezed to a stop and was racked by coughs. Gunnar lunged forwards to catch him in case he fell, and led his suffering king away, back to his litter.

Watching the rebellious jarl die and hearing the king's plan, his confidence, the simple fact he was able to stand upright when many had thought he would die, put a little life back into the army. Men got up and gathered what little they had with them without complaint. The fittest and fastest men were gathered and sent out in groups, setting off on their long and difficult journeys to carry the king's message through the deep woods. They would later split up into pairs and go in every direction, except that which led towards the pursuing Crusader army, with its fringe of ever-watching horsemen.

Ordulf levered himself to his feet and sulkily walked off to rejoin the group. No one acknowledged him. No one helped him with food or greeted him with a kind word. He stood awkwardly to one side as the men prepared to march, for this was the army of the free men of the North. And he was just a slave.

Two armoured riders dragged the prisoner into the clearing and dumped him on the ground in front of the Saxon lord. 'We caught him in the woods, my lord. He tried to run.'

'Thank you, well done.'

Count Adolf stepped over to the prone man, who was

struggling against the ropes that bound him tightly to no avail. 'Send for that slave we freed, the one who speaks their tongue.' The count sneered down at the now still Norsemen with distaste and waited for the translator.

After a short time, a strong young man was brought into the clearing. He was a Saxon who had been in slavery in a town near Lund for five years, working on a farm. He hated the Norse with a passion and had volunteered to serve as an interpreter with the scouts. Adolf had found he was also an effective interrogator. It was really very hard to interrogate via a translator, and the... persuasion this man applied really required a profound hatred, which the freed slave had by the spadeful. As his scarred and marked back would attest, he had not been treated well by his captors.

'Take this man into the woods over there, two men will go with you, and find out what he knows.'

The big scarred man smiled a gap-toothed grin down at the prisoner. 'Does he need to survive the questions?'

'Not once he has given all the answers, no.'

'Perfect.'

The methods did disturb Adolf, it was beneath him to engage in this type of behaviour, but the results were undeniable, and he himself took no part in the actions. That was what he told himself, anyway. He gave the doomed man a last look of distaste and strode off. He wanted to be out of earshot when the questioning began.

An hour, later Baldwin and Duke Welfard were listening to Adolf's messenger report.

'So, their king is with that small army? We are certain?'

'Apparently so. He is wounded, and his army is starving and weakened. But as they have nothing to carry, no supplies or baggage train, they are still faster than us.'

'And what is their plan?'

'They are moving inland, going to a place called Jönköping, a town on a big lake one hundred miles north of here. This man was one of a few sent out to carry a message to all the Norse forces that the king will go there with his army, that we cannot follow, and the rest of the Norse army is to wait until spring to re-group.'

Baldwin's eyes widened at this news. 'Their king is isolated and weakened! My, my, gentlemen, this seems to be a God-sent opportunity, does it not?' He looked around the small group. No one dissented. All the dissenters had long been purged from the smaller command meetings he conducted while on the march. Sent to the rearguard or vanguard or simply ignored.

'Our plan to proceed along the coast securing all the towns, securing a base for attacking Uppsala in the spring, seems a wise one, should we deviate from it?' asked Duke Welfard, rubbing his chin nervously.

'A good commander changes his plan to accommodate new information, does he not?' said Baldwin with a self-satisfied smile. Welfard couldn't disagree with that principle, but the change still worried him.

'How will we supply our army if we move away from the coast?'

'We will take care of that, establish a harbour on the coast, bring the supplies into there, then transport them overland to the army. We will make a road as we go. Roland, you will attend to those arrangements?' The count waved his hand as if these were small concerns as one of his aides nodded in assent. Welfard thought they sounded very large concerns indeed. There was an army of nearly ten thousand at their backs. Moving them through the forest where there was nothing but trails sounded implausible at best.

'I am not sure…' Welfard began.

'We have them, by God, we have them!' The count slapped his thigh in pure glee, ignoring Welfard's quiet voice in the excited crowd. 'We have their messenger, we know their plans and their weakness. This is the time! This is the time to strike, and strike hard! We shall set off into the forest tomorrow and run down our quarry, this king with a broken wing!' Baldwin tittered to himself at the rhyme and a polite burble of sycophantic laughter broke out around the gathering. Welfard frowned further, his misgivings turning to deep discomfort.

'This is it, my lords, the great victory we came to win!' Baldwin shouted in a shrill voice.

'In God's name!' shouted an armoured French lord.

'In God's name!' the crowd shouted back.

When the excitable meeting was dismissed, Welfard went to find Count Adolf with his deep sense of unease. Adolf would bring some sense to the matter, he always did.

'We are doing WHAT?' Adolf exclaimed. He had been leading the vanguard for a solid week and he was filthy, tired and fed up with marshland and mosquitoes.

'The commander believes we should go after their king, and eliminate him and his army while he is isolated,' Welfard explained.

'He wants to march ten thousand men into the deep forest, to hunt down a thousand starving refugees! We should let them march off into the woods, it keeps them out of our way. If they wall themselves into a town in the deep forest, then good! It keeps them away from us, it stops them from using their ships to move around, it paralyses them. Who advised against this madness?'

'Nobody.'

'Nobody!' Adolf was open mouthed now. 'I thought we were finally on the path of sanity, and now we are veering off it into stupidity once more, on a whim?'

Welfard shuffled uncomfortably. 'I thought it best not to argue, there was no support in the meeting for disagreement, I would simply have caused a schism for no avail. After all, you and others who ever disagreed with him have been banished.'

'But you are the co-commander, he can't banish you!'

'Careful how you speak to me, Adolf, I respect you hugely but I am still your senior.' Welfard wagged a thick finger at Adolf reproachingly.

'My apologies, my lord, it is not you I am angry with, but that child who leads us.' Adolf swallowed and regained control of his emotions.

'Well, I don't see anything we can do except to try to make the best of it, as usual. What can I suggest to him that might help the situation without trying to change his mind?'

Adolf absentmindedly scraped some mud from one shoe with another, mostly just smearing it around ineffectually. 'We need to divert as many men as possible from the main column. Suggest contingents be sent on to continue up the coast, pacifying the towns and villages. Suggest a significant garrison be left at the proposed harbour, detachments to be set up at regular intervals to patrol this new road we will have to cut and escort supplies along. Anything. Anything to get men away from this nonsense.'

Welfard nodded. 'I will see what I can do. Perhaps I will offer to command the detachment. As his co-commander, I would have the right to a large contingent, and it would get me out of his hair, he might go for that.'

'That might work.'

'Then we are agreed. Here are your orders.' Welfard handed Adolf a tied scroll. 'We head into the woods tomorrow and you will be replaced in the vanguard.'

Adolf sighed and took the scroll, opening it briefly to read it. 'I understand. Thank you, my lord.'

Welfard waddled away back down the path and Adolf was left with his scroll and his worries. He climbed the small rise ahead of him where his men had made camp and looked out from the summit. On the right was the sea, glistening in the sun with its promises of ships and support. Ahead of him, the gentle curve of the broad bay carried on towards the horizon. Golden sands and small coastal villages backed by fields and marshes. To his left, perhaps two miles distant, the forest loomed. He had no maps of it, no scouting reports, no knowledge other than it was vast and sparsely inhabited. As he stood there looking at it, he was gripped by a cold shiver, like he was looking into the maw of a great beast. He looked again at that beautiful stretch of golden sand and calm sea and wondered if he would ever return to see it again.

The first contingents of an army of seven thousand men set out into the forest that afternoon. Welfard had been given a force of three thousand, mostly Germans but not including Adolf's Saxons, and had been tasked with keeping the coast, harbour and roads open. By the day's end, most of the army had not even entered the forest, progress was so slow. The new and inexperienced French vanguard was cutting a road like a chisel being hammered into wood with a brick. All brute force and no skill. No one was sent to scout a proper route, no supply caches or camps were pre-set. By evening only one mile of progress had been made, and the army was forced to simply sit down in the fields and sleep where they were.

Count Baldwin was furious. He called the French vanguard commander and Adolf to an audience. Adolf did his best to dress himself smartly and went to the commander's campfire.

'Count Adolf, why did you not give Baron Anselm appropriate directions and scouting reports with which to progress the line of march?'

Adolf thought for a moment, trying to translate the gibberish question into sense, too tired to really be offended or angry.

'My lord, we have ample scouting reports of the line of march we were on, but none of the forest, which we had no responsibility for. We could not scout a route for a road that yesterday we didn't know needed to exist.'

Baron Anselm bristled and looked embarrassed. Baldwin went red in the face and shoved a finger in Adolf's face. 'I don't want excuses, I want to go into the forest. Your job as commander of the vanguard is to anticipate your commander's needs and be prepared for them.'

Adolf didn't bother to argue with that nonsense, he just stood there impassive. 'I'm sure Baron Anselm will do a superior job to me, and he is fully prepared for the route tomorrow.' He cast a knowing look at the young French baron, who opened his mouth like a landed fish.

'I'm sure Anselm is well prepared. Aren't you, sir?' Baldwin waited for the baron to answer.

'My lord... I... We were going to scout the route tomorrow,' he tailed off lamely.

Baldwin stared at the hapless French lord with stinging reproach. 'Surely the time to scout the route would have been today?'

'Uh, yes, my lord. Sorry, Count Baldwin...'

'Enough. Count Adolf, you are such an expert, you take over tomorrow again and continue as the vanguard. We will find something more suitable for Anselm to do.'

Adolf bowed curtly, arguing would have been pointless. He turned to walk away without waiting for dismissal, the young French baron mumbling his apologies as Adolf passed him.

CHAPTER 25

DEATH IN THE DEEPWOOD

RAGNVALD WAS CONCENTRATING on putting one foot in front of the other. The gnawing pain in his stomach, persistent cramp in his left leg, tingling and numbness in his wounded arm, he was trying to ignore all of them. Their march into the woods was not progressing as well as they had hoped. Twenty men had not joined them when they left their makeshift camp that morning, the second day of their march into the forest. Either dead, dying, or simply too weak to continue. The whole army was starving. Those who had bows were out on the fringes and ahead of the army, killing whatever animals they could, gathering whatever edible plants they could find, but it was never enough. There was a reason very few people lived out here in the deep woods. Little lived or grew under the dense firs.

Sigurd called a meeting with the jarls and they gathered around their king as the army took a rest during midday.

'This march is harder and slower than I expected. I want to discuss if we have any options. This town we are headed for, Jönköping, how close is the nearest road that leads to it?'

One of the local jarls spoke up. 'The town sits on a cross-road, four great roads lead from it, south-west to Lund, north-east to Linköping and Uppsala, west to the coastal towns of southern Norway and north-east, along Lake Vättern to Arbugæ and the northlands.'

'So, the closest road is the Lund road?'

'Yes.'

'How close?'

The jarl grimaced while he thought about it. 'About three days' march to our west.'

'And how long would it take to march from that point to Jönköping?'

'Another four days, at least. We would be no closer than we are now, just on a better road.'

The king sighed. 'It is as I thought.'

'There is another problem,' Ragnvald said. The king set his bloodshot, sunken eyes on the Swedish jarl.

'What?'

'We don't know how closely the Crusader army follows us, or if it follows us at all.'

'Why would they not follow us? They have been following us since the battle at Åhus. Surely their purpose is our destruction,' one of the other jarls replied.

'Perhaps, but perhaps they were simply headed along the coast, and we happened to be on the same path,' Ragnvald mused.

'It's possible, but it doesn't matter what their intention was, we don't know if they follow us, so we must assume they do.'

'They follow us,' said Sigurd.

'How do you know?' asked Ragnvald.

'All the men sent out with messages were given the same story to tell if they were captured, a story too enticing for the Christians to ignore.'

Ragnvald raised an eyebrow. 'You didn't tell us this.'

'No, what use is a secret if I tell men who might themselves be captured? Now it is too late for that.'

'You want them to follow us?' said another jarl, in shock.

'Of course. If they follow us, they are not marching on more towns we cannot defend. Let them come into the deep woods, it will treat them just as poorly as us, if not worse, and winter will soon be upon us.'

'It is a trap, with us as the bait,' said Frode, with a thoughtful expression.

'Yes,' said the king, solemnly.

'And if none of them were captured to tell this lie?' asked Ragnvald.

'Two brave men agreed to make sure they were taken, and to sell this false secret dearly.'

The king coughed heavily and waved Ragnvald's further concern away. The group was silent for a moment as they digested this news.

'Well then, if we turn west for the road, the Christians will more easily catch us, or at least come across our path as it angles in front of them. If they follow it, it will lead them to the road, which they may not know about, and on the road...' Ragnvald looked around the gathering. 'They will march much faster than us on the road. In the forest, we can stay ahead.'

Sigurd thought about this and nodded. 'Yes, going to the road will not help us with them, but it will likely provide us with more food. There must be settlements along the road.'

'Not really, the road has always been a dangerous place to live. Desperate people sometimes use it, raiding parties and armies. Settlements stay away from the roads unless they are big enough to defend themselves,' said the local man.

The king sighed in defeat. 'Then it is decided, the road is no salvation for us. We must head for Jönköping and suffer the journey. We will gather what food we can as we go. I see no other way.'

No one around the circle spoke up, none saw an alternative. The jarls wearily separated to return to their men, to rouse them to their feet, and find out if there were any that could not.

The king was growing stronger every day, that was a blessing, Ragnvald thought, as he returned to his men near the front of the column. He was given the best food to help him recover, no one envied him for that, he was the heart and soul of this ragged army and every man cared for nothing more than they cared about his recovery. Without it, they would be finished. Sigurd walked a little further each morning before needing to be carried. The strongest men took turns to carry his litter over the rough ground of the forest, winding as they did around marsh and lakes. Even Sigurd's famed cloaked huscarls were struggling, starving with everyone else.

The column shook itself out and continued the march. A while later that day, they passed another small ridge in the land, a lump in the endless sea of pine. The men at the front of the column shouted out in excitement, a ripple that worked its way back down the army. Ragnvald perked up and shuffled his way to the front, going as fast as his legs could carry him.

The woods thinned out after the brow and laid out before him was a glimpse of paradise. A small lake lay off to their left, around the right side a broad meadow and fields. Fields of freshly harvested crops, surrounding a tiny village on the edge of the lake, perhaps five buildings and some sheds. Ragnvald could even hear the lowing of cows. To a starving man, it was a vision of Valhalla itself. To the residents, it must have seemed that hell had opened, and spewed forth an army of ravenous dead.

The army descended on the settlement in an uncontrolled mob, ignoring the shouts of those like Ragnvald who roared orders to stop. The terrified people hastily barricaded themselves into one longhouse but were quickly evicted by the careless warriors, who pushed them into a huddle beside the lake, the two men who resisted with weapons left lying forlorn in pools of their own blood.

The king was carried into the village and shouted hoarsely for order, but he was ignored, left looking around with a shocked expression as his partly feral army stripped the village of every scrap of food, clothing and anything else of use while the survivors wailed and cowered by the lake and his huscarls and anyone else not given over to the madness futilely tried to stop the looting.

By the time order was re-established by the more disciplined men with fists and axe handles under the direction of Ragnvald and the other jarls, it was too late. Much of the food had been eaten, even that which was uncooked, and Sigurd ordered what remained to be piled up on blankets in the centre of the village and glowered at his sheepish army. He was furious beyond words.

He brought the survivors of the village into the small square and levered himself off his litter to kneel before them as Ragnvald and the army watched.

'I am King Sigurd Magnusson. I beg your forgiveness for the behaviour of my men. I am shamed by it. They have dishonoured themselves and me in front of the gods by attacking those they are sworn to protect.' The king knelt there, shaking with shame, and the pain of his wounds, until an old woman approached him.

She slapped him, hard across the face. 'That is for my son.' Stunned silence held around the watching men. Then she slapped him again, so hard she almost fell over. 'And that is for my grandson.' The king hung his head in misery and did not resist the assault.

The woman stood before the king for a moment longer and then turned away. She gathered the rest of her family and spoke to them. They recovered some possessions and what food they could carry and walked away, Ragnvald knew not where, perhaps a neighbouring farm, and the men parted silently to let them through.

Seeing their king humiliated, allowing himself to be humiliated due to their actions, chastised the men in a way Sigurd could not have. As the king rose to his feet, no one would meet his gaze.

'Who killed the sons?' he said quietly.

A man shuffled forwards, blood still staining his trousers.

'It was me, lord king,' the man admitted, downcast and humble.

Sigurd did not even look at the man. 'Pick up that rock over there, and walk into the lake. Do not come back. Wash yourself of your sin and us of your shame with your death.'

The man looked around, horror etched into his face. 'Please, lord king, let me die by the sword, like a warrior. Please!' Sigurd paid him no heed.

Gunnar walked around to stand next to the condemned man, hand on his sword. 'Don't shame us anymore. Do as your king commands.'

The man looked around for support, but saw only shame and anger in the faces that looked back at him. His shoulders slumped in resignation and he stumbled over to the rock, weeping openly. Picking it up and clutching it to his chest, he looked around the silent gathering for the last time and then walked out onto the lake shore. As he headed out into the gently sloping lakebed, water rose over his knees and then his waist. He was shivering with fear and the bitter cold of the water.

As he reached the centre of the small lake, the water was only up to his armpits, a final insult. He turned to look at the shore for a moment, seeking some deliverance, but receiving none. Then he leaned back, mouth wide open. He dropped back into the water with a splash and a rush of bubbles, the rock on his chest taking him down to the bottom, and the lake's surface stilled as if he had never been.

Sigurd moved his gaze back from the lake to the crowd. 'Never again. Never again will a man of this army harm one of our people. If they do, I will kill him and every man of his crew. I will put the blood eagle on his back and leave him for the crows.'

He limped over to the pile of food. 'We will cook this properly and divide it. Every man to have a share, those who greedily ate their fill already will not claim any more, or follow their brother into the lake. Set fires from the wood in the wood piles and leave the houses untouched. These people may wish to return one day, if the Christians don't come this way first.'

The king led them out the next day to continue the march. Each man had had a good meal, but almost nothing remained except a small portion of dried or cooked meat per man. A whole winter's supply of food for three families had been devoured by a starving army in a single evening.

Despite the food, a few more men were succumbing to injuries. Men whose wounds had rotted and slowly poisoned their bodies. The last of them would die soon. After that, everyone who had been wounded at the battle would either recover or already be dead. That at least they could be thankful for.

Two more days followed without a proper meal. It was pitiful as Ragnvald watched the scouts bringing in two small deer and a few birds and rabbits to cook and share. A mouthful or so of meat per man, each man staring and salivating as the meat was cooked. Breathing in the rich smoke as if it would give them sustenance. The offal and even the lining of the hide was cooked and shared. Men ate the dirt that the dripping fat had landed on. Ragnvald was too hungry to be disgusted. He would have done that too, if he had thought of it first.

On the fifth day, they found another small settlement. But it was much poorer and had little food. Just a single small family scratching a living in the woods. Sigurd did not allow a single man to enter the settlement; he went to speak to them alone. Some time later, he emerged with the people, each carrying their clothes and belongings.

'I explained that we need their food, that I will give them rich lands somewhere else of their choice in exchange for everything they have. They agreed, they are coming with us. See how it is right to behave,' he said, pointedly, staring around at those who were close enough to hear him, men who could not meet his angry gaze in their shame.

By the eighth day, men were dropping out of the march like fruit from autumn trees. Ragnvald could not think of it any other way but in terms of food. His every thought was about food. Starvation had set in deeply. Eating the dead was openly discussed, although it was not done, so far. They had not seen another settlement, or evidence of one, since the fifth day. The scouts were too weak to do much hunting, it involved far too much extra walking. Men were eating mushrooms and berries and whatever else they could find. Those poisoned by eating the wrong types added to the trail of moaning bodies the army left behind.

The dead and dying were left where they fell. No one had the energy to move them off the path. No one even counted them anymore as the number grew into the hundreds. Ragnvald thought they had maybe fifteen hundred men remaining, but he was not sure. All he knew was that more would not continue the next day. What worried him most was that Leif was fading. His best man was dying in front of his eyes, and they did not know how far they were from Jönköping, he was not even sure they were headed in the right direction.

The only blessings, although they seemed slight, were that the weather held out and the Christians were nowhere to be seen. The army would be beaten by a single crew of children with sticks in its current state. He had no idea what would happen if they reached Jönköping just in front of the Crusaders and had to defend it. Most of them would not be able to swing a sword, let alone fight a battle.

His thoughts were interrupted by a cry from the front of the column, they were always good news, no one bothered making a noise about bad news anymore. Perhaps they had caught a deer. The thought of fresh meat made Ragnvald uncontrollably salivate.

The column continued its slow shuffle forwards through the undulating forest until Ragnvald saw what had raised the excitement. The road. Four paces' width of packed, well-worn earth. To Ragnvald, who had been tramping through the soft leaf litter, up and down hills and through streams, it might as well have been the path to the doors of Odin's hall.

Sigurd was standing by the road, welcoming each man onto it as the army passed. 'We are nearly there, lads, this is the road to safety. Pick up your chin there, we will find food at the end of this bloody path.'

Ragnvald reached the king and smiled weakly at him. Sigurd was swaying as he spoke, exhausted and weak as the rest of them.

'Stay a moment with me Ragnvald, I only stopped because I could not keep walking, but I can't let them see that.'

Ragnvald nodded and stood next to the king, supporting him with a friendly arm across his shoulders as the army passed. He smiled and nodded to all his men, patting some on the shoulder. He saw his slave Ordulf pass, eyes averted, and he said some small word of encouragement, ignoring the sullen look that was returned from sunken eyes. When the last stragglers were moving past, limping, holding each other up, gaunt and slack jawed, Sigurd turned his face to Ragnvald. 'I do not think I will last much longer.'

'Nonsense, we are nearly there,' Ragnvald said, panic gripping him but trying to soothe the big man.

Sigurd struggled to free an arm and lifted his tunic. Ragnvald saw with a wave of nausea that the king's side above his ribs was blue and yellow and covered in angry red veins.

'I think a rib is broken, I stumbled and fell two days ago. My men don't know. No one knows.'

'You have been walking for two days with this injury! You madman, why?' Ragnvald hissed at him.

'They are too weak to carry me. But they would have killed themselves trying.'

Ragnvald had no answer to that. It was the truth.

'If I don't make it to Jönköping, you take over the army, you lead them to food, to safety. You carry on the fight.'

Ragnvald nodded, tears falling unbidden from his red-rimmed eyes as he supported the wasting man who used to be the unbreakable bear of a king. This starving wraith he supported, whose breath he could hear wheezing out from cracked lips.

'We will fucking make it. If I have to carry you every step of the way.'

'Well, that's lucky, because you might have to do just that.' The king laughed weakly and grimaced at the pain it brought to his side.

On the tenth day, a party of hunters was travelling down the road from Jönköping and thought they had stumbled across a line of dead men by the road. A carpet of withered bodies as far down the road as the eye could see. Slumped against trees, lying curled in the pine needles or passed out on the path itself. They stopped in fear and were about to turn and run from the horror when one of the bodies sat up and called out to them.

'You, come here,' called the corpse.

'It must be a wraith,' said one of the hunters, watching the road nervously.

'Nonsense, I'm going over.'

'It's an army of the fucking dead, don't go over there, you idiot.'

'I'm going, coward.' The other hunter was an old man, a proud warrior before the years robbed him of that life. He wasn't going to turn away from a starving man in a ditch. He walked over to the man, who had prised himself to his feet. A blue cloak and other clothes hung loosely off him, a sword in a belt at his side, skin on his face sunken and sallow. *Perhaps it really is a fucking wraith*, thought the old warrior, but he carried on cautiously nonetheless, one hand on his large seax.

'Who are you?'

'I am Gunnar, Huscarl of King Sigurd.' The man gestured down the road. 'This is his army.' The trader stared down the road in disbelief.

'This is an army?'

'Yes, we were defeated on the coast, near Åhus, we have walked for nine days through the forest, trying to get to Jönköping. Please, tell me, is it far?' The man's face was desperate, pleading.

'Jönköping? No, it's just two miles down the road. We left there this morning. You walked from Åhus!' The trader just shook his head in wonder.

'Only two miles? Thank the gods. Please, go back and tell the people, their king needs them. Bring food, bring water, bring carts to carry those too weak to move. Please. Hurry.' The shrivelled warrior then wavered, stumbling against a tree to support himself. Other men were getting up now, peering at the newcomers in shock, or shaking their fellows awake.

'Of course, yes. We will go back to the town.' The hunter turned and ran back to his companion. After a brief conversation, they started running back down the road.

Before noon had arrived, a wave of townsfolk arrived at the withered army. They brought food, they brought water, they helped men who could not walk and carried those who could not stand. But salvation had come too late for many. The townsfolk piled the bodies of those who had not survived the night in carts, three deep. Nor was rescue the end of the tragedy, Ragnvald realised, as he stumbled back to town alongside the cart carrying the unconscious king, chewing voraciously on half a loaf of flatbread that was the single best thing he had ever eaten.

Men died in the arms of those that were carrying them back. Men took a bite of food and died with it in their mouths. Men died on the straw mattresses that had been laid out in the town square. Men can live for a while after their body has died, Ragnvald learned that day, and no power on earth can save them after that. Fifty men died that morning, more victims of the disaster at Åhus, but Ragnvald stayed with the king, hoping desperately he would not be among them.

The afternoon wore into night. All the men were found shelter, food and water. Clothes where they needed them, wounds were tended to, broken bones set as best they could be. Starving men have brittle bones, and many were broken in minor falls on the path. That was another horror Ragnvald learned that long week.

In the morning the king was still alive, in a deep fever, but clinging to life. Leif was improving, unable to stand but eating and drinking. Over a thousand men of the army still lived. They were an army of scarecrows, but they had survived. Of the Christians there was no sign.

The town's gates were closed, the food and people brought in from the surrounding farms, but nothing appeared on the road behind them. Ragnvald offered his silent thanks to the gods for their deliverance.

Ragnvald went to see Leif and some of his men who were all together in a longhouse by the lakeside. He walked around the room, stopping to talk to each man, trying to keep the despair off his face. His men, his superlative hird of nearly two hundred ferocious warriors who had set out with him two months ago now littered the rooms of the town's buildings like old men, just a hundred and twenty of them. It could have been worse. One Swedish jarl had seen his crew of fifty-five reduced to seven. Although, Ragnvald remembered, he hadn't seen the end of that, the jarl had died himself the previous day beside the road, just a few miles from salvation.

But moving around that room of withered men, Ragnvald felt the weight of their loss keenly. His people, his friends. A generation of families back home who would never see their sons and husbands again. His lands would take years to recover, even if this was the end of it, which he knew it would not be.

As he was sitting exchanging meaningless words with one of his men, a healer who was going round the room checking the men noticed his bandaged arm.

'Show me your arm.'

'What? No, it's nothing.'

'I will be the judge of that,' the healer said. She stretched out the arm, noting his barely concealed grimace of pain with concern. She carefully unwrapped the bandage, tutting and huffing.

'I changed and washed it every day,' protested Ragnvald with a lie, like a child defending himself from a fussing mother. 'Well, most days.'

The last layer of bandage came off. The wound was a mess. Even Ragnvald winced when he saw it. He had been ignoring it for a week, the worry and pressures of the desperate march taking precedence. The rough stitches that had been put in at the time of the injury had split, spread and opened across most of the wound. His skin was loose anyway from the starvation, so the wound, although partially healed, was not closed. A mess of scab and exposed, dried muscle tissue filled the opened gaps.

'This is not good,' said the healer, almost reproachingly.

'How bad?'

'Flex your fingers, grip my wrist.'

Ragnvald tried to close his fingers around the woman's small wrist and hissed with the pain. He was barely able to put any pressure on her.

'The wound has healed onto the muscle, which is damaged. It's too late to fix or re-stitch. You will have to keep it clean and hope the wound does not fester. It will heal over and if the gods favour you, you will have good use of your hand.'

Ragnvald paled. 'And if not?'

'If not, your hand will stiffen and become weak. You must use the fingers, every day, many times a day, stretch and grip, stretch and grip. I will give you an ointment to rub into the wound, to soften the scar. It will hurt like fire, but it will help.'

'Thank you, læknir.'

'Bretta, my name is Bretta, Jarl Ragnvald.'

'Thank you, Bretta, how do you know who I am?'

'Your man Leif sent me to you, he was worried.' Ragnvald nodded and looked around at Leif, who was studiously pretending not to be listening. Bretta stood and went over to the next man in the line, whose face was partially healed from a sword wound, one eye fading to milky white.

As Ragnvald watched her work, a man came into the long-house and called for him, peering into the gloom to see if he could find him.

'I am here, what do you want?' Ragnvald didn't bother to stand up or move, he felt he wanted to sit for a month. The man came over, it was one of the king's cloaked huscarls.

'The king wants to see you.'

'He has awoken, he will live?' Ragnvald was jolted into interest.

'He wouldn't need you if he was dead.'

Ragnvald laughed. 'His need for me would not end with his death, I promise you that.' He let out an exhausted sigh and levered himself upright, fighting a wave of weakness that threatened to make him sit down again. He shook it off and followed the man out of the longhouse.

They walked down the main street of the town. Jönköping clung like a limpet to the southern tip of Lake Vättern. A broad valley led from the lake southward, narrowing towards a point, down which the road to Lund led. For a little over a mile to the west and east of the town, flat land was given over to fields. In the south, they extended nearly two miles and beyond that, gentle slopes were forested in every direction.

On the north side of the town, the lake shore was open and lined with docks. The lake was rich in life and great racks of drying fish dominated the shoreline outside the strong palisade walls that encircled the landward side of the town. It was to the shore and the docks that the huscarl led Ragnvald.

When they arrived, Ragnvald saw that there was a lone man standing next to a bed, perched on the end of one of the docks. He could see the top of a great hairy head poking out of the furs on the near end. The king.

The huscarl stopped and jerked his head in the direction of the dock. Ragnvald followed the unspoken direction and walked down the grey weathered boards until he arrived at the bedside. Gunnar was the man standing there, at the king's side as ever.

The man was thinner, but seemed to have recovered well from the desperate journey already.

As he was looking at the huscarl, there was a grating laugh from the bed next to him. He looked down to see the king's pale face looking back at him with mirth on his sunken features. 'It's fucking annoying, isn't it. He barely looks ill, and I nearly died. Yet I am supposed to be the king!'

Gunnar was expressionless as the king cackled and coughed to himself.

'But you did not die, and you are still the king,' Ragnvald replied.

'True, and I owe both to you two more than any other man.'

Ragnvald was embarrassed, he had done nothing compared to Gunnar, who had helped carry Ragnvald across half of southern Sweden. But the huscarl was still impassive, unmoved, as if he was not really there.

'Let's not waste words, I can make few enough.' The king raised himself on one elbow and regarded Ragnvald with his sunken eyes. 'I need time to recover, the army needs time to recover. Men will soon arrive, I hope, brought by those of our messengers who survived the journey.'

Ragnvald did not know how many of the messengers would have succeeded, but others would spread it from those settlements which received it.

'We can't go anywhere, so we might as well make a stand here. This town has strong walls, and the land around is, as we know, quite tough.' Ragnvald grimaced at the understatement.

The king carried on in his hoarse voice. 'We will make this town our anvil and the winter will hammer the Christians against it, break them in the forge of frost. The Christians will not bring their great siege engines here, not up that road in the autumn rains. The road will turn to mud, the fields are already cleared, and the snows will come. They will have the choice of enduring it while they besiege us, or leaving and returning to Lund.' The king stopped to regain his breath.

'What if the Christians did not follow us after all?'

'It does not matter, we must prepare as if they did. If they went along the coast towards Uppsala, then there is nothing we can do, and we must hope they cannot take it before the snows come. I must leave you to organise the defence, I cannot. I also cannot let the men watch me like this. The healer says there is an island, out there,' Sigurd pointed a wrinkled finger out into the lake. 'An island where I can go and rest, a fort where I will be secure.'

Ragnvald nodded with a smile. 'Visingsö. It is appropriate. You own it.'

'I what?' Sigurd looked confused.

'It is a royal island, the property of the kings of Sweden since ancient times. Everything on that island belongs to you. Some say it is a sacred place, but perhaps the kings themselves started that rumour.'

Sigurd's eyes blazed as Ragnvald spoke, with an energy he had not seen for a while. 'Ragnvald, sometimes the gods make these things happen, I am sure of it. I have been brought here, we have been brought here, for a reason. You will command the army here, delay the Christians if they come, hold the town fast against them, make them suffer in the forest as the snows come. Then, in the spring, I will call the army, and we shall drive them from our lands.'

The king was trying to sit up now, and for the first time Gunnar moved, to help his king struggle up, help that was angrily refused.

'Hold the town until spring, we will supply ourselves by water, we will raid their camp and ambush their wagons on the road. Yes. I see it now so clearly. It was not defeat that brought us to this place, it was the gods who gave us this opportunity, one that we had to suffer and earn, as is their way.'

Ragnvald felt himself quail at the thought of having to hold the town with their battered army, of having to put his men into the shieldwall once again. But he pressed his hand into his king's shoulder, as much to stop the man from trying to stand up as in agreement. 'We will do as you command, my king.'

'I know, Ragnvald, I know. That is why I called for you.' Sigurd clasped Ragnvald's hand, with surprising strength, and locked eyes on his. 'I will come back for you Ragnvald, hold here, and I will return. Together, we will defeat them, I believe it was always fated thus.' The king let go of Ragnvald's hand and lay back down in the furs as his men gently bore him away.

CHAPTER 26

THE ROAD TO VICTORY

'GOD DAMN THESE fucking trees!' Adolf shouted as he helped a work party wrestle with a stump. His men and a Bavarian contingent had been working the road for ten days, fighting the trees and the landscape to create a workable route for the army. The previous morning, his scouts had found a road to the west, ten miles or so away. The road led north and they were now hacking their way towards it. Fifty miles into the forest, in ten days. Progress was steady but excruciating. September was slipping towards October. October would bring the rains. Or so the guides said.

Baldwin was furious, he was always furious. He had expected to do ten miles a day, as was normal for the army in open terrain. He had no conception that it would be so much harder in a forest where you have to make your own road, no understanding of the difficulty, he hadn't even visited the vanguard to see the problem, he simply sent angry messages every day accusing Adolf of every incompetence under the sun. Adolf didn't even accept them anymore, returning them unread.

But now they were just two miles from the road. Two more miles of misery and tree stumps and they would be free to march on a road wide enough for their carts to pass unhindered. His scouts had also kept track of the route the Northmen had followed. It wasn't hard, an army walking through the forest left a trail a blind man could follow at the best of times. But this one left a string of dead men. The blind man would be able to follow just by smell alone.

But despite leaving such an obvious trail, the Norse had no carts, no supply train, and could go where a road could not follow. So Adolf had broken away from their route, and had been forced to take several long detours, one of which had by fortune taken them close enough to the road to stumble upon it. He was certain it led back to the lowland around Lund, the forest's edge that Baldwin had refused to probe, making this entire enterprise a total waste of time and effort as they could simply have marched to the road and then followed it, but he filed that away in his list of grievances and just got on with the job. And at the moment, the job was a particularly big and well rooted stump, right in the middle of the path.

Adolf slipped in the churned-up dirt and fell, awkwardly, knee twisting as he went down.

'FUCK!' He rubbed and stretched his tender leg and one of his men, just as dirty and streaked as he was, nodded his head towards their camp. 'Leave this to us, lord, no use you getting yourself hurt. We can get the last bit.'

Adolf was too tired to argue. The man gave him a kind smile and helped the count to his feet. A week slogging through the woods with his men, working alongside them, had given him the kind of respect that you could not earn any other way. He limped back down the rough path to his hobbled horse and got into the saddle with the help of a step up from a fallen trunk.

When he got back to his camp, trouble was waiting for him. 'Count Baldwin,' he said, reining in his horse and dropping gingerly from the saddle.

'What? Who are you, I am here to see Count Adolf, call him here immediately, where the devil is he?' Baldwin barely looked at the filthy man dressed in a simple tunic.

'Reporting as ordered then, my lord,' said Adolf with a resigned smile.

Baldwin turned and stared at him before recognition finally came across his features. 'Count Adolf? What on earth do you think you are doing, what is wrong with you? Rolling around in the mud like a peasant! No wonder this vanguard is in such disarray if its commander has lost his mind and behaves like an animal. What have you been doing, explain yourself!'

'What have I been doing?' replied Adolf calmly. 'We have been building a road. As a good commander, I have been sharing the burden with my men. They know their business and there is little commanding to do, so I have been helping them the only way I can, with my hands.'

Baldwin spluttered in rage. 'Don't you lecture me on command! If you don't know how to behave like a gentleman and get the most from your men with good discipline, only by debasing yourself to their level, then I will replace you with someone who does know their place.'

'Like Baron Anselm?' Adolf replied coolly. 'He knew his place, he is a proper gentleman. He sat on his horse while his men made no progress whatsoever.'

'ENOUGH! Take your men and return to the baggage train. Perhaps we will find a task for you that is suitable for your level of incompetence!'

Adolf smiled wearily. 'We can be relieved? I thought this was a punishment detail. In any case, we have nearly finished, just in time for one of your brainless lackeys to take over and claim the credit.' Adolf didn't care anymore, he left the French count speechless with rage and started shouting orders at his men. They stopped work, packed up their tools and trudged back down the line of march without a backwards glance, suddenly filled with the hope of rest, and for their first good night's sleep in two weeks.

The next afternoon and the army still hadn't moved. Adolf was sitting in front of his tent when a flushed French knight appeared. 'Message from Baron Anselm, my lord, he wants your report on your scouting of the road.'

Adolf shrugged. 'So, send him here and he can get it.'

The knight bristled. 'He requires you to attend to him, he is busy.'

'We haven't moved all day, he can't be very fucking busy can he? And *Baron* Anselm would do well not to tell counts what he requires of them.'

'You have been relieved of your position in the army by Count Baldwin, your feudal rank doesn't matter here,' the knight said with a sneer.

'Really? Fucking fantastic. In that case, I will pack up my camp and me and my men will return home.'

'What, you can't do that!'

'Why not? You just told me I have been dismissed from the army, releasing me from my oath to the Crusade, which means I am free to take my men and go home. Please convey my thanks to Count Baldwin for this kindness, and my best wishes for the rest of his Crusade.'

'What, no, you must remain and do your duty!'

'You aren't very smart, are you, young sir… what is your name?'

'De Hart.'

'Whatever, I don't care. As I have been dismissed, my only

duty is to my men and my lands, so I will be going to see to them. And it couldn't concern me less what some ponce of a French knight or a foreign count thinks about what I and my thousand or so men should do now. So kindly fuck off out of my camp.' Adolf pointed into the woods where the man had come from. 'That way will do.'

'How dare you! You German peasant, you jumped up farm...' Adolf ripped his sword from his scabbard and held it pointed at the knight's throat, stilling the man's diatribe in an instant.

Adolf's mock friendly face was gone now, and his eyes promised pain and death. A circle of his men had formed, hands on weapons, around the knight and his two nervous companions. 'You go too far, sir. Beg my forgiveness or draw your sword and prove your statements true. I am the Count of Schauenburg and Lord of Holstein and Stormarn, the governor of the province of Jutland, and you are nothing, a one-manor knight from some French backwater. If you were not a man of the Crusade, I would take your life where you stand, and hang you from that tree by your guts, for what you just said to me.'

The French knight shook with anger and his fingers twitched near the hilt of his sword, eyes looking around to judge his position. 'I will not beg,' he said through gritted teeth.

'Then draw your sword and defend your words.'

The knight just stared back, unable to decide what to do. One of his companions hissed at him, urging calm.

'Count Baldwin will gut you for this,' said de Hart through gritted teeth.

'Baldwin couldn't gut a dead fish if I caught it for him, nailed it to a board and held his knife hand steady.'

The knight flushed at the insult but said nothing.

'Fine, dog. If you cannot make a decision for yourself, let us call for your master.' Adolf dropped his sword to his side. 'Take him. Don't hurt him, tie him up.' His men swarmed in and disarmed and tied the shouting and struggling knight before he could react.

Adolf pointed at one of the Frenchmen who had come with de Hart. 'You, go to Baldwin and tell him what happened here. Don't lie, or I will have you killed afterwards. You understand?' Adolf said flatly, no hint of a boast in his tone.

The man looked nervously back at him and nodded, turning to run back down the line.

Adolf turned to Sir Hans, who had only just arrived back with the column. 'Stand the men down. Disarm. Whatever happens when he comes, take no action against him. We will not provoke a battle. This is a matter of honour between me and them, my men will take no part.'

Sir Hans's face was a mask of concern. 'Are you sure?'

'No, but if this goes wrong, you are to leave if you can, as you see best in the situation. Perhaps you can return to Duke Welfard. But I will not have our men massacred over this, this is my fight and Baldwin's men are too many.' Sir Hans nodded grimly and turned to start shouting orders.

Baldwin returned at the head of two hundred fully armed knights as the day wore into evening. He looked around in anger and confusion at the circle of tents, with Adolf standing alone with his humiliated prisoner in the open space in between. There were other men around, but none were armed and armoured. Only a couple of knights in tunics wore their swords, as was their right.

'Count Baldwin, why do you come here so armed? This is a dispute between me and this knight, there is no need for those men you have brought here.'

Baldwin looked around suspiciously. 'I was led to believe there was mutiny, and given it was you, I believed it.'

'Well then, you were lied to, I made it clear to the messenger they should tell the truth, but clearly they could not be trusted.'

'Then what did happen here?' Baldwin stayed mounted, with his knights beside him, and did not dare enter the circle around the fire.

'This de Hart told me I was dismissed from the army. When I told him to inform you I would be returning home with my contingent, he insulted me; he called me a peasant, a jumped up farm animal. So, he and I have a matter of honour to settle, that is all. However, he was too cowardly to settle that matter himself, so I called for you.'

The bound knight struggled and mumbled through the rag that gagged him, desperately looking at the count, shaking his head. He was being humiliated in front of his entire peer group, who had unknowingly turned up in full armour to save him from his mistake. Many were visibly regarding him with disgust.

'Why is he gagged?' said Baldwin with distaste. He was aware of the turning mood in his men, but he was trapped, unable to send them away without losing face, or risking the trap he still suspected.

'Because he was unable to control himself, so I had to do it for him,' Adolf said with a frown.

'Ungag him if you would, I want to hear what he says.'

'Certainly!' said Adolf. 'Although I take no responsibility if he is as rude to you as he was to me.' Adolf stooped and cut the gag, deliberately nicking the man's ear as he did, eliciting a cry of surprise and anger.

The man spat the filthy rag out and glowered at Adolf with rage.

'So? What do you have to say for yourself?' called down Baldwin from his horse. 'Did you call Count Adolf a filthy peasant?'

The miserable knight sagged, looking around the circle at his fellows, who had spread out to watch, all atmosphere of potential violence dissipated at the obvious lack of threat. 'Yes, lord,' he finally managed to admit.

Baldwin's face darkened. Much as he hated Adolf, the system of rank that gave him his position was his dearest and most profoundly held belief. There was no excuse for a knight to speak like that to a count. 'Why?'

'Because he refused to follow the orders you sent to him'

Baldwin shuffled on his horse, unable to decide how to proceed. 'Count Adolf, why did you refuse the orders he brought you from me?'

Adolf spread his arms. 'Because the man told me I was dismissed from the Crusade, so the orders no longer applied. You cannot order a fellow lord to do anything without that authority. I explained this simple principle to him, but he did not understand it.' Adolf indicated his hand lazily at the kneeling knight with indifference as he spoke.

Baldwin opened his mouth to reply but then shut it again. Adolf knew at that moment that Baldwin had ordered his dismissal in a rage and not understood the implications. Probably everyone in the circle knew it too. Adolf seized on the opportunity. 'I expect he was mistaken, Count Baldwin, that I was dismissed. The dolt must have spoken in error?'

Baldwin swallowed and straightened in his saddle. Seeing the way out he was being provided. 'Yes, yes, of course. He has mistaken my orders.'

'Excellent, in that case I and my men shall not be leaving! I am glad that it is resolved.' Adolf smiled at the count but made no move.

'Then you can release my man?'

'Afraid not, my lord, the matter of honour is not settled. As you know, and as all the gentlemen that you have brought here will agree, what he said cannot go uncontested.' Adolf pointedly looked around at the circle of the assembled chivalry of northern France. 'Does any man here think his words were acceptable?'

No one spoke or moved. Baldwin finally dismounted and walked over to Adolf, who smiled pleasantly and unthreateningly. 'There must be some way to resolve this,' Baldwin said quietly, so only Adolf could hear. His face was miserable, he was trapped and he knew it.

'Of course, my lord. Someone must correct the matter of honour. Either him as the offender, or his feudal lord.' Which, inconveniently for Baldwin, was himself.

'I could command you to release him.'

'Of course, but you won't. You of all people cannot allow a knight to talk to a count in that manner. Imagine the example it would set?' Adolf almost whispered with glee. He knew Baldwin's vanity would not allow him to risk it.

'So what must be done?' The French count choked at the pain of his submission.

'He, or his lord, must beg my forgiveness, or fight me for his honour,' Adolf replied.

Baldwin swallowed nervously and nodded after a brief pause. He turned to the kneeling knight, who looked up at him with pleading eyes.

'Beg Count Adolf's forgiveness, then beg my forgiveness for causing me this humiliation. You could have settled this yourself like a man, not called for me and my men to come and save you, like you were a lost dog caught in a fence.' Baldwin raised his voice so that the words carried to everyone watching.

The knight's face fell as the words cut into him. His life was over, one way or another, humiliated beyond recovery. He looked around the circle of men who had once been his peers and friends, and saw nothing but indifference and disgust.

He scraped his last shred of dignity together and lifted his chin. 'Swords,' he said, simply. 'I choose swords.' Adolf felt a wave of nausea, he hadn't expected that, the knight was young and probably skilled, and Adolf was exhausted.

Baldwin stared at the man, deep in thought, clearly also surprised. And then set his eyes on Adolf. After a moment, he walked over to Adolf, so close the men could touch. 'If you die, would your men continue on the Crusade?'

'Perhaps, if you have not dismissed them,' Adolf said.

'But the morale of the army would suffer, it would be very bad for me for one of my men to insult you and then kill you.'

'Yes, but perhaps I will kill him. I have killed a lot of men in the last months.' Adolf smiled wolfishly, with courage he didn't feel.

'Perhaps you and I can come to an understanding to end this nonsense,' Baldwin said carefully.

'That would suit me.'

'Do you have a suggestion?'

'I do, you respect my military knowledge and ability to lead men, and I will respect your command position and make sure you are seen to be in charge.'

Baldwin's eyes flicked to the man on the ground.

'I assume Baron Anselm is having more trouble than expected with the road?' Adolf asked innocently.

Baldwin grimaced again. 'Yes.'

'So perhaps I was not all that incompetent?'

Baldwin stared daggers at the older count but wilted. 'Perhaps.' The Frenchman thought for a moment and then looked away again and made his decision. 'So, we are agreed?'

'Yes,' said Adolf agreeably.

'I saw you limping when you came back from the road. You are hurt?'

'It is nothing.'

'It is not nothing. Do you have a man who could stand in your place?'

Adolf bridled but confirmed it, speaking the name in Baldwin's ear. Baldwin turned towards the kneeling knight and walked past him. He turned to address the whole gathering.

'Count Adolf was injured during his construction of the road. Despite his stated desire to do so, he is unable to participate in a fair honour duel. He will nominate a second to fight in his place. You may have heard of him,' he said looking down at his kneeling man. 'Sir Hans Mettel.'

De Hart's face fell as he knelt in the mud, mouth open as he looked up at his lord, but he nodded and set his mouth, accepting his fate.

The two men faced off in a circle of watching men. Sir Hans in his green surcoat and cap a pied maille, silent and immobile behind his faceless helm. De Hart stood across from him, equally armoured, but face still streaked with dirt under his open-faced nasal helm. He drew his sword and set himself to face the metal monolith that opposed him, not a trace of humanity visible in the dull reflection. An arrogant pup he may be, thought Adolf as he watched, but not lacking courage. He was worried for Sir Hans, who was only just recovered from his serious injury and would not be at his best.

The French knight looked on in confusion as his opponent didn't react. He slowly advanced forwards and brought his sword up in a high guard, neither man with a shield, Sir Hans's choice as the defender, for his weak arm was his shield arm. Not that de Hart knew he was weakened. As de Hart closed, he slid a foot forwards through the dirt and took a fast cut from high to low, diagonally towards Sir Hans.

Sir Hans snapped a cover in return from his relaxed position, stepping back as he did, his blade connecting with the oncoming sword and deflecting it away and down into the dirt. De Hart recovered with a half step retreat, avoiding the cut back from Sir Hans's left. The two men separated after the rapid exchange and faced each other again. Sir Hans attacked next, a low swing, followed by a rising cut from that feint that caught the Frenchman a painful blow on the upper sword arm, but it ran off the maille sleeve.

De Hart growled and attacked again, sweeping a cut at shoulder height, and when Sir Hans backed out of range, shoulder charged him and shoved him aside to clear space. Sir Hans took the shoulder charge in his own wounded side and staggered, de Hart looking in confusion as his opponent reeled and hissed in from the pain at the minor blow. He seized the advantage and stepped into a series of cuts, targeting the green knight's weak side, all of which were dodged or deflected. Sir Hans's healing ribs might have been weak, but there was nothing wrong with his legs and he moved like a dancer.

De Hart focused again and again on the injured side, trying to get an opening. He got one glancing blow on his opponent's ribs but all it did was make Sir Hans angry.

He swung another blow at the ribs, not very powerful, and while he was unbalanced, expecting Sir Hans to block it to protect his weakness and allow himself space to re-set. The green knight simply ignored the swing, trusting his armour, and snapped a perfect thrust into the throat of the oncoming Frenchman. It was a glorious stroke, fast and true. De Hart was spitted on the sword, gurgling and thrashing as he slumped to the floor. Sir Hans reeled back with a cry of agony as the Frenchman's sword thumped into his ribs. Leaving his sword embedded in his dying opponent, he sat down heavily against a tree.

Adolf rushed over in concern and helped Hans's fluttering fingers remove his helmet. 'That wasn't very smart.' He grinned as Sir Hans's grimacing face was revealed.

'I'm alive, aren't I?'

'Seems so.' Adolf held out a hand to help Sir Hans gingerly to his feet. 'Thank you,' he said, as the man held onto his shoulder for support, looking over at his dead opponent. Sir Hans smiled back through the pain. 'Anytime my lord, anytime. Except now, that is. If you piss anyone else off, you are fighting them yourself.'

Adolf barked with laughter and let go of Hans, who went to retrieve his sword, unceremoniously dumping the dead Frenchman off the blade. Baldwin came over to Adolf and shook his hand. 'A regrettable incident. Settled now, I think?' Baldwin looked tried, drawn out.

'Indeed,' replied Adolf, with something approaching a genuine smile. 'Now, I think you were saying young Anselm needed some help again in the van?'

CHAPTER 27

A TASTE OF IRON

FIVE DAYS PASSED from the king's departure and the army still festered in the town like an unhealed wound. A pall of mourning and depression hung over everything. Even Ragnvald was affected, unable to rise with the sun each morning, even as his strength returned to his limbs and his wound itched and dragged at the edge of his mind.

Despite the responsibility given to him by the king, he could not bring himself to begin the preparations for the siege, for preparing for a siege would mean rousting the surly army from its well-earned rest and recovery, earning their ire, and accepting the truth: that more of them were going to die here.

As he sat on his borrowed bed, trying to decide if this day was finally the day when he would begin the work, Leif, still drawn and gaunt, but with no trace of his usual humour or spark in his eyes, pushed open the door and came into the room unannounced. Ragnvald bridled at the intrusion into his privacy, embarrassed that he was still on his bed while his men were already about their business.

'Do you have any orders, lord?' Leif said in a tired voice, one that was heavy with implied criticism.

Ragnvald frowned and cast a furious look at his huscarl. 'When I have orders, I will tell you,' he said curtly. Leif was unmoved by his anger, a look bordering on contempt crossed his face, before he controlled himself and turned to leave.

He paused at the door and stopped with a sigh, gathering himself and turning to speak again. 'If we are not ready, more of us will die.'

'More of us will die anyway,' rasped Ragnvald.

'Yes, but fewer if we are well prepared.'

'Then see to the preparations yourself!' snapped Ragnvald.

'We have been, but there is a limit to my authority; however much it carries your name, we cannot command the other jarls. The men need their leader.'

Ragnvald itched around his angry wound and grumbled to himself. 'The men are tired, and weak, and need the rest.'

'No, the men are fed and rested and their strength returns. They need a leader, and they need him now.'

Ragnvald snarled and rose to his feet. 'Do not speak to me in that way, even alone.'

'What will you do?' said Leif with a shrug. 'If you punish me, at least you will have done something, shown some strength, some resolve.'

Ragnvald grunted in shock as the blow landed, and gathered himself to shout his man down as his anger rose to a red heat. But Leif held up his hand and spoke first. 'No! The king has left us, winter is closing in and we cannot return home. Every man here has lost more brothers this month than in his entire lifetime before now, and the army hangs by a thread. They need a leader to believe in and they need to believe we can survive the winter here. Enough of your brooding, you cannot undo the past.'

Ragnvald gaped at Leif in anger and then shame. Looking away and unable to meet the man's eye. Finally he spoke. 'We need to arrange to bring in everyone who still remains outside the walls, and all their food and supplies and tools of any kind. Burn anything left outside the walls, leave no shelter for the Christians, no well for water, nothing to help them at all.'

'Many of the people have already come in, but I will see to the scouring of the land around,' Leif replied with a stilted smile.

'Arrange it for sunrise tomorrow, give the people a day to save what they can.'

'It will be done.'

'Good.'

Leif nodded and turned to leave.

'Leif,' said Ragnvald with a growl, and his huscarl turned to face him again, a hint of nerves on his face.

Ragnvald met his gaze with a steady eye for the first time and his hand clenched and unclenched. 'Thank you,' he finally said.

'Of course, Lord Ragnvald,' Leif said with a mischievous grin, and left.

The jarl walked straight to the biggest longhouse in the town with a renewed sense of purpose, assuming it would be where the local leader lived. No one had presented themselves as in charge of the town. The central hall was deserted, a solitary thrall there had told them the jarl was dead and shrugged, not knowing more. The whole place seemed leaderless, but he decided it was time to find out if that was true.

When he opened the door and entered, he found more than a dozen people huddled around the two fires. A family, or two; men, women and children. An older man stood, hand moving to the handle of his seax.

'Who are you?' he rumbled at the jarl, eyeing him suspiciously.

'Jarl Ragnvald,' the jarl replied, drawing himself up a touch in displeasure over the rude welcome. The man appeared entirely unimpressed, in fact he sat down again and muttered something to the woman beside him.

'Do you know…'

'Yes, I know who that is, Lord Ragnvald. The king appointed you commander of this town's defence.'

'He did. Is there a problem?'

'I hear we are to be besieged, you are going to use this town as your battlefield. So we are likely to starve, or die, or both. So yes, there is a problem.'

Ragnvald crossed his arms over his chest and glared at the man. 'We fight to defend this kingdom, and everyone in it, your family included. Would you rather we left you to the mercies of the Christians? I've seen them burn towns like this to the ground, seen the helpless people fleeing from them, with nothing but what they carry on their backs.'

The man waved away the little speech and implied threat away irritably. 'I know, and I'll help you in whatever way you need, just don't expect me to be happy about it.'

'Good,' said Ragnvald in a tone that implied it was anything but. 'Now, I am looking for who rules this place. Are you the man I am looking for?'

The man shook his head. 'The jarl died, some months ago, we have not yet met to replace him, too many men are away hunting, or fighting in the war.'

'He died fighting the Christians?'

'Gods, no,' replied the man with a frown. 'He was gutted by a boar.'

'Then who do I talk to about organising the defence? Who will lead your people, will you even fight?'

'I don't know who will lead us, I can go and talk to some of the other karls, see if we can come to an agreement.'

Ragnvald closed his eyes and pressed his fingers into the bridge of his nose, squeezing it painfully as he tried to control his temper. 'There is no time for this, do you even understand what is coming, can your people even fight?'

'Everyone in this town can use a spear and a bow,' said the man with a snort. 'These walls aren't for show. We face raiders every few years and everyone here learns to fight, and everyone here is armed. Half the women in this town can stand on the wall if need be.'

Ragnvald finally looked pleased.

'But it won't be you who leads them,' said the man simply. 'We don't trust outsiders, and we aren't going to fight under your word. When a foe comes to these walls, we will stand on them and defend them, but on our own terms.'

Ragnvald was fuming, but seeing that it was fruitless to press further, he scowled and left the room. Going out into the square, he found Ulf and Bjorn and a dozen or so of his other men walking through and they looked up at him in surprise and stopped. 'Where are you going?' Ragnvald asked them.

'To help on the eastern wall, it needs repairs,' said Bjorn, eyeing his jarl cautiously.

'Good, you see to that. Ulf, you come with me to the southern gate.' Half the men split off with Bjorn and headed east, and Ulf and the others went with Ragnvald. They walked through the half dozen rows of longhouses until they reached the southern gatehouse, which was a sturdy double gate the width of six men hung between the two ends of the wall, cut into a gap in the earthen embankment that the palisade stood atop of.

'I want to make preparations to seal the gate. When the Christians arrive, it will be the closest to them, and most vulnerable.

We won't need to use it, anyway. You are the best carpenter we have, so it will fall to you to arrange.'

'Yes lord, it can be done,' Ulf said with a shrug. 'But we will need cut and seasoned timber, we have no time to prepare it.'

'Take what you need from barns or stables or even an abandoned house or two if needed.'

'And if the owners object?'

'Pay them, explain it, but then do it anyway regardless. The people here are leaderless, but we need to avoid making them our enemies.'

Ulf nodded. 'Some roof beams and wall posts will certainly do.'

'Good, see it is done.'

'Horsemen, on the road!' cried a voice from the wall top, and Ragnvald looked up, then ran to the nearest steps up to the walkway. He reached the man who had cried out, and followed his outstretched arm. He saw it too, in the distance, where the road exited the trees on the southern edge of the town's fields, a small clump of horsemen was coming to a halt and looking back at them.

Ulf stood up beside him and squinted at the far figures. 'Christians?'

'Undoubtedly, and sooner than I had hoped.'

'Bastards,' replied Ulf simply.

'Yes. Forget what I said about preparing to seal the gate, start now, do whatever is required,' Ragnvald said with concern. 'We have already lost too much time.'

Within an hour of the first horsemen being sighted on the road leaving the forest, the first column of soldiers came into view, dressed and arrayed for battle. Ragnvald stayed on the wall watching them all day as the Crusader army arrived, giving his orders as men came to him and left on the tasks he gave them.

With the enemy finally spotted, a new sense of urgency prevailed, and the town's recalcitrant people finally held a meeting to discuss the threat. The man Ragnvald had spoken to earlier that day came to find him as the first evening light settled on the landscape.

'Jarl Ragnvald,' he said from the wall top behind him.

Ragnvald looked around and grimaced when he recognised the man, but he nodded at the man to speak.

'We have held a meeting.'

'You have elected a jarl?'

'No, but I have been made the leader until the siege is over. I am Arvid Lendilsson.'

Ragnvald nodded. 'You will fight under my command?'

'No, but we will fight alongside you. We know this town better than you, but I know you would not submit to my command.'

'No, I would not,' said Ragnvald, with a hint of contempt. 'But it is acceptable.' He leaned on the wall and gestured out into the fields. 'Have you seen our enemy?'

'Briefly. There are more than I expected.'

Ragnvald laughed. 'This is less than half of their army.'

'Half?' Arvid said with alarm. He moved to the wall and stared out over the fields. Lines of infantry had formed facing the town, and behind them a line of wagons was moving into the fields, the leading wagons already stopping and being unloaded. Horsemen flitted through the trees to the south-east and south-west, probing and observing, ensuring no hidden forces threatened the main body, and examining the town's defences.

'Yes, most of the force that hunted us is not here yet, although I suspect they will come soon.'

Arvid looked shocked. 'I have never seen such an army.'

'There has not been one in this land for a generation. I've been watching them all day, it is always hard to count, but I think four thousand, maybe five, and more to come.'

'What will they do?'

'If I was them? I would attack, as soon as possible, while we are weak.'

'Odin protect us, can we hold them?' Arvid said, aghast.

'Well, I can put nearly a thousand men on the walls, but most are weak or wounded. So, alone? No. We will need your people. Every spear, every bow and everyone who can carry them.'

Arvid looked crestfallen. 'And if we do that, many of our people will die.'

Ragnvald nodded sadly. 'I know that only too well, but the alternative is the death of everything we have, our history, our future, the freedom to rule ourselves. If we don't make these sacrifices, we will never have the choice again.' He looked at Arvid solemnly. 'Will your people stand with mine?'

Arvid looked at the disciplined lines of enemy soldiers standing motionless in the fields for a while and then looked back at the jarl with a worried expression. 'I will bring everyone I can.'

The Crusaders set their camp that evening and made no attempt on the town. As night fell, Ragnvald left a strong watch on the walls and went to eat his evening meal and meet with the leaders of the army, and with Arvid, in the empty hall.

'Leif, what of the clearing of the land around?' Ragnvald said when everyone had food and was seated.

'Everyone around for three miles has either fled or been brought into the town. We have brought all the food and weapons we could find, and burned or destroyed anything useful we left behind, and fouled the wells.'

'Good. Bjorn?'

'We have strengthened the bad section of the eastern wall, but it needs more work.'

'Do you think its weakness is noticeable from outside?' asked Ragnvald.

'No, the damage is only apparent from within.'

'Good, continue to work on it, but hide your activities from the enemy. Ulf?' He looked at the old shipmaster.

The man looked annoyed. 'We struggled to find good timber, lord – by the time we had it, it was too late to fully block the gateway.'

Ragnvald grimaced. 'Why?'

'We needed to tear down a house, needed the wall beams.'

'I found them trying to take a house apart with the families still inside!' protested Arvid incredulously.

Ragnvald looked at the local leader with a furrowed brow. 'You understand the seriousness of the situation?'

'Yes, but the family losing their home did not, and I had no power to enforce it on them.'

'You offered payment?' Ragnvald said to Ulf.

'They refused it. Weren't going to leave their home for no man, they said,' Ulf shrugged.

'So what did you do?'

'We found another family willing to move for silver. But that was only in the evening, we've barely got the wood out of the walls, the gate is not blocked yet.'

'When will it be done?' asked Ragnvald with concern.

'Tomorrow sometime.'

'Work through the night. We may be attacked at dawn.'

'You think they will attack so soon?' asked Arvid with concern.

'I would,' replied Ragnvald simply.

'Hard to do that kind of work at night, lord, very hard. No moon tonight, clouds everywhere, hard to find enough torches,' Ulf said dismissively.

'Do what you can, the gate needs to be able to withstand an attack by the morning.'

Ulf grumbled. 'I'll do what I can.'

'Good. Everyone should get what sleep they can, every crew needs to be up before dawn, armed and ready by the wall. Your people, too,' said Ragnvald, looking at Arvid, who nodded grimly.

'Leif, come and find me when you have eaten your fill,' said Ragnvald, standing up and making for the door.

Leif came to Ragnvald's borrowed quarters soon after. 'We have prepared what we can, but I have my doubts about the strength of the walls, and the local people to stand firm on them,' Ragnvald said gravely.

Leif looked troubled. 'What do you want to do? Leave?'

'No, we cannot leave, not all of us.'

Leif was taken aback. 'What do you mean, not all of us?'

'Tomorrow, if they come, we must avoid a total defeat. I want you to prepare whatever ships and boats are on the shore, make them all ready to leave in a moment. If the walls fall, we will save whatever of the army we can. Tell no one other than those who are required.'

Leif nodded. 'Those boats all have owners, and those owners will all be trying to leave in them too.'

Ragnvald shrugged. 'Then we may have to fight for them.' He held up a hand to forestall Leif's protest. 'I will say to you again, we will do what we must. However dark the path that leads us on.'

Leif looked troubled but he nodded. 'I will do as you have said.'

CHAPTER 28

THE DOORS OF SALVATION

THE FIRST WHISPERS of dawn were not yet over the city when Bjorn came to wake Ragnvald and found he was already awake. 'You slept, lord?' he asked.

'I did,' Ragnvald lied. 'I will see you at the gate.'

Bjorn left a simple lamp and went into the main room of the longhouse, and Ragnvald heard the first stirrings of life from it, followed by the crackle of a fire.

He walked out into the main room where a dozen of his men, mostly his huscarls with the exception of Leif and Ulf, were sombrely preparing for the battle that they might face. There was no time to cook, but food had been prepared the night before and left cold, and men were eating cold pork and half-stale flatbreads and washing it down with weak ale.

Ragnvald put his equipment and the lamp down on a bench and the room grew quiet as most of the men turned to look at him. 'There is no time for fine words, we all know what is expected and what we must do. We will stand on the walls of this town and defend it as if it is our home.' He looked around the men with a sense of pride. 'Now, let us arm ourselves, brothers, and prepare to stand in the storm of steel, may Odin judge us worthy of victory.' Men touched their amulets and growled their agreement, voices low in the morning, knowing that the empty pre-dawn air carried sound so much better than in the light of day.

Ragnvald was already in his tunic, but he sat and carefully wrapped his shins and calves in thick wool, trying it behind his knee. He took his maille shirt and Sebbi helped him into it, shrugging the shoulders into place and trying his belt tight around his waist so that it spread the weight around his hips. He twisted and checked it was free and comfortable.

Drekitunga went around his waist, the swordbelt adjusted so it hung just right on his hip for a quick draw. He hung his seax from his belt at his belly and checked it was firmly in its sheath. He took his dragon-crested helm, with its skirt of maille, and put it firmly on his head, eyes adjusting to the gloom visible through the broad eye slits. He finally put his armrings on, every one he had with him. If this was to be his final day, he would fight and die in the full glory of his status as a warlord of the Svear, a bringer of war and despair.

When all the men were armed, he led them out quietly into the dark, finding their way through the streets by the first shreds of light, and by a few carefully shielded stone lamps. All around them, other buildings were also disgorging warriors, quiet columns of metal-clad phantoms in the darkness, all moving without words to the same purpose, spreading out to different places on the walls.

They reached the southern gate quickly, the only place that was well lit, and found Ulf and a party of exhausted-looking men still working there in the glare of torches. The old shipmaster wiped his brow and came over to Ragnvald. 'It is done, best we can.'

Ragnvald nodded, looking at the work. They had dug four

postholes behind the gate, and put stout timbers in them, pressed up against the doors of the gate, supported by big angled beams behind whose tips were dug into the earth of the road behind the gate. To open them, the Christians would have to break the hinges from the wall, or rip the posts from their holes, before the gate would move at all. Ragnvald was satisfied and patted the wiry man on the shoulder. 'You have done well. Go quickly, get some food and arm yourselves. I know you need sleep, but I fear you will not get it yet.'

Ulf sighed and nodded, slinking off with the half dozen men who had been working with him.

Ragnvald climbed the steps to the wall and joined the men who were carefully watching the darkness of any sign of the enemy. Nothing was visible outside the walls, it was a murky blackness that shifted and lied to the eyes, a light fog coming off the lake making swirls and shapes that half a dozen times made Ragnvald think he had seen something.

He looked left and right down the wall and saw men gathered at the base behind him, waiting for any sign of an attack to race up the steps and man the wall.

There was nothing left to do but wait, and he stood watching with the others, nervously fidgeting with his sword hilt, eventually deciding to walk down the wall rather than stand inactive. He passed Leif, who gave him a measured nod, and then fell in behind to follow him. He whispered jokes in low tones to his men as he passed, and then words of encouragement to men of other crews.

As he was perhaps fifty paces from the gate along the wall top, he heard a low commotion behind him and saw, coming out of the narrow streets from the town, another dark mass of people bearing weapons and torches. He watched as the shapes herded towards the steps of the wall and started up them, pleased they had the sense not to bring the lights up with them but cursing their noise and indiscipline. He wondered what crew this was and made to intercept them.

He came face to face with the first man up the stairs and hissed at the man to keep his crew quiet.

'Lord Ragnvald?' the man asked, and he recognised the voice of Arvid. He looked beyond the man and saw a few large warriors in helmets and maille, but behind them on the stairs, still lit by the lamps and torches below, he saw a female archer, a boy holding a spear near twice his height, men in nothing but fur caps carrying shields and axes. The entire people of the town, come to the walls as promised.

'Keep them quiet, we don't want the Christians to know we are ready,' he whispered to Arvid.

The man nodded and directed his people to spread out along the wall. Ragnvald watched as men and women with every weapon imaginable, many with just a shield or no shield at all, filed past him with exaggerated care, until a hundred or more had passed him and yet more were still coming.

He smiled at Arvid appreciatively, before realising that the man would barely be able to see the gesture. 'You really have brought everyone,' he said quietly.

'Yes,' the dark figure said back. 'Half are here, the other half went to the other side of the gate.' The voice was tense and full of nerves.

'Good man, let's…' Ragnvald paused, and looked out into the darkness. He thought he had heard something, a clink of metal on metal. He squinted and tried to parse the swirling shadows out there from reality. Dawn was just beginning to take hold over the trees to his left, and he could see a little of the lie of the land, just make out the road leading from the gate, and the fields nearest the wall, but beyond that the road was still concealed by shifting darkness.

Then he tensed. The shifting darkness wasn't the fog. Someone at the gate called it out a moment before he opened his mouth to shout. 'They're here!' he heard, right before he bellowed at those around him to make ready, as the swirling shadow resolved itself into a dense mass of slowly moving men.

As soon as the cry went up, arrows started zipping out from the wall into the mass, and the first cries of pain rang out. Having been discovered, the enemy roared as one and broke into a run, crossing the fifty yards to the ditch in front of the wall with terrifying speed, and before all of Ragnvald's men could even get onto the wall, the enemy arrived.

Ragnvald saw ladders being brought up and raised, and a moment later one thumped into the wall beside him. He drew Drekitunga and raised his shield and resisted the temptation to look over the wall to see who was climbing it. A townsman next to him made that mistake, peering over and receiving an arrow in the shoulder that caused him to reel back and trip, falling down the back of the wall in a welter of dirt and agonised cries.

A helmet appeared at the top of the ladder and Ragnvald speared his sword tip into the dark space underneath it, feeling a wet crunch, and the enemy sighed and dropped back, nearly dragging Ragnvald's sword with him.

Another form quickly followed, and a woman on Ragnvald's left stuck her spear into the chest of the dark Crusader with a wild cry and that man too fell back off the ladder. Ragnvald left the woman and two of his men fighting at the ladder top and tried to survey the scene. Leif was behind him, guarding his right, and Bjorn was beyond that, just finishing off a fallen enemy on the wall top.

Arrows were whistling through the air now in both directions. As he watched, a Norseman in a thick wool hat was hit by an arrow under the ear and his whole body tensed rigid, before he soundlessly toppled backwards, tumbling himself and an unfortunate boy off the wall into the town below.

Two more men stepped forwards to close the gap in the wall, and Ragnvald saw that it was safe, for now. He turned back and saw the woman who had stood alongside him on her knees, gurgling her life away through a ragged hole in her throat, even as the Christian who had killed her was shoved back over the parapet by one of Ragnvald's men with a caved in skull.

It was chaos, but the wall was holding, and there were still plenty of his people on the wall, and more of the men of the army still arriving at the top. He called to Leif and Bjorn and pushed along the wall back towards the gate where two ladders had come up together and the enemy had managed to force their way onto the wall walk. Enemy with shields and spears were holding the tiny gap open as more of their comrades climbed up to join them.

Ragnvald forced his way to the front of the press, hollering at men to make way, and arrived just as one of the enemies facing him put his spear into an unarmoured townsman to his right. Ragnvald whipped Drekitunga down and cut off the spearman's outstretched hand, sword biting into the shaft of the spear and shearing off a great chunk in a bloody spray of splinters.

The enemy yowled in pain and pulled back, having the sense to cover himself with his shield as Ragnvald pressed the attack. A fresh enemy squeezed himself past the maimed man and set his shield, Ragnvald ineffectually trying to fish around underneath it for his enemy's groin, but everything was too pressed and tangled together.

Bjorn swung an axe from behind Ragnvald, and it thunked into the back of the head of a man defending the other side of the tiny press of enemy, and the man dropped like a sack of grain. A Norse warrior pressed himself into the gap, and Leif wrestled his opponent off the wall, throwing him down into the town, and suddenly the little knot of enemy collapsed and, where there had been an organised attack, there were suddenly just dying and panicking enemy.

No sooner had they finished off that group and toppled the ladders to the ground with spear points than a fresh breach of the defences happened behind him, near the stairs from the ground. More enemy this time, pouring from four ladders, a dangerous assault. 'Go,' he shouted at Bjorn and Leif, and they ran off down the wall to face the new threat.

Ragnvald became aware of a noise that had been nagging at the back of his mind, a rhythmic thumping. He looked around in confusion and then realised it was coming from the gate. He made his way down there, past bodies and men still holding the wall, and a pair of women still pouring arrows down into the enemy. He risked a look over the wall, trusting his helmet, and saw what was happening.

A dense mass of enemy was at the gate, and they were hammering at it with a makeshift ram, a tall pine tree stripped of all but the stumps of some of its branches, which they were using as handles to carry it and repeatedly smash it into the gate. Between hits, a half dozen men with big axes were hacking at the weakened timbers, and Ragnvald saw with concern that the gate was moving inwards with each hit, and he could hear splintering and groaning.

He looked down over the wall behind the gate, and saw that the posts were sagging in their postholes, starting to lean back more drunkenly with each hit. *Fuck.* The huge ram was more effective than anything he had expected them to have.

He looked back in the direction he had come from. The enemy were still on the wall between him and the stairs, it was a twelve-foot drop to the ground by the gate, too far to jump in his armour and war gear, and he had no other way down there. There were very few men inside the gate, he had forgotten to post anyone there in reserve and he cursed himself for relying on the gate's strength alone.

The gate shook again and a post, an old timber from a house, unseated from its hole, tearing the packed earth away. Now the only thing that was keeping it from toppling was the cross beam that tied all four of the posts together and the gate's locking bar. Ragnvald shouted at a man who was near the base of the wall. 'Gather some men! We must defend the gateway!' The man looked up at the figure shouting at him uncertainly, perhaps not even hearing him over the din.

The gate shook again and a thick board in the gate splintered, pieces falling inside and landing on the ground. Ragnvald felt the gorge rise in his throat, the gate would not hold for long. As he stood there and despaired, a half dozen running figures appeared on the street behind the gate and he looked down, recognising Ulf and the men who had been with him, armed and ready for battle. He shouted at Ulf, waving his shield in the air. 'The gate! Ulf, the gate.'

Ulf looked up at him and did not break his stride, leading his men towards the shuddering wooden structure and then sending one of the men off running east, Ragnvald didn't know what for. Ulf ran urgently over to the damaged part of the new structure, even as it received another huge impact. And Ragnvald heard him swear.

'It won't hold!' shouted Ulf. 'You have to stop the ram! Give me time!'

Ragnvald nodded, looking around. He saw the two women with their bows and lunged over to them, grabbing one by the shoulder. She looked around at him in confusion and he pointed at the men wielding the ram. 'Them, shoot them!' She nodded and drew her bow, sending an arrow down at the men at the front of the tree trunk, it narrowly missed the front man and thunked into the wood.

The other woman saw and joined in, the two of them quickly hitting first one man, and then another. The front of the log dipped as several men dropped their branch handles to take cover from the arrows, and shouted at others, who tried to cover them with shields. For thirty heartbeats, the ram was stilled as the enemy tried to respond to the arrows, and Ragnvald looked down inside the wall to see that Ulf and two men were desperately trying to wrestle the dislodged post back into its hole.

More men were arriving at the gate now from the eastern wall, and Ulf shouted at them to push back on the structure to help his men get the post back into line so it could be re-seated. There was a sharp cry behind him and turned to see one of the women had been hit in the face with an arrow, she dropped her bow on the walkway and reeled around, one hand clamped to her cheek, the arrow shaft jutting between her fingers.

Ragnvald sheathed his sword, leant his shield against the wall and picked up the bow. There were still several sheaths of arrows resting against the wall, along with several empty ones. The woman still firing her bow gave him a single grim look and returned to her work, grunting as she drew and fired, ducking back to nock another arrow as the enemy organised more men to fire back at her.

There was another crunch as the ram hit the gate again, and a string of curses from below. Ragnvald looked down to see the post had been ripped from its damaged hole again, and Ulf and half a dozen men leapt to re-position it, while others tried to brace the gate.

Ragnvald looked out over the enemy and nocked an arrow with cramped fingers, trying to remember the skill from last time he had used a bow, years before. He took a breath and straightened his left arm against the curve of its belly, raising the stave and leaning into it as he drew his elbow back past his ear until the back of his thumb brushed his cheek.

He tried to focus on the lead man on the ram, the man covering him with a shield was only half protecting him. He let his fingers relax but he snatched at the string as it slipped off them, and it lashed at his exposed forearm, the arrow wildly veering off course and harmlessly hitting the shield.

He cursed and nocked another arrow, ignoring the sting in his forearm and taking another breath. Others on the wall had seen what they were doing now, and spears, arrows, rocks and axes were pouring down onto the attackers around the ram, picking men off and fouling the attacks. Ragnvald drew again and fixed his eyes on a man who was trying to drag a body to the side to clear the path; he loosed, fingers smoothly sliding off the string this time, and he saw the tail of the arrow swerving and then snapping back into line and thumping into the centre of the man's back.

His target spasmed in pain and toppled onto the body he had been trying to clear, and Ragnvald chose a new target and drew again.

Below him, Ulf and his men wrestled and shoved at the post, trying to get the gate back into line with brute force. As they did, the men with axes outside finally broke down a second and third timber, and a hole big enough to climb through was opened. An arrow lanced through the hole, hitting one of the men with Ulf, and stopping the rest who were wrestling with the post as they cursed and grabbed for shields and weapons as the first brave enemy forced his way through the hole.

Within moments, there was a vicious fight over the hole in the gate, and the dislodged post and damaged hole was impossible to fix as the enemy got close enough to touch it. Ragnvald saw the men outside abandon the ram as men surged into their path and tried to force themselves through the gate, and he fruitlessly sent two more arrows down but there was just a forest of upraised shields now, so he abandoned the bow.

The first of the dawn was finally breaking and he could see both ways down the wall in the dim light. There was still fighting all along the wall; Leif and Bjorn were still contesting the top of the stairs in a fight that had degenerated into a bloody brawl over a pile of bodies, both sides packed together too closely to achieve much.

Below him, he saw Ulf shouting at the men with him, urging them on to push back the enemy struggling through the hole in the gate, so that he could replace the post. The gate was sagging dangerously, and if it gave up much more, space would open between the doors, and the whole enemy army would be able to force their way through and pour into the town, with barely thirty men down there in the street to oppose them.

Ragnvald saw this and understood. And Ulf looked up and gave him a grim look and Ragnvald saw that he understood too. He realised that there was nothing else he could do to help the gate from where he stood, and jogged down the wall to join the fight there. He pulled a bloodied and exhausted Leif from the press and put his mouth to the man's ear.

'The gate may fall, if we don't clear this and get down there, we will die up here and the town will be lost.' Leif looked at him, and then back over his shoulder towards the gate, and nodded in understanding. Ragnvald drew his seax, his sword no use in the press ahead, and with Leif at his side shoved his way into the brawl, shield up, seax working underneath, stabbing at anything that wasn't a Norseman, kicking and pushing and screaming and wrestling.

Inch by bloody inch, they pressed forwards, and he tasted the blood of his enemies on his lips, and heard their ragged breaths in his ear, and stared into their wild eyes, pressed close as lovers, but unable to do more than grunt at each other. He felt the sweat run in rivers and the fear grip his insides as his shield was shoved out of position.

An enemy blade found his stomach, but it had no power behind it and his maille held. The blade jabbed again and again and fished and wriggled and there was nothing he could do but withstand it as the tip prodded and scratched at his skin through the maille and the pain of the cuts and the impacts spread through his bowels.

The man holding the blade screamed at him over their locked shields and Ragnvald struggled with all his remaining strength to free his other arm, bringing the seax up and lashing out with it at the other man's face, all desperation and fear, no skill, as the man tried to tilt his head and use his helmet to protect himself, while still trying to shove his own blade through Ragnvald's maille.

Finally, something gave, and his feet freed up a measure, and he managed to get his shield down more and push the enemy's now trapped arm down and expose his shoulders. The man was desperate as more and more of him became vulnerable, and shouted in fear as Ragnvald's seax found the top of his maille shirt, and screamed as the tip went above his shoulder, and whimpered as it was forced down into his body. He collapsed around that invading steel like a punctured waterskin, unable in the press to even fall to the ground away from it, having to simply suffer it as it reached into him and took his life.

No sooner had Ragnvald freed his blade from the body than the press gave way. A dozen Christians, alive, wounded, and the one dead man, collapsed on top of each other in a pile, and suddenly the exhausted Norse were scrambling all over them, stabbing the hopelessly trapped men repeatedly as they struggled to free themselves.

Finally, the gruesome work was done, and nothing moved in the mass of bodies, and no more enemy dared the ladders. Ragnvald waved to the men with him. 'The gate!' He was too out of breath to say more, and they pounded down the steps and jogged towards the gate, where the sound of fighting was still raging.

He arrived at the gate with several dozen men and found the enemy had hacked a hole wide enough for two men to pass through, and, even as he watched, the gap between the sides of the gate was widening, enemy hands lining the edges, trying to force it wider against the groaning structure holding it closed ever more precariously. The rough timber braces were straining, the ground around the temporary post holes cracking, the panels of the gates themselves splintering and bowing under the assault of ram and axes.

'Force them back!' shouted Ragnvald, pointing his re-drawn sword at the gate, and his men jumped to the gate, slamming it back half a pace and narrowing the gap just as the first enemy forced his way through, hacking at a Norseman bracing the gate, who was trying desperately to defend himself with his shield as he did it.

There was a great shout from the other side of the gate and a crash as a coordinated mass of bodies hit the other side, forcing them back half a pace again. The gap reopened and a second man joined the first. Ragnvald nervously looked back over his shoulder, trying to judge if it was time to leave.

'We have to get the post back in, then hammer a wedge in to hold it,' said a voice, and Ragnvald turned to find the strained face of Ulf. Ragnvald dropped his thoughts of fleeing and nodded. 'How? We cannot reach the post.'

The post was now between the enemy still fighting through the hole and the ones now shoving through the gap in the gate. Anyone trying to move it would be cut down instantly.

Ulf looked wild. 'Force them back, or it's lost. If they pull another post out, the gate will open.' He pulled out his long knife and went back to the fight. Ragnvald shouted at everyone who was not already at the gate. 'Push them back, close the gate!' he roared, and a dozen men added themselves to the press. A Christian who had breached the gate was cut down, and then another, and the gap closed a handspan, leaving the next enemy unable to get through. He instead fought through the gap with his spear, jabbing at anyone who came too close.

The gate creaked back another handspan as the Norse bellowed and shoved at it, and Ragnvald watched in uncertainty.

Then Ulf ran forwards with two of his men and they threw themselves at the unseated post. Ragnvald called out in alarm as the unprotected men put their shoulders into the timber and shoved at it, and the enemy in the gap in the gate angled his spear and jabbed at them, scoring one across the ribs.

A Norse warrior tried to clamber across to shield the men, but in front of the gap in the gate he was cut down by an arrow fired through the gap, sprawling on the timbers. One of the men with Ulf was run through with a spear as Ragnvald added his own shoulder to the press, heaving on the post, hoping his maille would protect him.

The gate shoved back another measure and the post nearly reached the hole, but the spear lanced out again and went into the thigh of the man next to Ragnvald and he howled and fell to his knees, leaving Ragnvald and Ulf wrestling the post alone.

Ulf looked up at him with horror in his eyes. They could not get the post back into position with the enemy so close, could not force the enemy back while the opening in the gate existed.

The spear licked out again, thumping Ragnvald in the ribs, his maille holding but pain shooting through him. A sword came for Ulf but Ragnvald desperately fended it off. The post ground back another handspan under the pressure. Ulf batted away another spear thrust as another Christian forced his way through the hole in the gate and came for them, only to be cut down by Bjorn.

Ragnvald put his shoulder to the post again and looked at Ulf, who nodded at him, fear etched into his features. 'Get it done.' He turned and threw himself at the spear that was jabbing at them, knocking it to one side and grabbing hold of it, dropping his seax as he pulled and wrestled with it, trying to drag it back from the enemy.

'PUSH,' roared Ragnvald, heaving on the post, his feet scrabbling in the blood-soaked earth for purchase as he felt the gate give a measure. A handful of men joined him as Ulf cleared the enemy at the gap, and Bjorn covered their flank from the enemy at the hole in the gate, and Ragnvald felt the door give a handspan, and put everything he could into moving it back more.

Ulf howled in pain and rage as the spear he was clinging to was pulled sharply back and he was slammed against the gap in the gate, he could not let go or the spear would get him, and he writhed and shouted as unseen blades bit into him and he blocked the gap with his body. Ragnvald gave one last heave and felt the post catch in the hole and then he shoved at it, trying to force it down into the earth.

One of Ulf's men arrived with a rough wedge of wood and shoved it bodily into the ground at the back of the hole, then stood back and hammered at it with the back of an axe, driving it into the hard earth and wedging the post in place as the gate finally closed and the gap sealed. Ragnvald looked up and saw Ulf standing in front of the closed gate, hands clutched to his belly, shivering and twitching.

He rushed over to the man even as his legs gave way, and Ulf tipped back and Ragnvald caught him and slumped to the ground with him. 'Get it done,' mumbled Ulf. 'Get it done, get it done,' he whimpered, and Ragnvald looked down and saw the ruin of Ulf's stomach and groin and the blood pouring from a dozen wounds, and he felt a shuddering breath leave the old man's body and did not feel another one enter it.

He lowered Ulf to the ground with tears in his eyes and looked back at the breach in the gate. Bjorn was standing there, bloodied and exhausted. The enemy on this side of it were dead, and his men had piled loose beams against it, blocking the hole. Above him on the wall, more men were firing arrows down into the enemy and throwing stones at them and then he heard a wave of ragged cheering break out from the top of the wall and spread to his left and right and he knew it was over.

CHAPTER 29

A FINAL JOURNEY

THE CRUSADERS RETREATED to lick their wounds and did not return. When Ragnvald finally tore himself away from watching their camp, pushing away the nagging doubt that they would try again as he would have done, the sun was high in the sky. The townsfolk and his men were already clearing the bodies, leaving the stench of death and battle hanging devoid of its source.

Ragnvald made his weary way back to the longhouse, the patchwork of scabbed over shallow cuts and scrapes on his stomach itching and tearing as he walked, the still unhealed wound on his arm fizzing and complaining now that the battle fugue was over. Though the fight on the walls and at the gate had been desperate, it had been limited in scale, and no more than a few hundred had died in total on either side. It had been more of a test than a full, determined attack.

Whoever commanded the enemy army, they were still cautious and careful. In all the time since they had first fought at the Trelleborg they had never overextended or committed rashly, but also, Ragnvald noted, they had never truly chanced their full strength. Perhaps something that could be exploited.

He reached the longhouse and went inside. There was a murmur of conversation inside that rapidly died as the occupants, about twenty men, saw their lord had entered. Ragnvald peered around in the darkness, trying to see who was there. He spotted Leif standing with a few other men, and then Ragnvald spoke into the silence.

'Where is Ulf?'

'Over here, lord, we were just about to carry him to the pits,' a man replied from the smoky gloom, standing by a bloodstained linen wrapped bundle on a bench.

The pits were the shallow graves outside the town walls where the townsfolk had buried those whose bodies had been recovered from the road, or who had died after arriving. They had been buried in long rows, with little or no ceremony, with few of their friends having the strength to send them on their way with the proper observances, and not enough precious firewood to burn them all with winter fast encroaching. It was something that grated at all of them.

Now they were being filled with the bodies of those who had fallen in the dawn assault, both enemy and friend.

'No, not Ulf.' Ragnvald looked around. 'We had not the strength or the time or the space do the right thing for our brothers before, but we will send Ulf to the gods in the old way. He earned that.'

There was a sea of nodding heads and downcast eyes in the dim light.

'He wanted to be burned in his ship, and be set out to sea so the flames would carry him home, but the Christians stole that from us,' the man beside Ulf's wrapped body said. It was Sebbi,

Ulf's closest friend, if such a man of the sea could have been said to have friends beyond the wind and waves.

'We will find another boat, and we have the lake. It is the best we can do for him.'

'We will need every boat here for the siege, to carry supplies and men,' said Leif cautiously.

'We can spare something. Find an old one, to match Ulf, something old and gnarled and stubborn, but that is still sound, and buy it.' A few men laughed quietly at this, and the tension was broken.

'Aye, lord,' said Sebbi. 'I will see to it.'

'Tonight we will send Ulf on his last voyage, and remember all those who we have left behind in death. Then tomorrow we'll set about the tasks left to the living, to the continued defence of this town and, by that, our homelands.'

There was a fierce grumbling of assent and Ragnvald looked around at each man, nodding and meeting their stares. 'Sebbi, make the arrangements for the funeral.'

Ragnvald had a dozen tasks to complete before he could attend to Ulf's final journey. He remained in his maille, partly to avoid having to deal with his wounds, and partly because he was certain the enemy would attack again. The gate needed repairing, the remainder of the bodies cleared, weapons, equipment and arrows collected, and the town's food collected and carefully accounted for, so that they could ration it for the siege ahead.

He came across Ordulf as he walked back to the hall and stopped him with an outraised hand. 'I did not know you survived the march,' the jarl said gruffly. 'What have you been doing?'

'I have been helping your men,' Ordulf half lied.

'With what?'

'Whatever they wanted me to do,' Ordulf said, as neutrally as possible.

'You did not come to seek instructions from me?' Ragnvald growled. 'You are my thrall, not theirs.'

'I am sorry, Jarl Ragnvald,' Ordulf said, in the same neutral tone, staring at the jarl's chest to avoid making eye contact that he knew would seem hostile or resentful.

'Well, I will put you to better use now, come with me.' The jarl strode off again without another word or a glance back, and Ordulf sighed quietly and followed.

The town's smithy was modest but well appointed. Much more a blacksmith than a place dedicated to making weapons, as with most Norse smithies outside the largest towns, it did both. The smith was a balding, thickset man with a full, wild beard and a red and bloodshot nose that was quite unpleasant to behold. Ordulf wasn't sure if it was badly broken, or if several decades in the frozen North and the heat of the forge had destroyed it, but it was so odd he found himself staring at it, and found the smith staring back with a hostile glare.

Ragnvald spoke as the two men stared at each other. 'I am Jarl Ragnvald. Arvid said you could help us to make and repair weapons.'

'I can, and who is this?' the smith said, pointing at Ordulf.

'My smith, I'm leaving him here to help you.'

'I've got three lads, all the help I need.'

'I wasn't asking,' said the jarl, his voice grating as his patience wore thin. 'I've had my fill of those who refuse to do what I say – take him, and use him. We need weapons repaired, and we need more spears made, and arrowheads, as many as you can. I'll strip every good feather and every bit of wood that can be made into a shaft from this town, and we will need every arrowhead you can make.'

The smith thought about this and nodded. 'Fine. Can you

make good arrowheads?' he said, pointing at Ordulf with a calloused finger.

Ordulf shook his head dumbly.

'What kind of smith can't make fucking arrowheads?' said the Norseman in disgust.

'I'm a swordsmith,' said Ordulf, with a thick undertone of arrogance.

'Oh, really? Well, ain't no one going to be fucking making swords in a siege, and don't take that tone with me. You ain't a swordsmith here, you're just shit in my forge.' The smith looked at Ragnvald with a cocked eyebrow. 'Who is he to you? Important?'

'He is my thrall, a captured Christian smith.'

The smith looked again at Ordulf with sudden surprise and interest. 'I thought you sounded funny. A Christian thrall, and he talks to us like that?' He looked at Ragnvald in confusion.

Ragnvald looked at Ordulf with annoyance. 'He has a bad habit of talking when he should be silent, and of forgetting his place.'

'I won't have that here, not in my forge.'

Ragnvald nodded. 'I understand. If he disrespects you, do whatever you feel is required to get him out of that habit.'

The smith sighed but relented. 'Fine, I'll take him. At worst, he can shovel charcoal.' Ragnvald nodded and was about to leave when he stopped, and shoved his hand into a pouch on his belt, coming out with a small collection of ragged hacksilver, which he held out to the smith, who accepted it and examined it dubiously, the tiny pile dwarfed in his big hand.

'For the arrows,' said Ragnvald defensively.

'For some of the arrows,' the smith corrected him.

'For the rest of the payment, I'll stop the Christians burning your town and everything in it,' replied Ragnvald, his irritation spilling into his voice again.

'And if you don't succeed?' said the smith, still unflustered.

'You may recover the rest you are owed from my body, it will be on the walls.' And the jarl turned and walked away in his blood-stained armour, leaving the smith tutting to himself and muttering his displeasure at being landed with the paltry payment of silver and the surly Christian slave.

'Talk to me like that again, without your lord to protect you, and I'll put out an eye and consider the damage deducted from what he owes me,' said the smith, without even looking at Ordulf.

Ordulf bridled, and the smith's eyes snapped up and narrowed. 'You even look at me like that again, thrall…' Ordulf felt chilled to the bone by the intensity of the stare, not disbelieving for a second that the man meant it. He forced the anger off his face and nodded, casting his eyes at the ground.

'Better. Now get inside, I'll find something useful for you to do.'

Ordulf left the smithy dirty, tired and with one side of his face aching from an enormous backhand blow the smith had given him, the taste of blood still in his mouth.

The smith had cared nothing for the fact he was just recovering from starving half to death. He had spent the rest of the day hauling charcoal to the smithy from the town stores, moving stone anvils and equipment around the smithy as they set up to make the arrowheads, and being given every menial task that didn't involve swinging a hammer. The smith, whose name he still didn't know and did not care to learn, had started pounding iron into rods, and then the rods into socketed arrowheads, while a junior smith did the same thing at a different anvil. Ordulf had watched the process with interest as he shovelled charcoal into the greedy forge and otherwise stayed out of the way. He had found the process interesting, and remarkably simple. He had been sure he could do it easily, although it did not appear he would be given the chance.

He had made the mistake of saying so, and the smith had invited him to the anvil with a knowing shrug. Ordulf had hammered the iron out into a round rod with ease, and then set about trying to forge the socket of the arrow. It had looked easy, flattening the end of the rod and then rolling it around on a spike anvil to form a socket, but he forged one area too thin, and when he tried to roll it, the hot iron cracked and collapsed. The smith had laughed at his failure and embarrassment, a cruel laugh. 'You are wasting my time, thrall.'

'I can do it,' said Ordulf with resentment in his eyes.

'You can try, but you will just waste my time and iron again.'

Ordulf seized the rod and cut the ruined end off, then thrust it once again into the fire, concentrating hard as he once again hammered out a fan of iron from the end, checking repeatedly that he was not overdoing it. Then he set to rolling the iron, but realised with fury that the iron fan was too narrow, and in his attempt to correct it, it buckled and the socket did not meet up at the back.

'I can fix th…' His head had slammed to the side as the smith's gnarled hand connected and knocked him back.

'I told you not to waste my time and iron.'

Ordulf was still furious with the Norseman, and with himself for his arrogance. The forming of the socket looked simple, but clearly took time and practice. The smith had made it look so easy. The shame of appearing a fool in front of another smith hurt worse than the blow to his face.

As he reached the longhouse, he saw that all the warriors were leaving together, armed and dressed for war still, but sombre and unhurried, not rushing to the walls again. He stopped and watched them in alarm, but no one gave him an explanation. He wondered if there was another attack, but the men were all heading down in the direction of the lake.

Confused, Ordulf went inside and to the corner he had been sleeping in, cursing when he found someone had taken the ragged fur he had been sleeping under. He wandered the empty house for a while, considering stealing another, but even in his anger, decided against it. The consequences if he was found out would be dire.

Eventually, angry and riled up, his curiosity got the better of him and he pulled on his spare woollen tunic and set off into the cold night to find out where everyone had gone.

As he walked along the mostly deserted street that led down to the lake, he reached the two hundred or so yards of the open shore where the beached boats and fish drying racks stood. The town's main dock was in the centre of the bay, reaching out into the shallow water like a fallen tree trunk. The dock was lit with torches, and torches were also carried by many of the small crowd of warriors who stood in a group on the shore.

Ordulf walked over, staying up the shore and behind the crowd, none of whom were facing his way. He reached the place where the main street led down from the town to the head of the dock, and sat down on the side of an upturned boat. He watched as a single figure detached himself from the quiet crowd and walked slowly out in front of them.

Jarl Ragnvald walked down the old wooden boards of the dock and towards the boat that would carry Ulf on his final journey. The boat his men had purchased was an old fishing hull with three oars a side. Small enough for a pair or trio of fishermen to manage, large enough for Ulf to lie on his bier of firewood along the centre, in the space created by hacking away the two rowing benches and the mast-step. He would need neither.

Tears had pricked unbidden at his eyes as they had laid the old shipmaster to rest on his timber bed, but those were gone now, and he was full of his purpose, of the duty he owed to this man's service.

There was no priestess in Jönköping, no one to chant their strange songs, or to fill the air with the smell of their burning herbs. But Ulf had always been a follower of Ran, the goddess of the undersea, who kept no temple and sought no priests or blessings. Ran only demanded one thing, the sacrifice of brave men and stout ships into her care, and that often.

Ragnvald walked to the edge of the dock with his torch and paused, letting the firelight play over the body of his old friend, dressed in borrowed finery of coloured wool, arms crossed over his chest, axe in one hand, an oar in the other. 'I'm sorry, brother, that we could not take you back to the sea,' he said, almost in a whisper, so that no living man would hear.

He cast the torch into the boat, and the tallowed wood caught immediately, the fire crawling around the base of the bier, starting to smoke at the wool wrapping Ulf's legs.

Calm in the heat of the growing blaze, Ragnvald took hold of the sternpost in his right hand, and the bow rope in his left, and started walking the boat down the pier, putting his weight behind it and gaining speed, until he reached the end of the dock. He let go of the rope and gave the sternpost one final shove, letting the boat glide out into the deeper waters of the lake.

A gentle breeze blew from his back, which would take the boat out into the lake and spare it the ignominy of drifting back to shore. That, along with the stones laid in the bottom of the bier, should ensure Ulf's final voyage went smoothly.

Ragnvald watched the fire growing, flames leaping above the sides of the boat as it slowly receded into the lake, until he was satisfied and turned to walk to the head of the dock. He collected his shield from a hirdsman, and turned to face the blazing boat, the flames now rising high and burning from stem to stern.

He drew Drekitunga and raised it, glinting in the firelight. The men behind drew their swords or raised their spears and axes with him and he looked out over the flame-lit lakeshore and sang out Ulf's tribute.

'Go well with the wind, brother. Let it take you calm over Ran's raging waves. Let the wake run true and clear at your back, and the sun welcome you into the dawn's embrace. We will raise a stone to honour you, for when we are gone, only the sea will remember your name.'

They lowered their weapons and stood in silence, that reduced and ragged warband, as their brother burned. Then a warrior detached himself from the line and stood on the shore. 'Let Ulf carry the soul of Grimar Thennsson, who fell bravely in battle at Åhus and whose body was lost to the Christians. Let him find his way to Odin's hall.'

Ragnvald nodded to himself at the gesture. He had seen Grimar fall in the desperate battle at the camp.

'And Arne Bosson,' shouted another man.

'Halfdan Suneson, who will forever remain in the deep woods,' called Leif from Ragnvald's side. A fellow huscarl, gone and not yet replaced.

'Bjorn Gormrund!'

'Svend Ander!'

'Trygve Knudson!'

The names rolled out along the line, spoken by the friends and comrades who had most felt their loss. Half a hundred names and more were called, adding their souls to the blazing ship, the pyre of their memories; the fire of the fallen. Ragnvald stood in silence and wept unseen in the darkness as the names of his lost warband were called out over the lake. He cuffed his tears away as the crowd fell to silence and did not notice the man who appeared beside him.

'Would you allow us to join?' Ragnvald looked around, and saw Jarl Frode standing next to him with a sad smile. He nodded curtly, and Frode gave him a friendly grasp on his shoulder and walked forwards a few paces, then bellowed into the night. 'Harald Karsten, my kinsman, who fell protecting his lord, his uncle, upholding his oath to me with until his last act. May I meet him in Valhalla to thank him.'

Another voice spoke up from the left, and Ragnvald turned, seeing that outside the ring of torchlight cast by his men, more warriors were arriving on the shoreline. He looked up and down the waterline as dozens and then hundreds of men walked onto the beach, and shouted the names of the lost into the deepening darkness, rolling out into the emptiness until, finally, the last of hundreds of souls was called into the night and silence fell once more across the water.

Eventually, the flames of Ulf's pyre burned out when the charred keel of his boat slipped quietly beneath the shimmering surface, and the darkness of the night fell upon the ranks of men like a cloak once more, but a little less heavy and dark than before.

Ragnvald embraced Frode, and up and down the beach, men stood in huddles and spoke of their comrades in the darkness as the few remaining torches started to give out.

'It was well done. The gods take note of such things, I believe,' said a quiet voice behind Ragnvald. He turned to find Tormund standing there in his hooded tunic, he recognised the odd-looking man at once and was disquieted.

'I did not know you were here, why are you not with the king?'

'I go where I am drawn, or where I am needed. I was drawn here to your side, and the king does not need me.'

'What draws you here? I do not need you either, unless you can wield a spear and shield,' Ragnvald said with a dismissive air.

'I can, but I do not. I am drawn here by my dreams, and the

power of fate that clings to this place. This town is the centre of the gods' focus now, I am sure of it. You have honoured them this day, tomorrow, they will stand in your support.'

'I honoured my men,' Ragnvald said with a weary scowl, wishing the strange seer would leave him and bother someone else with his mysteries.

'It is the same thing, don't you think?' said the seer, unperturbed. Ragnvald grunted noncommittally.

'And what will happen tomorrow?' asked Ragnvald, curiosity itching at him.

'That is not for me to say, Lord Ragnvald,' Tormund said with a shrug as he fiddled with a pouch on a thong around his neck.

Ragnvald turned away, bemused.

As he stood there, Leif came up to him through the crowd and spoke urgently in his ear. 'My lord, a message from the scouts, they report a body of men is coming in from the north-east.'

Ragnvald looked surprised. 'Ours?'

'Yes lord, men from Ostergotland, the first to receive our messages.'

'How far away, how many?'

'Three hundred men. They will be here tomorrow morning, before the dawn, before the Christians know they are here.'

Ragnvald smiled. 'They will be most welcome. Thank you, Leif. Let the men finish here, and then tomorrow we will rise before dawn, and be ready to welcome our kin into the city.'

Leif nodded, and set off through the crowd, speaking to the men in quiet tones. One cluster at a time, the message passed through the crowd, and the warriors started to melt back into the town. Ragnvald was left deep in thought, until he realised he was almost alone on the beach, just the silent seer standing behind him, and a few of his men politely waiting for him to leave, vigilant as ever.

Ragnvald grunted and made to walk up the beach, eyes

meeting Tormund's, who showed no sign of triumph at his little display of foreseeing. Ragnvald told himself that the man must have overheard the scouts talking, and rushed to the beach to appear to have known, but he did not truly believe that was possible. The strange man showed no reaction either way, and turned to walk with him up the beach, Ragnvald's men forming up in front and behind with fresh torches to light and guard the way.

As they went up onto the street leading into town, Tormund's eyes locked on a man sitting on the side of a boat in the half shadows as the torches lit up his face. Ragnvald looked across and saw it was Ordulf, hands tucked under his armpits against the cold. He saw Ordulf's bitter look, and then the slave looked away at the ground as his eyes met the jarl's.

Ragnvald heard Tormund draw in a sharp breath of shock, and felt the man's stride break for a moment as they passed. He looked at the seer inquisitively, and saw that he was now looking over his shoulder at the slave.

'Who was that man?' asked the seer with a hushed voice, turning his head to meet Ragnvald's gaze and showing the burning intensity in his eyes.

'The man on the boat? He is my thrall. Why?'

'I have seen him in my dreams. Dreams of power and war and fate that I do not yet understand.' The seer turned to look back again, but Ordulf had disappeared into the receding shadows.

Ragnvald let out a dismissive choking laugh. 'Him? You must be mistaken. He is no one.'

The seer stopped and brought Ragnvald to a halt with a surprisingly strong grip on his shoulder. 'No, it is you who is mistaken,' Tormund said, before turning to walk away, raising a hand over his shoulder and pointing a finger at the sky for emphasis. "Keep him close, Lord Ragnvald. He has Odin's eye upon him, and he *reeks* of destiny.'

Epilogue

Lundjen, Nordland
September 2015

THE MEETING WAS tedious and Halfar had never been good at following these bureaucratic affairs. All they did was talk, these government types, and he had trouble forcing himself to listen to them say things in a hundred words that could clearly be expressed in ten. But it was a situation they had to deal with. The department of culture owned the sword and the university was publicly funded and overseen by the government, so nothing would happen without their permission.

Halfar suddenly realised there wasn't any talking going on to listen to and snapped his eyes down from the ceiling to find everyone silent and looking at him.

'What do you think?' said the head of the bureaucrat pack, who was the deputy assistant minister of culture for antiquities and ancient monuments, a loathsome little man called Bertrand Lang. He was staring at Halfar with as much contempt as Halfar felt for the man in return. Halfar silently hoped he or Bertrand would just explode under the stares and thus end it. When they didn't, he raised a hand to rub his eyes and said, 'Sorry, about what?'

There was a collective sigh and Bertrand repeated himself. 'What do you think of the museum proposal? Its location in Lundjen in an annex of the university? Can we confirm this decision now?'

'Oh, that, yes. Fine. The more closely tied to the university the better. Professor Hallsson will be a superb steward for the collection.'

Originally the Ministry had wanted to make the display part of the National Museum of History in Lundjen, but the museum was out of date, too small and, frankly, entirely focused on revisionist Christian-centric history of the Crusades and the great purges. Halfar despised it and regarded it as the Ministry of Culture's historical propaganda department. He had set up his own museum as a direct consequence of a visit there. The museum covered the Norse history of the country as if it had happened somewhere else, almost as a footnote.

'So, we move onto the proposals for the display of the artefacts and how we present them. We must remember, not just the eyes of the nation will be on this, but also the world's. Now, we have reviewed the three proposals for the display and we in the ministry heavily favour option C.'

Halfar rubbed his eyes and sat up. 'Three?' he asked. 'We only presented two proposals for the annex at Lundjen,' he said, face screwed up in confusion. 'Option A was to consolidate the entire collection in the existing university history museum, along with the displays about the history and culture of the period, which would require a new building. Option B was to spread some of the components over different buildings, which would require alterations and a small extension, and shuffle a few of the current displays about to make space.' He had ticked the two options off on his fingers as he went and pointed back to the first. 'We strongly suggested option A to avoid making the museum seem disjointed and to avoid impinging on very limited space. What is option C?' he asked, with dread creeping into his mind.

'Option C was to use the existing building for the displays and cut back on the content in order to fit it all in one building without significant changes to current displays. This is regarded as the fastest and most cost-effective method,' replied Bertrand, with a hint of nervousness in his voice.

'The proposals we wrote clearly showed that not only would the existing buildings not be big enough to do that, would not have space to display all the accompanying items and historical context, making it a genuine educational display worthy of the university, but also that the cost of the new building or extension would be paid for by already pledged donations, and that it wouldn't cost the government anything.' Halfar looked between the assistant minister and his flanking minions before his face darkened. 'Did you even read our meticulously researched and detailed report?'

'Yes, we did,' Bertrand replied defensively. 'We have just decided we prefer another way. A smaller and more efficient museum that will free up funds for renovating other historical collections and artefacts.'

Halfar's mental alarm went from red flashing lights to little men screaming and running around on fire inside his head.

'So, to be clear,' he said, slowly and deliberately, 'Your preference in this situation is to use the money gained from the renewed interest in the Norse history of this country, which is drastically under-represented, misinterpreted and maligned, to boost funding for other parts of our history instead, whilst minimising the history the funds were intended for? Perhaps another display on how the purges were good for the region's economy in the 13th century, ignoring the fact that it was partly because the Crusaders killed all the locals and replaced them with their own rich descendants? Perhaps on how the integration of the Catholic faith allowed the region to trade and freely travel like never before, ignoring the fact that the Norse had the widest and most diverse trading network in the world at the time and traded everywhere from Sicily to India except for the western Christian states?'

Bertrand's face was stone and he snapped back across the table, 'It's about best use of funds, not pet projects.'

'Okay, so where is this proposal for my review? Why are we voting on it before I have even seen it?' Halfar asked, twisting in his chair, comedically looking around the room and under the table as if the presentation would be hiding somewhere for him to find.

Bertrand sighed and nodded to one of his flunkies, who stood up with a folder and walked around the absurdly large table to the far end to hand it to Halfar.

Halfar perched his glasses on his nose and opened the binder. 'Give me the summary while I read it. Actually, don't. It's your fault I didn't get it so you can just sit there while I read and then I don't have to hear your spin on it.'

Bertrand sat and fumed while Professor Hallsson shook his head like a father of two squabbling children. He liked and respected Halfar a lot, but the man really did enjoy needling Bertrand too much; it was getting in the way of the project almost as much as Bertrand's unsuitability for the job.

Halfar became more and more agitated as he read the proposal until finally, after ten minutes, he slammed the folder shut and pointed glared across the room.

'No wonder you wanted to try and railroad this proposal through the committee without further scrutiny. This would reduce the museum to a sideshow and leave out almost all of the supporting displays! You basically intend to put the sword and its replica in a glass box in the middle of a room and leave out the historical context!' He was visibly fuming with rage.

'That's not true, there will be pictureboards about the cultural impact of the myth, a diorama showing recreations of parts of the myth and a short documentary on the discovery of the artefacts,' Bertrand answered, trying to contain his anger.

'Oh great, a video, how brilliant. That will make up for the total lack of historical context from contemporary artefacts. Why is my entire proposal for the displays on the history of the Crusades and the backdrop of the legend left out? Why, in this entire proposal, can I not see anything about the events that surrounded this legend's development?'

Bertrand shuffled nervously in his seat. 'We feel that the link between the sword and the events of the unification of Nordlandia are speculation only and should not be presented as history. There is no clear proof that the legend is even linked to the northern Crusades and thus it should not be presented alongside them. Thus we feel it should simply be presented as the myth that it is, not woven into disputed historical events that would confuse the matter. We also feel that those events are amply covered in the National Museum.'

There was a stony silence while Halfar sat with his mouth open and his fist slowly pounding on the table. 'Who decided this was disputed? Which historians? Which experts on the period?' he demanded, his voice rising with each question.

'Well, our in-house experts,' Bertrand stated, raising his chin in defiance and folding his arms across his chest.

'Oh, that's okay then, your in-house "experts", who have no academic qualifications or published research that I am aware of, have overridden the conclusions of all of our country's leading historians on the period, including Professor Hallsson's?'

Bertrand sat like a stone, meeting Halfar's glare. He looked guilty and qualified the statement. 'Look, Halfar, it's not just a historical issue, it's a political one.'

Halfar's eyebrows climbed even further up his forehead at this statement.

'It's a what? Are you serious?'

'Absolutely. Look, if we present the legend as you have proposed, it could cause serious… difficulties for the government. The story of the hero who stood up to the Crusaders is already gaining a lot of traction in Norse nationalist circles. If we build a museum that could, in any way, be seen to support that idea, well… We are worried about a rise in division and disharmony in the country,' Bertrand finished, lamely.

Halfar closed his eyes and removed his glasses, carefully placing them on the table.

'How can you come in here and suggest we whitewash history to avoid affronting your political sensibilities? This is why history is not the responsibility of governments. This is why spineless propagandists like you are not supposed to be the custodians of our past. This is why the National Museum is such a revisionist disgrace, because political hacks like you have been rewriting the exhibits to be convenient to your chosen story for thirty years.' Halfar was bright red with anger now. Bertrand squirmed in discomfort at the far side of the room as everyone else sat in shocked silence at the outburst. 'I will not sit by and watch you revise this find to suit your needs. The moral and intellectual bankruptcy of that is so unacceptable that I'm surprised you don't die of shame even suggesting it!'

Halfar paused for breath and then continued, overriding Bertrand's feeble response.

'If you will not tell the story of this sword, I will. I assure you of that. Your attempts to cover it up will only make you look worse.' Halfar stood abruptly and picked up his papers, turning to leave.

'Halfar, please, we can work this out, don't remove yourself from the process,' said Professor Hallsson, gesturing to his friend.

'You cannot co-exist with that attitude,' he said, jabbing a finger at the deputy assistant minister. 'History should not be written in political compromises. I refuse to be a part of it.'

He walked to the door. Bertrand's assistant, Felix Meyer, stood to open it for him, giving him a sympathetic smile while his back was turned to the room as Halfar stormed through. Professor Hallsson followed him out, half jogging to catch up with the furious man.

'Halfar, please. Don't abandon this.'

'I am going back to my home, to my museum, and I will tell the story from there. Abandoning this is the last thing I am doing, I assure you.'

'I'll need your help here, to deal with this properly.'

Halfar stopped and looked at Hallsson sympathetically. 'I'm sorry, old friend, I know this will be difficult for you, but I was never going to move here anyway, and I cannot work with that charlatan, I cannot be dragged into it. I'm going back to the mountains, that is where the story began, and that is where it will be told, not in some airless conference room in the city.' He proffered his hand. 'Best of luck, old friend, you are going to need it.'

Afterword and Historical Note

They say that the second book is the hardest. The first comes after years of thought and preparation, and then you have 12 months to do a second, while still spending your time worrying about the life of the first one. Well, I must have been lucky, for although this book was indeed challenging, I loved writing it.

The world truly is getting dark for our two combatants in this great war between cultures. The Norse have been shocked to their core by the relentless and disciplined advance of the Crusader lords. The Crusader lords, in their turn, are torn by infighting and political machinations, so certain of their victory that they are on the verge of turning in on themselves to claim the rewards of a prize they have not yet earned.

Winter is closing in on the battered armies of the Norse and the Crusaders, locked in a fight to the death deep in the wild woods of Southern Sweden, and only time and book three will reveal who will triumph, and whose bones will litter the forest floor for generations to come.

Speaking of those woods, and my constant desire to inject as much realism and accuracy into what is, after all, a fictional alternative timeline, I must admit those woods were not as empty and foreboding as I made them out to be. Known at the time and today as Småland, or 'The small lands', the forests and lakes of southern Sweden were full of small pockets of settlements and petty kingdoms that defied outside control for generations. Hence their name.

Eventually the kings of the Svear did partially subdue them, and there is a whole fascinating history to that, and their people. But there just isn't room in this book to cover everything and it was simpler for the story to hide these people away, rather than have Sigurd and his army have to negotiate their way through these disparate, and possibly hostile, petty kingdoms.

So, I erased most of the people of Småland from the narrative, and I beg forgiveness of their shades.

As with book one, I tried to use only real people, searching the historical record for figures from history that were suitable for this story. This book sees the introduction of another very real historical figure, Reinhard of Blakenburg; Bishop of Halberstadt. Reinhard, from what is recorded of him, was very active in the political machinations of the empire and knew some of the other characters in this series.

In 1115, he joined with Duke Lothair of Saxony in open conflict with the Emperor Henry, one of dozens of conflicts spurred by the ongoing Investiture crisis and Emperor Henry's conflict with Pope Paschal. Now, as a reminder from book one, the alternate timeline in this series sees that conflict between Pope Paschal and Henry ended early, in 1112, as they set aside their differences to focus on an external threat: The Norse. A threat brought to the fore by the murder, in a Saxon church in the lands of Duke Lothair, of Pope Paschal's nephew and close confidante. A murder committed by one Jarl Ragnvald and his warband of Vikings.

So, in this timeline, Lothair and Reinhard never join together to fight the Emperor Henry, and instead I have directed their efforts and ambitions North, towards the ancient enemy of the Christian people of North-western Europe, the Pagan Norse.

Reinhard, as a particularly active and ambitious Bishop, one not averse to involving himself in war, and someone who interacted with some or many of the other characters in this series, was too perfect to ignore. I find it completely fascinating taking these real people, learning what I can of them, and re-directing their lives. It gives me a basis for what they might have been like, and a liberty to build on that in my own way. Every Crusader lord in this series, from Count Baldwin of Flanders, through Adolf and Lothair, to Reinhard, Baron Hugues and Duke Welfard is a real person, just... re-purposed, to a different story.

I love this period of history, and these places and people, who are so often misconstrued and misrepresented: The Vikings as heartless raiders and destroyers, the Crusaders as either perfect saintly knights, or fanatical mass murderers, depending who you ask. I've tried to show both sides as what I am sure they were; people, with all the varying traits, desires, ambitions and flaws that actual people have.

I have also tried to research how people lived in that time, the tools and weapons they used, and the culture and society they lived in. I don't pretend to have it all correct, and I take some liberties for the good of the story, but if you want to know more about the Norse and their way of life, I highly recommend Hurstwic as a starting point. This group of re-enactors and historians have a website that is the best resource for a casual history buff like me that you could hope to find, and the starting point for a dozen deeper dives through the internet. They cover every aspect of Norse life and culture and have spent decades painstakingly recreating Norse combat from the archaeological evidence, descriptions in the sagas and their own practice sparring to find out what does and doesn't work with those weapons. I have taken heavily from what I learned from their website and their wonderful series of videos recreating famous fights from the Icelandic sagas.

Lastly I wish to thank everyone who has supported me through this, fellow authors and colleagues, friends and family, who are too numerous to list. They know who they are.

If you have made it this far, I thank and congratulate you. As a debut self-published author writing in my spare time in the age of Amazon and social media, my publishing career will live and die on reviews, tweets, facebook recommendations, goodreads write-ups and 'likes'. So if this tale entertained you and you wish to see more, go to the nearest internet portal and let the world know. Each review makes it more likely I will be able to continue to write. Thank you all so much.

You can also sign up to my reader's club, 'The Warband' on my website. My reader's club will give you a vaguely monthly newsletter (no spam, no referrals), information on upcoming releases, my bladesmithing, and most importantly – discounts, sales, signings, freebies and giveaways. All my giveaways will be solely to list members. So join the warband today, it's completely free!

Anyway, enough of all that. The saga of *Ljós a Norðan* will continue. The stage for the mythical sword is set, and its story will be told. The siege of Jonkoping will come to its conclusion in the cold and darkness of winter in the deepwoods, and the fate of the North hangs in the balance.

All this and more in Book Three: A Forge Of Frost,
Will be published in Summer 2022.
James C. Duncan. August 2021

GLOSSARY

Named Characters

Adolf, Count of Schauenburg and Lord of Holstein and Stormarn: A Saxon lord of Duke Lothair's patronage, a senior commander of the First and Second northern Crusades

Aurick: Father of Ingrid, discoverer of the sword Ljós a Norðan

Baldwin VII, Count of Flanders: Son of the famous Robert II, 'The Crusader'. Commander of the second Crusade

Baron Anselm: One of Baldwin's leading vassals

Baron Hugues: Brother of Folmar, Count of Metz

Bertrand Lang: Deputy assistant minister of culture for antiquities and ancient monuments

Bishop Reinhard: Senior clergyman sent to oversee the new church in the captured lands

Bjorn Lendirsson: Swedish Huscarl

Brunhild: A Norse slave girl in the service of Jarl Ragnvald

Dengir: The Norse master Smith at Uppsala

Felix Meyer: Assistant to Bertrand Lang

Fenrir: Huscarl of Jarl Ragnvald previously killed by Leif in a duel

Gjaldir: Legendary Norse warrior

Gunnar: Huscarl of King Sigurd

Professor Hallsson: Head of the history and archaeology department at the university of Lundjen. An expert on the northern Crusades and medieval Scandinavia

Halfar Asleson: Curator of the Røros museum of Norse history and culture

Halla: Wife of Ragnvald

Henry V: Emperor of the Holy Roman Empire from 1111AD until the events of this book

Ingrid: Eleven-year-old girl who likes history and hates fishing. Discoverer of the sword Ljós a Norðan

Jarl Birgir: Ally of Jarl Harnsted

Jarl Erling: Swedish jarl

Jarl Frode: Swedish jarl, ally of Ragnvald

Jarl Gustav 'The raven's claw' : Swedish jarl

Jarl Harnsted: Swedish jarl, cousin of King Eric and one of the contenders for the throne

Jarl Kjartan: Norwegian jarl, ally of King Sigurd

Jarl Rangvald Ivarsson: Leading jarl and warlord of the Kingdom of Sweden

Jarl Steinar: Norwegian jarl, close associate of King Sigurd

Leif Leifson: Huscarl of Jarl Ragnvald

Lothair, Duke of Saxony: Contender to be the next Holy Roman Emperor, First Crusade leader

Orbert: Saxon campmaster

Ordulf: German smith from Minden in Lower Saxony

Eric of Sweden: King of Sweden from 1105 to 1116

Sebbi: Huscarl of Jarl Ragnvald

Sigurd Magnusson: Son of Magnus, the King of Norway

Sir Dietmar of Eresburg: A leading knight of Saxony

Sir Hans Metel of Oldenburg: A leading knight of the Saxon contingent, revered as a great swordsman

Sten: Brother of Fenrir

Ulf: Shipmaster of Jarl Ragnvald's hird

Welfard (Welf the Fat) Duke of Bavaria: Leader of the German contingent of the Second Crusade

About the Author

Hi there! I'm James Duncan. As an author I am fascinated with history and fantasy. I write historical fantasy/fiction based on our world, but in an alternate timeline, past, present, or future. Each book or series asks and tries to answer a question of 'What if?' This series asks the question 'What if the Norse didn't convert to Christianity, and instead the Viking raids continued.' And posits the answer, which you will have to read the rest of the series to find out! I do not create new worlds, I mess with the history and future of ours, grounded in our own past and the laws of our universe, but tweaked in events and often adding a soft sprinkling of the divine or fantastical, resulting in relatable historical and future fantasy.

Upcoming books include the questions:

'What if the black death was actually a coverup of something much, much worse.' - 'The Black' -An alternate history of the time of the black death, based in southern and eastern Europe, coming out in 2022.

'What if the human race develops a race of gene engineered

worker drones, but they are turned against us.' - 'Outriders' - A post-apocalyptic fiction set in the 22nd century in Poland and Hungary, est. release date late 2023.

Outside of authoring I am a professional engineer, and split my spare time writing, reading, and being an amateur bladesmith. My bladesmithing work, and more information about my life and authoring, and the ability to contact me and talk to me directly, are available on my website.

www.Jcduncan.co.uk